The Grapples
of Wrath

Uncorrected bound proof

Also by Alice Bell

Grave Expectations
Displeasure Island

The Grapples of Wrath

Alice Bell

> A note to reviewers: please note that this text is uncorrected, and changes may be made before the book is printed. The appearance and contents may not resemble the finished book. You have received this proof on the understanding that neither the proof nor any of its contents may be reproduced before publication of the finished book without the publishers consent. This proof may not be sold.

Published in hardback in Great Britain in 2026 by Corvus,
an imprint of Atlantic Books Ltd

Copyright © Alice Bell, 2026

The moral right of Alice Bell to be identified as the author of this work has been asserted by her in accordance with the Copyright, Designs and Patents Act of 1988.

All rights reserved. No part of this publication may be reproduced, stored in a retrieval system, or transmitted in any form or by any means, electronic, mechanical, photocopying, recording, or otherwise, without the prior permission of both the copyright owner and the above publisher of this book.

No part of this book may be used in any manner in the learning, training or development of generative artificial intelligence technologies (including but not limited to machine learning models and large language models (LLMs)), whether by data scraping, data mining or use in any way to create or form a part of data sets or in any other way.

This novel is entirely a work of fiction. The names, characters and incidents portrayed in it are the work of the author's imagination. Any resemblance to actual persons, living or dead, events or localities, is entirely coincidental.

10 9 8 7 6 5 4 3 2 1

A CIP catalogue record for this book is available from the British Library.

Hardback ISBN: 978 1 80546 343 6
Trade Paperback ISBN: 978 1 80546 344 3
E-book ISBN: 978 1 80546 345 0

Printed in Great Britain.

Corvus
An imprint of Atlantic Books Ltd
Ormond House
26–27 Boswell Street
London
WC1N 3JZ

www.atlantic-books.co.uk

Dedication

1

Opening Curtain

With the benefit of much hindsight, Basher's first mistake was to say, 'Do not, under any circumstances, bring home a dog. I do not want to open the door and find you holding a dog when I get back.' Claire did not need hindsight and realized immediately, upon the words exiting Basher's mouth, that he had made a fatal error. She had been friends with Basher and Alex for less than a full year, but it was very obvious that if you forbade Alex from taking ownership of a dog from someone who had advertised online that they needed to divest themselves of a dog, then Alex would, in fact, make it their business to become plus one dog at the first opportunity.

Sophie, who was Claire's best friend and had been more or less constantly by her side since they'd been at school together, also knew this.

'I look forward,' she said, glancing between Basher and Alex as they all sat at a table in a mid-bougie

Brighton café one sunny morning, 'to helping Basher and Alex come up with the name for their new dog.'

Thus neither Claire nor Sophie was at all surprised when they called round to the flat Alex and Basher shared, early on the evening of the same day, and Alex opened the door with a small but energetic Jack Russell terrier under one arm. It was white, with large caramel-coloured splotches.

'This is Wyatt,' said Alex, grinning very broadly. 'She's a year old, so not a proper grown-up yet.'

'Yes, you have that in common,' said Basher's voice, floating through from another room. He sounded much put-upon. But then he usually did.

Alex was an extremely outgoing nearly-twenty-year-old and lived with their uncle, Sebastian, because each was the only member of the extended family the other still talked to. Alex bore Basher's style of theoretical parenting in good humour, while Basher insisted that Alex was pushing him to some sort of nervous breakdown.

Alex – who was growing into themself enough that they were no longer gangly, and was currently sporting hair that was dyed deep pink down one side of their parting and their natural pale blond down the other – moved aside so that Claire and Sophie could walk down the narrow hall of the flat. They found Basher in the front room, slumped on the sofa with one hand over his eyes. Bash was shorter and stockier than Alex, but they both had clear grey eyes and the kind of natural high-cheekboned facial structure for which people would pay a cosmetic surgeon many thousands of pounds. Basher, an ex-policeman and a perpetually tired, bookish Shakespeare enthusiast, was less adventurous with his own blond hair and kept it shaved close to his head. He usually had a day's growth of stubble as well, giving him the air of a very attractive peach.

'Could you put the kettle on, Strange?' he asked, employing his nickname for Claire. He didn't open his eyes or turn his head. 'I fear they have killed me this time.'

Despite saying this, Basher made no objection when Wyatt, released by Alex, ran and jumped onto his lap. He scratched her behind the ears, and she began to playfully chew his thumb. It was evident that Wyatt would be a permanent fixture.

Claire went to the kitchen and flicked on Basher's kettle, which was so ancient it was probably an antique and vibrated and roared so loudly that she had been given to wonder several times if it was not some sort of medical Victorian sex aid that had been repurposed. Sophie followed her and pointed out Alex and Basher's favourite mugs in the cupboard.

'Remember, sugar for Alex ...' she said.

'... and no sugar for Basher – right, I know, I've done this loads,' Claire muttered. She used Sophie as a sort of portable external hard drive for storing data on, such as passwords, birthdays and days on which she had promised Basher she would go to the cinema to see a special screening of a Hungarian film about a stuffed whale, and therefore couldn't lie in bed eating Twiglets and listening to her favourite episodes of true-crime podcasts. Claire was aware that Sophie was much smarter than her – even though Sophie always dressed in a bright-turquoise velveteen tracksuit, which was the uniform of someone who was cool in 2007, not someone who took homework seriously – but she did find it a bit galling when Sophie acted like Claire didn't know how to do normal, everyday tasks. Granted, she did have trouble navigating the interface on the Sky Box to find the shows she had recorded, but she'd be able to figure it out, if Sophie ever gave her enough time to do it herself. Anyway, Alex was on at her to get rid of Sky. They said it was unethical to let Rupert Murdoch into her home, let alone pay him for the privilege.

Claire tried not to get too annoyed, because she had a suspicion that Sophie was actually attempting to be nice and helpful. They'd had a huge falling-out at the start of the year over two different but entirely unsuitable men, and Sophie had behaved worse over it. To the extent that she had nearly got Claire killed. Even though it was now nearly summer, there was an unspoken sense that Sophie still hadn't made up for it.

They went back into the front room. Claire sat on the sofa and found space amid the piles of books that lived on the coffee table, and which Basher was about to get round to reading any day now, to put down the mugs. Basher picked his up and put Wyatt down on the floor, because she was trying to put her whiffling little dog snoot into his tea.

'Alex has promised to train her properly,' said Basher, eyeing the dog. 'But I am sceptical.'

'I would be too,' said Sophie. She nodded for emphasis, which set the chestnut-brown curls of her hair, swept into a tight, high ponytail, bouncing.

'All right, fucking hell! I s'pose I shouldn't be surprised it's "have a go at Alex" day, because that's every day. I have enriched our lives,' said Alex. They bent over to look at Wyatt. 'Haven't I? Haven't I enriched our lives with the best dog in the world? Yes, I have. Yes, I have!'

Wyatt snorted in agreement and came up to Claire to start investigating her trainers.

'Have you personally enriched your bank account by getting a job?' asked Basher.

Alex had quit their part-time job in Brighton Library a few months ago to focus on their weird pop-culture embroidery projects, a venture that hadn't yet taken off. But Basher could literally afford to give Alex some leeway, because he had succeeded in selling his family's old country house to a hotel chain and thus also paying off the mortgage on his flat. Claire, for whom having close friends beyond Soph was a new experience, was happy for him, but she and Sophie paid rent to live in a basement flat under a newsagent's, next to a busy road and a set of traffic lights. Every time Alex and Basher did anything that she believed was an unconscious demonstration of their inherited wealth – such as not having to get a job – Claire chiselled the chip on her shoulder a little deeper. But she was fairly sure that neither Basher nor

Alex knew this and wouldn't mind if they did, because – after much anxiety that they didn't want to be friends with her – Basher had succeeded in persuading Claire that they did in fact like her and wouldn't hang around with her so much, if they didn't.

To everyone's surprise, even possibly their own, Alex pointed their finger at their uncle. '*Aha*! I have,' they said, in triumph. 'Well, sort of. Maybe,' they added, after thinking about it for a second and apparently deciding they needed to revise expectations down. 'I've definitely got Claire a job anyway. I've got one for me a bit.'

Claire perked up. 'You have?' Her income as a freelancer was variable and subject to more competition in her field, since she'd moved to Brighton.

'Sorry, how can one have a job *a bit*?' asked Basher.

'And why does your dog have a name like someone from Texas?' said Sophie, who had apparently been considering this point for some time.

'Hmm, who should I answer first? Decisions, decisions ...' said Alex. They flopped on the floor, and Wyatt came over and rolled into their lap, where she promptly fell asleep. 'Wyatt is named after a wrestler. So you know I got Wyatt off of some randomer? Turns out he's not a randomer, he's the owner of a local indie wrestling promotion, Sussex Wrestling Federation, and they were all practising there when I went to pick up Wyatt. And it was so cool! So he says I can enter their training school when the next intake starts in a couple of weeks, and I can help set up and tear down before and after shows. And if I'm good enough, I might end up performing sometime, and then I get a cut. Isn't that cool?'

'I am going to predict that this training school will cost money,' said Basher. He raised an eyebrow.

'Well, yeah, you can't expect people to train you for free,' said Alex.

'Right. I think that what you're describing sounds very much like the opposite of a job,' continued Basher.

'Speculate to accumulate, Uncle B,' said Alex cheerfully. *Chisel, chisel*, said Claire's treacherous brain.

'What sort of training is it? Like, for regionals? For the Olympics?' asked Claire.

'Ohmigod,' said Sophie. 'Can you imagine Alex leading Team GB, waving a flag?'

'Not that sort of wrestling,' replied Alex. They sat up a bit straighter. 'We, my friend, are talking about *pro-wrestling*. The magnetic and dangerous world of sports entertainment. That's a whole different bowl of potato salad.'

Basher rolled his eyes.

'What, like ... that guy who goes "Wooo!", and The Rock, and all that? It's fake, but not fake, and they get cross if you say it is. Really?' asked Claire.

'Bit out of date with your references, C, but yeah, broadly speaking,' said Alex. 'It's fake in that they decide who wins the match beforehand and they're not really trying to hurt each other, but the heroic feats of strength and hurricanranas off the top rope are all real, innit.'

Alex pulled up a video on their phone and then made it appear on the big TV screen. A man who resembled a sort of oiled Stretch Armstrong doll, glistening like the tears of gods, walked down a huge ramp as lights strobed and fireworks went off around him. He waved a hand in front of his face. The crowd screamed. Alex switched to another video, this time of a man who looked like the lead singer of an emo band, circa 2005. He climbed to the top of a metal ladder, which was balanced inside what looked like a boxing ring, and then leapt from it in a beautiful reverse swan-dive. He seemed to hang in the air for a second before he flipped over and went straight through a pane of glass set up on the outside of the ring. It was apparently there for the sole purpose of causing this man bodily injury, and it shattered in spectacular fashion. Claire was alarmed and impressed in equal measure.

Alex was in the habit of encountering a hobby or subculture that was hitherto unknown to them and then getting terrifically excited about it in short order, and learning all the necessary information to be an expert. They stuck at new special interests at a rate of about 10 per cent, which was why they were a very skilled embroiderer and could alter clothes, but no longer had any interest in baking olive bread or knitting fingerless gloves. It was more than possible this passion for pro-wrestling would wear itself out in about three weeks, but it was unwise to mention this to Alex when they were in their honeymoon period with it.

'I wouldn't have thought pro-wrestling was very you ...' Claire said, with some caution.

'Pro-wrestling as a theatrical performance of heteronormative masculinity is post-ironically cool,' said Alex, with a withering glance. 'Besides, there are a bunch of gender-diverse wrestlers now, and a history of performers being subversive and inclusive. And, like, at what point do you not just have to be the change you want to see in the world?'

'Right. Should have known, I suppose,' replied Claire, suitably chastened.

'I think it's well cool,' said Sophie. 'And Alex'll probably be quite bad at it, which will be funny,' she added. She sat down and started waving her fingers at Wyatt in a futile attempt to get the dog's attention.

'I will be as graceful as a gazelle,' said Alex, who was quite confident for a young person and had never run into anything they wouldn't try once, short of heroin – and even then Claire wasn't sure Alex wouldn't decide they'd be able to do it once and then stop. This sort of devil-may-care attitude was possibly why Basher worried so much about Alex as they took their first steps into the world as an adult.

'What's this other thing about Weirdo-here getting a job?' asked Sophie. 'I wouldn't have thought pro-wrestlers would have much call for a freelance medium who isn't very good at it.'

'They're quite superstitious actually,' said Alex. 'And that's exactly where C comes in. This guy – Ken, he's called – his dad died a few months ago and he reckons he's being haunted now.'

Claire was interested, despite herself. 'What, by his dad?'

'That's what he says. Should be easy enough to sort out, right?' responded Alex.

Claire looked over at Sophie, who shrugged. 'Could be fun. Like Alex said, either his dad is hanging around as a ghost or he isn't. Being haunted is kind of a binary issue, LOL.'

Claire was about to reply, but then Wyatt surprised everyone by running full pelt at Sophie and trying to leap on her. Because Sophie wasn't physically there, the poor dog skidded into the wall, turned and began to growl at Sophie in obvious affront.

'Er,' said Claire, 'can your dog see dead people?'

2

The King Is Dead

As a natural-born Popular Girl, Sophie's attitude towards most things she encountered in life was to be aloof. She had grasped far more quickly than other teens that if she acted like nothing anyone did or said impressed her, many of her peers would only redouble their efforts to do so. The fact that Sophie had died young meant she never got old enough to test this behaviour in adulthood. Most people who do so find out that it offers diminishing returns.

Claire had never been confident enough to use this tactic in the first place, and approaching her mid-thirties and being haunted by the ghost of her best friend, who was forever trapped as a teenager and had an extremely short attention span, had not increased her ability to socialize. When Soph had been alive and had, for reasons still unclear, decided to make Claire her best friend on the first day of big school, Claire had developed a circle of other friends by osmosis; when Soph disappeared six years later, at the age of seventeen, she no longer provided a layer of insulation between Claire's natural bent towards being a bit anxious and odd and everyone that Claire came into contact with. The oddness and anxiety were only reinforced by suddenly being able to see ghosts. Quite apart from the unexpected reappearance of her missing best friend precipitating a nervous breakdown – Sophie had turned up at Claire's elbow a few weeks after she'd gone, at a candlelit vigil for herself, loudly expressing disappointment at the numbers she'd pulled – from that day on, Claire could see all ghosts, everywhere. She became an even more strange, cold, twitchy sort of a person, often caught talking to thin air and, before she got good enough to tell a ghost apart from a living person on sight, avoiding eye contact. When ghosts figure out you can see them, they become more desperate for a conversation than – as Claire had recently found out – a Sky customer-service rep when you try to cancel your account.

Claire was working on being more assertive and self-confident, though, and, especially with Alex's encouragement, had accepted the idea that she was good at stuff and had things to offer the world. These things were perhaps very specific, but still.

Anyway the point was that, because she had been dead for a period of more than fifteen years, Soph had never encountered a living creature that didn't get on with her. And it was extremely clear that Wyatt, though she did not have the knowledge or ability to say as much, thought Sophie was a hideous affront to nature of the sort that should not be walking the Earth. Whenever Sophie went near her, she growled and yipped until Alex picked her up.

They were presently walking along a quiet-enough street in north Brighton, which Basher had parked at the end of, and Wyatt was getting so agitated that Alex had to ask Sophie to move further away. Alex couldn't hear or see Sophie's reply themself, of course, but Alex was the only person Claire had met who cheerfully acted as if they could, no matter the situation. Although Claire sometimes suspected that Alex could ... not *hear* Sophie exactly, but pick up impressions of her meaning sometimes. It was the nearest thing to another medium Claire had ever run into, and she was keeping a close eye on the situation to make sure she wasn't imagining it. In any case, Alex's attitude was quite embarrassing for Claire, who usually did the opposite, but in conversations with Alex and Basher she did at least repeat what Sophie said and did, for their benefit; it was usually rude. In this case Sophie stuck her tongue out at Alex and Wyatt.

They passed some rundown mixed-use units – the sort with an off-licence, hairdresser and purveyor of definitely real handbags on the ground floor, and little pebble-dashed flats on the first floor. Alex took them past the corner and down a little walled lane that was mossy at the edges, and Claire had the sense that if you walked down it during the night you'd feel a bit edgy, because there were no street lights. Alex turned off at the end of the lane and before them was a sort of village-hall-meets-barn kind of building, with breezeblock walls covered in thick white paint and a tin roof.

Above the door was a sun-faded sign, with the letters S.W.F. emblazoned on it in large black letters. Underneath, in slightly smaller ones, it said 'SUSSEX WRESTLING FEDERATION !' The kerning between the N and the exclamation mark was slightly off, and it made Claire immediately ill-disposed towards the owners.

'Bogey at ten o'clock,' muttered Sophie. She'd seen another ghost.

Claire glanced over and saw a short, balding white man in wide-legged jeans and a dark hoodie, which was covering the kind of taut, low beer-belly that made him look like he was smuggling a basketball. His whole vibe spoke of someone who had only stopped wearing a wallet chain because his long-suffering fiancée had told him she wouldn't go through with the wedding unless he did, and Claire really did not want to have a conversation with him. He was holding a notebook and was approaching them with what Claire considered to be an expression of horrible intent.

Luckily Alex had already barged through the door of the SWF – which was their favoured way of going through any portal – and stopped short, because the room was empty and there was, therefore, nobody to whom they could make a dramatic entrance. Basher quietly pulled the door closed behind them all, and the clunk of the handle was very loud in the quiet room. Claire noticed with relief that the other ghost had not followed them, which suggested that he couldn't, for some reason. Alex dropped Wyatt on the floor almost immediately, and Basher, with similar speed, scooped her up.

'Oh, would you relax? She used to live here,' said Alex.

Wyatt did, indeed, look quite bored, although she began to growl again as the relatively small size of the room forced her into closer proximity with Sophie. The air started to get cold, as it did when a ghost was in an enclosed space. Claire pulled down the sleeves of her jumper without thinking about it. She owned and wore a lot of warm clothes.

She was actually surprised at how small the place was, though. It was basically the sort of office you get when you move into an office that used to belong to a different company and make minimal changes. The carpet was faded blue and the texture of a Brillo pad, and towards the back of the room was a single wooden desk and an old computer. The walls had T-shirts hung up, with big, bold designs reminiscent of band-tour shirts. Sophie walked over and examined one section that had tees saying 'PNK' in Barbie-pink neon, others reading 'CPN' in gold and yet another that said 'PINK CHAMPAGNE' in elegant, sparkly script.

Soph tipped her head. 'Tag team maybe? Right?' She turned to look at Claire, who shrugged.

'Beats me,' she replied. 'I don't know anything about this. Why isn't anyone here?' She looked around again. It really didn't look like the sort of venue where you could watch two muscly beefcakes throw each other around.

'They're probably all out back in the main bit,' said Alex. 'Let's just go through there.'

'This is not our building. We will wait,' observed Basher. His serious tone was only slightly undercut by the juvenile terrier in his arms, which was squirming around and trying to lick his chin.

'I'll go and look,' said Sophie, and she strode out through the desk and the back wall with the directness you can only get when physical objects pose no barrier.

Claire started to shout, 'No, wait!' but Soph moved too fast. Claire staggered forward and into the desk, knocking over the computer screen. There was a muffled 'Ohmigod! Fucking – ow!' from the other side of the wall, matching Claire's own furious and pained swearing.

Neither Claire nor Sophie was exactly sure how, or why, Sophie was a ghost – or why anyone was a ghost really – but they had established some basic rules of hauntings through years of observation. The most important of these was the first one:

1. Ghosts are stuck in one area, usually where they lived or died, and a variable radius around that point.

In Sophie's case her area was, for some reason, Claire. They were tied together via a sort of force that Claire thought of as the tether, like an invisible thread of steel wire attached around her naval. A few months ago, while on a disastrous holiday, they had managed to stretch it to the point of breaking, which had caused them both a phenomenal amount of pain, and now it was extremely short and still very sore. When Claire had explained this to Alex and Basher, Alex had said it sounded like a footballer's hamstring, and Basher said that Alex didn't know anything about football and was just trying to show off; and then Alex asked who would they be showing off to – none of us like football anyway?

'Arses,' said Claire, with some feeling. She rubbed her knees, because she wasn't altogether sure the impact hadn't relocated her kneecaps to the back of her legs; and if that were the case, she'd have to walk like a goat, and people would film her in public to put on TikTok, and then probably very intense mothers' groups in America would accuse her of being the Antichrist, which was the last thing she needed.

Claire's runaway-thought train was interrupted by Alex coming over and starting to reset the bits and pieces that Claire had knocked over. Closer inspection revealed that the computer was merely a screen that wasn't attached to anything, and basically everything on the desk was the sort of stuff that was there because nobody had got round to throwing it out. Alex casually nosed in the desk's single drawer and Claire heard the rattle of a load of pens.

Basher, who was a former police detective and annoyingly good at accurately assessing the seriousness of a situation, asked Claire if there was any harm done, but in a tone of voice indicating that he already knew she was fine. 'Close that drawer this instant,' he added. 'And that pencil pot was on the other side of the stack of packing envelopes.'

'Yeah, but it makes way more sense where I put it,' replied Alex, the chaotic, vibes-based yin to their uncle's yang.

Sophie had by this point returned to the office and was doing slow breathing, like a yoga instructor during child labour.

'Sorry, Weirdo,' she said. 'That was a bad one. I keep forgetting.'

She was being unusually contrite about this one specific issue because it was inarguably entirely her fault. It was the same reason she was being nice and helpful.

'There's a guy coming, anyway,' Sophie continued. 'He's wearing a T-shirt with the sleeves cut off, so I assume he has no friends or they would have grabbed the scissors from him.' About most things, she was still offhand and rude.

Seconds later a man did indeed come through the door in the back wall. He was a short, fake-tanned white man – and was, as described, wearing a black SWF-logo T-shirt with the sleeves cut off, the better to give out free tickets to the gun show. In the small room he seemed approximately as broad as an articulated lorry, if lorries could be made out of beef. He was so big-featured and good-looking that he would have horseshoed back around into being bland and unforgettable, were it not for the terrifying size of him on the horizontal plane.

'It's like looking at a giant sack of oiled pumpkins,' said Sophie, in a tone of some respect. 'There's a horse hospital somewhere missing its entire supply of steroids.'

'Oh, hi again, Alex,' said the Jolly Orange Giant. His voice was deep, but he immediately switched to a widdle baby-talk voice to greet Wyatt, who had started to wriggle in Basher's arms. 'Hello, best girl! Who's the best girl in the whole world? Yes you are!'

He tickled Wyatt under the chin and she made a spirited effort to lick his entire hand in one go.

'Oh, sorry – I'm Ken King, operator of the Ess Doubleyoo Eff.'

He stuck out a hand the size of a loaf of bread, and Claire and Basher introduced themselves. Claire had expected her own hand to be crushed, but Ken carried himself with the careful and gentle air of a man who did actually know his own strength.

'Training school doesn't start for another week, Alex,' Ken went on. 'And you probably shouldn't be bringing Wyatt back here this soon. Poor kid'll get confused.' Ken seemed not to be registering how cold the office room was. He showed no signs of feeling temperature at all. His skin was so hairless and shiny that it was possible he was, like his more famous namesake, made of plastic.

'I know, I know. But Uncle B wanted to see the place before he signed me over to you for controlled bodily harm, you know? And I brought Claire about ... about the other thing, right?'

'Oh! You're the medium?' Ken studied Claire with renewed interest. She was sure she would be found wanting. People expect – and sort of want – mediums to say vague but significant things, wear a lot of eye make-up and swathe themselves in scarves. Claire had badly dyed black hair, a pink-tinged nose from being constantly cold and wore big baggy jumpers and skinny jeans. She had the vibes of a standard millennial mum who was still trying to look cool, but didn't have everything together – if a millennial mum was terrified of children, because she had no idea how to speak to them. The fact that she could see and talk to ghosts made being a freelance medium basically the easiest career path available to Claire, but because it's hard to do theatrics when a translucent pensioner is shouting at you about how much they hate their neighbour's son, it was also the biggest barrier to being a successful freelance medium. Which, Claire thought, was wildly unfair.

Ken was still looking at her.

'Oh. Er, yeah. That's me. Alex said you had a ghost.'

'She's honestly very good. Sort your haunting in two seconds,' asserted Alex, in a show of support.

'Well, I'm at the point where I'll try anything,' said Ken. He paused and looked back at Alex. 'I could swear you didn't have hair like a drumstick lolly the other day, you know.'

Basher and Sophie barked a surprised laugh at the same time. Claire thought that, by matching Alex at their own game, Ken had shown to Basher that he would, at least on one level, be able to look after Alex. The little policeman behind Basher's eyes made a note. Claire wondered if Ken had done this knowingly, and if he was able to size up everyone he met that fast.

'Come into the main building.' said Ken. 'We use this for the box office on show days and as somewhere for deliveries to leave stuff, that kind of thing.'

'Oh, right. Er, how did you know we were here then?' asked Claire. 'We didn't ring a bell or anything.'

Ken pointed to a tiny digital camera up in the corner of the ceiling. 'We're basically never in here, to be honest, and there's nothing worth nicking, but just in case anyone buggers off with a T-shirt, we'd know who it was.' He got out his phone and opened an app, and suddenly they were looking at a tiny version of themselves staring at Ken's phone, which was displaying an even tinier version of themselves. Claire did not think about this too hard because she had a tenuous grip on reality versus fantasy as it was, and spending half an hour pondering recursion and whether the little versions of them all in the phone went on for ever would do nobody any favours.

'See, there's a live feed and it sends an alert to your phone if the motion sensor picks up anyone in here. Good, right? Wasn't that expensive, either. Dad was chuffed with it. There's one covering the door to the locker room as well, because the wrestlers leave their gear there.' Ken tapped the screen again and brought up the view of an empty corridor somewhere else in the building, and then closed the app. 'Okay, follow me and I'll show you around. We'll go into the proper office first.' He jerked his head towards the back door, and they all trooped after him as he went through it.

The door opened directly into a large space that looked like a school gym, but Claire only got a glimpse of it before Ken led them off to the side into another office, this one obviously used all the time. There were a couple of filing cabinets, a desk with a plugged-in computer, and stacked chairs and boxes. The desk was covered in paper and the filing cabinet was partially open. Ken went over to close it and seemed, for the first time, a bit embarrassed. Here was a man who spent his time jumping around in tiny pants in front of crowds. Was he really abashed at a bit of mess? He settled in the chair behind the desk and laced his fingers together in the attitude of a businessman.

'Do you do this sort of thing a lot then?' he said.

'Oh, you're talking to me?' Claire realized. She could sense Sophie rolling her eyes, without even needing to look. 'Er, a bit,' she replied.

'Yeah, right. Haven't done a proper seance for months,' said Soph.

This was correct. Claire's business as a ghost-talkerer had undergone a small boost when she moved to Brighton, because it was the sort of place populated by people ready to believe in ghosts; but it un-boosted quite quickly because it was also the sort of place populated by Tarot readers who were more than ready to light incense and talk about how your grandmother wanted you to know you're worthy of love, which was the flavour of observation Claire found actual ghosts didn't really bother their arse to make. Your grandmother was more likely to go on about the fact that you didn't visit her enough when she had a bad foot that one time. Dying didn't make people beatific angels, it simply made them dead. Claire was on the verge of asking Mr Przybylski, who ran the shop above her basement flat, if he had any shifts going. The commute was ideal.

'Well, I dunno how much Alex told you, but SWF is a family business, right? My dad, my uncle and, well, the pair of them, founded this place, and now we're the largest pro-wrestling training school in the area. We put on regular shows and we're one of the only big indies still making a living outside London, cos a huge multinational company started its own official feed for new talent and – look, that doesn't really matter. What matters is that my dad built this place up from nothing, and he died a couple of months ago.'

'Was it a shock? Or, like, was it peaceful?' asked Claire, who was just about considerate enough to know one probably shouldn't ask a recently bereaved person, 'Was your father's death violent?'

'Sort of "no" on both counts, I suppose,' replied Ken. 'He had high blood pressure and we were trying to persuade him to step back from in-ring performing. He'd already had a heart attack last year and was on medication for the blood pressure, so when he died here after a workout ... I wouldn't describe it as peaceful, and it was sudden. But it wasn't exactly a shock, either, you know?'

'Who found him?' asked Basher. There was an edge of impatience to his voice, and Claire sensed that it was less because he wanted to get the conversation over, and more because his ex-copper instincts were kicking in and he felt she wasn't getting enough salient facts.

'Mum. It was the morning of a show and he'd left some paperwork behind, so she took it over and found Dad on the floor. It wasn't pleasant for her, as you can imagine.'

Basher nodded. 'The police cleared it fairly quickly, I imagine,' he said.

'Yeah.' Ken frowned slightly. 'Why wouldn't they? There wasn't anything suspicious about his death.'

'Of course. I just mean that it is routine to double-check, when someone dies unexpectedly,' said Basher.

'Yeah, that's what they told Mum,' agreed Ken.

'Uncle B used to be filth,' said Alex, with a helpful grin. It earned a frown from Basher and a chin tilt of acknowledgement from Ken.

'Ah, right,' he said. 'Didn't know that.'

'Did your father die with any regrets? Stuff he wanted to see happen that didn't?' Claire asked.

She saw the corners of Basher's eyes twitch, as if he wanted to smile, as she dragged the interview back to her own, more paranormal side of the tracks.

Ken raised his eyebrows in some surprise at this. 'Wow, is "unfinished business" actually a thing? I thought that was only in stories.'

'Unfortunately it is,' muttered Sophie. This was rule number two on the list of Things Claire Knew About Ghosts:

2. Ghosts usually hang around if they have some kind of unfinished business. Getting rid of the unfinished business will often get rid of the ghost. The meaning of 'unfinished business' is, however, unhelpfully flexible. It can range from 'being murdered' to 'Everton haven't won the Premier League since the 1980s' and 'I wanted to call my sister a bitch one last time.'

In Claire's experience, solving a murder was sometimes the easiest bit. But Sophie was growing more annoyed at her own circumstances, because the current chances of her own murder being solved were about as high as Everton's. Her disappearance was officially a cold case.

'Yeah, it can be,' replied Claire cautiously. 'So do you think your dad had any?'

'Maybe,' said Ken. 'I suppose the first step is if you just tell me whether Dad's here. That I'm not going off my rocker. And then we can figure out the rest, regarding you … I don't want to say "exorcise". But if Dad is here, he needs to move on, doesn't he?'

'Why do you think your rocker stability is compromised?' asked Basher, leaning slightly forward. He often tried to pretend he was above the shenanigans that Alex got Claire involved in, but equally he often couldn't resist poking his nose in if it caught his interest.

In response to the question, Ken rubbed the bridge of his nose and looked around.

'Oh, he's finally got a bit shy about thinking there's a ghost knocking around,' said Sophie. 'Big, physical man like him, terrified by a bed sheet? Where's his street cred?'

'I was telling this lot: wrestlers are a bit superstitious, right?' said Alex helpfully.

'Well, yeah, with pre-show ritual stuff and that, but ghosts is a bit ... Things move,' said Ken. He was clearly uncomfortable. 'Doors slam shut by themselves. I hear things, late at night when everyone else has gone. The performers are complaining about the temperature, and sometimes you get a proper all-body shiver. I know you can have natural explanations for all that stuff, but it's only been happening since Dad died, and it's not like a window has been left open. Plus, I had to get rid of Wyatt. She started tear-arsing around and barking at nothing, out of nowhere. It was driving us all up the bloody wall.'

Claire glanced at Sophie, who shrugged. They had not encountered a dog that could see ghosts before. It was possible Wyatt was just a weird dog.

'Well,' said Claire, 'I can't see anyone in this particular room, apart from us lot.'

She double-checked. Some ghosts could disappear, but every ghost made the area cold, so a sudden chill was either a ghost trying to poke you or an indication that you'd left the freezer door open. But it was also a reminder of point three:

> 3. It is important to sort out unfinished business as quickly as possible, if you can, because ghosts – if they hang around for too long without any purpose – start to become less human and solid-looking. They can lose their emotions, memory and eventually their voice and form entirely. Old ghosts are just insubstantial, freezing mist.</D1>

Claire hated those ones. You couldn't even tell if it was the right ghost. Someone could have hired you to chat to their great-great-grandfather and it might as well have been a fog machine. Ken's dad was a recent death, so if he was a mist ghost, something had gone catastrophically wrong.

'Well, I've got no problem with you checking the rest of the place. If you follow the corridor around, there are toilets, a locker room and showers, but it's mostly – well, I can show you,' said Ken. He got his confident little grin back. He beckoned them to follow him out and they got a proper look at the SWF gym for the first time.

Claire hadn't been expecting a huge arena with seating tiers, but neither had she thought it would so closely resemble an English primary-school gym. She got this impression because the floor was varnished wood under spot-lighting, and a handful of people in loose gym gear were practising rolls and flips on gym mats. There were a lot of slaps, and occasional grunts as someone landed heavily. Towards the back of the room was what looked a lot like a boxing ring – which is to say, a square platform about three feet off the ground, with three-ring ropes going around all four sides, making a sort of fence. Two people were in the ring and were taking turns picking each other up and flipping each other over. Every time one of them landed there was a loud bang.

'Good, isn't it?' said Ken. 'The ring itself is made of planks with padding on them, so they rattle individually, and it makes a great noise. On show nights we have live mics under the ring – gives an even better effect.'

'I thought you said training didn't start for a couple of days?' said Claire.

'It doesn't; these are just some of the usual gang putting in extra time.'

At this juncture Wyatt squirmed so much that she sort of back-flipped out of Basher's arms and dropped to the floor. Jack Russells were apparently very robust, though, because she bounced back to her feet and capered over to the nearest wrestler. This was a fit, muscular woman – though not so muscular that she looked like she would burst if she encountered a cactus, like Ken – who was notably very miserable.

'She's doing Florence Pugh sad face,' remarked Sophie, who had been introduced to Florence Pugh, and her various expressions, only a couple of weeks ago when Alex had made them watch *Midsommar*.

The miserable woman became momentarily happy

again at the appearance of Wyatt and immediately fell to her knees to receive a face-wash. The other wrestlers around the place made their way over too, and started cooing as if the dog was in fact a baby.

Sophie gave a little alert whistle and jerked her head. The two wrestlers in the ring were still practising, and a third person was watching them from the side. Point four of the essential nature of ghosts:

4. Ghosts can look like they did when they were alive, or like they did when they died, or like whatever state their body was in, which meant that Claire was now quite philosophical about skeletons and head wounds.

If you knew what you were looking for, ghosts were easy to tell apart from living people – even the ones that didn't have a gunshot wound or were a bit decomposed. They went see-through in bright light and more solid in darkness, for example. Once you'd seen a few of them, you could tell a ghost from a mile off because they had a certain wrongness to them, like someone who had been green-screened into reality.

Sophie was the kind of ghost who was going to wear exactly the same clothes she'd died in for ever, including the little butterfly hairclips and the white trainers. It seemed that Ken's dad was similar, because he was wearing nothing except a threadbare blue towel tucked around his waist.

It was a prodigious waist. King Snr was big and strong, but fat rather than muscled, and was the same pink colour as cooked ham. He was also entirely bald. It was giving Charlie Bronson.

'Terrible fucking form!' he shouted at the two in the ring.

They, of course, didn't hear him, but Claire had unwisely winced at the volume of his yell, so he immediately turned on her.

'You can see me, can't you?' roared Mr King, in a tone of triumph that cost him nothing in volume. 'Don't pretend you can't! Right, you have to tell my boy – I've been trying to give him the message for weeks. That bastard Nate killed me, and I'm not going nowhere until he's gone down for it.'

'Interesting. We should be used to this by now, I suppose,' said Sophie. She yawned a bit too theatrically for Claire's liking.

'Fucksake,' said Claire. It was almost the last thing she'd wanted to hear from Daddy King. 'I hope you're not an Everton fan as well,' she added, after a moment's consideration.

3

Long Live the King

If Mr King – who introduced himself as Eddie, and Claire lost a few seconds trying to figure out if Eddie King was a good name for a wrestler or if he would have been better off as, for example, starting a long-haulage business, because Eddie King would look good on the side of a lorry – was correct and he had been murdered, it would technically be the fourth murder Claire had encountered in less than a year. It was upsetting to her that the average kept increasing. Previously she just had the one murder victim hanging around all the time. Technically, she supposed, she probably had run into a lot of long-dead murder victims still kicking about, because by the law of, you know, maths, a non-zero percentage of the ghosts she saw in her life would have been killed by someone else. But it's not like she asked them all the time. It would be rude.

'Who's Nate?' she asked. This seemed the most pressing information for any amateur detective to discover.

Until recently Claire had been a true-crime fan of many years' standing, and she'd always suspected that she'd be able to solve a murder if it came down to it. She had turned out to be right – a lot of help from Sophie notwithstanding – but it hadn't made her happy. It had made her stop liking true crime as much.

Eddie opened his mouth to reply, but one of the wrestlers in the ring had heard her and said, 'What?'

'Rookie move, Weirdo,' said Soph. She was right. Normally Claire only slipped up and talked to a ghost in front of other people if she was very tired or specially annoyed. She had a Bluetooth headset that she usually wore when out and about, to make it seem like she was always on the phone, but she'd taken it off to talk to Ken.

'What was that?' asked the wrestler again. He was a tall, lithe Black man with warm reddish-brown skin and mid-length dreadlocks tied back in a ponytail. He was breathing hard as he came over, and flopped his arms over the ropes to talk to Claire. 'Did you ask about Nate? He's not in today, I think he's over checking on Trudy.'

'Bet he is, the greasy fuck,' spat Eddie.

'Oh – I ... I don't actually know anyone. I, er ...' Claire tried to think of a plausible excuse.

'Come on, I thought you were getting better at thinking on your feet,' commented Sophie. 'You have a legitimate reason for being here, remember?'

Claire coughed to cover a sort of nervous burp and took a deep breath in. Sophie usually offered her own commentary on conversations, but it was often unhelpful.

It meant that Claire either left long pauses while she listened to what Sophie was saying or had to ask people to repeat themselves several times, because Sophie talked over them.

'A friend of mine is going to start the training-school thing soon, maybe,' she replied. 'And, erm, Ken invited us to look around here.'

Claire, despite having been doing it as her main source of income for about fifteen years now, was still a bit embarrassed by having to say that her job was being a medium. Most people, reasonably, didn't believe her and thought she was a weirdo at best, a charlatan taking advantage of people's grief at worst. Besides, she wasn't sure if Ken wanted to broadcast that he suspected – correctly, as it turned out – that the SWF was haunted by his dead dad.

'Oh, right, sound. I'm Guy, this is Ruby. Rubes, c'mere.'

The other wrestler in the ring, who had been stretching her arms behind her head, came and flopped on the ropes next to Guy. She was a very tall white woman and was built like a bodybuilder, the same colour as fine porcelain, but of inverse fragility. Ruby had dark, mischievous eyes and a dyed blonde buzzcut that was uncannily similar to Basher's hair, although Ruby looked as if she could snap Basher in half like a breadstick.

'I bet they're the tag team,' said Sophie.

'We're a mixed tag team,' said Ruby. Sophie looked smug. 'We wrestle together as "Pink Champagne".'

'Oh, cool. We saw your T-shirts in the little storefront office-thing,' replied Claire.

'Yup,' said the distractingly unclothed Eddie. 'They'd be our biggest draw, wrestling as singles, but they insist on booking as a tag team. Anyway they've been off their game recently. Terrible form.'

Eddie radiated the attitude of a man who would self-describe as 'I speak as I find', who would call a spade a spade and, furthermore, knew the difference between a spade and a shovel. Eddie knew how to rewire a plug, put up a shelf, and when he saw what he considered shit form in the ring, he'd call it out. Claire thought he would not have been particularly nurturing as either a father or a wrestling trainer.

'Who's joining the school?' asked Guy.

'Oh, er, Alex.' Claire pointed. 'With the two-tone hair.'

'Ah, they took Wyatt, right?'

'Yup. They're ... enthusiastic.'

Ruby laughed. 'Well, that can get knocked out of you the first time you take a bump. There are always a lot of people who sign up but don't come back for the second lesson.'

'Lot of kids think it's easy,' sniffed Eddie. Sophie shushed him, so he wouldn't distract Claire, which struck Claire as very 'do as I say, not as I do'.

The wrestlers' commentary was promising, though. Alex wasn't any kind of a gym bunny and also smoked a lot of weed, which, as substances went, wasn't really a get-up-and-go motivational kind of drug. On the other hand, Claire was pretty sure Alex was going to fall instantly in love with Ruby and do anything to impress her.

'Nate'll probably be at the first lesson,' said Guy. 'He's the owner.'

'Oh, I thought Ken was the owner,' replied Claire, realizing that she had made the classic rookie-detective mistake of an assumption. It was one of the worst things you could do as a detective on her favourite police-procedural TV show *Murder Profile*. It was second only to allowing a suspect to ask for a lawyer without getting them to confess first.

Guy shrugged. 'Well, for whatever reason, Eddie left all his share of the business to his brother Nate, not his son. Doesn't really make a difference to us, and Ken doesn't seem bothered.'

'Yeah, neither does Trudy,' said Ruby, with what might be considered a definite tone. She snickered. 'Eddie was going to retire soon anyway, so him dying sort of moved things up a bit, I suppose.'

Guy gave her an elbow and a stern look and said that they needed to get back to practising. Eddie watched them with a face like a slapped arse.

'Come on then,' said Sophie. She prodded Eddie's towel-covered stomach, and he slapped her hand away.

'Come on, what?' he growled.

'Who's Trudy? Why d'you think you were killed? Explain your fuckin' self!' said Sophie, undeterred by Eddie's prickly demeanour. 'You can't just walk up and say you were murdered without expecting basic enquiry afterwards.'

Eddie slapped a hand to his forehead and slowly wiped it down his face. Claire half-expected him to transition from a frowny face to a happy face, like a weird semi-nude mime, but it turned out to be a method of mastering himself in a frustrating situation, because he took a deep breath and relaxed his shoulders.

Claire was aware that, to any onlookers, she was standing still, away from everyone else, doing nothing. She looked at the ceiling and contrived the attitude of someone who was interested in cobwebby light fixtures, and then looked at the floor and scuffed her foot as if she had seen a stain, but it made an alarming squeaking noise. 'Could we go outside or something?' she muttered.

'Can't,' huffed Eddie. 'I'm stuck in this bleedin' building.'

She wondered how to best continue a conversation with invisible people in a big echoing room, and noticed an arrow sign indicating that toilets could be found through a door on the opposite wall. Once inside them, Claire was relieved to discover that the toilets were extremely clean, but there were no showers in evidence, so the locker room and showers that Ken had mentioned must be hidden somewhere else in the building. The SWF was much like the TARDIS – that is, it seemed much bigger on the inside (and also it felt like a lot of bisexuality had hitherto been left subtextual, so as not to alienate the more conservative elements of the audience).

Claire checked under the cubicle doors. She huffed in the increasingly cold air, as the two ghosts in one comparatively small place started to make the place frigid enough to turn the tip of her nose Rudolf-red.

'All right, same question,' she said, less self-conscious now, and at a more normal volume. 'Who is Trudy?'

'Trudy is my wife,' said Eddie.

'Your ex-wife,' Claire said automatically.

'Nah, more like he's her ex-husband,' replied Sophie and cackled. 'Get it, Eddie? Because you're *ex*, like as in—'

'Yes, I bloody get it!' responded Eddie, going from an attitude of 'man at an even keel' to 'man who has had his pint of Stella slightly spilled during England v. Scotland at the Euros' at record-breaking speed. 'How long have you been dead? Cos it hasn't been long for me, and it takes some getting used to, all right? Do you want me to tell you what's wrong or do you want to keep interrupting with smart-arse comments?'

Claire inclined her head. Sophie raised her hands in a gesture of truce. 'All right, fair enough, Eddie. Apols. Go on.'

'Trudy is my bloody wife, okay? Childhood sweethearts, we are. Together nigh-on forty years. Only Ruby and Guy, and half the bloody locker room, think she's stepping out on me with Nate.'

'Stepping out? Is this the 1800s? Are you Queen Victoria's youngest son?' said Sophie. Claire snorted, and covered it up with a bad fake sneeze. 'Anyway,' Soph went on, 'that doesn't mean Nate killed you, does it?'

'No, but I know he done it, because I saw him!'

Claire felt her eyebrows rise. That was quite compelling testimony. Sophie had tipped her head on one side, which meant she thought so too.

'What do you mean, you *saw* him?'

'So, I was here. I'd just arrived to do weights and cardio, like I usually do, cos I got to keep my core fitness up, yeah? I went into the locker room, got changed, took one of my pills, did a workout. I finished up and had a shower, but I'd been feeling weird the whole time. I had a tummy ache and it got worse, and then I started to feel prickly in my chest. I couldn't breathe properly, my heart was going mad and I felt sick as a dog. So I went to go outside and get some air, but I never got that far. I yakked up on the floor and everything.'

'In fairness, that sounds like you were poisoned. Are you sure you didn't overdose or something by accident?'

'No! I take those damn pills all the time – nothing like that ever happened before.'

'Mhmm,' said Sophie. 'And at what point did you see your brother?'

'Twice. The first time I'd just arrived and gone into the locker room. I got an alert on that security-app thing that someone had come through the front office. I didn't think anything of it, but when I checked on the app I saw it was Nate, and something about him looked strange. He was in his gear as well, so maybe he had come to practise before the show too, but he'd not mentioned it.'

'Sure, he probably wasn't about to tell you he was planning your surprise murder,' said Sophie. 'Hurry your story along; this is taking fucking ages.'

'Don't rush witnesses,' said Claire.

'Thank you,' sniffed Eddie. 'Anyway, I go out there to check and Nate's gone, so I go outside, in case I can catch up with him, but no sign. Go back into the locker room, take my pill like normal and a couple of hours later I end up face-down on the floor, don't I? I hear someone walking over to me and the next thing I know, I see Nate's wrestling boots in front of my bleeding face. Signature red leather, white stars up the sides,' continued Eddie. 'No one else wears them. And muggins here thought to himself, "Oh, thank Christ – Nate'll call the ambulance, I'll be all right." So, as you can imagine, it was an extra-large shock to me when I reappeared looking down at my own dead body.'

'Boots aren't exactly a smoking gun. A smoking shoe. Maybe Nate was there for another reason and got scared,' she suggested.

'I know what I saw,' Eddie replied. He folded his arms and stared Claire down.

'But what if someone else put on his gea—'

'Nobody else ever wore his gear,' said Eddie, speaking to Claire as one would to a child who was struggling to understand why changing ten quid to ten dollars did not mean you literally had more money. 'Nate is a lot of things – and one of them is really superstitious, and a really traditional wrestler. He was wearing those boots years ago when he was training in Mexico. He narrowly missed splitting his head open in a bad fall, and now he won't work without them. And if anyone else put on any of his gear? They'd be on a hiding to nowhere. He'd bar them from the whole gym. They'd never work a show here again.'

'Ah, come on—' Sophie started to say.

'I'm serious, it wouldn't happen.' Eddie crossed his arms. End of conversation.

'All right, fine. But like I said, it's pretty obvious from your description that you were poisoned,' she added. 'That's usually a woman's murder weapon, did you know that? And the point with poisoning is that the murderer doesn't have to be anywhere near you when it happens.'

'Well then, why did Nate come here, see me dying, and do nothing about it?' Eddie asked. It was clearly a rhetorical question, because he viewed 'because he fucking murdered me' as the obvious answer.

Claire had to admit, if only to herself and not out loud, that Nate's logic was fairly compelling. She tugged at her lip, thinking. 'I guess we need to find those meds then. To have them, er, analysed or whatever.'

'Well, I've no bloody idea where they are, do I?'

'Maybe the police have them,' she said to herself. She remembered something else. 'Are you slamming doors and moving people's stuff around?' she asked.

'A bit,' replied Eddie proudly. 'If I concentrate really hard, I can sometimes move stuff. And I think if I concentrate and shout really loud, you can hear me a bit. I tried to shut doors in Morse code and that, but it didn't work, cos once I manage to get one shut, I have to wait for someone to open it again.' He rubbed the back of his head with a reflective expression. 'I don't know Morse code, either.'

'Well,' Claire replied, 'knock it off. You're freaking people out.' She became aware that, to everyone else in the gym, she was either having the world's longest piss or a big poo. 'Ugh. Right. Fine,' she went on. 'Step one, I'm going to talk to some people with a pulse and figure out some things. You'll have to bear with me.'

Eddie did not have the attitude of someone who bore other people with much equanimity. He hurried after her as she left the toilets, making noises like a small steam engine.

Alex shouted a 'hey-o!' down the hall as Claire emerged back into the gym, so Claire walked over to where they stood with Basher, Ken and a bunch of wrestlers taking it in turns to stroke Wyatt. The ghosts accompanied her. Eddie still looked a combination of frustrated and angry, and Sophie seemed marginally less bored than normal. Claire noticed, too, that while Sophie made a careful effort not to walk through people, Eddie did not. He walked as if he still expected people to move out of the way for him, but it meant that as he clipped into them, they got a sudden full-body-shudder moment, which explained the sensations Ken had told them about. It wouldn't make the gym seem *not* haunted.

The initial excitement of Wyatt's return abated, and people began returning to their own practice areas, or else rolled up mats and got ready to leave. Ken was talking to Alex and Basher – who had retrieved Wyatt – and had an arm around the miserable-looking woman who had earlier greeted the excitable little dog.

'Hey, Claire,' he said. 'This is Lila, my wife.'

Claire shook Lila's hand, which had the same confidence and grip as a used tissue, despite her obvious muscle tone. 'You're a wrestler too?' she asked.

'Yeah. Trying, anyway! Ken has been helping me with my character work.'

'We've been pushing a new gimmick,' said Ken proudly. 'It's going to get her over any day, I know it.'

'It's bleedin' rubbish,' grunted Eddie.

Claire winced, and Alex clocked it immediately. 'Any sign of spooks, C?' they asked, not bothering to lower their voice.

'Er, yeah. I suppose so,' replied Claire awkwardly.

'What d'you mean, you suppose so!?' said Eddie, enraged. 'I've been bloody murdered – you need to tell my son about it right now!'

'He's quite loud,' mumbled Claire.

Eddie reached out in his anger and slapped a hand on her shoulder. But nothing happened. This was unusual. Normally Claire felt a strange tingling *zip*, which meant that a ghost had managed to plug into her life energy and was draining it like a battery. Sophie went to slap Eddie's hand away, but then frowned as she registered that he hadn't even touched her.

Still, Claire shuddered all over. She'd nearly died

recently from a ghost using her as a battery with malicious intent, and consequently she was anxious about even Sophie doing it to her now. It was, unfortunately, a centrepiece for when they did seances, which was another reason why Claire hadn't done any big proper shows for months. She'd have to get over it soon, because her bank account was feeling the strain and she was having to reach for the really cheap instant ramen packets again. The kind on the bottom shelf, with noodles made of powdered cardboard and flavour names like Super Chicken Classic. She didn't want to go back to eating plain rice.

'What was that about?' asked Eddie.

'Mind your fucking beeswax,' snapped Soph.

Claire looked at her feet, partly to avoid looking at Eddie, whose expression was thunderous.

'What's going on?' asked Lila.

'Look, Ken, your dad is … He's here, right? And he's …' Claire paused, because people generally wanted good news from their dead relatives and if she made a murder accusation, it dawned on her that most people would interpret this as *her* making the accusation, rather than delivering one on behalf of a ghost. 'Well, let's say he's definitely got some unfinished business to talk about.'

Lila put a hand to her mouth.

'Well, what is it?' asked Ken.

'Er, I think I'd rather talk to you a bit about it first.' She glanced at Eddie, who had clenched his fists and looked like he wanted to chin her – being dead notwithstanding.

'It's a pretty simple message to pass on, love!' he said.

'Oh, put a fucking cork in it; it's not like you've got a fast-approaching time limit, is it?' snapped Sophie.

'It's very unattractive for a young lady to swear,' replied Eddie, glaring at her.

Eddie clearly wasn't as good at reading people as his son. Letting Sophie know that she could annoy you simply by swearing was like opening a floating abattoir off the beach at Amity Island.

'Suck my dick,' said Sophie. Her tone was mild, but there was intense glee in her eyes.

'Maybe we could talk about it ... outside?' Claire suggested. She realized she had once again been silent for several seconds longer than was normal, watching an argument that nobody else could see. Her suggestion made Eddie even more furious, but since if they went somewhere else they wouldn't be near him, this didn't worry Claire in the immediate.

'Sure, okay. You know what, I'll clear this lot out anyway,' said Ken. 'Lila, can you help with packing up, pet?'

Ken stuck two fingers in his mouth and whistled, then told everyone they didn't have to go home, but they couldn't stay here.

'You know who does have to fucking stay here? Eh?' Eddie roared, as Claire and Sophie retreated outside to wait, where Eddie could not follow. Alex, Basher and Wyatt soon followed, and a few moments later the gym door slammed open and disgorged Ken. Lila was skip-walking behind him to keep up. He turned and threw some keys at her, which she dropped, then asked her to lock up even as he continued his stride towards them. He reminded Claire of a much shorter Terminator. A brick wall would provide only a momentary barrier to Ken's determined walk. Claire had a vision of him appearing, nude (although she imagined Ken was smooth like a Ken doll) in an alleyway, and trying the clothes/boots/motorcycle thing in his London-lite Brightonian accent.

They walked a little further away from the gym building, up to the wall bordering the area, which Ken leaned heavily against while they waited for the wrestlers who'd been practising to file away. Alex let Wyatt flop to the ground and both dog and owner stretched.

'The bogey is back,' said Sophie. The bald, bearded, notebook-wielding ghost from earlier had clearly not left while they'd been inside the SWF and was awkwardly jogging over to the group.

'Hello, ladies,' he said. He sounded like he had a boiled sweet in his mouth, but Claire wasn't sure if that was because he had died choking on one or because he had one of those slightly damp, unfortunate-sounding voices.

Sophie turned on him with the stance and hiss of a cornered alley cat. 'Shut up and fuck off!' she snarled. It worked by about half, in that he shut up, but didn't fully walk away and hovered on the edge of the conversation out of Sophie's eyeline. Claire tried not to look at him.

Ken didn't shiver, but Claire could see goosebumps appearing on his arms, as two ghosts suddenly made the air temperature drop a few degrees. He pulled at his lip with one hand and stared at Claire. It was disconcerting and she took a step back, and then thought that wasn't the sort of thing a seasoned detective who stared death in the face every day would do, so she stepped forward again.

'You look like you need a wee,' said Sophie. She picked at invisible hangnails, which was her favourite thing to do when she was affecting boredom.

Ken shifted and slid down the wall until he was on his haunches. It was an odd situation, because theoretically he had put himself in a position of weakness, if you subscribed to the kind of alpha-dog bullshit that said you should never extend your arm more than halfway when shaking hands. Ken was sitting while everyone else was standing, so he was looking up at them all. But he seemed perfectly at ease, and Claire felt like she was the one at a disadvantage. Granted, she felt like that most of the time, which may have been a factor.

'All right, go on then,' said Ken, after what Claire felt was an uncomfortable length of time spent studying her.

Basher had stepped up beside her, which made her feel better.

'Er, well, it's like I said – and like you thought. Your dad is haunting the … I dunno, would you call it a gym? Venue? He's, um, slightly embarrassing, but he's in a blue towel. Like he's had a shower and mostly dried off, but he's not got dressed yet.'

Ken's expression didn't change, but his eyes flickered.

'You hit home there,' said Sophie.

'What else?' Ken asked.

'He, well, he's heard some people talking in the locker room about, erm, about your mum and your uncle. People think there's something going on. But also your dad is pretty ... he's pretty sure that your Uncle Nate killed him. He says he saw it. So, that's ... um, that's everything, I think.'

Ken kept looking at her. He seemed to be thinking again. He almost, Claire thought, looked relieved.

'Honestly I'm happy to hear I'm not going mad,' he replied. He stuck his hand out. 'I don't know about murder. Dad had a temper; he probably got his wires crossed. I just want you to help him pass over. Whatever it takes. Can you do that?'

Claire cleared her throat. 'Uh, I mean, I can try.'

'Good.' Ken paused. 'You should come to our show tomorrow.'

Next to her, Claire heard Basher say, very quietly, 'Oh, for fuck's sake.'

4

The Squared Circle

According to Ken, and the SWF website, they had a show every month (although in years past it had been twice a month). Despite Basher's loud protestations, tickets were bought for the next evening. Alex was excited, Basher was practising his 'I am incredibly weary' face, Claire had no idea what to expect and Sophie was practically vibrating.

They left Wyatt behind – Alex swearing that they had definitely walked her, so she wouldn't pee anywhere and she would 100 per cent not chew anything – and made their way to the SWF gym. Sophie had started calling it a barn, because it was a big shed full of beef, and Claire was struggling not to say that out loud. Doors were opened at 5 p.m. for a show start at 6.30, which seemed quite early, but Alex helpfully explained that the shows could go on for *hours*, which made Basher actually groan. There was a steady stream of people, skewing heavily to the demographic of young men in video-game T-shirts, bypassing the fake little office room and heading straight to the gym, and Alex confidently joined them with the single-minded determination of a salmon fighting its way to the spawning ground.

'Oh, wow,' said Sophie as they turned the corner. 'I'm starting to be impressed.'

The gym and the concrete expanse in front of it had been transformed with, if not showbiz magic, then showbiz magic's non-union fell-off-a-lorry equivalent. Multicoloured fairy lights picked out the edges of the walls and roof of the gym and outlined the windows and doors. There were folding tables set up everywhere, decked with more lights, where you could buy cans of Monster Energy, bags of Doritos or mini Mars Bars, all emblazoned with 'MULTIPACK – NOT TO BE SOLD SEPARATELY'. The most popular corner held a pair of stocky men with a pair of stocky coolers, full of ice and cans or bottles that they were selling for £3 a throw. The second most-popular area, and certainly the largest set-up, was a double-table-spread of T-shirts for the wrestlers who would be on that evening. The entire enterprise was, obviously, cash only. Opposite the doors, and powered by a generator making the same noise as a ride-on lawnmower, was a small black food van called 'SLATER'S TATERS'. It sold very large baked potatoes.

'I will get us some drinks,' said Basher. He was very admirably suppressing any instinct he might have had to narc on everything.

Alex made a beeline for the potatoes, despite having had dinner about half an hour previously. And making a beeline for Claire, as she saw, was the bearded ghost who had been eavesdropping the day before.

'I thought I told you to shut up and fuck off,' said Sophie, as soon as he got close enough.

'Right, yeah,' he said. 'It's just, if I did that every time a woman said so, I wouldn't be engaged!' He laughed nervously.

'It's not a brag to say your fiancée didn't like you,' said Claire absent-mindedly.

'Oh, wow! So you really can see me,' he said.

Claire sighed. She had to go through the same rigamarole almost any time she met a ghost, and she looked at him to assess how much of a nuisance this one would be. He had eyes the same shade as the water in a vase of flowers if you didn't change it for weeks, and a muddy-coloured untrimmed beard. Clean, but not groomed. A standard-issue Englishman.

'I thought I might be able to help you,' he said.

Sophie stuck her hands on her hips and snorted.

'Help me. With what?' Claire asked.

'All this SWF stuff. I'm Miller.' He said this not as if he was introducing himself, but as if saying his name meant he needed no introduction.

Claire and Sophie stared at him.

'Owen Miller? I run the *Fight Forever* blog and podcast? It's the most popular wrestling blog in the UK, south and south-east.' He said 'south and south-east' after a pause, and more quietly. Claire could hear the brackets falling into place around it.

Sophie rolled her eyes. 'Oh, of course, *that* Miller.'

'So you haunt outside the gym, but can't get inside it?' asked Claire. 'Were you here the night Eddie died?'

'Nah, that was before me. I died about a week after him. Unrelated. My fiancée killed me,' said Miller. Claire raised her eyebrows at him. 'I know, right?' he went on. 'Liz was going on at me to clean the bathroom while she was at brunch, because I never pull my weight, so I poured drain cleaner down the bath plug and then sloshed a load of bleach in. Double-cleaning, right? Except that makes some kind of toxic gas, apparently. Would have been all right except for my asthma. So I hope Liz is pleased with herself.'

Sophie was staring at Miller as if she had never been less impressed by a human in her life.

'Well, if you didn't see anything, and you can't go in that building, how on earth can you help me?'

'I overheard your conversation yesterday, so I know Ken didn't actually tell you anything useful.'

'Overheard, eavesdropped – potato, po-tah-to,' said Claire.

'What d'you mean by "useful", pal? We're just going to do a seance to finish some unfinished business,' replied Sophie. 'We don't need your big boy's encyclopaedia of wrestling moves to do that.'

'But how are you going to find out what his unfinished business is, if you don't know the *wrestling* business?'

said Miller, who looked quite pleased with his very basic wordplay. 'Plus, if what Eddie wants is you to shop Nate for his murder, you'll need to find evidence, and that's assuming Nate's really guilty. If he isn't, it's a bit unfair on him. So you'd have to convince Eddie that Nate *didn't* kill him. Either way, you need to find out what happened.'

'Hmm,' said Claire.

Miller took this as a good sign. 'Look, there's definitely something funny going on. I can tell you're interested, and nobody else can see Eddie, so you're the only one who can help. I know everything about everyone, me – I can give you a suspect list.'

Claire shrugged and opened a fresh page in her notebook. Miller tried to jab at it, but his finger went straight through it.

'All right! Nate King is Eddie's brother, and the scuttlebutt is that he and Trudy King, Eddie's wife, are having an affair.'

'Eddie told us that,' said Sophie. 'Next!'

'All right, how about Lila King? She's unpopular as a wrestler. I hate to say it, but it's true: women don't have the stamina needed. They're not as good to watch, and a lot of them try to skate by on a bit of T&A, you know?'

'I do not,' replied Sophie, narrowing her eyes again.

'Well, anyway, Lila seemed a lot happier for a while, even though the crowd hated her, and I heard rumours that there was a big storyline involving her coming up. I predicted she was going to turn heel and I posted about it on my blog, but she outright denied it. All the storylines are sort of getting reset now that Eddie has died, and Lila's been mopey. You should find out what that story would have been.'

'The fuck has that got to do with Eddie?' asked Claire.

'He had total creative control of the company. And look, write down Ruby and Guy on here, the tag team.'

'Oh yeah, we met them.'

'They know all the gossip. Off the record, but one of them was a great source for me. Very ungrateful to the Kings, though. They had beef with Eddie over their bookings, and I heard word from other independent wrestlers that they were actively trying to dig up dirt on Eddie.'

'Anything else, apart from hearsay?' said Sophie.

'I protect my sources,' replied Miller, with the gravity of a Fleet Street reporter about to break the story on how Princess Di *really* died.

'Interesting …' Claire wrote down explanatory notes, based on what Miller had said, so her newly minted suspect list ran thus:

NATE KING: *brother/new owner of SWF*

TRUDY KING: *wife, possibly having affair with Nate??*

LILA KING: *Ken's wife, appears weepy, wrestling not going well?*

GUY & RUBY: *tag team called 'Pink Champagne', digging up dirt*

After a bit of thought she added:

KEN KING: *son, manages SWF, hired me*

'I think you may have overestimated how useful you can be,' she said to Miller.

Miller drew himself up to his full, extremely average height. 'I know stuff, I'm telling you. I might not know exactly *what* I know, you know? Plus, there's one thing I know that you definitely don't.'

'Which is?' asked Sophie.

'I won't say – you have to come back to talk to me,' said Miller. 'I can't go anywhere, can't go inside the gym. Can't even doodle because this bloody pen doesn't work.' He scribbled on his ghostly paper with his spectral ballpoint to demonstrate. 'Besides, I want to help. Chivalry isn't dead, you know.'

'Oh please, if chivalry was depending on you to stay alive, it'd have Dignitas on speed-dial,' said Sophie.

'Okay, fine. I want to write a last post on my blog. To settle a few scores. If I tell you what to write and give you the log-ins, you can do it for me, can't you?' He looked eagerly at Claire.

'I'm making zero promises,' she said.

'Buzz off, our friend is coming back,' added Sophie.

Basher returned, and Miller sulked away and stood on the edge of a group of men dressed similarly to him, as if he were part of the conversation. He laughed when they all laughed. Claire felt a twinge of something like sympathy.

'I have some drinks,' said Basher, hugging the offending items to his chest. This turned out to be a very accurate description, because the cooler guardians had not given him any choice in beverages; he had asked for three drinks and, lo, three were provided.

'Would you prefer a bottle of Stella, a purple-variant Strongbow or a can of Carlsberg?' he asked.

'Er,' replied Claire. It wasn't a great selection. She asked for the bottle of Stella, because beer always tasted better out of glass, but it turned out to be one of those awful plastic bottles that you got in nightclubs sometimes, and her misery was unconfined. She could feel it going warm from her hand almost instantly and tried to surreptitiously stick the bottom of it into Sophie's side.

'Absolutely fuck off with that – I'm not a freezer,' said Sophie, instantly noticing this gambit.

Alex wasn't allowed in the venue with their second dinner, and Houdini himself could not have made two giant potatoes vanish with more speed. Alex showed no signs of eating less, just as they showed no signs of stopping growing. Being almost twenty now, they were in danger of breaching the six-foot barrier. The reason they had two potatoes was that Alex always insisted on getting Sophie a portion of food whenever they ate in her vicinity, which was a reason why Sophie really liked them. Alex always ate the second meal, and Claire had no objection as long as, you know, she didn't have to pay for it.

'They're going to feel sick,' said Soph. 'They always do when they eat something too fast.'

'And an entire first dinner as well,' said Claire, idly wondering if Hobbits had second dinner as well as second breakfast, and maybe second lunch as well, and then thinking that Hobbits would be hit particularly hard by the cost of living if that were the case, what with the increase in food prices. A Hobbit nuclear family consisting of two adults and two children would be absolutely destroyed by austerity, even without weed expenses factored in.

'I'm a growing child,' Alex said. They turned to Claire. 'Bean face?'

'Face clear of beans, good to go,' she confirmed.

'Right,' said Basher, apparently to himself. 'Once more unto the breach, dear friends ...'

And in they went.

The space had completely changed. When they'd been in there before, the ring had been close to the back wall, but now it was almost at the centre of the room. Around the sides were rows of cheap folding chairs – as many as the space would allow – and a TV screen hung against each of the walls, playing a repeating, punky-graphic animated logo for the SWF. Alex explained that they played entrance graphics for wrestlers, and pretend backstage interviews and things like that. Sophie pointed out a man behind the controls of a spaceship, which Alex helpfully explained was the mixing desk for lighting and sound control. This was a more advanced set-up than Claire had been expecting.

The seating appeared to be a free-for-all, and after some strident but high-speed arguing between Basher (who wanted to go at the back) and Alex (who wanted to go right at the front), they settled on the compromise of sitting somewhere in the middle of a block of seats, off to one side of a velvety curtain. Claire was on the very end of the row, so Sophie had somewhere to stand that wasn't in someone, but she very heavily suspected that this put her right on the aisle where the performers would enter, and she was nervous about this.

'It's a bit like the circus, isn't it? Or the theatre,' Claire said to Basher.

'I believe that is the idea,' agreed Basher. This made Claire more nervous. How theatrical was it? Would the wrestlers crawl over the seats, like in *Cats*? 'I really do not think this is conforming to maximum-occupancy rules,' Basher added, as an afterthought.

'Nerd,' said Sophie. 'Safety pervert. What time is it? Is it starting soon?'

Claire waved a hand to shush her, although history suggested this wouldn't really work. Besides, the show would actually be starting in the next five minutes, because although the potato had been eaten in record time, Alex had queued for quite a while to get it. Claire craned her neck to look around, but the dead former owner was not in evidence. She took a sip of her body-temperature beer for something to do and grimaced.

'You would have thought they'd postpone it,' Sophie said. Claire could hear her above the crowd very easily.

Ghost's voices appeared in her ears as if the sound didn't need to travel to get there, almost like a lover talking very close, which had been incredibly unnerving for the first few months of seeing ghosts, until Claire got used to it.

'Hmm?' she said, keeping her voice low.

'Eddie fucking *died* not that long ago,' replied Sophie. 'Wouldn't it be more normal to cancel the show, or push it down the line or something?'

Claire shrugged with one shoulder. 'It was months ago, remember … Funeral's done. Money needs making. The show must go on, I guess?'

'Yeah, s'pose,' Sophie snorted. She sometimes got a bit iffy about how living people thought about dead people. It seemed like time didn't pass in the same way for ghosts. Their thoughts weren't as elastic. Claire could try to explain that, for example, Ken wouldn't really forget his father, it was just that some days he wouldn't remember him, but the distinction wasn't there for Sophie. Claire wondered, sometimes, if they should go to visit Sophie's mother. But it didn't seem like that would go too well for anyone concerned. She opened her mouth to say something – she wasn't sure what – but suddenly all the lights in the room cut out.

The crowd fell into a hush, one that lasted maybe a second before, as if on a predetermined cue, they all roared and clapped. There were whoops, and at least one '*Yow!*' from somewhere off on Claire's left.

A voice boomed over invisible speakers. 'Laaaaaadies and geeeeeentlmen!' it said, the balance way off, so that at the points where it got too loud it transformed into a *blahwahwah*, vibrating in Claire's chest. Suddenly spotlights clicked on over the ring, revealing two men standing in the centre. Their appearance felt, genuinely, a bit magical.

'They scuttled down the aisle here when the lights were off, bent over, so there was less chance they'd be seen,' Sophie observed. 'It's all smoke and mirrors, right?'

One of the men was Ken King, wearing a black-and-white striped polo shirt. But he wasn't fully in the spotlight. That was taken by another man, equally meaty and shiny. Even at a distance, Claire could see the family resemblance in the broad, open-featured face, if not in the large vanity muscles. This must be Nate.

'Does he look murdery? Murder-ish?' asked Sophie.

'Ken looks pissed off, at any rate,' said Claire.

'I can't hear a fucking word you're saying. This'll be fun, won't it?' Soph replied.

Nate was milking the audience like a herd of dairy cows – almost too much in fact. He wore the international costume of a wealthy but cool businessman: bootcut jeans, T-shirt, dress blazer. In his case, his bulk meant that everything looked slightly uncomfortable. The blazer in particular looked very strained. Nate's arms resembled sausages about to burst their casing, and it didn't help that he kept raising them as he turned, taking in the applause. He was also wearing an actual crown, at a rakish angle, and it sparkled as he moved. Ostentatious. Garish.

Ken stood quietly beside him, arms behind his back, eyes unfocused and cast out over the crowd. His face was carefully unemotional, but his body language was radiating anger.

Eventually Nate raised the microphone to his lips again.

'Sensation-seekers of all kinds!' ['*YOWOWOW!*' from the left.] 'Welcome ... to ESS! DOUBLEYOO! EFF! *THE RESET!*' Nate ended the sentence in a roar, and anyone in the crowd who wasn't already standing leapt up – Claire too, because she wouldn't have been able to see otherwise.

'Hmm. Oddly mixed reaction,' said Sophie.

Claire frowned, but after a moment she realized that Sophie was right. Running under the cheering were small but very identifiable pockets of booing. Claire looked around and saw a few members of the audience had their arms crossed and lips pressed together, wanting their disapproval to be obvious, but not going so far as to actually *voice* it. Onstage Nate seemed unaffected by the booing. Ken's body language had reached his face, though, and he looked as if someone had pissed on his chips with total completeness.

The crowd sat again, and Nate launched into what turned out to be – in Claire's opinion – a far-too-lengthy speech. It was a lot about honouring his brother's legacy, but elements of looking to the future started to creep in, until it became apparent that what the whole speech was about was that everyone was looking to the future, and the future was the best way to honour Eddie's legacy; and it was in fact Nate – Nate *was* the future, the future was definitely not anyone else in the family, the future was not his nephew, the future was Nate; Nate was indeed the future. The future was getting quite sweaty.

'Okay, I quite like this Nate guy already,' said Sophie. 'He's done a coup. He's done a coup on his nephew and he's cementing it *in front of him*! And they're live onstage, so Ken can't do anything about it.'

Claire leaned over towards Basher and Alex. 'Has Nate done a coup?' she asked in a hoarse whisper.

'In real life or as a storyline?' Basher replied. 'No, wait – I am sure I do not care.'

'Maybe both?' said Claire.

Alex's contribution was to wiggle their eyebrows and say, 'He's worked himself into a shoot, brrrrrother!'

Claire understood all of the individual words, but the sentence as a whole was an impenetrable mystery, so she just sat up straight again without responding. She looked across at Sophie, whose eyes were glittering with the reflected glow of the spotlights.

'Ohmigod,' she said. 'Pulling the rug out from Ken when you killed his dad. In public! Making yourself the centre of attention. Potentially brave. Definitely stupid.'

'Well, I always say: if you're going to do something wrong, do it right,' whispered Claire.

'LOL. You've never said that in your entire life. Never. I would remember if you had, because I would have made fun of you over it for several days – and I'd do the same now, but you're about to be saved by the actual bell.'

She was right. Nate was wrapping up, which was good because his nephew looked like he was doing a cost/benefit analysis on 'getting arrested for committing murder in front of a live audience' versus 'at least that piece of shit would be dead, though.'

'So without further ado,' said Nate, a man who had indeed done a lot of ado up to that point, 'let's get this show started!'

The audience had got a bit bored and restless – aside from '*Yow*' man and some other diehard yellers – but this phrase activated them like sleeper agents ready to throw aside their suburban children and soccer-mom duties to kill some goddamn capitalists. Suddenly they were all on their feet again, yelling and clapping as the house-lights were mostly raised. Nate disappeared from the ring and ran out past Claire and Sophie.

Ken remained in the ring as the evening's referee. For a few seconds he stared blankly at the ring mat – a robot that had short-circuited – until another '*YOW!*' shook him awake from his thoughts. He took up the mic to announce the opening event, a women's singles bout.

The music switched from off-putting cock-rock to a mid-tempo, slightly haunting reed organ. It was also off-putting, but in an entirely different way from the cock-rock, a version of the song that Claire didn't know the name of, but which was recognizable as 'that music that plays in a circus when the clown runs on and trips over loads'. Claire leaned over to Basher again.

'What's the name of this—' she began.

'"Entrance of the Gladiators",' Basher, a repository of much general knowledge that is useful in a pub quiz, replied without letting her finish.

The audience actually groaned, and Claire turned to see a woman dressed as a clown fight her way through the curtains. It was Lila.

Hers was an odd costume. Claire understood that women in pro-wrestling wore more or less sexy outfits, in that – similar to the men – they basically wrestled in spangly underoos. Lila was wearing a sort of bikini top, if a bikini top had big puffy custard-yellow sleeves attached. Her wrestling pants were sparkly blue, and she was wearing laddered tights that, rather than more normal wrestling boots, ended in big flappy clown shoes. It was an extremely confusing look, and was not enhanced by the clown nose and green pigtailed wig.

She was holding a custard pie. Claire leaned away, sensing trouble.

The most remarkable thing was that the audience hardly reacted at all. Claire felt the energy leaving the room like it was a slowly deflating balloon.

It was hard to tell if Lila was just clumsy or was being clumsy as part of the clown bit. Her entrance took a while because she pinballed from one side of the aisle to the other, in a sort of 'Wh-wh-whoa!' act, which unfortunately led her right into Sophie, who didn't get out of the way in time. The shock of suddenly being icy cold caused Lila's whole body to spasm involuntarily, and she tripped over for real. The pie hit a man near the front in the back of the head. He was not charmed, but it at least elicited laughs from that half of the room.

The clown version of Lila got to her feet and climbed into the ring, visibly shaken. There was a smattering of good-natured clapping and some whistles, but she didn't bother to vamp and instead sat down and began to unlace the huge boots, the picture of misery. Claire could have cried for her. Ken, still in the ring to referee, quickly patted the clown on the shoulder and introduced her as 'The Original Prankster!' This was greeted with the same lacklustre boredom.

'Ohmigod!' Sophie exclaimed. 'I feel so sorry for her.'

'Poor thing,' agreed Basher.

Lila's opponent was a woman they didn't know, who was chubby and attractive and was also doing a gimmick, dressed as a sort of scene kid from circa 2005 – closer to what Lila had dressed like in real life, which seemed almost cruel. She had black-and-red checked jeans and one of those flat square studded belts. Claire was punched right in the nostalgia. They went back and forth in what Claire assumed was a technically competent match, where the crowd was firmly on the scene kid's side, even though she was playing the role of the baddie and kept cheating.

'I hope we get to see Ken wrestling,' she said to Sophie. Ken was refereeing in a very energetic way. He waved his arms, shouted to the crowd and slid on to all-fours whenever he counted out one wrestler almost pinning the other, his head low with his arse in the air.

'He looks like he's presenting to a bigger dog,' said Soph drily. 'Are you watching what they're doing? It's clever. See, whenever one of them kicks the other? She slaps her own thigh when it lands. Makes a big noise.'

Sophie was, Claire could see, really enjoying herself. She was watching the show like a puzzle to figure out, while Claire was trying to understand the story it was telling. Sophie was usually a better noticer, which would be yet another item that she added to the litany of reasons it was unfair that Claire wasn't the one who'd been abducted and murdered by (presumably) a pervert.

'You're ruining the magic,' Claire hissed, largely out of jealousy for not having spotted the trick herself.

In the ring, the baddie picked up Lila and proceeded to drop her heavily onto her back. It made a loud, clattering kind of noise.

'Ken said it was a load of wood, didn't he?' mused Sophie. 'Like a bunch of planks. I wonder how it all fits together under the padding. I'd love to get under there.'

'Don't you dare,' said Claire.

Lila eventually won, but that became a big moment of drama, as the scene kid complained that Ken only awarded it to Lila because they were shagging, it was biased and the SWF was corrupt, and so on. Everyone was shouting, and Nate came out to add to the shouting and sent Ken off, saying he wasn't allowed to referee for the rest of the night. Claire tried to catch his eye as he left, but he was head down, power through, seemingly unaware of the audience.

'That was all planned,' Alex said helpfully, as the crowd hubbub returned in the break between matches.

'Yeah, I got that, I'm not a fifty-eight-year-old estate agent trying to use TikTok for the first time,' replied Claire.

'You're not what?' said Alex. 'I can't hear.'

'Can you both stop leaning over me, please?' said Basher, who was sitting between them.

Alex grinned and ignored their uncle. 'Is S enjoying it?' they asked.

Claire looked back at Sophie, who was glancing up and around at the lighting rig over the ring, turning back to look at the curtain and clearly wishing she was able to walk further away from Claire. She took another step forward as Claire watched, straining the tether between them. It stretched out painfully, but it was bearable.

'I think so?' said Claire. 'I think she'd rather be haunting you, to be honest.'

'Eh, who wouldn't?' said Alex.

Basher was looking slightly glazed over, radiating the 'Oh, it's not my sort of thing really!' energy of an Oxfam bookshop volunteer who has accidentally ended up at a Gojira gig. For her part, Claire wasn't sure whether she was enjoying it or not. This was, unfortunately, her approach to life in general.

Her thoughts were interrupted by another blast of music, and the curtain was swept aside to reveal an extremely hairy man and a woman who was a normal amount of hairy, both clearly going for a kind of

Celtic-tribe theme in their outfits. A new referee had appeared and introduced them as the 'Bonny MacBrides'. The majority of the crowd leapt to their feet and yelled enthusiastically, so this pair must be Names of some description. Claire checked her phone and realized the show had been going on for over half an hour, which surprised her because it had really dragged so far, but the fact that she'd just heard the loudest 'YOW!' yet gave her hope that it was about to get more interesting.

Coming out as opponents to the MacBrides were Pink Champagne, the mixed tag team. They looked, it had to be said, fantastic. They were wearing their own merch T-shirts, but Guy's was cut into a fringe halfway down, and Ruby had tied hers into a crop top and had cut slashes across her chest, half-exposing a black-sequinned bra top. Both wore sequinned booty shorts, but with accents in respective gold or pink, and Guy had very subtly highlighted some of the muscles on his arms and legs, the high points of his cheeks and even the hollow of his throat in a gold shimmer. The lights had changed to a warm red, so Ruby's pale skin looked rosy all over, and Guy shone less like he was wearing body make-up and more like he was lit by magic from within. They looked like Artemis and Apollo, deigning to step down from Olympus to momentarily amuse themselves by visiting a small regional pro-wrestling show on a Thursday night. The effect was such that the crowd forgot to cheer for a second, but when they remembered, the noise broke over Claire like a rogue wave.

'I mean ...!' said Sophie.

'Fucking ... wow!' yelled Claire.

'Agreed!' Basher shouted back.

Alex was performatively overcome, screaming and grabbing at their uncle like a teen at a K-pop concert (a thing Claire grasped that Zoomers were into these days) and enjoying the experience all the more, simply because they were acting so much like they were.

Pink Champagne v. The Bonny MacBrides was the match where Claire sort of understood why people enjoyed wrestling. The female MacBride could perform acrobatic flips that were almost balletic; Guy launched himself from the middle rope like a cannonball; and at one point Ruby sprang over all three ropes and onto a MacBride to try and force a win by counting him out on the floor. It was athletic and brutal but strangely graceful at times, like the way an Olympic diver seems to hang in the air and you're fooled into believing they might be able to fly, until they crash into the water. Except the wrestlers weren't crashing into water, they were landing on almost solid ground. And doing it in such a way that they didn't get seriously hurt, but acted like they were hurt a bit. The contrast between the death-grip-tight hold that the two tag teams had on their presentation and the literal sad clown that Lila had been was night and day.

Sophie was watching everything super-closely, like a cat. Ghosts were often enthralled by proximity to *life*, and the room was crammed with emotion. The wrestlers in the ring were alive to their fullest extent, stretching the possibility of life as far as they could without snapping it. Pink Champagne won, but they hugged the Scottish wrestlers (at least, Claire assumed they were Scottish) with what seemed like genuine love and respect.

Still, though. Ultimately, Claire thought, it wasn't really for her. She wondered idly how much longer it would go on for, and then wondered if now would be a good time to look around backstage or if it would actually be a terrible time. The crowd was standing and thumping their feet, and Pink Champagne were taking their time leaving. She could go in the back rooms, right? She worked for Ken. What was the worst that could happen? Someone would just tell her that she shouldn't be backstage, and they'd call security, who would try to detain her; she'd panic and run away and trip over, accidentally punching a child in the face in the process, at which point she would be arrested by the police and there'd be nothing anyone could do to stop her going to prison for the rest of her natural life.

Even Claire had to admit that was verging on the dramatic. She employed the tactic Basher had suggested to her, which was to imagine the best thing that would happen, add it to the worst and divide by two, thus getting the actual most likely result: someone would tell her she wasn't allowed backstage and make her go and sit back down. Which would be embarrassing, but still. On impulse, she stood up and jerked her head at Sophie.

'What – where are we going? I want to keep watching!'

'I need a wee,' said Claire. It was half a lie. Really you're only ever a few hours, maximum, on either side of a wee, aren't you?

Claire self-consciously creep-walked her way down the aisle, skirting the crowd, and self-consciously wondered if anyone was watching her, and then self-consciously dithered about going through the curtain, and then took a deep breath and slipped through it. It was on a boxy frame and covered the regular door to the office areas. This somehow surprised her – as if the layout of the building might have been transformed by the power of fairy lights. She pressed the handle, found it unlocked easily and opened the door into Nathan King.

'Well, I wouldn't piss on him if I were you,' said Sophie solemnly.

5

Deep Cover

'You can't be here, love,' he said. 'Staff and performers only.' Nate King had the same blank-but-handsome face as his nephew. He was only a couple of inches taller than Claire, rather than tall and fat like his brother, and though he was bald on his head, he had a tight-cut blond beard, turning to grey. He was no less intimidating, though, because also like Ken, Nate was so broad that he was almost square.

'How much do you reckon it costs to get that big?' mused Sophie. 'Like, you'd be able to destabilize a government surely? What if you go on holiday: do you have to work out for eight hours a day while your family sits on the beach?'

'I'm, er, I'm with Ken,' Claire squeaked.

'I see your assertiveness is coming on in leaps and bounds,' said Sophie.

Nate let the door swing shut. His vaguely polite vibe was evaporating like piss on a hot pavement. He walked away from her, but his angry whisper-shouting was loud enough that Claire could still hear him. He had a naturally booming voice. 'Ken! Who's this girl? She says she works for you – are you spending company money? Have you signed someone without consulting me?'

Ken stuck his head out from an open doorway, next to the toilets where Claire had interviewed Eddie the day before. He frowned and came over. He had changed into his wrestling gear, which was, like everyone's wrestling gear, basically just a pair of pants.

'Ken's already on the warpath,' Sophie observed. The air in the hallway was taking on a definite nip, from her loitering. Claire could see the hairs on Ken's arms starting to stand up.

You'd have thought that being fully clothed would give Nate the psychological advantage in an argument, but Ken didn't seem to find being nearly nude at all undermining. It probably went with the territory of being a pro-wrestler, Claire thought, remembering Eddie's lack of embarrassment in his barely-clothed death.

'As I think you already know, I've hired her to help Dad move on to the afterlife,' said Ken. 'And as far as I'm concerned, she can look around wherever she wants.'

Upon hearing this, Nate's entire demeanour changed. His body language shifted: chest up, arms held away from his body, chin jutting upwards. Rather than trying to keep his voice low – or low-ish, at least – he began projecting, talking to Ken but sort of looking at Claire.

He had a rich, sticky sort of voice, theatrical. Oozing up to you and trying to sell you something.

'Well, you can do what the hell you like, but all the fans out there know, this whole locker room knows and, hell, the whole damn world knows that Nathan King' – here he slapped his own chest for emphasis – 'Nathan King is the head of this promotion!'

'Er, nice to meet you,' said Claire. She didn't really want to interrupt, but it did seem quite important to talk to Nate, as the alleged chief suspect in a possible death. 'I'm Claire. I'll probably need to talk to you at some point actually.'

'Well, I must apologize, but as the owner and manager of the SWF – the most electrifying, stupefying, death-defying promotion in all of sports entertainment, a truly independent nation fighting the good fight for quality shows, night after night after night after night – you can imagine that I have a lot of calls on my time!' he replied. The words were enunciated slightly unnaturally, the Rs rolled a little, the pauses milked. As a performance in the ring, Claire was sure, it would read well. At a distance of two feet, it was a social sandblaster to the face.

'These people are head-fucked, I can't handle it,' said Sophie. 'We should let them all kill each other.'

'Er, okay. Well, I just wanted to ask, you know, how are you doing with everything? There have been a lot of changes recently,' Claire went on.

'Ma'am,' began Nate, and consequently had part of the rest of his sentence obscured by Sophie laughing and repeating 'ma'am!', because she thought anyone calling Claire that was very funny. 'I've been a professional wrestler for nearly forty years and, let me tell you, the only constant thing in this business is change, and I'm here to tell you a second thing: that I'm carrying on my brother's legacy, hand to God, exactly like he would have wanted.'

'Oh, right,' said Claire. 'How do you think Ken feels about that?'

Nate slammed his fist into his other open palm, possibly performatively, possibly using some genuine anger in the performance. The tendons in his neck looked very tight.

'My nephew is a sorry son of a bitch if he thinks he's the man to carry the King legacy!'

'Okay, but, er, in real life or, like, part of a storyline …?' said Claire helplessly.

'Storyline?' said Nate, an exaggerated expression of confusion on his wide face.

Claire looked at him for a few seconds. She didn't understand what was happening, except that talking to Nate was fast becoming a fucking nightmare. She looked at Ken, who didn't appear to feel insulted and was standing with his weight on one hip, rubbing his temples in an attitude of extreme exhaustion.

She turned back to Nate. 'So you know I'm here because your brother is haunting the gym, right?' she tried.

'A story put about by my nephew. He has no honour, and he's trying to undermine me,' said Nate. 'Ghosts aren't real. What's real is two men out there giving it their all for the crowd!'

'Two people,' said Sophie automatically, and in time with Nate adding, 'I mean, two people,' in the voice of someone who had recently had a talking-to about this and had attended some kind of HR presentation.

'Well, anyway,' said Claire. 'You ... that is, someone saw you in your costume at the SWF, the night that Eddie died.'

'Impossible!' said Nate. 'I was at home that night.'

'By yourself?' Claire prompted.

Nate didn't say anything.

'Ding for the "no alibi",' said Sophie.

'They were very specific about seeing your boots,' said Claire, waiting for a reaction.

'It's true, I have lucky red boots. They saved my life, and I won't wrestle without them. And I tell you what, there's no man in that gym—'

'Person,' said Claire.

'There's no *person* in that gym who'd wear them. They wouldn't dare.'

'Right, I've been told that.'

'He's right,' grunted Ken. 'Nobody would.'

'Now just you listen to what I'm saying, ma'am. I won't wrestle without them,' said Nate. He was looking wide-eyed straight into Claire's face with a strange kind of desperation. Claire noticed his top lip was sweating. 'You understand? *I won't wrestle if I don't have them!*'

It felt very artificial, like it was performed entirely for Claire's benefit, but she didn't know how to continue the conversation, so they stood in silence for a few seconds.

Ken half-sighed, chewed on his tongue a bit and then said, in a much more perfunctory tone, 'Well, I guess we'll settle this out in the ring. I'm the man who's really fit to carry on my father's line. And so on.'

Nathan nodded, apparently satisfied, and walked back through the curtain towards the ring.

'What was that about?' asked Sophie.

Claire agreed. 'Er ... what ...?' She looked at Ken.

'Kayfabe,' replied Ken, as if that was an explanation. He noticed her expression, sighed and expanded. 'Old-school wrestlers act like it's all real, all the time. Never let their character drop, never talk shop in front of a punter. When you talk to Nate, he'll be talking to you as Nathan King the wrestler and manager character, because you're an outsider.'

'That's ... something,' said Claire.

'That's fucking *mental*,' said Sophie.

Claire was inclined to agree. It struck her that it would be much more difficult to interview Nate if he was constantly pretending to be a different version of himself.

'Don't worry about it,' continued Ken, looking over her shoulder. 'Listen, I'm pretty busy here. You can look around, because I don't want Nate to get the idea he's in charge of me, but don't get in anyone's way, okay? In fact stay out of the way of the entrance here – people will be coming through.'

'Hey, are we going to just stand around all night? I'd rather go and watch the show. Or you could follow Ken,' said Sophie. She flapped her arms at Claire.

Ken had walked back to the room he'd come from. It was the locker room, so Claire immediately stepped back, in case someone was getting changed, but actually everyone was already in costume. She peeped in a bit further. There were different groups standing around in different corners, almost like school cliques. Some were stretching or wrapping their hands, others were carefully applying tape to parts of their shoulders or knees. A pair right by the doorway were deep in conversation. They looked like they were made from a build-a-boy shop, where you could swap out modular facial hair and tiny pants, then stuff them full of muscles before you took them home in a cardboard box. This would, Claire thought, be a very popular shop in the local shopping centre, albeit not one aimed at children.

'I've got Valium and I've got Tramadol,' said one. 'And weed, obviously.'

'Oh, nice,' said the other. 'My guy is out right now.'

'We're never dry here. Eddie found a guy who can get basically anything you need, even regular stuff on the cheap. I don't think any of us go to an actual pharmacy any more. Your knee is still pretty bad, huh?'

'Davey! Gee!' shouted Ken, standing in the doorway. 'You're up, come on, you should have been at the door already. Fifteen minutes, excluding curtain.'

A couple of tall wrestlers brushed past Ken. 'Call sheet says curtain-to-curtain,' said one of them gruffly. The other, almost under his breath, added, 'Get your shit together, man.'

Ken shrugged it off by clapping and saying things like, 'Come on people, look alive!' Moments later the tag teams barrelled back and Claire had to step out of the way. Ruby noticed her and gave her a little nod of greeting. They were sweating and breathing hard, and there were whoops and claps from the locker room as they entered.

Sophie, who had no qualms about walking as far as possible into a dressing room full of partially clothed people, stretched the limit of the tether between them again.

'Any sign of ... the guy we're looking for?' Claire muttered.

'EDDIE!' Sophie yelled.

Claire was not expecting it and she jumped.

'No,' Sophie continued. 'He's not there. Although I think we should take a closer look. A thorough search.'

'No. Come on.' Claire walked out.

'Such a waste of a heartbeat, you know that?' grumbled Sophie. Despite many furtive teenage sexual fumblings before her death, Sophie had never actually got around to losing her virginity, and did not believe Claire when she said it wasn't all it was cracked up to be.

Davey and Gee were standing in front of the curtain. It sounded like they were running moves one last time: '... then I'll hit you with the topé suicida, yadda-yadda-yadda, back in the ring for the suplex, yadda-yadda-yadda ...'

'Give me an iggy for the suplex, though – you fucking took me by surprise in Durham.'

Sophie and Claire kept walking, into the gloom of the corridor.

'You're like that weird baby in *Interview with the Vampire*,' said Claire. 'Old and young at the same time, and going mental because of it.' She opened a door that turned out to be a side entrance to showers alongside the locker room. The water was going, so Claire assumed there was an adjoining entrance that went straight to the lockers. She backed out quickly.

'At least she got to eat people,' replied Sophie. She kicked an imaginary stone down the hall. 'I get to do fuck-all. I wish I'd haunted a millionaire instead. I could have seen the world.'

'You'd just have seen the inside of a castle while the millionaire went unusual and spent every hour God sent on social media complaining about gender,' said Claire. 'I wonder if those were the showers Eddie used?'

'Hmm. I wonder what this building was originally for?' said Sophie. 'It surely wasn't purpose-built for wrestling. Speaking of complaining about gender: if it was built to be a gym or, I dunno, for some other sports thing, you'd expect more than one shower and locker room, right?'

'The layout of this place is confusing,' said Claire.

'No, it isn't. Stand still a second.' Sophie had a much better sense of direction than Claire, and she began to draw a map in the air in front of her. 'The gym bit is like a big rectangle in the middle, right? The door we came through to get here is the same door we went through the other day to get to the toilets – we've just gone left down the corridor, instead of right, this time. So we're in a strip of smaller rooms along the right-hand side of the gym, if you're looking at it from the front entrance. And to the left of the main entrance were those admin rooms.'

'Okay. So?'

'So nothing, I'm only saying. One big gym room with a corridor down each side. Question is: do they join up around the back of the building like a horseshoe?'

'My question is: where the fuck is this bloody ghost?'

'Less of that; you know he doesn't like language from young women.'

They carried on down the hall. The walls were thin, so Claire could hear the roar of the crowd like a distant sea, or a party heard from the room next door. Which was what it was, really. A couple of times someone – maybe Nate – went on the mic and it became a louder, half-heard sentence that made Claire try to squint, but with her ears. The overhead lights were cheap white fluorescents, and some of them had started to flicker. It was like the whole building was buzzing. They passed errant stacks of chairs and old bunting, and then a cardboard box full of posters that, once unrolled, revealed bad art depicting old shows: Eddie in his prime and, latterly, less prime.

'These haven't been here long,' remarked Sophie. 'There are loads of dust bunnies and dead spiders, but these posters and the box are dust- and dead-spider-free. Which means …?' she prompted, in a condescending if broadly encouraging way.

'It means … someone took them down recently and put them out of the way here.'

'Exactly. But from whence were they tooken?'

'And by whomst?' added Claire.

'Hey, look, there is a connecting corridor round the back!' said Sophie, with a note of triumph. 'That must be a door onto the main room.'

Claire opened it a crack, surprised it wasn't locked, and saw that she was indeed behind a bank of seats. Emboldened, she opened it further and realized that she was opposite the main entrance and kitty-corner to where they'd been sitting before. She could just about spot Alex's hair. The two gruff, unimpressed wrestlers were in the middle of a match, overseen by Nate. Ruby and Guy were in the audience, unshowered and rabble-rousing for effect. Claire closed the door again and turned back.

The corridor was cramped, with most of the space taken up by more stacks of chairs. The lights were more broken and flickery here, with a general air of 'We can neglect this bit, cos most people never see it and we only store the seats here.' Claire ran a finger along the wall and felt a chilly condensation.

'Eddie?' she ventured.

There was a pause. Then, 'G'way, pet.'

Claire leaned over and saw a pair of meaty feet a little further down the hallway. She clicked her tongue at Sophie.

'Ho, big man!' said Soph. She jogged down the hall a bit too enthusiastically and Claire winced as the tether pulled against her.

'Not so fast,' she reminded Soph.

Sophie waved her away. 'Here, Eddie. What're you doing cooped up here? You don't want to watch the show?'

Eddie was sitting up against the wall. He'd had his knees bent, but he straightened his legs as they approached, which Claire was grateful for, because otherwise they'd have got an eyeful of the King's metaphorical jewels.

'Didn't feel like it,' replied Eddie. 'Can't get any further away from the ring than sitting here.'

Claire watched with some interest, and not a little sympathy, as a middle-aged straight white Englishman grappled with being sad.

'Can't you do the – you know – vanishing thing?' asked Sophie.

'I don't bloody know how to do that, do I? Dunno how any of this works.'

'Yeah, to be fair, I can't disappear, either,' said Sophie. They had met some ghosts who could go *somewhere* – disappear into the stones, the earth – and come back when they wanted, but Sophie claimed she didn't know how. Claire sometimes suspected she just didn't want to.

'Um, well. I wouldn't worry, anyway. The show's not that great tonight,' Claire said.

Eddie looked up. 'Really?' he asked, a little shyly.

'Ohmigod, yeah,' said Sophie, ably catching on. 'You're making the right choice. Lila did her whole clown thing and everyone hated it.'

'I told Ken it was daft,' said Eddie, shaking his head.

'Yeah, she fell over and everything, dropped a pie on someone in the audience.'

They all giggled the conspiratorial giggle of people having a little bitch about someone.

'Poor girl. She deserves better than Ken gives her, you know. And they didn't even boo?'

'Nah. Isn't it bad to get booed, though?' asked Claire.

'No!' said Eddie. He got awkwardly to his feet and adjusted his towel. 'You want heat from the audience, right? Now, ideally you want people to cheer if you're the face – the hero, you know, the good guy – and boo if you're the heel. But if you're getting *some* heat, you can switch things up. Maybe … I dunno, maybe if you're getting booed you lean into it and do a heel turn, or you switch up your angle, think about how to change the storyline track you're on, right?'

'Oh, we spoke to a guy called Miller just now. He died a bit after you, in a … let's call it an accident,' said Claire.

'Really? Daft bugger. He's still here too?'

'Yeah, only he's trapped on the outside, looking in,' said Soph. 'He said you had some big storyline something-or-other planned with Lila.'

Eddie shrugged. 'There are always a lot of story ideas floating around; doesn't mean any of them will make it to the mat. Miller always thought he knew a lot of things. He wanted to be a wrestler, but he didn't have the bottle. There's a whole class of fans like that, who can't just be fans, so they have to make out they know more than everyone else, like they're part of the inner circle. Are they fuck!'

'Makes some sort of psychological sense that he can't get in here then, I guess,' said Claire.

'Point is, even if Lila turned heel with the clown character, it wouldn't have helped. Boos you can work with. But if you're getting nothing? Well, that's proper shit, to be honest. Ah, Ken's never had the feeling for it, God love him.'

'Is that why you left the business to Nate?'

Eddie waved a hand, as if to suggest there were many reasons.

'What's down here?' asked Claire, pointing.

'The main office. It's probably empty right now,' said Eddie.

'Oh, let's look! Maybe we'll find something incriminating in there,' said Claire.

'Beautifully non-specific, LOL,' said Sophie. 'Although I agree we should search the office.'

'Well, maybe Eddie's pill bottle got left in there, or something. What colour were the pills?'

'Little blue tablets,' said Eddie. 'But I don't think they'd be there.'

'Nothing ventured,' said Claire. Eddie seemed to have perked up, given something to do.

They had reached roughly opposite where they'd started, the other side of the horseshoe. As a centrist would have put it, they'd started somewhere around libertarianism and were coasting towards antifa. In practical terms they were next to, as predicted, another set of showers and lockers, although these seemed largely disused and were storage for more chairs and at least one rolled-up carpet of dubious provenance. The cheering was louder again, both because the crowd was appreciating something one of the beefy gladiators had done in semi-real combat, and because they were closer to the ring once again. At the end of the corridor was another door and Claire walked up to it, but hesitated.

'Ohmigod, come on. If you stand right here, there'll be enough give in the tether for me to go through,' said Sophie. Her time-to-boredom rivalled that of the average toddler.

'In the what?' said Eddie.

'It's this thing ...' Claire started hesitantly.

'For fuck's sake. Okay, Eddie, you know how you can't leave here?' said Sophie. 'Well, I can't leave her. Come the fuck on, anyway.'

She didn't wait for Eddie or Claire to answer, and instead stepped right up to and through the office door, and Claire had to skip a few yards forward to avoid the tether hurting them both. She hesitated further, immediately anxious about being found with her ear pressed to the door and having to pretend she was dusting or something, like in a gothic thriller where a maid overhears the master of the house engaging in sexual sadism with a prince, or whatever. She compromised by leaning very close while hanging on to the doorframe on either side, which meant that when Eddie walked through her, the cold shock made her almost head-butt the door.

'Sorry, pet,' he said, coming back through. 'I forgot I shouldn't do that.'

'Yeah, who hasn't heard that before. It wouldn't work on a magistrate,' said Claire. Although she thought about it for a second and realized it probably would, and might in fact have been an excuse used by Eddie in the past. 'I told you to fucking knock off walking through people.'

'It's empty!' shouted Sophie, rendering the discussion moot.

Claire opened the door and she and Eddie both went through it normally.

It was the same working office that Ken had shown them, as opposed to the tiny empty office that was only used on show nights. There were three entrances: the one they'd come in through, another leading off to the main gym and a third that looked as if it led directly outside. This immediately spiked Claire's anxiety.

'One of you go and keep an eye out, would you?' she asked, and began her search.

Her approach was not forensic. The room had a few shelves and they were largely full of the kind of ephemera that accumulates when someone says, 'Where should I put this?' and gets the response, 'Just put it in the office for now – I'll sort it out later.' There were more old posters, boxes of unused flyers, at least one sock and several pieces of merch and costume. There were some filing cabinets, which were locked, as was the computer – and Eddie said the password had been changed, so Claire didn't get to flex her elite hacking skills.

There were a few cardboard boxes stacked in the corner and she opened one of them. It was a large mix of Lycra, sequins and fake leather in many colours, all jumbled together in a way that reminded Claire of Alex's room.

'It's all old gear. It's a shame to throw any of it out, cos it's all done custom. I go to a lady who does wedding dresses normally,' said Eddie, very proudly. 'You can reuse it as well. Sometimes we let new wrestlers put stuff together from the mishmash here.'

Claire was about to investigate further when the door handle turned, and she jumped like a cat presented with a cucumber. She had no time to hide, so all she could do was crouch behind the stacked boxes, not moving, and hope they were tall enough to hide her.

'It's Ken, you doink, you don't even need to hide,' said Sophie. 'The tag team are with him – you know, Cheap Prosecco. Who did you think it was going to be: the Grim fucking Reaper? Anyway, calm down. Breathe. Stand up.'

But at this point Claire felt the embarrassment of standing up would be so great that she might never be able to leave her depressing flat ever again, and her impulse to remain hidden proved a good one, when Ruby and Guy immediately rounded on Ken.

'Right, do you want to fucking explain yourself?' said Ruby.

'Do you really want to do this right now?' asked Ken. His tone was already conciliatory, so even Claire knew he'd be a soft touch in any sort of fight that might happen.

'Yeah, because I'm extremely fucking angry, and my therapist says if I don't work out my aggression in constructive ways, then I'll carry that tension in my body,' Ruby growled.

'Look, it doesn't need to get nasty. Ruby isn't happy because you screwed us on the running order *again*,' said Guy. He sounded much calmer than Ruby. 'We're one of the biggest draws this promo has. Why aren't you booking us properly?'

Ken spread his hands in a gesture of appeal. 'You barely ever agree to work in singles matches, and we can't book you as main-eventers every month because there aren't enough mixed tag teams to go against you,' he replied. 'Look, you're already over. What will putting you further down the call sheet do for you?'

'This is exactly the shit your dad used to say,' spat Ruby. 'He had us doing jobber work.'

'He just hated tag teams, that's all,' said Ken. 'That's not me.'

'Correct,' Claire heard Eddie say flatly. 'Give me a good professional singles match any day.'

'Ruby has got all close to Ken and poked him in the chest,' said Soph, providing helpful commentary. 'He's still basically naked, by the way.'

The ghosts had talked over the argument, and Claire had only caught half of what Guy had said to Ken.

'Come on, don't be like that,' said Ken.

'I'm warning you,' continued Ruby. 'Your dad wasn't a popular man. We don't want to do anything drastic, but we've done it before.'

There was the sound of the door slamming. Ken swore quietly to himself and then, to Claire's amazement, opened the Headspace app and did an anxiety breathing exercise. She bit her lip to stop herself groaning out loud, because she knew from experience that it was five minutes long. The entire time the ghosts were complaining about being bored. By the time Ken finally left, Claire's thighs were cramping so much, and her nerves were so shredded, that she felt the experience was probably comparable to SAS selection.

She crawled out from behind the boxes and exhaled, which made dust billow up from the carpet and into her recently-ex-smoker-no-really-I'm-definitely-trying-to-give-up lungs, which almost immediately went into spasm. She starting to cough so hard that Eddie became concerned.

'She's not going to die, is she?'

'Chance would be a fine thing,' said Sophie gloomily. 'She's just a massive fanny. What did you do all that for?'

'There's a drink in the desk, in the side-cabinet bit there,' said Eddie helpfully.

Claire clawed the desk drawer open, which revealed a sloshing bottle of Tesco Imperial Vodka. Claire glared at Eddie in mute fury, as she continued to cough and felt herself going the colour of a ripe strawberry.

'Well, it's better than nothing,' said Eddie.

'It ... bloody ... is ... not!' Claire gasped. She felt weak from the coughing fit and swallowed experimentally. 'What did Guy say? Something about Eddie being gone, but you were both talking over him.'

'He said he thought that, as I was gone, things would be different,' replied Eddie.

'*After*,' corrected Sophie. 'He definitely said "after Eddie was gone".'

'Are you sure?' asked Claire.

'Yeah! Well. Pretty sure. Quite sure,' said Sophie.

'What difference does it make?' said Eddie. 'Before, after – I'm still bloody dead.'

'Because,' said Claire wearily, 'one is expressing disappointment at a situation, and the other is an indication that they knew you were going to die somehow.'

Sophie tipped her head, an affected habit she'd practised as a teenager to look winsome and curious, and which she now did without thinking about it. An unintended effect was that it made her look a bit like a cocker spaniel. She seemed to be thinking about what to say next.

'Eddie, is there a single person you knew in life who didn't hate you and want you to die a bit?'

Eddie looked shocked, then angry, and blinked himself out of existence.

'I'd say he's figured out how to disappear then,' said Sophie. 'Wish I could.'

'Yeah, me too,' replied Claire.

6

Not a Wife Guy

Claire's attitude towards the SWF investigation was bleak. For one thing, her assumption – as it was about almost everything in life – was that she was probably going to crash and burn and fail and gag and bomb. For another thing, it wasn't even officially sanctioned by her client, who just wanted her to get rid of his ghost dad, and finding out who murdered said dad was an interpretation of that remit wide enough to fit Ken himself through it. And as a final point, Basher was, predictably, not on board with any kind of investigation whatsoever. But this was kind of balanced out by Alex, the sun to Basher's angry little moon, who was very excited. And Basher would get over it.

'What's he like?' they asked. 'The dead dad, I mean.'

'Almost naked, and fucking furious,' said Sophie. 'And, I might add, sexist in a weird old-fashioned way.'

They were walking into town. Claire was catching

the bus back up to the SWF, and the others were going shopping, although Alex was keen to go with Claire and Sophie. Alex's lessons were due to start the next afternoon, which they approved of because it was a Saturday. On Saturday mornings they might have a hangover, but by Saturday afternoon it would have basically cleared up. As a young person, Alex's hangovers were the nail in an action film that the brave protagonist could remove and then forget about, whereas Claire's hangovers were the brutal tetanus and sepsis that festered and nearly killed them at the top of the second act.

Basher rubbed his eyes with his free hand. 'May I take my last opportunity to register second thoughts about the wrestling training? Also, why does this dog not have a lead? And why am I holding her? This is your dog, Alex. I refuse to be the main carer for this dog.'

Alex rolled their eyes and took the much-mentioned dog. 'We're going to buy a lead right now – that's the point of this trip. Okay, maybe I shouldn't have brought the dog. But this is definitely a thing, right? Something for Claire to work on,' they said. 'We should get champagne too!'

'I fear that Claire will escalate this into investigating a murder that did not happen. If Eddie's death was actually suspicious, someone would have picked it up,' said Basher, a man with both faith in the system and an unnerving ability to predict Claire's behaviour.

'Eddie's description of his death *does* sound like he was poisoned,' said Claire, with mild defiance.

Basher, who operated at a base level of exasperation at all times like the little depressive who could, let out another huff. 'I thought you had agreed that it is bad to try to be a detective, because both times you have done it you nearly died yourself. Remember?'

'Yes, obviously I remember. *God,*' Claire replied. 'But I did solve all the murders, didn't I?'

'To a hammer, every problem is a nail,' replied Bash.

'This is actually great,' said Alex. 'Uncle B, you can get hold of Sami and ask her if Eddie's death ever pinged on her police-detective radar, right? Maybe she can dig out autopsy files or whatever?'

'I absolutely am not going to do that,' said Basher. Sami was his former work partner and was still a detective. 'She is annoyed with me at the best of times.'

'And I can be your sleeper agent, undercover in the wrestling school,' said Alex, without pausing to acknowledge their uncle's response. 'At some point I'll forget which side I'm on. I'll think about betraying you for a life on the road with my new wrestling family. It'll be very dramatic.'

'When is Alex not very dramatic?' asked Sophie. But she didn't say it like an insult. Sophie genuinely really liked Alex. 'Anyway, Ken has already hired us to hang around the SWF a bit, so that much is definitely not up to Bash.'

Alex waved their arms at their uncle. 'Thwarted! Anyway if you don't think anyone has been murdered, then you can't object to me doing wrestling training, on any grounds. At what point is you trying to shield me from harm only going to lead to more material harm for me in the future?'

Basher pinched the bridge of his nose. 'Alex, we will continue this discussion at home. Claire ... well, you always do exactly the opposite of what I think is sensible, so I do not suppose this time will be any different.'

They deposited Claire at the bus stop and she enjoyed another hot, sickly twenty-minute ride to the SWF. Except, they weren't actually going there. Ken had given Claire his mother's number, and Claire had arranged to meet her. Trudy King lived in a maisonette above the hair salon that she ran. It was so close to the SWF that they'd walked past it when they'd first visited it two days before.

'I don't think you're prepared to interview her, you know,' said Sophie. 'Like, ohmigod, do you even know what you're going to ask her?'

'Shut up, I'll figure it out,' replied Claire. She was determined not to let Sophie bring down her mood any further. She was very early for the meeting because she got anxious about being at things on time anyway. What if, on the comparatively short walk to Trudy's house, she fell into a hole or got hit by a car, or got mugged, or any number of things?

'There you go. Fucking hell, sometimes it's really like you don't live in your own body. Even more than me – and my body can't even touch stuff. Big weirdo. Above the hair salon, right?'

The hair salon was called Curl Up and Dye, which made Claire as well disposed towards Trudy as much as the SWF sign had made her ill-disposed towards Trudy's husband and son. The strip of retail units looked a little rundown, and the flats above were the blocky, ex-council-house type, with plastic-framed double-glazed windows. The salon was all done up in a nice slate colour, which looked very good next to the rundown pet shop with a single rope chew in the window display on one side, and the ubiquitous e-liquid shop on the other, but clashed with a red-and-white 'TO LET' sign in the window.

There were planters out the front, full of lavender. Alex said everyone should disapprove of lawns, which were like green deserts that destroyed biodiversity and frogs and bees, and so on, and Claire broadly agreed and would definitely rewild her garden, should she ever actually get one (she had hung a bee hotel in the depressing little square of concrete outside her flat, but bees obviously didn't consider it a worthwhile holiday destination). So she wondered if Alex would think a planter in what was otherwise a paved street was better, or worse, than a lawn.

Trudy had texted her to say she'd shut up the salon so that they could have a cuppa, so Claire went straight up the stairs to the second level and went to number six. It had a scrupulously clean front door. There were more plant pots by it, with purple pansies in them. Claire waited in front of the door and looked at Sophie. Sophie didn't move. Claire raised her eyebrows significantly. Sophie looked behind her.

'What?'

'Go on then,' Claire prompted her, in a conspiratorial whisper.

'"Go on then" what?'

'You know – case the joint. Make like a tree and walk through a wall.'

'Oh! Right, yeah. Sorry.'

Sophie walked through the door. It didn't make a noise, and Claire had always been faintly disappointed by this. There was no *Star Trek* whoosh or a frosty *sksssh*, or a faint violin trill, like there would be if life had SFX done by an A24 horror film. Sophie just walked straight through the door as if the frame was empty. It was something she forgot to do sometimes, especially when she was with Claire, because Claire could see her and automatically did things like opening doors for Sophie. Apart from habit, and it sort of psychologically making sense to open doors for someone who appeared solid, it would be rude to slam doors in Sophie's face. For similar reasons, Claire always said thank you to Siri. She reasoned that, when Skynet happened, as it surely would eventually, she would be the last to die at the big meaty hands of the T-1000.

There was a little twinge as Sophie tugged at the tether between them. Claire looked down at the street, in case a curtain-twitcher was watching her and thought she was preparing to do a murder or was a poorly dressed Mormon, and then she wondered if Mormon women were allowed to doorstep people, or if they just stayed at home making lacy bonnets for the parade of babies they had to have. And then she thought that 'curtain-twitchers' was too old a term, because nobody drew their curtains during the day really, even if they lived in a ground-floor flat, and so it was probably from when people still had lace curtains, which weren't really a thing any more, and maybe all the lace was used up on Mormon baby bonnets.

Soph stuck her head and shoulders back through the door. 'Can't see her. Not that I can go any further than the pissing hallway these days – which is full of pictures of Eddie, and of baby Ken and an off-puttingly yoked teenage Ken, by the way. He really grew into his giant muscles. Come the fuck on – knock on the door.'

Claire did as she was told and pressed the doorbell for good measure, because she held no confidence in the rousing power of her knock. After another minute the door swung open to reveal a middle-aged white woman with a dark-red feathered bob and the kind of entrenched wrinkles/tanned skin combination that one gets from alternating Silk Cut with the Canary Islands on a near-permanent rotating basis. An exemplar of the aforementioned cigarettes was delicately gripped between the fingers of her right hand as she enveloped Claire in a swift one-armed hug.

'Hello, darling,' she said, simultaneously pulling back and ushering Claire through into the hall. 'You must be Claire. I'm Trude. Come through to the garden, I'll pop the kettle on.'

'It's lucky we're from England,' said Sophie, as she peered at the photos on the wall more closely, 'because the first thing that happens when you go somewhere is the host goes and makes tea, without even asking if you want some. Always gives you time to look around a bit. American mediums must be up instant-coffee-creek without a paddle, hey?'

'Mmm,' said Claire. She sort of thought that, since Trudy was the recently bereaved one, she should be making the tea, while Trudy lay weeping and fainting on a sofa or, ideally, a chaise longue. But then again, she didn't know where anything was, and a stranger bumbling about in the kitchen and fucking up the arrangement of your sugar pot viz. the angle of the kettle and the spoons drawer was the last thing someone needed when their husband had died.

Trudy indicated that Claire should head through to the outside again, smiling. 'Go on, love, I won't be a mo.'

'She's awfully cheerful for a widow, isn't she?' said Sophie as they walked down the hall, which was papered in pale lilac.

'Like the Scottish fucker in the ads for that life-insurance company,' muttered Claire, keeping her voice low and hoping Trudy wouldn't hear over the boiling kettle. 'In her sexy red-lined black cloak. Bet *her* husband's life-insurance policy was pretty hefty.'

'I s'pose you can ask Trudy if she took out a completely coincidental policy against Eddie for a million quid, half an hour before he carked it.'

Claire nodded and remembered the 'TO LET' sign. She wondered how long it took to end a lease. Probably not as long as you'd think.

'Mind you,' Soph went on, 'that does seem like the sort of question you'd need to work up t— Well, fuck me ... purple!'

Sophie's sudden exclamation was because what Trudy referred to as the garden was a small balcony, angled well to catch the sun, but she had contrived to make it a flowering jungle in different shades of purple. There were tall stalks of mauve bells that Claire just about recognized as foxgloves, sticks of drooping little hoods in royal purple, a vine climbing up the wall with saucer-sized flowers that were almost white, and lavender and more pansies around the sides. It was a bit overwhelming.

Claire was about to say something, but Trudy was coming out with a loaded tray. She set it down on a wrought-iron table and sat on a matching chair, which had a purple cushion on it for comfort. She patted a second chair next to her and Claire sat down gingerly.

'Now then,' said Trudy. She picked up a black teapot and swirled it around gently, before pouring Claire tea into a matching cup, with saucer. There was a fig roll perched in the saucer at a rakish angle, like a fascinator. The incongruity of this image – a saucer at Ascot Ladies' Day – made Claire chew the inside of her lip so that she didn't smile at an inopportune moment. Sophie noticed this and made very deliberate eye contact with Claire.

'So as soon as you texted me to arrange coming over, I called Ken. Just to check you were telling the truth about him hiring you – nothing personal. Ken tells me that Eddie says he was murdered?'

Claire pursed her lips, unsure how to respond. She looked down and saw that the cup she was holding was not, in fact, black. It was a dark aubergine. She took a big gulp of tea for something to do.

When she was very sure that Claire's mouth was full, Sophie said, 'Here, what d'you reckon Trudy's favourite colour is?'

Claire sprayed tea all over the table.

Trudy was quite gracious about everything being covered with droplets of spitty tea, although she did go and make up a fresh tea tray with an unsullied, differently purple tea set.

'Sorry,' Claire said again, having lost count of the number of times she had already done so. Sophie was still hooting like a chimpanzee. Claire did try not to get *too* annoyed at Soph, because she had been trapped as a teenager for almost two decades, and even if she'd been an adult when she died, material pleasures are extremely few for the dead. But it still seemed wildly unfair that any consequences of Sophie's behaviour now were received by Claire.

'You're all right, my love. Least said, soonest mended,' said Trudy. 'I suppose you take funny sometimes, if someone who has passed tunes in unexpectedly.'

'Yeah, something like that,' muttered Claire, glaring at Sophie.

Soph composed herself. 'Come on, it was pretty funny,' she said. 'I only thought you'd choke on it a bit, I didn't expect you to explode like a faulty fucking fire hydrant, did I?'

'Well, no harm done. I've always wondered if I might be Sensitive. My granny's great-aunt was a Tarot-reader,' said Trudy, a note of expectation in her voice.

'Oh, er ...' replied Claire, unsure what was actually expected of her.

'That's an in, Stupid. You should humour her,' said Sophie. 'Like when a very loud person from Boston orders "a pint of the black stuff" in a pub in Dublin and the barman is like, "Ah, didn't my grandfather only know your grandfather, to be sure, begorrah" and quietly charges them a bit extra for a bowl of chips.' Having spent approximately four days in Ireland six months ago, Soph now considered herself an expert on the country.

'Ooh, yes,' said Claire, feeling like a bit of a shithead. 'I could tell that about you. That's probably why, er, I connected strongly with a spirit just then,' she said. 'They must be drawn to, um, your energies here. Yes indeed.'

She was leaning a bit close to manipulating a bereaved person. She and Sophie had faked seances with cold reads in the past – in fact they'd done so the first night they met Basher and Alex – but only if no ghosts turned up for a chat, which was quite rare. Even so, they'd talked and decided they wouldn't do it again, after Alex gave them a big lecture about Arthur Conan Doyle and the reason the rise in the English interest in spiritualism coincided with the World Wars, and so on. There probably were a bunch of other genuine mediums out there, because it seemed unlikely there wouldn't be, but Claire had gone to a few who advertised their services to check, and she was starting to feel like other mediums existed in the same way that NASA said there was alien life in the universe. The ones she'd seen put on a very good show, so Claire wouldn't describe them as untalented, but she was an aggressively unhelpful client for cold reads. She had gone to one seance in a leather jacket she'd borrowed from Alex, and when the smoky-eyed pretendo-witch had said, 'Why am I seeing a motorbike?', Claire had crossed her arms and replied, 'Beats me.' Given that none of the mediums she'd been to could see Sophie yawn or make rude gestures in their faces, Claire had her doubts about their authenticity.

'Do you think it was Eddie coming through just then?' asked Trudy, leaning forward.

This question actually made Claire more comfortable, because she could answer it more honestly.

'No, it wasn't him. It was someone else. Someone—'

'Glamorous,' filled in Sophie. 'Luminous. Outstanding.'

'Mischievous?' suggested Trudy.

'Oh, I could say so many things,' replied Claire, plumping for vague but technically accurate. 'Eddie is up at the SWF building. And yeah, he thinks he was murdered. Specifically, by his brother.'

Trudy nodded. 'That does sound like something he'd think.'

'Oh, *interesting*,' said Sophie. 'She's just like, "Oh yeah, my husband was in the habit of suspecting his brother of wanting to kill him." We're going to find out so many weird things about this family, I swear to God.'

'Why do you say that?' asked Claire.

'Because the Kings are clearly several planks short of an Ikea flatpack!' replied Sophie.

Claire pinched the bridge of her nose. Sometimes having two separate conversations at the same time was very wearing.

'Sorry,' she said. 'It's hard to tune ... er, the spirits ... out sometimes. One in particular. Sophie is – I suppose you'd say my spirit guide, but that's not quite right. She's the ghost I see most often.'

'That's all right, love. I wish I could hear her too!'

'I doubt that,' muttered Claire.

Trudy seemed not to notice. 'Eddie never really got on with Nate. He always said that Nate was their mum's favourite.' She was looking over Claire's shoulder, slightly unfocused, as she watched memories playing back in her head. 'Eddie was always jealous of Nate, I think, because he got on with people better. But they'd do anything for each other, you know? They weren't *emotionally* close, they didn't share things and they didn't like each other personally, but the only person who can say something bad about a King is a King. When push comes to shove, Nate will have Eddie's back, and Eddie has his.' She paused, realizing she was in the wrong tense. 'Had,' she corrected.

'Eddie was quite, um, insistent,' Claire continued. 'I know this is tough to hear probably, but Eddie said he actually saw Nate do ... it. Although I'm not sure how much he really did see. So I wondered if you could tell me what you remembered from that day, and the morning you found Eddie? If it's not too painful. We just want to get as much information as possible to help him, er – you know – move on.'

Trudy sighed. 'Well, there's not much to tell. It was a normal day. Eddie often stayed late, either going over schedules or training. He trained a lot, worked out a lot, to keep up with the younger kids, you know? He'd rung to let me know he'd be there late, so I had some carbonara and watched *The Repair Shop*, and went to bed like normal.'

This wasn't really a sound alibi, but Trudy did seem like the sort of person who would like *The Repair Shop* (a demographic that, in complete fairness, included large swathes of the country).

'It wasn't odd that he was late, or anything?' Claire asked.

'Well, not really, has e trained late quite a lot. I woke up and assumed he'd left early and all, because it was a show day. But I saw he'd left his show plan here, and I don't usually go to the gym, but I'd get it in the neck if he didn't have his plan. So I took it over there, except the door was locked, so I had to come back and find the spare key, and then I was a bit peed off – until I saw him spark out on the floor. Silly old sod,' said Trudy. 'Can't really be annoyed then, can you? I tried to wake him up and, when I couldn't, I called the ambulance, but I think I knew already. He was ice-cold, you see. And the paramedics, nice young boys, they called the police. And I called Ken, and that was that.' Trudy looked into her cup of tea and sighed, but she didn't seem at all sad. It sounded more like she was describing the annoyance of your sofa suddenly breaking and having to figure out how to get it down to the dump.

'Was Eddie taking steroids or testosterone or anything?' asked Claire. 'I know that's a weird question, but—'

'It's a good question!' said Soph. 'They're all at it. It's not like it's the Olympics. I wouldn't accuse The Rock of doing anything untoward, but if he gets any bigger, he's going to have to change his name to The Geological Anomaly.'

Claire thought this wouldn't be a good career move for Dwayne, because, 'Can you smell what The Geological Anomaly is cooking?' was nowhere near as catchy.

'Don't forget to ask about the door being locked,' added Sophie. 'Unless he normally locked himself in, that shows someone else must have locked Eddie in, after the fact.'

'No, I know why you're asking,' said Trudy, oblivious to Claire's distracted thoughts about America's largest future president. 'The police asked all the same things, cos that stuff can affect your heart, can't it? He might have been, but Eddie wouldn't have told me, either way. I wasn't really involved in all that wrestling stuff. I let them get on with it. But I don't think so, because Kayleigh – I do her hair for her – she was telling me a while back that her boyfriend was taking it for his bodybuilding and she said she was fed up with it, because he lost his rag just because she ate one of his chicken-and-rice lunch boxes one day because they'd run out of bread, and she didn't see what the fuss was about, because it was plain cooked chicken and it didn't even taste that nice, and who gets that angry about bloody chicken, for God's sake?'

'Er, right,' said Claire. She was unwilling to stop Trudy mid-flow and, like a regional coordinator supplying all the KFCs in the Greater London area, she just had to hope the chicken was getting somewhere she needed it to go.

'Well, nobody – that's what I mean,' said Trudy. 'Because if anything, Eddie had been more laid-back recently. And look, being honest, we sort of lived separate lives. You should probably be talking to whichever little dolly bird he was knocking off, not me.'

'Hmm,' said Soph. 'Bold to be like "my husband cheated on me routinely and our marriage was basically loveless" in a conversation about murder. The rumour is that Trudy was shagging Nate, isn't it? That isn't incompatible with what she's saying so far.'

Claire inclined her head. That was a good point. And she wouldn't have described the ghost they'd met as laid-back. She tried a different tack. 'Eddie had a heart problem, though, didn't he? And that's why the police said it wasn't, well, suspicious or anything,' she continued.

'That's right. He had high blood pressure, but he only found out after he had a heart attack a year or so ago. They got Eddie on some pills for it after that, and he's been fine on them mostly, although for a while he wasn't remembering to take them, and my cousin's husband

David said that he was the same, and he got one of those pill-box planner things. We got one of those and Eddie was right as rain with the pills after that, and I was a bit disappointed in a way. I thought he could do with a scare. But he didn't slow down at all.' Trudy sipped her tea after this pronouncement.

'I hate to say it,' said Soph, 'but score one for you. If Eddie was using a pill organizer, why would he have been found with a bottle?'

Claire tried to remember to look up how heart illnesses worked later on, because she was still unclear. Did high blood pressure sort of make your heart explode? And was it possible the pills weren't what had poisoned Eddie? If they weren't, what else could it have been?

'The other thing I have to ask is ... er, it's a bit of an awkward question,' said Claire.

'Faint heart never won fair murder case,' said Soph, who had accurately guessed that Claire's social embarrassment would be strong enough to prevent her asking a murder suspect something that might make them not like her. 'Your weird investigator team on that TV show you like wouldn't shy away from it. They'd spit in Trudy's face and call her a scumbag, and not let her call a lawyer.'

'The thing is, I was talking to some people when we were up at the SWF and they said, er ... well, I mean they mentioned some rumours,' Claire went on. She was sort of hoping Trudy would finish the thought for her, but it didn't seem like she was catching on at all. 'Erm, so the rumours are that you're – that you and Nate are ...' she tried.

Trudy just looked at her with an expression of honest and open curiosity.

'They thought you were having an affair, Trudy. You and Nate.'

To Claire's surprise, Trudy burst out laughing and didn't stop. 'Oh, that's good,' she said. She laughed so hard she had to wipe her eyes. 'I needed that, you know. Nate and me – ha! I wonder if anyone has told him; he'll find that dead funny as well.'

'That's a "no", then,' said Sophie flatly. 'Although nobody ever confesses to having an affair when questioned, do they?'

Sophie was right. If shows like *Murder Profile* were anything to go by, people would deny they were having an affair that would serve as a motive for murder until at least after the second ad break, at which point they would confess some of the details but insist it wasn't relevant, and that they only hid it because they didn't want Agent Smitty to suspect them. Rookie mistake.

'Is there anyone else you think we should talk to? I've got a list of names, but I wondered if you could add any suggestions.'

'Ah, "we" meaning you and your spirit companion,' said Trudy, nodding knowingly. 'Let me look at this now …'

Claire took the opportunity to stuff down another fig roll. It was slightly odd talking to someone who so unquestioningly believed that she could talk to ghosts, as soon as they met her. Alex believed in them quite quickly after a bit of a run-up to the idea, but Claire was pretty sure Basher still had major doubts. Of course most of her clients believed, or they wouldn't have asked her to hold a seance in the first place, but the majority of people in the UK didn't believe in ghosts, even if they had some vague believe in the afterlife. Day to day – and certainly the times when she'd accidentally been in the vicinity of a murder – most people were extremely suspicious of the idea that she was a medium. They generally received the news with the same body language and tone of voice employed when you open the door and are confronted by a local election canvasser and say, 'Actually I'm just on the phone to the bank.'

'Yes, of course talk to Nate, if everyone is getting the wrong end of the stick about him. He's got a lot on his plate, now that he's the owner of the promotion. I think he'd prefer that Eddie had left it to Ken instead.'

'Yeah, I bet Eddie would prefer it too,' said Sophie.

'Interesting ...' said Claire. Trudy continued down the list, tutting to herself.

'Eddie complained about Ruby and Guy a lot, but they know all the stuff going on backstage. I suppose it's worth talking to Lila; she's a sweet thing and has been really cut up about Eddie. She brought me a lasagne or a pie, or something, every couple of days, and I couldn't find a nice way to tell her to stop because I wasn't arsed. Plus, it was during that hot spell and you don't want to eat a whole load of mash-and-mince when it's hot, do you? They think that probably contributed to it, you know. The heat. Overworking Eddie's heart. Anyway I ran out of fridge room and had to throw most of it out in the end, and that made me feel bad.'

'Right, way too hot,' said Claire, who would in fact eat mashed potato if it were handed to her in the middle of the Sahara.

'Trudy doesn't like Lila,' observed Sophie. 'She just doesn't want to say it outright. She's being polite.'

'Yes! Anyway, Lila had been doing a lot more admin for the SWF recently, so she might be able to help you with the comings and goings.'

'How long have Lila and Ken been together?' Claire asked. Sophie gave her a big thumbs-up, which made her feel pleased.

'I think about four years now,' said Trudy. She fiddled with the teapot and sniffed. 'Married for two. Which might seem quick, but they'd already known each other a long time. They seem very happy as a couple.' There was a very slight, almost-not-there emphasis on 'seem', and Claire realized Sophie was right.

'Do you like Lila?'

'Oh, of course,' said Trudy. 'They've known each other since they were both born really, that's why I thought it was odd tha— Anyway, she's a nice enough girl.'

'That's very helpful, thank you,' said Claire. She slurped down the last of her tea. 'I'll leave you to it,' she continued and went to stand up, but Sophie hissed, 'Locked door, Weirdo!' at her.

'Oh, yeah, I nearly forgot. Was it usual for Eddie to have locked the door when he was training alone?'

Trudy thought about this seriously. 'No, I don't think so,' she replied. 'But you'd maybe have to ask someone else. Like I said, I wasn't involved with the wrestling stuff. I was hoping Ken wouldn't fall into it, to tell you the truth, and I'm relieved he didn't get the SWF in the will.'

'Do you know why that was? It seems unusual for a father not to leave his business to his son.'

'It does, unless you know the Kings. Eddie changed his will so much, I expect he had his lawyer on speed-dial. I always got the house, but if he and Nate had a big blowout, he'd change his will and leave the SWF to Ken; if he and Ken had fallen out, he'd switch it back to Nate. I've no idea what it was this time, though.'

Trudy's mild but persistent dislike of the SWF seemed strange.

'What is it about the wrestling you don't like?' asked Claire. 'It seems pretty important to your family.'

'Gawd, where do I even start?' said Trudy. 'It's successful in terms of indie wrestling, but all that really means is that it doesn't *lose* money, and I've been at Eddie to move to Spain for years, but he insisted we had to be near the bloody wrestling.' She began to tick things off on her fingers. Claire realized she had unwittingly blasted open a dam.

'They work too hard, I never bloody see them, they're both always injured, there's no pension in it, Ken didn't even finish any qualifications cos he said he'd rather be training and Eddie supported that. I had to keep being a hairdresser, even though I'm getting arthritis in my hands, and we didn't get a proper honeymoon because Eddie didn't want to miss a big show. It just eats them up.'

'Fucking hell,' muttered Sophie, when Trudy stopped to draw breath.

Trudy had been chain-smoking the entire time they'd been talking, and the table was now liberally speckled with ash from her gesticulations.

'Things got worse in the past few years. To hear the lads tell it, it's because a big American promotion stole all the talent who would work the indie shows. But the wrestling has been the bane of my bloody life since well before then,' went on Trudy. She sighed heavily. 'But I haven't got anyone to blame but myself. Eddie was a wrestler when I met him, I just thought he'd eventually do something different. Like, I don't know, teach PE. He never did. Most people only do it as a part-time thing. And then he dragged Ken into it after him. I always hoped Kenny would be a doctor.'

Sophie was looking at Trudy like she did when she was curious – head tipped on one side, long curls dangling. A spaniel who had found a hedgehog and wasn't sure how to pick it up.

'Well, she's not sad, not even a bit,' said Sophie. 'But she's *something*. I just can't tell what. I don't think Eddie was a wife guy.'

Claire had not really had any long-term relationships in her life, owing to the one she had with Sophie, but this analysis was not much of a recommendation for them anyway. She wondered how many women approaching retirement age grappled with something similar to Trudy: disliking your husband, but not feeling able to divorce, for whatever reason. Maybe Trudy thought her life had been a waste of time. Mind you, Claire had the nagging feeling she'd wasted her life too. At least Trudy got the occasional shag and a big purple balcony out of it. She was at a bit of a loss as to what to say.

'I'm sorry,' she settled on, after a pause. She decided to say what she'd quite like someone to say to her. 'It sounds like it's been hard for you. And you must have felt a bit on your own, even though you're not.'

Trudy nodded and sniffed. To Claire's surprise, it was now that Trudy started to show some emotion. Her eyes looked a little bright. She blinked and glanced up at the sky. 'Thank you. I can see you do have extranormal empathetic abilities,' she said.

Sophie rolled her eyes.

'And are you sure there's no one else you think we should talk to?' Claire asked.

Trudy shook her head. 'Not specifically. Try anyone who worked with Eddie. Because, love, I tell you now,' she continued, 'if you're making a suspect list, you're going to need to buy more paper. Never mind what Ken told you about him. Everyone hated Eddie.'

She paused and picked up another biscuit.

'Absolutely everyone.'

7

Déjà Vu

'Well, we didn't get much out of her,' said Sophie.

Claire walked back down the steps from Trudy's house to the street and chewed a bonus fig roll.

'We got some stuff. We got the personal-issues stuff. It's all colour,' she said.

'Yeah, but no actual fucking *facts*,' Sophie complained.

'Also not tr— Oh no, it's him again.' Claire cut herself off because Miller was advancing towards them from the direction of the SWF.

'Wait there!' Miller shouted. 'Wait!'

Claire was pinned to the spot by social embarrassment.

'You know we don't have to talk to him, don't you?' Sophie said, as he jogged over. 'Like, you can just leave and he won't be able to stop you.' She sounded mildly amused.

'So was what I told you helpful?' asked Miller. He was panting slightly from jogging. Claire noticed that ghosts tended to keep up breathing, out of habit.

'Bit far from home,' remarked Sophie.

'I can actually go quite far from the gym. But why would I want to? It's the not going inside that drives me mad.'

Claire noted that this was the kind of ironic afterlife punishment that someone would design on purpose, and filed this away in a drawer marked 'Never think about this again, because it's a scary idea.'

'Well, no, you weren't helpful, as it happens. Hence we weren't going to bother talking to you again,' sniffed Sophie. 'Your blog can go unpublished.'

'Whoa, look, okay. I didn't want to pull this ripcord so soon, but ... there's something nobody has told you about,' said Miller. He was rubbing his hands together nervously.

'How do you know what people won't have told me?'

'Because they weren't *allowed* to tell you. I'm talking about Chaz.'

'Well, who the fuck is Chaz?' Sophie asked.

'See! I knew it,' crowed Miller. 'I knew they wouldn't have mentioned him. Chaz Curtain is one of the original three founders of the SWF. He left about, oh, eight or nine months ago and Eddie forbade anyone to talk about him, ever again. I've been digging into it for months, trying to find out what happened, but couldn't turn up anything concrete. Chaz wouldn't talk; nobody here would talk. Proper mystery.'

'Huh. That actually is interesting.'

'He's a personal trainer now. You can find him really easily, if you search his name,' prompted Miller.

'Okay. Oh, I wanted to ask you about Nate's boots,' Claire went on. 'He said something to me about how he won't wrestle without them. Does that mean something?'

Miller rubbed his beard. 'Well, yeah. It was Nate's way of trying to tell you his boots went missing ages ago,' he said. 'Nate hasn't wrestled since before his brother died, and everyone knows it's because the boots went walkabout. I guess you wouldn't have realized that, if you weren't familiar with the SWF shows. I dunno why he would have wanted you to know that, though.'

'Maybe he was trying to tell me it can't have been him wearing those boots on the night of Eddie's death, therefore it cannot have been him who was here,' said Claire.

'Or maybe he's lying,' said Sophie. 'Because Eddie said he saw Nate on camera. I mean, who else could it have been? Are we doing an evil-twin thing? Mirror-universe Nate?'

'Yeah, you have a point,' replied Claire. She turned back to Miller. 'Who was putting it about that Trudy and Nate were shagging, do you know?'

'Could have been anyone. All it would take is anyone mentioning *anything* about it to anyone here and it'd get around, even if it was a joke to start with. It's a gossip mill, but I'll say that usually it's Ruby turning it. But I'm telling you, you should look up Chaz next. Maybe his leaving had something to do with all this.'

It was a vague hope, but Miller was at least correct that it was easy to contact Chaz Curtain. He had a basic website and his phone number was listed. Claire pressed dial, intending to leave a message, but was thrown because Chaz, being over fifty, actually answered the phone.

'Hello, Chaz Curtain,' said Chaz Curtain, although Claire immediately harboured the suspicion that she was talking to Harvey Fierstein, such was the painfully gravelly nature of Chaz's voice. Her throat started itching for a Halls Soother in sympathy. 'You have fitness goals? I can help you meet them.'

'Oh, hi,' said Claire. She regretted calling without a plan. 'Uh, to be honest, I didn't think this through very much before calling.'

The phone made a sound like a nail file, and Claire realized this was Chaz laughing. 'You'd be surprised how often people haven't!' he said, which seemed an outlandish claim for someone to make when they'd only been a full-time personal trainer for under a year. It didn't seem like it could have happened that often.

'Put it on speaker – I can't hear!' whined Sophie.

'Fine, but when the bus comes, I have to put it off speaker, okay?' said Claire, covering the phone. 'Hi, yeah, I'm sure I would,' she continued to Chaz.

'So what is it? You have a wedding coming up? Still struggling with post-lockdown indulgence? I have decades of experience in physical-fitness training, so I'm able to apply my skills to a range of situations.'

'Oh. Uh, actually, I wanted to talk about the SWF – and Eddie King?' said Claire apologetically.

There was a long silence. 'Yeah, well, I don't. Are you a reporter?' asked Chaz.

'Uh, no. Why would I be a reporter? Have reporters been calling?' Claire looked at Sophie, who shrugged.

Miller pointed at himself. 'He means me. Independent journalist,' he said proudly.

'No, no reporters have called,' said Chaz, deflating Miller like a hairy little balloon. 'It's just …'

There was another long silence. 'I've been hired to look into what happened,' said Claire.

'A private investigator?' asked Chaz.

'Er, yeah, basically. More or less.'

'Well, I don't have anything to say about what happened to Eddie. I haven't worked there for months,' said Chaz. He sighed heavily, in a rush of static. 'If you were any good at your job, you'd already know that.'

'I only just uncovered that you exist,' replied Claire. 'Nobody is allowed to mention you. Or *was*. It's unclear. I wanted to talk to you about why you left, in the first place. And whether there were any secret grudges at the SWF.'

'Psh, that place is nothing *but* secret grudges. And a lot of them weren't even secret. Nate and Eddie were always at each other's throats over who was the real face of the company, and as Ken got older, he was trying to muscle in on that as well.'

Miller nodded along, as if to confirm that he knew all this as well.

'Like George Harrison suddenly becoming another once-in-a-generation songwriter when John and Paul were already getting at each other,' said Sophie, who had watched exactly one documentary about The Beatles.

'What about Trudy?' Claire asked.

'What about her? She didn't ever get involved; she just didn't like Lila,' said Chaz. 'Ken was a mummy's boy through and through – that was normal mother-in-law shit. Besides, none of them really liked Lila, and I'm not even sure Ken likes Lila. I keep trying to get her to move on from there, and from wrestling, but it's tough. She's got the bug.'

'I heard some rumours about an affair,' said Claire, cautious to not mention who was having an affair with whom.

'Dunno anything about that,' said Chaz, perhaps slightly too quickly for Claire's tastes. 'I kept my nose out of other people's business. Head down, got my work done, let them duke it out over the big, famous wrestler shit. I ran the training school and handled the business side of things, and I guess they're struggling to find someone to do that now, cos that's not as fun as acting the big man, is it? That's real work, boring: answering letters and doing taxes, and that.'

'Huh,' said Soph. 'People really will run their mouth if they're angry about something, won't they?'

'Um, was that why you left then? Did you feel unappreciated at work?

'What? No, I liked how it was. Anyway,' said Chaz, appearing to realize that he had accidentally been submitting to questioning, 'like I said, I don't want to talk about it. Unless you can make it worth my while?'

'That seems unlikely,' chortled Sophie.

'Like, in what way?' asked Claire, who wasn't exactly at home with smooth PI talk.

'You don't have any interest in personal fitness at all?' said Chaz.

'Not really,' replied Claire, who treated her body less like a temple and more like a twenty-four-hour McDonalds in the back of a vape shop.

'Okay, well, the PT trade hasn't exactly been booming for me so far, so if you want to talk to me about it any more than this, then you're going to have to sign up for a private class.'

'Oh, for fu—' Claire started to say, before realizing this was an unprofessional tone to take. The agents on *Murder Profile* never swore, even when being tortured by a surgeon obsessed with snakes or hunting a hiker that made women into deer-suits, or whatever – although this may have been owing more to the puritanical approach to swearing taken by American TV networks than to the sensibilities of FBI agents. 'How much does that cost then?'

'Seventy-five quid,' said Chaz.

'That's daylight robbery!' exclaimed Claire.

'Well, if you want to know what I know, that's what it'll cost.'

Miller tutted. 'Bribery. Real journalism is above that.'

'As if you'd know. Anyway, it's paying a source,' snapped Sophie.

'Um. I mean, sure. But I don't even know that you know anything. I just wanted to know why you left the SWF suddenly,' replied Claire, trying to ignore the bickering.

'Oh, I know stuff,' said Chaz, an edge of bitterness creeping into his rasp. 'I know lots of stuff. I know stuff about who that Ruby has been talking to, and I know Eddie wouldn't have liked it. I know all the things Eddie was up to, and that Trudy wouldn't have liked that at all. Oh yes, all the skeletons.'

'I mean, he sounds legit,' said Sophie. 'Legit enough anyway. More legit than this clown.'

Miller glared at her.

'Do I have to do an actual workout or can I just give you money?' Claire asked.

'You don't have to do any exercise,' Chaz replied. She could practically hear him rolling his eyes down the phone. 'But I want you to give me a five-star rating on Google and a good testimonial as well. You can meet me at my house.' He gave her the address.

'Ugh, fine. I can be with you in like ... an hour, I think.'

'Not right now. This afternoon. I've got some stuff to work out. I'll text you on this number.' There was a pause. 'Cash only,' he said and rang off abruptly.

'So I *was* helpful,' said Miller. He bounced on the balls of his feet.

'I suppose this is a bad time to remind you that you haven't actually got paid by Ken for any of this yet,' said Sophie.

'Fuck. Fucksake! Okay, I'm going to ring him again – this is a business expense.'

'Yeah, threaten him with the small-claims court,' said Sophie.

Claire called Ken and left a message updating him on her scant progress in the case, adding that they needed to discuss payment. After some consideration she also messaged Trudy, letting her know that she was meeting Chaz, in case that flushed anything out of her; and texted Alex to tell someone at least vaguely trustworthy that she was going to a strange man's house by herself. She was pretty sure Basher would simply tell her off, whereas Alex always endorsed her stupid plans.

'LOL, okay, good work, Weirdo,' said Soph. 'You have an actual task to do! So you won't sit around being all depresso and forgetting to wash today.'

'I wash!' said Claire defensively, because sometimes it would indeed get to the end of the day and she'd realize she'd forgotten to shower.

'Is this also a bad time to ask when you'll update my blog?' Miller interrupted. 'I'll have to dictate it, of course.'

'Oh, bore off, she never agreed to that,' said Sophie.

'I said I'll think about it,' Claire conceded. 'Maybe when the case has been, er, resolved. I'm too busy to waste an hour sitting here with you.'

Miller looked a bit crestfallen as they walked away, and Claire proved herself wrong by spending a few hours rotting on the sofa, eating out-of-date cheese rather than doing anything more productive, because having an appointment in the afternoon made her brain go into

Waiting Mode and she felt incapable of doing anything else until the appointment had been achieved.

Chaz lived towards the Hove side of Brighton, and Claire was reasonably confident she could walk it without incident. This confidence soon evaporated because it was quite hot and she got sweaty, and then got lost in the back streets around Western Road almost immediately. It took her a while to find the street because she kept walking down it, assuming it was on the way to where Chaz lived, which she had mentally pegged as a dingy flat *above* a shop, making Chaz at least one rung higher on the socio-economic ladder than Claire herself. In fact Chaz lived in a disarmingly big detached house. It was red-brick, with a small tree in the front garden and a paved area for off-street parking. It was even gabled.

Sophie whistled at the size, but then stopped and looked up and down the street. 'Hmm,' she said.

'What is it?' asked Claire.

Soph wrinkled up her nose. 'Lot of spooks,' she replied.

Sophie had not spotted an unusual number of discreetly handsome MI5 officers surveilling the street, but a bunch of ghosts. Ghosts weren't really capable of loitering with intent, in Claire's experience, but they were world-class champions in regular loitering. In most cases it was the only activity they had. There were a few looking at her now: a late-middle-aged woman in a twinset from sometime in the seventies, if Claire was any judge; a fisherman of indeterminate decade (the really serious fisherman,

Claire had noticed, looked basically the same from the late 1800s to the 1990s); a sickly-looking Regency gent, who had probably been sent here for his ill-fated health; and another woman who looked basically fresh. There were also a couple of formless wisps. Claire kept her head down, because once ghosts figured out she could see them, they all wanted a chat. She was antisocial with living people, let alone with the vitally challenged.

She hurried up to Chaz's door and pressed his Ring doorbell. After a minute she buzzed again impatiently. Then a third and a fourth time. At Claire's urging, Sophie stepped through into the hallway and although she couldn't go very far from Claire, she was able to make out one very important piece of information.

'The door's on the latch,' she said. 'You can just come in, Weirdo.'

Claire pushed and the door creaked open. Chaz's entranceway was surprisingly clean. A bike was leaning against the wall, under a coat rack and next to neatly stacked trainers. It was bland, which in the circumstances made it somehow more frightening. Claire called Chaz's number. An extremely muffled rendition of 'Kickstart My Heart' by Mötley Crüe started playing.

'Ohmigod,' said Sophie. She started laughing. 'If you'd asked me what ringtone a middle-aged, semi-retired, unsuccessful local professional wrestler would have ... I mean, I probably wouldn't have guessed this exact song, but definitely something from Comrades Crüe's back catalogue anyway.'

'It's coming from upstairs,' noticed Claire.

'Yeah, and I hate to bring up murder traumas past, but I'm getting a bit of déjà vu here,' said Sophie as they cautiously advanced. Vince Neil's voice coalesced as they drew closer to the source.

Claire's foot touched the landing as the caterwauling singer asked some rhetorical girls if they were ready. *Bit on the nose, Vince*, she thought.

'I don't want to alarm you, Weirdo, but my spidey senses are tingling,' said Soph. She pointed to the door across the landing. It was slightly ajar.

Claire licked her dry lips. She could tell she was sweating under her eyes and down the sides of her nose. Through the mounting wave of her anxiety, she was able to register annoyance at Nikki Sixx for rhyming 'heart' with 'start' twice in one line, which was a hack move. She took steps across the landing with glacial slowness.

She thought she heard something creak. Was it her own footsteps? Was someone in Chaz's house? It could be Chaz himself, but then why wouldn't he answer his phone? Maybe he was waiting to ambush her?

Claire felt her heart rate increase, and adrenaline drop into her stomach, like coming up on a particularly un-mellow drug. She tried to count her breathing, but 'Kickstart My Heart' had a very high tempo.

She reached the door and paused to listen, but couldn't hear anything over her own blood rushing in her ears and tinny guitar. It wasn't like anyone helpfully labelled the doors to all their rooms, unless they were the sort of people who owned an ice-cream-maker, or listened to Tom Hardy doing *Book at Bedtime*, even though they didn't have kids. The other side of the door could be a wipe-clean orgy suite, for all Claire knew. She made wide eyes at Sophie and jerked her head, but Sophie just frowned and shrugged at her.

'I can go like six feet from you – you'll get three seconds warning, and your brain processes at a speed of five seconds, minimum,' she said.

Claire flailed weakly and jerked her head multiple times with more emphasis. She mouthed, 'Just fucking look, would you?' and Sophie reluctantly drifted through the partly-open door.

'It's like a TV room, type of thing. There's no one here,' she called.

Claire pushed the door and the un-oiled hinges screamed in protest, almost in concert with Vince. The ringtone was extremely loud now. It must have been at maximum volume. *God, why won't it ring off?* she thought.

'I'm getting some pretty bad déjà vu here,' she whispered.

'Yeah, I'm not feeling good about this, either,' said Sophie. 'I don't think anyone is here, though. Anyone else, I mean.'

'H-hello?' called Claire tremulously. 'Chaz? Are you there?'

She walked as quietly as possible up to the door, which was also slightly ajar. The ringtone was incredibly loud now.

Claire walked forward and rounded the three-seater settee just as Vince hit the bridge. There was an old but well cared-for television, a shelf of DVDs, a box of Carlsberg with a half-dozen cans scattered around the floor and – what Laurence Llewellyn-Bowen might call the main feature of the room – a very tall man lying face-down on the floor.

'How the hell,' Claire said, as she turned to stare at Sophie, 'did you miss *that*?'

Soph leaned over. 'Huh, I thought it felt off in here. He's on the other side of the sofa – I only came through the door.'

'Oh, great, so your surveillance sweep would have been foiled by a living man if he'd crouched slightly,' said Claire. 'Definitely dead?'

'Well dead,' confirmed Sophie. 'I thought there were more deados than normal on the street,' she added.

Claire hung up, and the sudden absence of guitar made her ears ring. The room temperature was normal, which meant Chaz probably wasn't hanging around as a ghost. On the one hand, that was good – especially for Chaz; but on the other, Claire was a bit disappointed that she wouldn't get to ask him any questions. Although she realized she was making an assumption that it was Chaz lying in front of her. In the circumstances, she felt like it was a safe assumption to make. She ambled over to the body at a speed that a normal person would have thought was callous and pressed her fingers to his wrist. It was weirdly cold, and she pulled a face.

'Why bother, he's basically chalk-white,' said Sophie, who had also come over and was examining Chaz's ear.

'I mean, I have to at least pretend, don't I?' replied Claire. 'I'm going to call the police now and when I say, "I checked for a pulse, Officer", it'll be true.'

She stood up and looked at everything in more detail. Chaz (she assumed) had a grey stubbly face and grey stubbly head, and was in some nondescript grey joggers and an equally nondescript black T-shirt. He wasn't as broad as the Kings, but he was in good shape for a middle-aged man. There was some orangey sick on the floor near Chaz's head that looked fairly old – it had soaked a bit into the carpet and seemed kind of filmy, like when rice pudding has a skin on it. Claire wrinkled her nose.

'Bleh,' she said.

'LOL. Looks like he got tanked at lunchtime,' said Sophie.

Claire frowned. 'That's not beer sick, though,' she said, with the forensic experience of someone who had drunk a lot of beer and subsequently thrown up over the years. 'If you're sick after having a load of beers, there's more of it and it's mostly beer. That's regular sick, so he must have already pissed the beer out.'

'Excellent work, Sherlock Holmes,' said Sophie.

'Holmes would definitely have thought examining puke was a viable investigation method,' said Claire.

'He's holding something in his hand – look,' said Sophie.

Claire peered. In Chaz's right hand was a pill bottle. She was about to pick it up for closer examination and then remembered that would be a bad idea.

She dialled 999, but had a brief moment of terror because she realized she had never actually had to call 999 before. What was the right way to call 999? How were you supposed to act? She didn't want the person answering to think she was an idiot.

She pressed the call button before she had time to overthink any more than she had already, and it was answered almost immediately by a very calm-voiced man.

'Hello, nine-nine-nine, where is your emergency?'

This immediately threw Claire, because she'd been ready to ask for the police.

'Oh, er, sorry, I'll just have to check the postcode,' she replied and took the phone away from her ear. She could hear the operator continuing to talk as she tabbed through to her texts and found the address, then read it off in a shouty way, so the operator could still hear her.

'Did you get that?' she asked, the phone back to her ear.

'I did, but what service do you require?'

'Police,' said Claire, on firmer ground now. 'And ambulance, maybe? I came to … well, it's not someone I know, exactly, but I had an appointment to see this guy, but when I turned up at his house the doors were open and I found him dead.'

'Okay, when you say he's dead, have you—'

'I checked his pulse. He's, sorry to say this, but he's one hundred per cent not with us any more. He's cold.

I think he's been dead a few hours, but obviously you're the experts.'

'Not me specifically,' replied the call handler, who was too professional to laugh at her. He told her the police were on the way, and asked Claire to leave the flat, but wait outside. He also asked if she had touched anything, and said not to touch anything else, if she had.

Claire waited out on the street, staring at her feet so that the ghosts still loitering there didn't make eye contact, and told the man on the phone when she heard the sirens.

'I'd give you an eight out of ten for the call,' said Sophie, as if reading Claire's mind. 'Not knowing where you were lost you some points with the German judges.'

The police made it in about seven minutes, which Claire felt was a highly respectable time. Two PCs got out of the panda car that drew up. One charged past Claire and into the flat while the other, a pointy-faced woman, took her gently by the elbow.

'Hi there. Are you the lady who called nine-nine-nine?'

'Yeah. My name is Claire Hendricks,' she replied. She had the bizarre impulse to ask the woman if she knew Basher, as if this would help her get on with the PC better – something that was, of course, important in this situation.

'Okay, no problem, Ms Hendricks,' she said. 'I just need to take an initial statement from you. Are you feeling okay?'

'Yeah?' said Claire, initially confused by the question. 'I mean ... Oh, yeah, it was a shock, obviously, but I'll be okay.'

'You're doing less good at the police questioning and, honestly, I'd have thought you were used to them by now, LOL,' said Sophie. Claire had, in fact, been interviewed by the police more times than the average person, because she'd now been involved in at least four times more deaths than the average person. Five, if you included Sophie.

'I'll take it from here, Madison; you can help secure the scene and chase up SOCO,' said a friendly voice that nevertheless cheerfully crushed Claire's hopes that she would get out of this situation without being told off. 'Claire Hendricks,' Sami Wilson went on, in a tone more deadpan than the Grim Reaper's skillet. 'As I live and breathe.'

'Hello,' replied Claire. She felt her cheeks flush and she stared at her shoes, as she was addressed by Basher's former police partner. Sami was a powerfully charismatic mum of two who – unlike the average dysfunctional alcoholic TV detective, whose family didn't speak to them and whose partner was about to ask them to choose between the job or their relationship – kept a vice-like grip on her work–life balance. She was also unnervingly good at her job, or at least the part of it that Claire experienced, which so far had largely been conversations where Claire had tried to tell what she considered harmless lies, and Sami had looked at her as if she were as opaque as cling film. But Sami was also kind, and had a lovely gap-toothed smile that took the sting out of embarrassing yourself in front of her.

'I'm going to choose to believe, if only for the briefest of moments, that I and my partner are attending the scene because we happened to be nearby, and yet somehow finding you here is one huge coincidence,' said Sami. She put her hands on her hips in a way that surely struck fear into the hearts of her children. Her new police partner – who was a lanky dark-haired woman, as if Sami had deliberately picked someone extremely different from Bash – glided past, talking quickly and quietly into her phone.

'Um, well, you know, he had to be found by *someone*,' said Claire.

'That's a very good point. And in this case that was you because …?'

'I'd go for the truth, you know, Weirdo – she's way too smart for you,' said Sophie.

'Okay, so I'm not here for, like, *no reason*, but I don't think this can really have anything to do with me this time,' replied Claire. She took a deep breath, but Sami held out a hand.

'If this is going to be a long, rambling story, as I suspect it is, then we will ask you to go down to the station. Give me some brief facts now, then one of the uniforms will take you back in a panda. Follow me.

Sami walked over to a long black Volvo and opened the back door and Claire slid inside, trying to radiate meekness and compliance. Sami got into the front.

'Right,' continued Sami. She sighed heavily and pinched her nose in a gesture reminiscent of Basher. 'If I start writing things down, are you going to say something about ghosts?'

'I mean, maybe,' said Claire.

'I recommend honesty again – you know what she's like,' said Sophie.

Claire took a deep breath and gave an abbreviated history of events up to that point, leaving out things that made her sound more unbalanced than usual (ghost blogger who got no respect from the wrestlers, for example).

'... and then I called you lot,' she finished.

'Right. That's a lot to deal with, isn't it?' said Sami. 'We're *definitely* going to need a bigger statement. Did you let anyone know you were coming here?'

'Yeah. Ken and Trudy. Oh, and Alex. Was that wrong?'

'I can check with them to corroborate some of what you're saying,' said Sami.

'Well, that's answering a different question from the one you asked,' commented Sophie.

'What do you think happened to Chaz?' Claire asked.

'I'm obviously not at liberty to comment, especially because I haven't even bloody been in that building yet,' replied Sami. She frowned and turned the key, so that she could start the heater. Her breath was misting.

'Yeah, um, only, I was thinking: someone left the front door open, and even if it was Chaz, it can't have been that long ago, because he would have realized and shut it,' said Claire.

Sami looked at her sharply. 'You can leave the detection to the professionals, Claire,' she said. No sign of her nice gap-toothed smile. She paused. 'Drink plenty of water and don't do anything exciting. I know you allege that you see dead people often, but seeing dead *bodies* is something else.' She got out and ushered Claire out of the car, before giving her the order to stay still.

The police had multiplied like high-vis rabbits. There were more cars and an ambulance, so that paramedics could officially pronounce someone dead, which seemed a bit of a waste of time, but Basher would probably go on about the need for a proper paper trail, and so on. It's not as if you could get all the way through a court case only for it to be thrown out because a paramedic hadn't said, 'Oof, yeah, that fucker's dead all right.' But then again, maybe you could.

There was police tape, and even a couple of rubber-neckers being told to bugger off. The street's ghosts were able to walk right through the cordon, of course. Sami was now deep in conversation with her partner, who was holding an evidence bag with a piece of paper in it. Claire looked at her phone and edged closer, as if she was only wandering in their direction by chance as she checked her texts. Sophie tried to walk up right behind them, and Claire gritted her teeth as the tether between them jangled in displeasure. But then Sami noticed her, and told her to put her phone away and move back again.

'I couldn't read it, but I heard the one that wasn't Sami say, "appears to be a note",' said Sophie.

8

The Sound of the Police

Despite her special interests, Claire avoided police stations. Early on in her career, spurred on by visions of becoming famous and being given her own reality TV series, where people like Amanda Holden came on as guests and Claire made them cry by describing their dead loved ones, she had tried to help solve a missing-persons case. The police had misunderstood that she could only help because the missing teen was already dead, so when his body had been found, Claire had no small amount of blame and shame heaped upon her. One of the reasons she worked on word-of-mouth was because there was no way ClaireHendricks.com would rank on Google search results above a horrible article in *The Sun*, even if it was nearly fifteen years old. Since then she'd been interviewed by the police a couple of times, but only once had been in a station, and it had been in Ireland, so she felt a safe degree of separation.</NI>

She'd never even walked past Brighton's police station before and, standing in front of it now, she was surprised at the large bright-blue facade and big blue chimney. It looked like something that could be made on *Blue Peter* with some poster paint and a shoebox. She was deposited in a sort of waiting area inside, which was not unlike a GP's waiting room in its uncomfortable conformity and bad carpet.

She called Basher, and he was very annoyed with her, as usual, which Claire thought was unfair, because it wasn't as if she'd planned to find a body and get taken to the police station; and then he had told her to call a lawyer. But she wasn't under arrest, and she couldn't afford a lawyer if one wasn't being provided for her, so Basher said to leave if she was asked a question that she didn't like, because it was a voluntary interview. As a former detective sergeant, Basher was usually a lot more positive about the role of the police in general, and Sami specifically. Possibly he was suspicious of Claire's capacity to find trouble, even when trouble was trying to hide from her. Basher also told her to look after herself and asked her again if she was okay, and said he'd pick her up from the station.

'See,' Claire said to Sophie, 'he's never angry with me for long.'

Sophie snorted.

Claire ended up waiting at the police station for more than an hour and a half, during which time Sophie got increasingly bored and petulant about the whole situation. But Claire didn't think she should leave, because if she left she would surely make herself look suspicious, even though she hadn't done anything. Plus, this was possibly a way to kick the whole dead-wrestler football into the police's back yard. 'I think my brother killed me,' was one thing, but 'there is definitely a big dead body in front of me' was another, and she'd had quite enough of it. If she could offload everything on Sami, she could simply bill Ken for the couple of days' work she'd done and go back to subsisting on off-brand Doritos.

She was still nervous, though, because she didn't know the right way to behave while being interviewed as a witness in Brighton police station. It didn't seem like it was the sort of thing you should google, either. Thus she found herself sitting in a bland interview room that looked sort of like an empty school classroom. She shifted her feet nervously while she waited for Sami to come back.

'Ohmigod, calm down, Weirdo,' said Sophie. 'You'll make a terrible impression. You look like you're guilty of something.'

Claire tried to speak without moving her mouth, in case there was a camera. 'I always feel like low-grade guilt. Usually I have just done, or am about to do, something that will upset someone,' she replied quietly.

'Yeah, I know. Terrible way to live. Another reason that if God were real, he would have taken you,' said Sophie.

Claire tutted. 'He didn't take you,' she replied, lowering her voice further. 'Statistically you were probably taken by a pervert who has kept your feet in a freezer.'

'Wow – uncalled for. I can see my feet right here, see?' Soph pointed at her white-trainered toes as evidence.

'Yes, but you have to agree that they're very cold, aren't they?'

Claire zipped her lip as the door opened and Sami came back into the room. She looked far less harried than she had been at the actual crime scene, which was fair enough. She even smiled, showing the big gap between her front teeth that made her wide grin powerfully charismatic. She reset her shining dark hair in its practical ponytail, tightening it almost like she bore a grudge towards her own scalp. This indicated to Claire that this was still very much going to be Sami in professional mode, despite the smile – as if the murder investigation left her in any doubt.

The other detective who had been at the crime scene followed closely behind Sami. She was wearing a crumpled blue suit and looked less friendly, although that might have been overspill from Claire assuming that all people she didn't know probably wouldn't like her.

'This is DS Madison, who you saw earlier. Madison is my partner and will be working on this situation with me,' said Sami.

Madison gave Claire a terrifyingly strong handshake. 'Hi, Claire, thank you for taking the time to come in,' she said.

'Yeah. Um, you too,' replied Claire.

Sami raised an eyebrow and grinned. 'Oh, we had to be here,' she said.

Claire and Sophie had harboured a suspicion that the police weren't entirely on the side of truth and justice, ever since a PC had confiscated from them, and subsequently poured out, a bottle of White Lightning circa 2006, on the basis that they were obviously not eighteen. Alex encouraged this anti-authoritarian streak in both of them. Basher often remonstrated with Alex for casually saying things like 'ACAB', made them say, 'All cops are bastards' out loud and asked if that included him, and Alex always said obviously not, because he had quit. So then Bash asked if it included Sami, and Alex thought about it and said that it did, insofar as they were discussing her role as a cog in a broken machine.

The thing was that, although Sami was very much a C, you'd be very hard pressed to think of her as a B. She had initially wanted to quit, because being British Indian and a woman put her in two out-groups of the boys' club at once, but unlike Basher, she didn't have 'inherited wealth while mooching about vaguely being a private investigator and working bar shifts' to fall back on. The hatchet was mostly buried, but she still sometimes referred to Basher as 'the sort of centrist who would listen to *The Rest Is Politics*', which Basher said was a deeply unfair characterization.

Sami led Claire past the main desk and into a kind of side-room, which had soft furnishings and an MDF coffee table. It was quite unlike the bare interview room with a two-way mirror that Claire had expected. There was, however, still a recorder on the table and a couple of slim files of paperwork.

'We'll be comfy enough in here, won't we? Don't want to be too clinical about it,' said Sami.

'God, she's very good at reading a room, isn't she?' commented Soph, observing that Claire had instantly relaxed a fraction.

Sophie was right. The first time they'd met Sami, she had seen Claire wince at the prices on a lunch menu and immediately insisted that Basher was paying for everyone, in a way that didn't make Claire feel awkward. Sami's ability to tell how someone was actually feeling, and act accordingly, was one of the things that made her so likeable. In the wrong hands, Claire noted, this sort of ability would be very useful to a sociopath, as had been the case earlier in the year when a handsome man had nearly charmed Claire into not noticing that he was a murderer. It hadn't taken much effort on his part. Claire was unused to men trying to charm her.

Madison started the recording and even did the thing where she said the date and time and who was in the room, which was thrilling, and then asked Claire how the tea was, which was a weird thing to put on the record.

'Er, it's all right, thank you.'

'Are you nervous?' asked Madison, which was a sudden change of tack.

'LOL. Bold choice to be good cop and bad cop at the same time,' said Sophie. 'That doesn't leave anything for Sami. Does she have to be neutral cop?'

'Um, yeah. Obviously. I'm in a police station.'

'Well, you've done nothing wrong, right?' said Madison.

'Oh, the old "the innocent have nothing to fear" line, is it?' said Soph.

'We just have some follow-up questions to get more context on Charles Curtain,' said Sami, smoothly breaking in and refocusing Claire.

For the next several minutes they went over again how Claire had found Chaz: the timing, the open doors, that she didn't touch anything. And then Sami started asking more about the context.

'In your initial statement at the scene you said that you wanted to speak to Mr Curtain regarding his former role at an independent pro-wrestling organization, the SWF, is that right?'

'Yeah. I'm not entirely sure what his job was. I was told he was one of the founders, but he used to do the books, I think. He said he knew where all the skeletons were buried.'

'Was your interest in one skeleton in particular?' asked Madison.

Claire blinked. She didn't know the police were allowed to be glib in interviews.

'Now's your chance, Weirdo,' said Sophie. 'What have you got to lose? Your reputation?'

Claire sighed. Soph was right, but there was no way she came out of this without looking several ducks short of a pond, so she might as well get ahead of the flock, so to speak.

'I spoke to ... Wait actually. Did either of you investigate Eddie King's death?' she asked, mindful that she might be about to insult someone.

Sami's eyebrows rose a fraction. 'Not personally, but I heard about it of course. He's a big local name. I don't think you would really say it was investigated, per se, because it wasn't suspicious. A man who has high blood pressure is warned to slow down a bit, does not and dies. Right?'

'Yeah, I s'pose,' said Claire. 'So, look, I get that you probably won't believe that I talked to Eddie's ghost or anything ...' She stared at her own hands, which were wrapped around a mug of tea, so that she wouldn't have to look at Sami or DS Madison's faces. She took a deep breath. 'But I did. And even if I didn't talk to Eddie's ghost, I think there is a lot about his death that is suspicious. So. Yeah.'

'Such as?'

'Go on,' encouraged Soph.

'Oh, right. So first of all, there's the door,' said Claire.

'The door?'

Claire was slightly disappointed. In her TV shows like *Murder Profile*, just saying something like 'the door' would cause Sami to look at her in sudden realization and respond with, for instance, 'Oh my God – the door ... Why didn't we see it before?' right on time for the ad break. It was constantly disappointing that real life didn't work on TV rules. So she explained in more detail: who had locked Eddie into the SWF after he'd died?; Eddie's wife had suspected him of having an affair, and seemed ambivalent at best about his death; he'd argued with his son about something and changed his will weeks before he died; two wrestlers had said something that sounded like they knew that Eddie was going to die; he had argued with Chaz, his lifelong business partner, so badly that nobody was even allowed to mention Chaz Curtain's name in front of him; and, finally, he seemed like a terrible prick. And, of course, there was the point about Eddie himself being convinced that his brother had killed him. She did mention this, but backed away from it quite quickly, because it made Sami and Madison exchange a significant look.

After she'd finished, Sami and Madison looked at one another again, for longer. Madison leaned back with one of the files and flipped through a couple of the pages. Sophie moved and tried to read over her shoulder, but Madison flipped it closed again.

'I think they're probably considering the internal politics of looking further into a death that was waved through by some less competent but popular broski, whose favourite T-shirt says, fuckin' "KEEP CALM AND BBQ ON" or something,' said Sophie.

'All right, well, investigations are continuing,' said Sami. 'And, I may add, will be handled by the professionals.'

'Cops being passive-aggressive feels like a violation of your rights somehow,' said Sophie.

Claire snorted, and Sami looked at her. She leaned forward. 'For the tape, and for you, Ms Hendricks, I am warning you to stay away from this matter. It is not something that needs your involvement, and you could find yourself back here again on a charge of perverting the course of justice.'

'Yes, something to take seriously. I think that's all we need from you, for now. We may be in touch again,' said Madison. She switched off the recording.

'Yes,' said Claire. She nearly added 'Miss' on the end. 'Can I not go anywhere near the SWF? Alex has training and stuff there.'

Sami pinched the bridge of her nose. 'You can still go to that building, as long as you're not harassing anyone about Charles Curtain or anything related. Believe it or not, there isn't anything in our training to cover mediums, so I'm not sure we can stop you communing with any ghosts that you or Mr Ken King believe are in the vicinity, because you are both private citizens. But I would tread very carefully, if I were you.'

'It's not like I *try* to get involved in stuff like this,' Claire protested.

'And yet ...' said Sami.

'Seems pretty fucking unlikely,' snickered Soph.

'I'll, um, do my best,' agreed Claire.

'Sami is being nice,' said Madison. 'But I transferred from Swindon. I don't know your friend. So if I run into you being a nuisance, I won't be so nice.'

Sami nodded. 'It's true. She's a horrible bastard.'

'That's police overreach,' mumbled Claire.

'Crikey, I'd better overreach here to open the door and escort you out,' said Sami.

Once they left the room, Sami sloughed off her serious-cop skin. She even walked differently. It was alarming, seeing how your friend could be two different people at once. It was almost like a wrestling persona.

'Nice to see you, Claire,' she said. She watched as Claire signed out of the visitor book, leaning easily against the front desk. 'Hopefully we'll chat again under more normal circumstances.'

'Yes, that would be nice,' replied Claire.

'Imagine,' said Soph. 'You and normal circumstances. Chance would be a fine bastard thing, wouldn't it?'

'Was he murdered? Chaz, I mean,' asked Claire sheepishly. 'I feel like it's my fault.'

Sami looked at her. 'I will say what Basher will, which is that if someone is murdered, it is the fault of the murderer.' She took Claire's elbow and led her outside, where she looked into Claire's eyes for a few seconds. Then she sighed. 'Completely off the record – and if this gets out, I will know it came from you and I will chase down every tiny indiscretion you have ever made – there was a note indicating Mr Curtain took his own life. There is no reason for you to feel guilty, or to involve yourself further.'

'Do you believe the note?'

'Oh, for goodness' sake,' said Sami. 'Go home. Drink plenty of water, like I said. Be with friends. Thank you for your cooperation.'

Sami pointed as she spoke, and Claire now saw that Basher and Alex were sitting across the street on some moulded concrete benches. They waved. Claire was so relieved to see them that she forgot to say goodbye to Sami before she rushed over the road. Alex and Basher both gave her a hug.

'Hello, Strange,' said Basher. 'Come with us. We shall get you a cup of tea.'

'Or something stronger, bloody hell, Uncle B.' Alex threaded arms with her, and together they all began to amble back towards the centre of town. 'He's having third thoughts about the wrestling training tomorrow,' added Alex.

'God, is it still only Friday?' Claire croaked.

'It is. You have been remarkably busy,' commented Basher. His hands were stuck in the pockets of a faded smoke-coloured hoodie. It made him look more blond, his eyes more grey, than they really were.

'If it makes you feel any better, Sami says Chaz – the guy who just died – she says he left a note and there's no reason for me to investigate. My head hurts,' she added, aggrieved.

'Oh, what – there's nothing wrong with you,' said Sophie.

'That does actually make me feel better,' said Basher. 'There is a pharmacy not far from here, so we can source some painkillers.'

He wasn't lying. They'd only been walking ten minutes when the neon-green cross hove into view. It wasn't the most salubrious part of Brighton, but then Brighton as a whole ran on small-batch coffee and vegan doughnuts to such an extent that it was a very relative measure. Still, as they all trooped inside and Alex began to examine the cheap nail varnish from brands Claire had never heard of, she was surprised when Sophie elbowed her in the ribs.

'Hey! Don't.' They had a long-standing agreement that Soph wouldn't touch her unless it was an emergency.

'Sorry, but – look. Over there, in the corner,' Soph said.

At the back of the room, off to one side, a youngish man with a name badge, who clearly worked there, was talking to another man, who was dressed all in light-blue denim and had his dark hair tied back in a rough, low ponytail.

'What?'

'Don't you recognize him? He's one of the wrestlers from last night! He was talking about painkillers.'

'Oh!' Claire said. She tried to keep her voice low. 'He looks so different with clothes on.'

Sophie urged her to get closer, and Claire wandered down the aisle in what she hoped was a very nonchalant way. Not nonchalant enough, because as she got closer, the wrestler hurried away.

'He put a little baggy in his pocket,' said Claire. 'Man, the oversight here must be like, zero, if he's dealing out of his own workplace.'

She glanced over towards Basher, who was buying two packs of paracetamol from an extremely elderly chemist, whose oversight clearly didn't extend far past his own nose. Claire had mere seconds to act decisively, which didn't play to her strengths. She walked over to the dealer.

'Excuse me,' she said. 'What did you sell to Eddie King?'

For a shot in the dark, it hit the bullseye. The young man blanched, then went strawberry-red. 'Fuck off,' he hissed.

'Threaten him with blond justice,' said Sophie.

'Er, right, except that guy over there is a cop,' continued Claire. 'I won't say anything, I just want to know what you sold Eddie. And if you don't tell me, then I'll, um, snitch.'

'Very convincing,' said Sophie. 'Sounded very natural.'

The criminal pharmacist grabbed her arm and pulled her towards the shelves of hair dye. 'Look, it's nothing funny. Some behind-the-counter painkillers, that's it. They're all at it. They get their steroids somewhere else, if that's what you're asking,' he said. 'Oh, and some Blue Diamond, but that's basically harmless.'

'Ready, C?' called Alex, from the other side. Basher was advancing down the shop from the tills. 'Oh, are you thinking of dyeing your hair? You should ask me about it.'

'Look I told you what you want, now fuck off,' hissed the dealer. His breath smelled unpleasantly of old coffee. He almost pushed Claire away, and she hurried back over to Alex.

Outside, Basher gave her a bottle of water and some tablets and she swallowed them gratefully.

'Find out anything interesting?' asked Alex. Their voice was carefully light. Claire and the pharmacist had clearly not been discussing L'Oréal.

'Yeah, we did,' said Claire. 'Eddie was getting meds under the table from a pharmacist, and that guy in there just said he was selling Eddie something called Blue Diamond, which is obviously slang for some drug. And Eddie said the pills he was taking were blue. What if someone switched them out? Maybe he overdosed accidentally.'

Basher stopped walking. He scratched the side of his stubbly face and put his tongue in his cheek. 'And he was found in nothing but a towel, was he?' There was a twinkle in his eye as he looked first at Claire, then up at the sky.

'Why are you acting like the answer is really bloody obvious?' Claire asked.

Basher actually laughed a little then. 'Maybe it is only obvious to a man. Or if you listen to a lot of American podcasts hosted by men? I think they all end up with the same ad-sponsor sooner or later.'

'What are you *talking* about, for fuck's sake?' said Sophie.

'Call it a hunch,' replied Basher. 'But to my tremendous relief, I think we might be looking at an accidental death after all. Or, to put it another way, I think Eddie might have been mixing his blood-pressure medication with something you definitely should not mix with blood-pressure medication. Come on, you can work it out. An older man, alone at night, in a towel, taking medication he thinks is a bit embarrassing?'

'Oh. Oh, shit! Oh, that's very funny!' said Sophie.

'Can one of you tell me what you're talking about, please?'

'You might have figured it out, if you ever got a shag, Weirdo,' said Sophie, who had started laughing as well.

'Viagra!' replied Basher, with some satisfaction. 'I would bet you any amount of money you care to name. I think Eddie was there to meet someone. Probably a woman, although I would not like to assume,' and he raised an amused eyebrow that was, like the rest of him, homosexual. 'But I do not think whoever Eddie was meeting killed him. I think taking Viagra at the same time as being on medication that lowers your blood pressure killed him. Because Viagra also lowers blood pressure.'

'Literally,' said Sophie. 'See, that was a good joke.'

'Get it? Because the blood goes—' said Alex.

'Yes, all right, thank you,' said Claire. 'What are the symptoms of lower blood pressure?'

'If memory serves: dizziness, blurred vision, nausea,' replied Basher.

'Well, shit. That's almost exactly what Eddie described happening to him, isn't it?' said Sophie. 'Horny old goat was killed by his own massive stonk-on.' She thought for a moment. 'Medium stonk-on,' she added. 'At best.'

Claire shook her head like a confused four-year-old. 'Argh,' she said. 'This is too much information to process.'

'Come here and sit down,' said Alex. They shot their uncle a look and helped Claire down on the steps of one of the old, tall flats that littered Brighton like discarded Magnum-lolly sticks. "You had a big day."

'Put it all in your little nark book,' said Sophie. Claire glared at her, but did after a moment retrieve her notebook. She opened up a new page and wrote 'VIAGRA' in the middle, and then did a little cloud around it.

'Okay, let's brainstorm this,' she said.

'Knobstorm,' said Sophie.

Basher sighed and leaned against the front railings of the house.

'Look, okay, we're saying Eddie was having an affair,' said Claire. 'I mean, it would explain why Trudy started checking up on what he was doing with other wrestlers.'

'They could *both* have been having separate affairs,' Alex pointed out. 'Or maybe he and Trudy were role-playing having an affair with each other, to spice up their marriage.'

'Don't people usually go dogging, or try to find a lonely and desperate thirty-something woman for that?' asked Soph. 'LOL. Lucky they didn't run into you a few months ago, isn't it, Weirdo?'

'I'm not *that* desperate,' Claire mumbled. 'It wasn't Trudy; she was very clear they were leading separate lives. Although if they were, why would she be arsed who Eddie was shagging? So definitely another woman, because I don't think he was gay …'

'Yeah, Eddie reads as, like, trad masc cis man who's homophobic but knows he shouldn't say that out loud any more,' said Sophie. 'Like, if Ken had come out to him, Eddie wouldn't have thrown him out, but he would have been uncomfortable using the word "boyfriend" and wouldn't have let Ken bring anyone over to meet him. It does explain why Eddie was in the towel, at least. He was making sure he was clean and sexable.'

'Maybe you can get the ghost to move on,' Basher waved a hand vaguely. 'Or whatever it is you can do to ghosts.'

'Annoy them, mostly,' said Sophie.

'You're being very unsuspicious, for a former policeman,' said Claire.

'My point is that it does not matter why Eddie was there, or who he was going to meet,' said Basher. 'We have a probably accidental death – albeit slightly different from what the police first assumed – followed by a probable suicide. You don't have to care any more, Strange. You can just go and lie down. No more getting into trouble.'

Claire stared at her feet. For some reason the whole thing made her feel extremely morose.

Alex brightened up. 'So I can definitely go to wrestling training tomorrow then?'

9

Very Serious Research

'I dunno what you're looking so sad about,' said Sophie.

'Seeing yet another dead body maybe?'

'Yeah, right. You'll just repress it, like all the other actually significant problems in your life. Apart from that, you've got reasons to be cheerful! You've done two solid days of work that you can bill someone for – except now you can leave everything to the cops. Isn't that what you wanted?'

'I know, but it … feels wrong. A guy offs himself hours after making an appointment to speak to me,' replied Claire. 'And it's about his old mate, who also died.'

'True, it would be less suspicious if he overdosed *after* meeting you,' said Sophie.

Claire grunted and mulled the situation over as she and Sophie schlepped up a shallow but long hill towards Brighton train station, having only just been released from the custody of Alex and Basher, on the insistence that she really wanted to have a nap. The station forecourt was home to a rotating crop of bougie food vans serving spelt bread and stone-fired pizza, to cater to upper-middle-class commuters. Claire only got one of those when she was feeling *very* sorry for herself, because they cost a fiver more than the frozen pizzas from Mr Przybylski's shop, which she now crossed over the road to enter.

Claire's basement flat (which Sophie liked to describe as *her* flat, an affectation that Claire didn't like and which she described as an affectation to Sophie's face, because she neither paid any fucking rent or, technically, lived there) was directly under the shop and was likewise owned by Mr Przybylski, a diminutive white-haired Polish immigrant and cheerful bastard. Claire liked him a lot, especially considering he was her landlord. People leaving Mr Przybylski's shop dropped their Solero and Twix wrappers directly into the stairwell that led to the flat's front door. Claire asked him to do something about it, but Mr Przybylski responded by saying that rubbish outside her flat was *her* rubbish, and indeed the amount of rubbish was making his shop look bad. So they found themselves at an impasse.

'Good afternoon, Claire,' he said, as the door sensor made a *bleeh-blaw* to herald her arrival. He was perched in his normal position on a high stool behind the counter, obscuring his lower half. Claire had never *not* seen him in that exact position and wondered if he was a gargoyle, or perhaps a centaur or Dalek hybrid. 'I see you have eaten a lot of Crunchie bars again.' This was not an incorrect statement, but he was making it because the stairwell had accrued a notable number of new Crunchie wrappers.

'Correlation, not causation, Mr Przybylski,' she replied.

'I dunno why he always thinks it's you,' said Sophie. 'The old fucker sees everything bought in this shop, and everyone who leaves it with said purchases.'

Claire bought a nearly-out-of-date loaf of bread to make toast and a likewise discounted microwavable lasagne, but Mr Przybylski was already shoving his phone at her again. 'Look, you see here?' he said. 'There is a camera above the stairs and I can see who is misbehaving outside my shop. And watch the recordings back, and show the police if there is a crime!'

His screen showed the door to his shop and the top of the stairs.

'I told you: I'm not the one leaving rubbish everywhere,' said Claire quickly. 'I swear!'

'Well, now we will know for sure.'

'Hey, is that like the system at the SWF?' asked Soph. 'What if there's footage of Nate still saved?'

'Oh, you're right!' agreed Claire out loud, without thinking. 'I mean, er, yeah, Mr Przybylski, you're right. You can see it's not me! Out of interest, how long does the footage stay saved for?'

'Joseph says it goes back as long as you want, if you have space in the Cloud. But he set it to auto-delete after a few months, because he says otherwise it will be like the most boring television channel in the world.'

'Smart man, Joseph,' said Sophie.

'Can you delete things manually?' asked Claire.

Mr Przybylski looked hard at her. 'Only myself and Joseph can delete what we want, with our log-ins. Even if you steal my phone, you don't know the password!' He waggled his finger. 'You can't delete evidence of you throwing all your this-and-that into the stairs.'

'All right, all right, I was only asking,' replied Claire.

She left and descended the steps to her subterranean cave, as Dante had descended to the first level of Hell. Her flat was so dark, and had such a general air of a place a goblin would live in, that Mr Przybylski had offered it for rent with bills included, which was basically the only reason Claire had taken it, because she could crank the heating on and be toasty warm all the time. Despite waking up every day feeling like a pot plant that got no sunlight, this flat was still an improvement on the one she'd had in London.

She made three slices of toast and put the lasagne in the microwave to heat up. Sophie sat down to watch her eat the toast with an intensity that would, had she been alive, have been very unsettling. It made Claire self-conscious, like a politician under scrutiny while eating a potentially ruinous bacon sandwich.

While she chewed, she reviewed her notebook and list of Official Suspects. She lingered for a few moments on a page she labelled 'MOTIVES':

NATE KING: *inherited the SWF from Eddie*

TRUDY KING: *ambivalent at best about husband, desperate to retire*

GUY & RUBY: *angry at Ken about billing – previously angry at Eddie over same issue. Implied threats and seemed to know Eddie would be dying soon??*

LILA KING: *unknown/none*

KEN KING: *Professional jealousy? But seems to be the only person who liked his dad.*

'Did I miss anything on this page?' she asked Sophie.
'I don't think so. But why do you care?'
'It's like there's a piece missing somewhere.' Claire wrote down:

CHAZ CURTAIN: *kicked out of the company he founded. Also, what's up with nobody mentioning him?*

From what she could tell, about eight months ago someone had tried to memory-hole Chaz Curtain out of existence. But they hadn't done a complete job. Any mention of Chaz on the official SWF channels had been wiped, but only up to the last twenty-four months. Before that, he still turned up in show-flyers and promos – whoever had been charged with his deletion must have decided that two years was a good-enough buffer. Plus, you could see the shape of Chaz from comments left around him: the occasional post on Bluesky replying to something long deleted, with a 'Looking good, Chaz!' or a 'Great match from Chaz tonight.'

The vibe was very much Stalinist Russia; the only thing stopping whoever at the SWF had made this edict from clumsily airbrushing Chaz out of any pictures he appeared in was that they didn't have access to Photoshop. Presumably the order had come down from Ken.

The question then became, 'Why had Ken tried to delete Chaz?' Ken had a temper, but Chaz had been one-third of the entire organization, so it had to have been over more than Ken waking up on the wrong side of the bed one day. Claire found an interview he'd done on Owen Miller's extremely tedious blog, where Chaz talked about how he and the King brothers had founded the SWF decades before, and that while Eddie was the owner and front man, he, Chaz, had a huge hand in the behind-the-scenes running of the promotion. 'I take care of most of the boring admin stuff, which leaves Eddie free to concentrate on booking talent,' he had said. Of the three founders, the one you could most easily retcon from your organization seemed to be Nate. Claire couldn't spot Nate in any photos, and he wasn't mentioned as really *doing* anything, other than being – the consensus was – very good at wrestling.

'I've no idea how the ownership of the SWF worked,' said Sophie. She was reading over Claire's shoulder.

'How do you mean?'

'Well, in this article Miller refers to Chaz as a founder. But as far as we know, Eddie left the *entire* gym to Nate, which he couldn't do if Chaz owned part of it. If he and Nate were all equal founders, how come they didn't get equal shares?'

'I suppose,' replied Claire dubiously. 'But either way, if getting ownership of a regional wrestling promo were a motivating factor in killing Eddie, you'd have thought whoever it was would have dusted off his murder years ago.'

'I was just wondering aloud about family drama, but you're still trying to solve a murder.'

'Look, I know the police don't seem to find any of this suspicious, but it is,' said Claire. 'We still can't explain why Eddie's death was staged, and what Nate was doing there that night, even if Eddie dying was a Viagra-related accident. But if it wasn't, and he *was* poisoned, we can narrow it down with "means".'

'You mean, whoever had the means to get hold of poison, right?' Sophie said.

'Yeah. But then again, because nobody bothered to test for poison, we don't know what it was specifically. They could have covered his pills in rat poison or weedkiller for all we know, which is pretty easy to get.'

'Well, we know at least one person who can explain away having weedkiller, right? A keen gardener indeed,' said Sophie.

'Wow. You're right.' Claire stared at her notes. 'But Trudy has such a weak motive.'

'Don't you, and your stupid shows, say it's always the spouse?' insisted Sophie. 'And poison is a woman's weapon and all that, like you said.'

'I dunno. I'm going to watch some *Murder Profile*,' said Claire. She loaded up a mid-run season (the show had gone on for fifteen years and was apparently getting a comeback season soon, which Claire was trying to stay chill about). Granted the team of crack FBI profilers usually dealt with very contrived serial killers who did stuff like kidnap brown-haired women and dress them as dogs, and someone on the team would very confidently explain this was because the perp's brunette mum left on *the very same day* his dog died, and so on. So the parallels to a ghost telling you they were murdered, in presumably a normal way, weren't exactly one-to-one. Also, Claire couldn't call on a private jet and loads of crime-scene examiners, or just get all of everyone's private data at will …

After two episodes she sighed. She'd got caught in a comfort loop of watching an extremely inaccurate TV show that made her feel better in the short term, which wasn't going to help in the long term.

She switched to YouTube and, almost without thinking about it, pulled up videos of pro-wrestling. The lasagne in the microwave pinged, so she ended up eating pasta with one hand while she looked up things about pro-wrestling with her phone in the other.

'Well, on the face of these videos, I'd say pro-wrestling is intensely homoerotic,' commented Sophie. 'Yet at the same time the number of "TAP OUT" shirts I can spot in the audience suggests their core demo does not like to contemplate the level of homoeroticism.'

'Ah, come on, what's straighter than stripping down, oiling up and hugging another nearly-nude rude dude?'

'Well, as long as the rude dude has a 'tude ...' said Sophie.

'Alex said that it's slightly more progressive these days. At least a bit, anyway. But reading these Wikis is like reading Cold War spy code. Look here: "Page used the Crossface ChickenWing complete with taunt, a reference to Scurll working at ROH." It's like an iceberg – eighty per cent of a wrestling match you don't see in the match itself. It's all built up over hours of matches beforehand, and shouting at each other and what *other* wrestlers are doing, or did years ago. If this was a murder, the motive might end up being very complex. I don't think I'd be able to figure it out, unless the SWF has a fan Wiki.'

'Buck the fuck up, pet,' said Soph.

She was looking at Claire's mouth, which made Claire pause in the act of unconsciously licking away a blob of sauce and wipe it off with her hand instead. 'You've solved two murders already.'

'Three,' replied Claire. The last two had happened at roughly the same time on a group holiday, but the killers were different, so Claire counted them separately.

'Call it two and a half,' said Sophie. 'So you totally could solve it, if you wanted to. Although my two cents are still that you should cut your losses and run. We need to work on stretching the tether and building up our regular clientele anyway.' She squinted at the screen. 'Unless you're more interested in a guy dressed in all denim and a T-shirt of his own face? I mean, I guess it's better than a literal clown.'

Claire sighed heavily. It was like prodding a bruise. She couldn't leave it alone.

'I can see why the police didn't think it was suspicious to start with,' she conceded.

'Sure,' agreed Sophie. 'Big man with a blood-pressure problem gets in some extra training the day before a show and – *kablooie,* his heart fucking explodes like Boxer the horse.'

'I dunno if that's exactly how Orwell described it, but something like that.' Claire looked up the symptoms of both high and low blood pressure and found that they were, indeed, very similar to what Eddie had described: dizziness, nausea, vomiting, fainting, and so on. This was another check mark in the column for Basher being right (and being smug about being right). 'I just think they're being pretty quick to brush off Chaz dying too, that's all. Plus, sometimes murderers return to the scene of the crime, don't they? Bash said sometimes they would interview whoever found the body a lot because they needed as much information as possible, and sometimes because they were probably the one who did it. So they could be hanging around the gym still. Maybe they're on the CCTV.'

Once more she internally lamented how far she had to go before she was as good at being a detective as the cast of *Murder Profile* or the hosts of podcasts like *Wine Girlies' True Crime.* Alex often pointed out that they all had editors, and also the TV shows and podcasts Claire liked were, quoting directly, 'a bucket of total horseshit' that were exploitative of victims and their families. Which did make them less fun to watch. Alex gave her things like non-fiction books about the history of women's magazines instead (she had read these and been appalled, and wondered if the cost of learning about things – that is, being depressed by basically the entire world – was too high, but Alex said that's why you Organize, with a significant O).

'If you're itching to feel useful, why don't you call Ken?' Sophie suggested. 'You can ask about all the stuff bothering you and get probably normal explanations. And maybe get paid.'

Claire scraped the last of the lasagne into her mouth. This was an achievable suggestion, although she hated asking anyone for anything at the best of times. Still, her bank balance wouldn't keep her in ready meals indefinitely. She psyched herself up and pressed the call button.

'Hi,' said Ken. 'Can we make it quick?'

'Hi, this is Claire,' she replied.

'Yeah, I have caller ID,' he said. 'How can I help?'

'Oh, er, yeah, well, I have a few things to check in with and I—'

'Sure, but it's not a *great* time, with everything going on. Can you call on me in a couple of days or something? I'll send you our address; text me to check where I am before you come over.'

'He sounds stressed,' said Sophie, which Claire thought was putting it mildly. 'Ask him about the security cameras.'

'Oh, right. Er, so I was wondering if you had a file with all the security footage from that camera at the gym that you showed us. Or even the log-in to the app. I, um …'

'Make up some ghost shit,' said Sophie. 'He'll eat it up.'

'I, uh … just wanted to check for spirit orbs and other phenomena, which might, you know, er, suggest when your father began haunting the area.'

'Oh, right. I suppose that's okay. I'll send you a dummy log-in, but you won't have administrator privileges. You can only look at stuff.'

'Got it. Thanks, Ken. Sorry about everything. Are you … you know, are you feeling okay?'

'Me?' He sounded surprised. 'Yeah, I'm okay. Look, we'll figure out meeting up, but I have to go right now, Lila needs me.'

He hung up abruptly, but did send Claire an invite to the camera app only a few minutes later, and she was able to log in and see a huge grid of videos, dating back a long time.

'That man has strange priorities,' said Sophie.

She watched as Claire swiped back through the videos. The camera only recorded something if it detected motion, so there wasn't as much as she'd been expecting.

'Hey, look,' Claire said. 'Here's the day before Eddie died.' There were a couple of videos – both of the man himself striding through the room with barely a pause. 'And here's the day after. Look, there's a video of Trudy going through in the morning, and then a bunch of videos with confused paramedics, and people coming in to collect the body and going through the wrong door.'

'So?'

'So there's nothing the day before. From the night he actually died. Even if Eddie lied about seeing Nate on the camera, we know *Eddie* went in there. And, what: nobody else went through the whole day? So someone has deleted the files, haven't they?'

'Huh,' said Sophie. 'That's a bit stupid. Wouldn't you delete *all* the files? Deleting just one day calls attention to it.'

'Mm. Maybe you'd have to be looking for it.'

'Anything else? Hey, try to find us.'

Claire did. She watched a small version of herself smash her knees into a tiny desk.

'Ha!' barked Sophie.

'I'm getting a massive bruise, thank you very fucking much,' Claire grumbled. 'Wait, what's this?'

After they'd come to visit, there was a really long file showing everyone streaming through and buying tickets for the Thursday-night show. But there was one lone video, the day after, that stood out.

'That's Trudy. She's got all those old posters we found, look!'

Trudy was indeed struggling with a large number of rolled-up promo posters. As they watched, she dropped a couple of the tubes and kicked them towards the door. She looked dejected.

'She told us she never went over there,' said Claire.

'You do say never to trust anything anyone says, like in *Murder Profile*.'

'Well, she also said nobody liked Eddie. Do you think that's true or not?'

Sophie considered this. 'Dunno,' she replied. 'You looked up Chaz before – why not look up Eddie's name on socials?'

This was a good plan. She started with a general news search, hoping that there may have been appeals for witnesses or useful info dug up by an ace newshound. There was nothing but a small local news piece, plus the specialist blogs like Miller's, which all had faintly obscene-sounding names like *Ring Insider* and *Big Graps Report*. None of these stories yielded anything new, so she moved on to Instagram, Facebook and so forth. When Eddie died, there had been a lot of tribute posts on Twitter and Facebook from wrestlers and wrestling fans that featured heart emojis, or the one that was actually a high-five, but people used as prayer hands: 'Eddie gave me a shot when I was just starting out; safe to say I wouldn't be where I am today without him [strong-arm emoji], RIP, big fella [prayer-hands emoji]'; 'Mr King was a proper gent of the old school, so sorry to hear the news of his passing [heart emoji]'; 'Anyone who wrestled with Eddie King came out a better wrestler for it; thoughts and prayers with his family [heart emoji, prayer-hands emoji, heart emoji].'

'Seems like he was quite well liked within the industry,' said Claire, scrolling. She took a massive bite of lasagne and pulled off most of a sheet of pasta, then flicked it back to swallow it like a zoo penguin being given an overly large pilchard. 'At least to the extent that you can trust what people say about someone as soon as they die, which I think is fuck-all,' she finished.

'How dare you; people said really nice things in that school newsletter about me, after I disappeared,' said Sophie.

'Yeah, exactly.'

Sophie mock-gasped and pressed a hand to her chest. 'I was very popular!'

'Yeah, but I mean … popular isn't the same as nice, is it?'

Sophie had actually been very nice to Claire at school. Her whim to make the mousy, nervous-looking girl in the playground her best friend had persisted for the next six years of Sophie's life, which meant that Claire – who would otherwise have been a target for the sort of bullying children only otherwise experience if they're the main character of a Roald Dahl book – had a relatively pain-free school experience until Sophie's death. She and Sophie had eaten marshmallows and got drunk in grim London public playgrounds after dark. They would probably not have stayed friends after leaving school, but circumstances had forced the issue. Now they could hurt each other in ways you can only do when you know someone as well as you know yourself.

'Like, I'm just saying …' Claire went on.

'Well, that guy seems to be pretty pass-agg about Eddie's death, look,' said Soph. She pointed at the phone screen, where Claire had half-scrolled past a tweet that said, 'You shouldn't speak ill of the dead, so I'll say nothing about Eddie King.' It had generated a lot of responses, by the look of things, but the poster – a man called Michael Doolan – had not elaborated in any replies. Claire clicked through to the full profile. It looked like the owner-operator of an indie wrestling promotion called Weegie Pro-Wrestling, based in Scotland.

'Huh, that's the home promotion for the tag team that Pink Champagne wrestled the other night,' she said, navigating to the other profiles. Weegie Pro-Wrestling had re-tweeted a picture of the four wrestlers post-match, all with big smiles.

'No such thing as a coincidence, right?' suggested Sophie.

'In real life they happen all the time.' Claire sighed. 'I wish we had one of those see-through evidence boards that they stick photos to and write on with markers.' Still, she picked up the TV remote and searched for 'PINK CHAMPAGNE WEEGIE PRO-WRESTLING' on YouTube.

There were a handful of results, and one in particular from about six months ago caught her eye. It was called 'MANAGER DOOLAN OFFERS PINK CHAMPAGNE A CONTRACT', uploaded by the Weegie Pro-Wrestling account. In it, a white man with slicked-back dark hair and a too-tight tartan suit (wrestlers seemed universally unable to buy clothing in the correct size) stood in a wrestling ring, surrounded by a load of other wrestlers of various shapes and sizes.

'You know, we've been trading blows back and forth with you in the SWF – in the ring and out of it – for months now,' he said. He had a strong Glaswegian accent, enough so that at least one comment under the video read, 'im american and i cant understand what hes saying lol braveheart.' The man went on with an air of quiet, controlled menace. 'I've been too polite to say what we're all thinking, what we all *know* in fact. And that's that there's not a one of you can stand toe-to-toe with my team. The team we've put together here isn't just the best in Scotland, isn't just the best in the United Kingdom, it's good enough to go toe-to-toe with any promotion In. The. World.' The pauses for emphasis were leaden, and the man stepped closer to the camera with each one.

'But there's one exception. I don't know how, but you've managed to find some of the best talent in all of your godforsaken country. In three weeks' time we're hosting the Fightful Monster Mash XL, and Guy and Ruby – the wrestlers otherwise known as Pink Champagne – are going to be there. So this part of my message is solely for them.' He held out his hand, and one of the group flanking him handed him some papers, covered in small printed writing, crocodile-clipped together.

'*These*,' he went on, flourishing the papers, 'are contracts. Contracts with *your* names on them. You're the only wrestlers worth a damn that I don't already have under my roof at Weegie. I want you here – and, well, I think you already know that Doolan always gets what he wants. So you come to Fightful Monster Mash XL

– tickets on sale now – and you wrestle with everything you've got, you leave your hearts on the mat. And then you think very carefully about who *really* appreciates you. Cos I don't think it's anyone where you are right now. I'll tell you something now. I'd kill to have you at Weegie Pro-Wrestling. And I think you'd kill to be here.'

Claire took a deep breath. 'We're going to Alex's training,' she said, in what she hoped was a very firm voice.

10

Impractical Fieldwork

'Differential diagnosis,' said Claire, employing a phrase she had heard on a lurid medical drama. 'Why would a business kick out one of its founders and try to erase the very memory of him?'

It was Saturday morning. Claire and Sophie sat with Alex on the bus. They had occupied a set of four seats right at the back. Wyatt, who was crouched on an empty seat opposite Sophie and behind Alex's gym bag, wore another brand-new collar and lead (dog accessories apparently being a new fixation for Alex) and a mutinous expression. Her small bullet-head was only just visible over the bag, and Claire had to try quite hard to not laugh, because she felt this would offend Wyatt's noble sensibilities. Wyatt seemed to have decided to stop barking at Sophie in favour of wary observation and, if Sophie got too close, a low growl full of ill-intent.

Besides, Wyatt was also distracted. Claire's base amount of low-level, grinding panic had increased early on in the journey, because Alex was eating the second of two Subway foot-long Meatball Marinaras, which seemed a wild food item to eat on public transport, and Claire was worried that if Wyatt made a lunge for it, it would cause a scene and they'd all be thrown off.

'God, too many reasons,' said Sophie. 'Maybe Chaz said something mean about Trudy. Maybe he ruined Eddie's best suit. Maybe they found out he's secretly a massive Nazi and was going to debut a Third Reich-themed character.'

Claire winced. 'That escalated.'

'Well, Nazis tend to.'

'Anyway, there wasn't anything grim like that around his flat, from what I saw,' said Claire.

'Has Uncle B cornered you again yet?' asked Alex. 'I told him you were coming today and he said he's concerned you'll end up breaking into someone's house or something.'

'He has texted me with a definite tone,' she replied.

'As he is wont,' said Alex, through a face full of sauce. They swallowed. 'Ignore Uncle B. He's just being a mizzog. You're allowed to be poking around annoying people until Ken officially tells you to stop,' they went on, cheerful and, if not pragmatic, assured that everything would turn out all right. They scratched Wyatt idly behind the ears, and Wyatt angled her head to quickly lick some sauce off the back of Alex's hand but, somehow, did not break eye contact with Sophie.

Claire said nothing and picked morosely at the fraying sleeve of her hoodie. 'Yeah. S'pose.'

'Are you working on your case notes and all that?' asked Alex. 'That always cheers you up.'

'She keeps getting depressed about it,' said Sophie. 'Like, you know when you tell everyone you're going to redecorate your bedroom and, as soon as you cover everything in dust sheets, you realize you've actually got to *do* it? And that you hate the paint you picked? She's like that.'

Claire glared at Sophie, but repeated it for Alex's benefit anyway.

'Yeah, I suppose with your other murder solves you got involved by accident, whereas this time you're doing it on purpose as part of a job,' said Alex. 'When you tell people you're going to stop smoking, you feel more pressure to do it. Which is why I have never claimed I will stop smoking weed. But *you* told someone you'd try to exorcise his dead dad.'

Claire sighed. 'I'm going the long way round to it. I think Ken is the least of my worries, to be honest. He just seems relieved to get confirmation that he wasn't losing it. The last time I texted him an update, he told me to do whatever it takes to help his dad move on. But that was before Chaz. I'm worried about how everyone is going to react to me now.'

'You're worried about stuff that hasn't even happened,' said Sophie. 'Stop it, Weirdo.'

'Oh, I'd not thought of that before – my anxiety has disappeared!' replied Claire, in a sing-song voice.

'Don't fight,' said Alex. 'You done with the sub, S? Atta girl, I'll finish it off. And you, C, can show me the case notes you have so far. And we can make another list, right? You love writing lists. It'll make the work more manageable.'

Claire fumbled in her rucksack and retrieved her notepad. There was a new heading marked 'POISONS', with some research about the sorts of things you could easily kill someone with, because she was still pretty sure that poison was the most likely culprit. Next to Basher's accident theory, anyway.

'We've assumed the poison was on his meds, but we don't know that for sure,' she went on. 'The other thing is, we overheard that tag team Pink Champagne having a go at Ken on Thursday night and their wording was ominous.' Claire was warming to the subject.

'Ahh, and that's why you asked me to bring you to training! See, you're being proactive!' said Alex. 'When we first met, you were basically afraid of making phone calls. What's your objective today then?'

Claire ignored the crack about phone calls, on the basis that it was essentially accurate, though felt she could have made the point that Alex's generation communicated through front-facing camera videos and interminably long voice-notes, and also couldn't watch TV without subtitles on, for reasons that weren't entirely clear to Claire.

'I'm not sure. Chaz's death seems like too much of a coincidence. Plus, someone must have cleaned up around Eddie's body, because he said he was sick and that. It's still all really fishy.'

Alex, their mouth full again, tapped the notebook meaningfully, so Claire flipped to a new page. After a bit of thought she wrote, very carefully and with her tongue slightly sticking out, 'NEXT STEPS'.

'Okay, so favourite would be getting the police to test Eddie's medicine. Assuming we can find it,' she said.

'That will take some doing,' observed Sophie.

'Aim for the stars and all that,' said Alex.

Claire split the difference and wrote it down, but put 'STRETCH GOAL' in brackets next to it.

'I should probably do follow-ups on everyone, because you have to fact-check everything and not get it confused and—'

'Well, let's start with the immediate future, right. One foot in front of the other and all that,' prompted Alex.

Claire looked up at them and they smiled encouragingly. So she wrote down 'INTERVIEW GUY AND RUBY'. Alex gave her a big thumbs-up. She wondered if this was the same experience Wyatt had every time she successfully sat on command.

'This'll be great,' said Alex. 'I'm super-ready for this. Carbo-loaded with the two subs, didn't I?'

'Er, aren't you meant to do that longer before the workout than a few minutes?' said Claire. 'I dunno if you'll be getting the full benefit …'

Alex flapped a hand dismissively. 'I'll be fine.'

*

About half an hour later, Alex was bent over with their hands on their knees, breathing raggedly. 'I'm going to die. I've got a stitch. For the love of God, Montresor!'

Sophie chuckled. 'Interesting. They might yak up everywhere. Odds on, d'you reckon?'

'Stop talking – save your breath for the reps!' shouted Ruby.

She and Guy were leading a class of about ten hopeful wrestlers, almost all of whom were men approximately twenty-five years old, many of whom looked as if they liked the idea of being a pro-wrestler far more than they liked the idea of eating half a dozen eggs and chicken sausages after a 6 a.m. gym sesh. But, Claire supposed, the SWF ran these courses less as a way of finding new and up-and-coming talent and more as a way of making some quick cash on the side.

Claire and Sophie were seated at the back, rather self-consciously – or at least Claire was; Sophie had never been conscious of herself as anything other than a blessing to all who knew her. Claire was doubly unnerved because Eddie King was also watching, but from the other side of the room, occasionally prowling amongst the class to shout obscenities about how they were all as soft as shite, the worst bunch of hopefuls he'd ever set eyes on, and so on. But Claire couldn't go and talk to him without drawing attention to it, so she stayed where she was. He seemed to have no interest in talking to her, at least for the moment.

Ruby and Guy had started by demonstrating a basic fitness-training circuit that the class could do without having to go to a gym: squats, dumb-bell reps (which Guy insisted one could do with a jug of milk), push-ups, planks, lunges, jumping jacks, and so on. Alex's initial high confidence during the warm-up phase had, in the sixty seconds of the actual workout, melted away like a delicate ice-sculpture beneath a flamethrower.

Ruby, wearing a matching leggings-and-sports-bra set in a multicoloured leopard print, was setting the pace, and it was probably quite galling to Alex that they weren't the best-dressed person in the scenario. Guy walked back and forth between the sweating, gasping bodies and occasionally clapped and shouted encouragement like a benevolent drill sergeant, and fixed people's form by adjusting their shoulders or feet.

'If you can't even do a basic body-weight workout, you're going to struggle. Come on, push through. Give me some power!'

'When I look at Alex, I'm not sure "power" is the first word that comes to mind,' murmured Sophie.

'Last rep, come on!' Ruby shouted, as she leapt up from a lunge into some energetic jumping jacks.

'She's like a fuckin' Duracell Bunny,' said Claire.

'All right, good work, everyone,' shouted Guy. 'Let's get on to the lesson.'

'Oh, fuck off,' said Alex. They were unusually dysregulated. 'I need a break.'

'First of all, don't ever tell anyone training you to fuck off ever again,' said Ruby. She strode forward until she was almost nose-to-nose with Alex. 'Anyone who takes valuable time out of their day to impart their hard-won fucking wisdom to you should be thanked.'

'Sorry,' replied Alex, who looked down at their toes in an unusual display of subservience.

'Say "thank you" to me,' insisted Ruby.

'Thank you,' said Alex, in a little voice.

'Good. Secondly, you did seven minutes. Ideally you'd want to be doing that circuit for twenty minutes a day, every day,' continued Ruby.

Claire relaxed slightly, because this indicated that being a pro-wrestler wouldn't be a long-term interest for Alex, who favoured never getting up before noon, if they could help it.

'You have to raise your general level of fitness and keep it there,' Guy was saying. 'That doesn't mean vanity muscles, unless you want them. I'm talking about core strength and stamina. But a really important part of wrestling is losing your fear. Sort of like being a goalie. You put your body on the line and, if you're afraid, you're actually more likely to fuck up and properly hurt yourself.'

Claire remembered what Trudy had said about the Kings always being injured.

'Yes?'

Everyone swivelled to look at her, and she felt a blush heating up. 'Er. Sorry. It's just that Alex is only twenty. Well, not even. They're not ... Like, how dangerous is this exactly?' she asked.

Eddie King made a loud 'Tch!' and folded his arms, and Claire tried not to look at him.

'All right, I don't need a third mum, thanks,' said Alex. Alex's mum had recently left their horrible dad and, in the process of divorcing him, had acquired a cottage-core lesbian lifestyle by the sea.

'Who are you again?' asked Ruby. It was probably the most brutal thing one person could say to another.

Sophie laughed, and Claire started to feel like she was being bullied by a gang of bigger kids, except that nobody else could see most of the gang.

'I'm a friend of Alex and their uncle,' she said. 'I'm here to check out the first lesson, so he feels comfortable with Alex continuing, which was the cover story she had agreed with Alex, if not with Basher. She only wished it didn't make her sound such a massive loser.

'For God's sake,' said Ruby. 'Alex is an adult. They signed their own forms. Are you joking—'

'It is pretty dangerous, though,' interrupted one of the interchangeable male students, in a tone of voice that indicated he would like to be told it was very dangerous and that he was a very brave boy.

Ruby turned and focused on him, which was a tremendous relief to Claire. 'It's not much more dangerous than boxing, if you do it right, it's just less socially acceptable,' she said. 'Think of it as being like acrobatics mixed with Shakespearean stage fighting …'

She began talking to the class at large about different styles of acting from different countries, most of which went entirely over Claire's head.

'The point is: accidents happen and its high-impact,

but it's not like Alex – or any of you – will be flipping off the top rope their first time out,' said Guy.

'I might be,' said Alex. 'I might turn out to be really good. I'm naturally talented at many things.'

'Yeah, they fucking nailed that medium-intensity cardio,' snorted Sophie.

'It's not solely about natural talent,' continued Guy, very seriously. 'That will only take you so far. It's about hard work.'

Guy and Ruby made everyone collect gym mats and arrange them in rows on the floor. Then they started the class on their first practical drill: taking a bump. This meant falling – or being tackled, or similar – to the mat without getting really hurt. Ruby demonstrated a standing flip forward, landing flat on her back. After a beat she started to groan and spasmed like a landed fish.. Claire was mildly alarmed until Ruby flipped to her feet again, grinning.

'That's what you're aiming for,' she said.

'But you're not there yet,' added Guy. 'You get to start on the first stage.'

This meant that Claire ended up watching a group of young adults doing forward rolls. Repeatedly. Guy told them they needed to do so many rolls that if they tripped walking in the park, they'd roll without thinking about it.

'This is boring now,' said Sophie, after a few minutes. 'I'm getting bored. I thought you were going to question them.'

'What am I supposed to do – interrupt the lesson?'

'It'd make me long for death less than this,' Soph replied.

'You're already—'

'Ohmigod, I obviously *know*; it's a figure of speech, fucking hell,' Soph snapped.

Eddie was eyeballing her again, Claire noticed, but he was sort of trying to pretend he wasn't. A slightly plump young man wobbled, going into his forward roll, and Eddie spat, 'Pathetic!' at him. It was a blessing in disguise that he'd never found huge success, because he'd have been a massive liability to any company big enough to need an HR department.

'Do you want to give it a go?'

Claire jumped. 'Argh. Ugh. Sorry, what?' she said.

Guy had wandered over without her noticing. He smiled at her in a faintly bemused way, which was not an uncommon reaction people had when encountering Claire, and her behaviour in general.

'Do you want to have a go? It might make you feel better to realize how slow we take this.'

Claire blanched, her earlier blush draining away completely to somewhere in the region of her toes.

'Idiot, you can talk to him while you're failing to do basic Year Seven gymnastics,' hissed Sophie. 'Come on!'

'You don't need gym gear or anything at this stage, honestly,' Guy went on.

'Um, okay,' muttered Claire and stood up. She slipped the end of Wyatt's lead under one leg of a stack of chairs, and the little dog yawned lazily and settled down on the floor.

Guy got Claire a mat. Ruby had sidled over and began chatting, while she and Guy kept an eye on the rest of the class. Claire, growing more self-conscious with every second, realized that Guy and Ruby were in fact just bored. She did a couple of half-hearted forward rolls, and performed them well enough that Guy suggested doing one from a sort of half-crouch. Claire grew anxious that he was asking her to do so because he knew she'd look silly. Eddie made his way over as well and stared unblinkingly at her, arms crossed in pre-unimpressed mode. The combined scrutiny made Claire lose all confidence in her ability to operate any of her muscles, in the middle of her attempt at a roll. How did one move one's arm? Had she always been able to do it? The notion of an elbow is ridiculous, on first principles! And she toppled over to one side like a slow-moving bicycle.

'Better than I thought you'd do,' remarked Sophie.

Claire got to her feet and brushed her thighs clear of non-existent dust, because it was better than doing nothing.

'No harm done,' commented Ruby, with a grin.

'That was the worst display I've seen in my life,' said Eddie. He jabbed a finger in Claire's direction.

'You don't have one,' said Sophie, curling her lip. 'Metaphorically or literally, Saddo.

'You need to commit to the movement and put more power through your thighs,' said Guy.

'You're bent over before you start; you need to be going up first, not forward, for Christ's sake, or you don't have time to complete the full flip,' said Eddie. 'These two are teaching it all wrong. Out of the bloody way – I'll show you how it's done!'

Claire had only a split second to be thoroughly alarmed at the prospect of Eddie flipping in a towel, something that even more briefly called to mind the image of a butcher's shop window. Eddie went to shoulder-barge her out of the way without thinking and instead stepped *into* her.

The next moment she felt her back snap tall, her leg muscles push energy up through her knees into her hips and she went up, but then *over*, and the momentum of her legs completed the arc to pull her down flat on her back. She lay there, arms out to the sides, chin and head tucked forward, knees bent and feet flat to the floor. She blinked. She felt like she'd been submerged in an ice-bath.

Eddie King stood up and looked down at her. He snorted derisively.

'What the fuck was *that*?' asked Sophie. Her voice wasn't raised, but it wasn't *not* raised, and she was looking at Eddie rather than Claire.

'Flip-bump,' said Eddie. 'Basic flip-bump.'

'You know what I bloody mean! Hey, get back here.'

Eddie had walked off and Sophie tried to follow him, but was pulled up short by dint of Claire still lying on the floor in a small amount of shock.

Ruby laughed nervously. 'That was …'

Alex's face appeared in Claire's vision, haloed by the horrible lights hanging from the ceiling.

'Bloody hell, C. Are you all right?'

'Wow, you're a natural,' cut in Guy. He offered Claire a hand and pulled her up. 'Leave it to the pros, though, yeah?' he added, more quietly.

'Good form, though,' said Ruby. 'Have you thought about actually joining the class?'

Alex looked between Claire and Ruby and rolled their shoulders. 'Well, no offence, C, but if you can do it, then it really can't be that hard …' And, without warning, they also attempted a flip-bump onto the mat.

'What did we learn?' asked Guy, as he applied an antibac wipe to Alex's head. They were sitting on the desk in the back office, looking very sorry for themself.</NI>

'To do as I'm told,' chorused Alex. They winced, but Claire did not believe they would take that particular lesson to heart for several years. Specifically, they'd definitely learned that they weren't a virtuoso pro-wrestler, and very specifically they'd learned that if you were quite tall and misjudged a flip, you could scrape your head severely and even sort of partially scalp yourself. This meant that everyone else in the class had learned that head-wounds bleed quite a lot.

'You're blood lucky you didn't break your neck,' said Ruby, prodding Alex. 'If you'd seriously injured yourself, we'd all be deep in shit, you know that?'

'My head hurts,' groaned Alex.

'Big surprise there,' observed Sophie. 'Are you still going to ask this lot what's going on or are we here for your health?'

'Can I still do lessons?' Alex asked.

'Well, yeah, eventually. Everyone hurts themselves at some point,' said Guy. 'But we should wait until your scalp heals up a bit.' He had staunched the bleeding, doused Alex's scalp in antiseptic and put a small dressing on it.

'Aw, what? Can I come and watch or something?'

'I mean, I guess? I'm sure there's something useful you can do around here,' said Ruby. 'Do you know anything about costuming?'

Alex's eyes lit up. 'Do I ever,' they said.

'Oh, great; well, there's a load of old ring gear in those boxes in the corner. They've been sitting there for ages because they need someone to go through them and find what's reusable.'

Ruby had barely finished speaking before Alex scampered over to the corner. They almost dived head-first into the boxes.

Claire sighed and parked the issue of possibly, sort of, being possessed by Eddie – who had absented himself once again and, to be honest, Claire was starting to wonder if she should even bother looking into his murder, because he was a giant bellend who didn't deserve closure – to think about a potential conversation starter with Guy and Ruby.

'So you'll be wanting to ask us about Eddie and Chaz then, innit,' said Ruby.

'Jesus. That was a freebie,' muttered Sophie.

'Um, yeah. What? I mean sorry, yeah I do, but how do you know that?' Claire asked, trying to stop her tongue stumbling over her teeth.

'Everyone knows that,' said Guy.

'What do you mean, "Everyone knows that"?' asked Claire, feeling somewhat affronted.

'Secrets don't stay secret around here,' replied Ruby. She shrugged. 'This wasn't even a secret really, was it? We all know Ken hired you because he thinks this place is haunted, and the news about Chaz got around almost instantly.'

'Poor guy,' said Guy. He shook his head. 'He didn't seem the type.

'I will say that if anyone was going to be a ghost, it'd be that horrible old bastard, Eddie,' Ruby added. 'He'd hang on just out of spite.'

'I've heard Eddie wasn't very popular,' said Claire cautiously.

'Understatement of the century,' said Ruby, with a snort. 'It's less "who wanted to kill him?" and more "who didn't?"'

'Well, I've also heard that it was blown out of proportion, because he was very, er, old-school?'

'Oh, you've been reading Miller's blog, have you? I'd treat anything you see there with a dump-truck of salt,' said Guy.

'Fucking loser,' added Ruby. 'You know people who want to join the police, but end up doing security for the nightshift at McDonald's? That's wrestling bloggers like Miller. I'm not happy he's dead, but I'm fucking delighted he can't hang around backstage, pretending he's one of us, any more.'

'Well, okay,' said Claire, making several all-caps, underlined mental notes about Miller. 'And you never thought Eddie's death was suspicious?'

'No, not at all. Why? Should we?' Ruby looked at her with an expression that was something like curiosity, but not quite.

'This is where one of us will say the same thing about Eddie as Ruby said about Miller – you know, like, "I'm not sorry he's dead, but I didn't kill him,' Guy added.

'G'wan then, Weirdo. If they want to make it easy for you, then hit them with it,' said Sophie.

'Uh, okay. So I overheard you in an argument with Ken. And it sounded like you knew Eddie was going to die. Is the only thing.'

'Which argument would that be?' asked Guy.

Ruby nodded. 'I have shouted at him quite a lot,' she said. She appeared unburdened by guilt.

'It was on, er, Thursday, after your match. You said you thought things would be different when Eddie was gone,' replied Claire.

'I didn't realize listening at doors was part of being a medium,' commented Guy, although his voice was even, rather than angry. 'We didn't know he was going to *die*, we thought he was going to retire. Rubes heard him on the phone to someone about it.'

'Yeah, he must have been talking to Trudy. He said he was "going to leave soon", and so we went to Ken about it, to ask that we got treated fairly when he took over. Ken said if he was in charge of booking, we'd be treated better. Just hasn't turned out that way.' Ruby shrugged, indicating it was a fuss about nothing. 'I mean, I'm not going to pretend I'm sad Eddie's dead, because I'm not. I don't think anyone who knew him is.'

'What about the guy in Scotland?' prompted Sophie, and Claire dutifully asked about him.

'The Weegie lot?' said Ruby. She laughed. 'Yeah, they're probably pleased Eddie is dead too. We did a whole storyline about will we/won't we leave SWF a year ago. It did really well. Cross-promo: bunch of us lot did shows up there, their lot came down here. Everyone wins. It's all normal stuff. In fact that storyline was Eddie's idea – you can ask people, they'll tell you – except that Eddie started being a massive prick about it, because Weegie got a bigger boost than SWF. There's a rumour he screwed Weegie on the back end somewhere, to get his own back.'

'We still go up and wrestle there,' said Guy. 'We wrestle different places, maybe twice a week. Everyone does, or your profile never goes up – you don't get respect. The scene in Scotland is great, everyone is doing well up there.'

'Okay. Thanks. Um, when was it you heard Eddie say he was leaving?'

'Dunno exactly,' replied Ruby. 'A while ago. Six months? Eight? Something like that.'

Claire made a note of this in her official-unofficial detective's notebook.

'And what about Chaz?' she asked. 'Would he have wanted Eddie dead?' She looked up from the notebook in time to see Ruby and Guy looking at each other. Ruby raised her eyebrows at Guy, and he shook his head almost imperceptibly.

Guy paused. 'I don't know about that,' he said, talking slowly, still figuring out what exactly he was going to say as he was saying it. 'Chaz left a while back. It was sudden, and there was bad blood between him and Eddie. It's not my place to say more, and I don't want to talk ill of the dead. Chaz was a decent bloke.'

'He didn't mind speaking ill of Eddie,' observed Soph.

'Eddie said nobody could mention Chaz in this building, or in his hearing, ever again,' added Ruby, all conspiratorial and apparently far less concerned about where her place was, and if she was in it. 'We were here one time when a newer guy accidentally did and Eddie went properly apeshit at him. I guess we all just kept up the habit.'

'Nobody knows why Chaz left? Were there any rumours?' probed Claire.

Ruby opened her mouth, caught Guy's eye and reconsidered. She pursed her lips. 'Only that they were both really angry at each other. People said there was a big shouting match in here one night, and then Chaz never showed up again,' she said finally. 'It's surprising Chaz never said anything himself, to be honest, because he couldn't keep the piss between his legs. He'd spill loads of gossip normally, so it must have been something pretty bad for him to button his lip about it.'

'Chaz always backed us, and Nate,' added Guy. 'The problem was Eddie got the final say on booking, and he hated tag teams. He was kind of a size-queen too. You know, he liked big, beefy, manly men with huge muscles. The lads you can't actually *prove* are taking steroids.'

'Do people take steroids?' asked Claire.

'Less than you'd think,' Ruby replied promptly.

'Well, I know about the painkillers and stuff.

'Sure,' Ruby shrugged. 'Nobody wrestles injured, but everyone wrestles hurt – that's the saying.'

'Okay,' said Claire, making a note never to mention that to Basher. 'What about Ken: is he a, um, size-queen?'

'Nah, Ken is a bit more forward-thinking. He likes different kinds of spots, less drama. He's much less of a bastard than his dad. Nobody liked Eddie, but everyone likes Ken. Which makes it more difficult that he's a bit rubbish at it,' replied Ruby.

'He's not a great booker, honestly,' agreed Guy. 'Look at Lila. She's a decent wrestler! She used to be fearless too – DDTs and atomic leg-drops all over the gaff. But Ken is forcing her to battle with this stupid clown-gimmick, show after show.'

'She started getting better, a year or so ago. The crowd was responding a bit.' Ruby rubbed at her nose and frowned. 'I think Ken's a bit jealous as well. Maybe he wishes he could be more of a spot monkey, you know?'

She was talking more to Guy than to Claire. 'He's just not built for high-flying, though.'

'That means he can't do as much of the acrobatic flippy stuff,' Alex called from the corner, with the confidence of someone who had not known any of this jargon until three weeks previously.

Ruby got a twinkle in her eye and started to quiz Alex. Between them, Ruby and Guy explained many things that Claire knew she would struggle to remember or even know whether they might be relevant: 'catch' being short for 'catch-as-catch-can'; why nobody really wants to be a 'jobber'; the Japanese strong style; the way referees will make an X with their arms if someone actually gets hurt, but because fans know that now, it's often used as a plot point for audience benefit; the difference between a 'work' and a 'shoot', and the time the two concepts collided in an infamous match in Canada in 1997; that pro-wrestling is so intense a form of entertainment that performers will sometimes cut themselves with razor blades at their hairline to cover their faces in a mask of blood; that this trick is called 'gigging'; why shouting 'Bah gawd!' is sort of a meme in wrestling circles (and, to a lesser extent, but for related reasons, 'That man is broken in half!' and 'That man has a family!'); and so on.

Claire saw that pro-wrestling had a culture that was, if not as respectable to old people as, for example, The Sealed Knot or Crufts, at least as complicated and impenetrable to outsiders, and she was impressed. She also knew – thanks to Alex's warning –not to, under any circumstances, suggest that because outcomes were predetermined, it wasn't 'real'. Here Guy and Ruby expanded on the concept of kayfabe, as introduced in the person of Nate. Claire sensed a new segue.

'I've spoken to Nate a bit. Do a lot of wrestlers stay in character outside the ring?' she asked.

'Not so much nowadays,' explained Guy. 'I think it's more common with heels because if you're a babyface, it doesn't break the spell if you're polite to fans when they meet you.'

Claire now knew that a babyface was a good guy, a hero, and a heel was a bad guy. Wrestlers frequently switched between the two – a change known as either a heel-turn or a face-turn.

'You don't think Nate could have killed Eddie?' Claire asked.

'You're doing unusually well here, Weirdo,' said Sophie.

Ruby considered this. 'Nah,' she replied eventually. 'Don't ask me why, I just don't think Nate has it in him somehow. Even though he has a great motive, what with the situation where he's shagging Trudy.'

'You said that before. Why do you think that?' Claire asked.

'Ruby ...' said Guy. His voice was mild enough that you probably wouldn't spot the soupçon of warning in it, unless you were looking out for it. If it was a warning, Ruby ignored it.

'A while back Trudy started getting twitchy. She was always texting people asking where Eddie was, when he'd be home, all that stuff. Seemed like she was keeping close tabs on him,' she explained, with some relish. 'And then it was all over the dressing room – sort of open knowledge that Trudy and Nate were going at it. No idea where it came from, though. I mean *someone* must have told me. I remember Ken asking me if I heard it, to please not pass it on.'

If Claire's assessment of Ruby was correct, she passed things on as quickly as Patient Zero.

'But you have to understand, none of us think Eddie was murdered,' said Guy. 'So I don't know why you keep bringing it up. I can't imagine this is what Ken intended you to do.' He was looking at Claire with a hard expression.

'I think it's a big coincidence: Eddie dying and then Chaz,' she replied. She lifted her chin and tried to appear defiant.

'From our point of view, a guy had a heart attack or whatever, and then a couple of months later someone he used to work with took his own life,' continued Guy. 'And maybe a stranger going around rocking the boat won't help.'

Out of the corner of her eye, Claire saw Alex half-turn to look at her.

'It's Lila I feel sorry for,' said Ruby. She stood up and cracked her knuckles.

'Huh? Why?' asked Claire. 'Is she not all right?'

'What do you mean "why"? Her dad just committed suicide. Of course she's not all right.'

11

Out with the Bathwater

'These people are so weird,' said Sophie. 'It's like when everyone in our friendship group at school started going out with each other.'

'Everyone in our friendship group was going out with each other?' asked Claire.

Sophie gave her a pitying look in response. Claire was looking in one of the boxes of old wrestling gear that Alex had left open. It was a riot of contrasting colours and fabrics, comparable to the average toddler's playroom. She pulled out a spangly gold woman's singlet and noticed the label was satiny-white and read 'Hannah's Belles', which must be the wedding-dress shop Eddie had mentioned.

'Trudy did say that Ken and Lila had known each since they were kids. I suppose we know what she meant now,' Claire said. 'We should go and talk to her.'

'We should go and talk to bloody Nate,' Sophie grumbled.

'Well, I was going to, and then Chaz dying happened,' said Claire. They were waiting in the office while the lesson finished up. Alex was helping roll up gym mats.

'Did you say Chaz is dead?' asked Eddie. He materialized in the office as he said this, and Claire dropped the lucha mask she was holding.

'Fucking hell, don't do that,' she said. 'Is that your new party trick?'

'Is Chaz dead?' Eddie insisted. 'Is that why the coppers were round here asking about him?'

'Yeah,' replied Sophie. 'Apparently killed himself yesterday.'

Eddie paused. Then he let out a sudden bark of laughter. 'Ha! Serves him bloody right,' he said. 'Tried to get one over on me.'

'Is that why he left? He tricked you somehow?' asked Claire.

'He was fiddling the books,' said Eddie. He crossed his arms. 'That's why this place never made any bloody money. Me and Nate never noticed because Chaz did all the books – said he'd take care of it, like he was doing us a favour.'

'That explains Chaz's nice house,' said Claire. 'But not why you didn't *tell* people that. Unless …'

'Mutually assured destruction!' exclaimed Sophie. 'He knew something about you too. Something you didn't want getting out.'

'Like maybe who you were having an affair with,' reasoned Claire.

Eddie glared at her and pressed his lips together.

'Every accusation is a confession, idiot,' said Sophie. 'We know you were taking Viagra, and nobody takes that for a long evening alone, do they? Unluckily for you, our friends now think that you died from combining that with your heart meds.'

'It bloody wasn't that – I'd taken them loads.'

'So you don't deny it!' crowed Sophie. 'Who was it?'

'If you haven't worked it out, then why should I tell you? You're supposed to be the one figuring all this out,' growled Eddie.

'Because it might be a motive, dipshit,' said Claire.

'Nate was the one who killed me. I saw him,' Eddie insisted.

'You saw his boots, which had gone missing before you died!' Sophie shot back.

'According to Nate,' said Eddie. He was raising his voice to match Sophie shouting at him. 'He could have been creating an alibi!'

'Oh, for fuck's—' Claire started to say, but then the office door opened.

Alex stuck their head in. 'C'mon, C, Uncle B is almost here,' they said. They were wearing an unflattering black SWF-logo beanie, which they had pulled from the costume boxes.

Claire looked around, but Eddie had gone.

Outside, the other hopefuls had already dispersed, but Basher wasn't in evidence. Miller was, though, hopping from one foot to the other.

'Oh, bloody hell,' said Sophie.

'There's another ghost,' explained Claire, for Alex's benefit, as Miller came over. 'He's a blogger who died after Eddie did. Unrelated.'

'Oh, is it Miller?' Alex asked. 'The others have mentioned him; he sounds like a total...' they paused, '-ly thorough blogger,' they finished.

'Well done,' said Sophie drily. She turned to address Miller. 'What do you want now? And why didn't you tell us that Chaz was Lila's dad?'

'I thought you'd find out,' said Miller. 'It's not like it's a big secret or anything. I didn't know he was going to be dead when you turned up, did I? The police came up here late in the afternoon and talked to people – at least I saw them go into the building. Anyway, are you going to publish my blog post now?'

'No, we're bloody not,' snapped Sophie. 'You've just been telling us half a story every time – you're not holding up your end of the bargain.'

'Did you know Eddie was having an affair?' asked Claire.

Alex, who was watching her have a conversation with thin air, went, 'Oooooh.'

Miller blinked and said, 'Yes, of course. I just didn't know if *you* knew.'

'Right, understood.'

'All right, fine, I didn't know he was having a specific affair this time, but everyone knows he's been having them for years.'

'Fucking Deep Throat over here,' said Sophie. 'More like Gag Reflex, LOL.'

'Great work,' replied Claire. 'What do you think of Pink Champagne's thing with the Doolan guy from Weegie?'

'Pink Champagne think a bit too highly of themselves,' said Miller promptly. 'They think they're too good for this place and, honestly, I wouldn't put anything past their ambition. Word on the street was that they were desperate to move up to Scotland full-time, but needed some assurances from Doolan about how many matches they'd get. Maybe Doolan asked them for something pretty big in return.'

'You said they were digging up dirt on Eddie, though, right? Maybe they found out who he was having an affair with,' Claire pondered out loud.

'Still doesn't make sense why they'd kill Eddie *and* Chaz over it,' Sophie pointed out.

'Hm, well. Thanks, Miller. If I have time, I'll come back and sort out that blog post for you, okay?' said Claire as Basher pulled up in his battered old Peugeot.

'Sure. Great! Thank you,' replied Miller. He seemed very relieved, and even waved them off as they got in the car.

'Hello, nibling, Strange,' said Basher, as they got in.

'And Sophie,' prompted Alex. They slammed the door and fastened their seatbelt. They didn't mention their injury, which is when Claire realized why they were wearing the ugly beanie.

'How was training?' Basher asked.

'Alex sort of hit their head, but not hard. Like they don't need to go to hospital for possible concussion or anything,' said Claire, plumping for a middle-ground kind of honesty that would get her off the hook once Basher noticed the dressing later, but that Alex would not view as an utter betrayal.

Basher pursed his lips, and Alex crossed their arms. There was a studied silence as neither party conceded ground by speaking first.

'Claire got possessed and did a front flip,' said Sophie. This caused a small uproar when Claire repeated it.

'It's never happened before,' Claire explained. 'I don't think many ghosts know it might be a thing, so they don't try it. It must be something to do with Eddie not being able to touch me. He can do this other thing instead, like a different version of using living energy.'

'What did it feel like?' asked Alex.

'Er, sort of normal. Weird. It was like I was doing things without deciding to do them.'

'What a fascinating morning you've had,' said Basher. He pulled away and drove back towards town.

'Yeah, and we found out that Lila, Ken's wife, is Chaz's daughter!' Claire added. Basher's lips moved as he repeated this to himself, as one does when trying to parse the events and characters of a complicated soap opera.

'I fail to see the ultimate significance. In fact I have a message to relay to you from Sami. It is a voice-note. Alex, please unlock my phone and play it for me.' Alex unlocked Basher's phone by holding it up in front of his face, which made him go, 'Not like that!'

'We're at traffic lights – he's such a safety inspector,' said Sophie.

Sami's voice filled the car, after a slight Doppler effect from Alex rapidly turning the volume up on Basher's phone. 'Yeah, play this to Claire the next chance you have. I'm almost one hundred per cent sure she will have ignored me and is still poking around, so let me be clear. We are handling this. Her involvement is not at all necessary, and both deaths in question are fairly clear-cut. It would be a professional bloody courtesy of her to trust me, and also interfering with a police investigation is, as I have pointed out, *a crime*. If I or my partner have cause to run into her again over this, it is highly likely she will be arrested. Over and out.'

Claire felt her face grow hot. She bit down on her embarrassment.

'I just think that Sami is being hasty – like does she even know about Ruby and Gu—'

'Strange, that is enough,' said Basher. 'Please take this seriously. If you do not trust Sami, do you at least trust me?'

'Yes,' replied Claire, in a little voice.

'Then listen to me when *I* tell you to leave this alone.'

Sophie stuck the Vs up at the back of Basher's head. Claire folded her arms. 'Fine. Can you drop me off in town, please?'

'For why?' asked Basher.

'Bloody hell, Uncle B, she's a grown woman,' said Alex.

'I want to talk to Ken about getting paid for the last couple of days,' Claire replied. It was not entirely a lie. 'I didn't solve anything, but I did *some* stuff and I should get at least a little bit of money. Or are you going to say I shouldn't?'

Basher sighed. 'Very well. Are you still going to come over for dinner?'

'I dunno, maybe I don't want to any more,' said Claire.

Basher merely raised an eyebrow and talked in a wry near-monotone. 'Please, no, do not stop visiting my home. I would hate it if you ceased scattering biscuit crumbs across the soft furnishings with your wanton refusal to use a side-plate.'

Claire glared at him. He smiled into the rear-view mirror, until she smiled back.

'Your company is a delight, Strange, and you are of course always welcome. Although I must insist that if you are to slide into a mild depression about all this, you do it in your own home, where I can visit and minister to you in the manner of Florence Nightingale.'

'What, wash your hands loads?' said Sophie.

'Yes. Well, I find depressive moods to be catching, and I am the one with a clinical diagnosis,' said Basher. He began to pull over near the town centre.

'I'm fine!' protested Claire.

'She is,' said Alex in solidarity. 'She did a forward roll.'

'Good,' replied Basher. He got out and opened the door for Claire, which was a typically old-fashioned Basher-y thing to do. 'Come on, give me a hug.'

Bash was quite slight and taut. Hugging him was sort of like hugging a warm scarecrow. His hugs were rarely meted out, so Claire felt pleased, but also concerned that she must seem really quite pitiable.

'In all seriousness,' said Bash, over her shoulder, 'if someone asks you to fuck off, off you fuck.'

'All right, all right,' Claire replied. 'I'm not totally incapable, you know,' she whined.

'Yes, in fairness, she's only *mostly* incapable these days,' said Sophie. 'You've been a really good influence.'

Ken and Lila's flat was only about ten minutes' walk away. Really, it would be silly *not* to go and see how Lila was doing, while Claire had a legitimate reason to talk to Ken.

'Aren't you going to text them to let them know you're coming or something?' asked Sophie.

'Nah, element of surprise. Often that's key in cracking a witness,' said Claire, trying to regain some confidence in her abilities as an investigator.

'Great, yeah, let's go ambush the recently bereaved. What if no one's in?'

'Well, then you can look inside. Not very far inside, obviously, but better than nothing.'

'The inspirational rallying cry of the private detective,' replied Sophie, in a voice that contained a multitude of rolling eyes.

Their route took them past a big church, which had a huge sign advertising a youth programme that alleged it would, through the power of Jesus, somehow make being young tolerable. Claire and Sophie usually avoided that side of the street, because the church was haunted by a terribly earnest Sunday School teacher who had died in the fifties and was still very upset with them because he had accosted them when Sophie was in a bad mood, and consequently was told to shove his Bible up his tight arse. He was distracted as they passed him, because some teenagers were skateboarding on an area that used to be a patch of grass and was now a car park for potential congregants, and the Sunday School teacher was very cross indeed.

'I wouldn't want to live in one of these, you know,' said Sophie, once they had arrived. 'It's too much like a specimen jar or something.' She was looking up at the newish tower block that Ken and Lila's flat was in. You could tell it was new because it was all too-shiny blue-tinted glass and exposed metal beams. The ground floor was a Big Sainsbury's. Claire would trade living below an inscrutable small business owner for living above a Big Sainsbury's.

'I wonder if you have to pay more for living higher up?' Claire said. She'd never thought about it before, but surely there was a point where it became *too* high and the rent dropped again. The higher you went, the more chance of being trapped by a fire or something. Plus, it's an arse getting shopping up. Although Claire never usually bought more than two meals-worth of food at a time. Maybe she was designed for high-rise life. 'What would happen if you stepped through the wall of a tower block?' she asked Sophie.

'How should I fucking know?' said Sophie. 'I'm not trying, before you ask.'

The main entrance had a communal lock. Claire buzzed to be let in, but then someone else was on the way out a moment later, and they did the thing that nobody who lives in blocks of flats is supposed to do, but which nevertheless most of them do, and held the door for her. So she had no cause to be worried that nobody answered her buzzing.

The hallways were off-white and identical enough that the building had the air of a horror film. When she came to the door of Ken and Lila's flat, the door wasn't pushed shut all the way. It looked as if Lila had dropped her coat when she came in and, as a resident used to the fire-safety doors of modern homes swinging closed, hadn't looked back and noticed that the sleeve had caught in the door jamb and stopped it closing. So Claire had no real cause to worry that the door was open.

When, however, her nervous but increasingly frantic calls of, 'Um, hello? Ken? Lila?' went unanswered, she did start to worry.

'That's the bath running,' said Sophie. 'So someone's definitely in. Nobody runs a bath and then leaves.'

'Um, depends on what you mean by "leaves",' said Claire. She got a horrible sense of déjà vu, that she had been in this anaemic beige identiflat hallway before, suffering this exact same nameless anxiety, and dealing with it by being flippant in a remote, unfunny way. The waterfall of the tap grew louder as Claire approached a varnished door that was shiny in a way that indicated it was MDF. She knocked on it.

'Lila? Hello?'

There was no response.

Afterwards, while Alex was laughing at her so hard they gagged, Basher suggested that escalating from knocking on the bathroom door one time to immediately trying to kick it in, only to discover that your four-year-old unbranded Converse rip-offs are not up to the job, and instead employing an Ikea Ekedalen dining chair sourced from the kitchen as a battering ram, was an uncalled-for escalation of events. Claire thought that she had demonstrated compassion and a cool head in an emergency, even if it was only an emergency that she had imagined because of heightened anxiety. And also that she was going to buy some Ekedalens, because there was a chair you could really rely on.

In the immediate, after the pretend wood around the bathroom door lock splintered under pressure from Swedish ingenuity, and Claire pulled a muscle after she, too, proved too weak for the task at hand, she was confronted by a naked and screaming Lila sitting in her bath. She was half-pressed to the side of the tub, trying to cover herself up, while some headphones dangled off her shoulders. She was not, as Claire had feared, in terminal distress.

'Ah, right,' said Sophie. 'I see what's happened here. Good for you, going all Rambo on the door – didn't think you had it in you. LOL. Bad for you, though, because you'll probably have to pay for it.'

After a few seconds Lila stopped screaming. Claire handed her a towel.

12

Domestic Bliss

'I thought you were someone coming to kill me,' said Lila. She had got dressed, but her hair was still wrapped up in a towel, and she had been so gracious as to make Claire a cup of tea.

'I thought you were going to do it yourself,' said Claire. 'Um, sorry, again. I didn't mean to go all "Here's Johnny!" on you. Just the stress of the last few days, I suppose. Well, I mean I don't have to tell *you* that.'

'It's okay,' said Lila. Her tone was flat. Her father's death had probably pushed Claire behaving in slightly deranged ways down the list of things to worry about. 'I don't know what I'll tell Ken about the door, though.'

'This place is the most depressing flat I have ever seen. It's somehow more depressing than yours,' said Sophie, spinning on the spot to take in the whole room.

Claire could see what Sophie meant. It wasn't that it was a horrible home, in the mechanical sense. It was bright and looked like it was probably a two-bed, at least. But as much as Trudy's home was stamped with her personal taste, this space was like a show home that nobody had moved into yet. It was scrupulously clean, and there was almost nothing on display that was personal. It was a v.0.1 flat, with fake-wood floors and furniture made of MDF with the same fake-wood veneer over it, so it sort of looked like the chairs had been extruded by the kitchen-and-living-area itself. Claire was surprised when she sat at the table and realized it was because she'd been subconsciously expecting it to feel warm and damp to the touch, like a freshly laid egg.

'So. This place is nice,' she said. She became aware that she was sitting on the chair quite gingerly, trying not to touch anything, lest she shed hair or skin cells on the pristine surfaces.

'Oh, thank you,' replied Lila. 'We've been here just over a year now. It's way smaller than where I grew up with Dad, but it's our own place. I don't think we have any biscuits to offer you, I'm afraid.'

'That's okay, I'd make too many crumbs anyway,' said Claire.

'Well, thank you for worrying about me. I'm all right, honestly.'

'Everyone always says they're okay, out of social embarrassment,' commented Sophie. 'Like, how fucking okay would you be a couple of days after your dad seemed to have committed suicide?'

Lila had turned away to put the milk back in the fridge, and Claire considered the back of her head, enlarged by layers of pink towelling.

'Well, um, it would be normal for you not to be okay,' Claire replied. 'After your dad dying.'

'It's not only that, it's …' Lila paused. She seemed to collapse in on herself like wet candyfloss. 'I think I should talk to someone about the night Eddie died,' she went on.

'Jackpot!' said Sophie. 'You keep lucking out with this. You're having to do zero interrogation yourself.'

Hope bloomed in Claire that Lila was about to confess to being a murderer: 1 x feather in her cap and 1 x one in the eye for Basher and the police. But really Lila didn't look capable of killing anyone. The woman in front of her projected smallness, despite the fact she was of average height and muscular build. In this, Lila reminded Claire a lot of Alex's mother who, since finding lesbianism in the same way others find Jesus, seemed to have grown three sizes almost overnight.

But Alex's mum Tuppence was middle-aged and tended towards cardigans and pashminas. Lila was around Claire's age, and wore black athleisure-wear and a T-shirt with indecipherable metal-band logos all over it. Her little pointed pixie face radiated the aura of someone who got a bit misty over the Sainsbury's Christmas adverts; who would go on marches against wars, but didn't have any friends who would go with her and was too scared to go by herself. Lila sort of vibrated with energy, but it didn't have anywhere to go; her hands were constantly moving, picking things up and putting them down, folding and smoothing out a tea towel that had been hanging over one of the kitchen drawer handles. She looked at the ceiling and then at her feet.

Claire swallowed. 'Er, look,' she said. 'We can't both be this anxious about talking to each other or we'll never say anything.'

This made Lila laugh, and she visibly relaxed a little. She came and sat at the table and started to draw little circles on it.

'You saw my clown-gimmick, didn't you? I try really hard, and Ken has explained to me why he thinks it's a good idea. But, honestly, it embarrasses me. I don't want to be a comedy wrestler – although there's nothing wrong with it!' she added hastily, as if Claire might know, and be close friends with, many wrestlers with a comedic gimmick. 'It's just not what I want to do. I want to be a serious wrestler, taken seriously, and my gimmick won't do that for me. I know you have to take your lumps first: you know, put the work in and show willing; and loads of funny wrestlers are over as fuck – I love Orange Cassidy, for God's sake.'

Claire nodded seriously as if this all made sense to her.

'But the gimmick I have right now ... it wasn't my idea, and it doesn't work.'

'Sure, that makes sense. I could see why you wouldn't want to be, um, a literal clown, you know,' she replied. She was trying to sound as sympathetic as possible. On paper, if you described the situation to an outsider without the emotional context, it did all sound quite silly. But obviously Claire wasn't going to say that, because it would be like when someone shows you a picture of them and says, 'God, I look awful in this' and you reply, 'Yeah you do!' instead of 'No-o-o, you've never looked more radiant.'

'It was only a bit of make-up to start with, but Ken kept adding to it over time because he said it wasn't *enough* of a gimmick and you can't go half-measures. But it doesn't work. I really want to get the crowd experience, you know? People used to say I only got booked in shows because of my dad. When he quit, I thought at least I would be able to prove myself. But now people say that the only reason I get booked is because I'm Ken's wife. And they're probably right, but not in the way that they think.'

'What do you mean?' asked Claire.

'Also, what does any of this have to do with Eddie dying?' added Sophie. 'Because I'm getting bored.'

'Eddie had started letting Ken book some of the shows, run a couple of storylines,' she said. 'My gimmick was his first big swing. And Ken didn't want it to miss. Ken is sweet, but he feels pressure to measure up to his dad and his uncle, so when they started telling him it wasn't working, he didn't back down.'

'But I've met Eddie – in a manner of speaking – so when you say he started telling Ken it wasn't working,' said Claire, 'I mean, I can't imagine he was very polite about it.'

Lila gave her a sad smile. 'You're right, he wasn't. And neither was Nate. It just made Ken dig in. Both sides got entrenched and became more and more angry about it.'

'And this poor loser ended up in the middle,' said Sophie. 'Genuinely feel sorry for her; imagine having to dodge your way through that knob-measuring contest.'

'I got more annoyed, the longer it went on, because I could see Ken wasn't really paying attention to how *I* felt about it,' Lila continued. 'And I can't wrestle at other promotions. Most wrestlers, they pay their dues by travelling and doing shows in tiny venues all over the place every week. Ken wants me to stay here while we get the gimmick ironed out.'

She paused and looked deep into her drink. 'Eddie was really nice to me about it. He could see how much I actually care about wrestling and that I want to do it for real. It's not a joke to me.' She looked down at her hands again before continuing. 'The thing is ... I was there the night that Eddie died. Every so often he'd ask me if I wanted to do some extra training, but it was on the quiet.'

'You weren't having an affair, were you?' asked Claire. 'We know Eddie was seeing someone, but he won't say who.'

Lila pulled a face, like she'd had a sour sweet forced into her mouth. 'The idea of that is disgusting, isn't it? Eddie was the one who would text me if he had an evening free, so maybe he had a busy extracurricular schedule. I did think he was, you know, probably seeing other women. I just didn't want Ken to know about my training thing, because it felt like a betrayal of his booking, his character-planning.'

'I suppose I know where you're coming from, but *you* know why Ken hired me,' said Claire. 'Eddie says Nate killed him. He says he saw Nate there the night he died. That's not something that should be left alone, is it?'

Lila exhaled slowly.

'Lila, did you see something?' enquired Claire.

'Dollars to doughnuts,' said Sophie. 'And by the way, I am highly sceptical of everything she has told us.'

'I didn't really see anything!' Lila replied quickly.

'But you were there that night?' Claire pressed her. *This is possibly the first time I've had a conversation with someone more anxious than I am. And I'm winning!* thought Claire, almost immediately chastising herself for regarding a conversation as a competition (even though most of them sort of were, in her experience).

'I ... I didn't plan on it. I had ... I parked nearby, down the end of the street. But I didn't go in at first because I saw—'

'You saw Nate!' Claire exclaimed.

'*Get her,*' hissed Sophie.

Claire thought this was a bit much, given that Lila's dad had just died. Lila kept starting and stopping crying a little bit, like the seal on her eyes was leaking.

'It was dark, but I think it was him,' she said. There was mounting horror in her voice. Claire would almost have used the word 'shrill'. 'Nate was in most of his gear, which wasn't usual, but at the time I didn't think anything of it. I thought he must have grabbed something from the office and left again, because he was only in there a few minutes. But when I went in, Eddie was dead and I ...'

'Oh my God, she didn't,' said Sophie. She put her head in her hands.

'I cleaned up,' said Lila. 'I wasn't thinking. Eddie was surrounded by all these pills, and I thought it looked embarrassing. I thought Ken would be cross. That he'd get upset, I mean. I really didn't want him to be upset about any of it. It wasn't suspicious! Everyone knew Eddie had high blood pressure, and later they said he had died of a heart attack, so I thought it was okay. But then the police told me what Dad's note said!'

She got up abruptly and disappeared into another room, returning with a creased, photocopied piece of paper. The original had been typed:

> I can't live with myself.
>
> It wasn't right, what I did to my best friend.
>
> I used wolfsbane on his tablets, and now I've taken the same. Don't pray for me.
>
> Chaz

'But ... that doesn't make any sense,' said Sophie. 'If she saw *Nate* that night, then what is Chaz saying here?'

'Typed note, as well,' murmured Claire. 'So anyone could have written it. That's why you're scared. You saw this note and you knew that if Eddie had been murdered, then it wasn't your dad. In your mind you're now pretty clear that someone killed Eddie *and* your dad.'

'And who knows who's next,' replied Lila. She exhaled sharply out of her nose. It was more like she was frustrated than despairing, and Claire felt silly for ever worrying about what Lila had been doing in the bath.

'Well, if you're that scared, you should maybe go to the police,' suggested Claire.

'They've already told me and Ken that their colleagues don't see either death as suspicious,' said Lila. 'I don't think I can trust them at all. I wish I could tell Ken what happened, but if I do that, I'll have to tell him what was going on.'

'And that's what she wanted to avoid in the first place,' said Sophie.

There was the sound of a key in the front door lock and Lila looked at Claire, slightly frantically. 'Please don't say anything,' she whispered. She wiped her eyes and looked up with a smile.

Ken came in, wearing the sort of grey sweatpants that make you uncomfortable to look directly at a man, and another sleeveless T-shirt, of which he had an apparently unlimited supply. He was carrying a shopping bag with a twelve-carton of eggs peeking out of the top.

'Hi,' said Claire. 'I came over to discuss, er, having a discussion about ... everything,' she added, in an attempt to sound professional, but which she suspected made her sound like a badly programmed robot.

Ken didn't seem to have noticed. He barely seemed aware that she was there at all.

'Well, I guess this is a Mormon household,' said Sophie, 'because these two are living on their own separate planets!'

Claire raised an eyebrow, but did not look at Sophie – not even when she did a stomp-clap and spread her arms like an MC waiting for applause from the crowd at a working men's club, circa 1975.

Eventually Lila pointed out that they had a guest, and Ken started and blinked like a dog seeing a cow for the first time. 'Sorry, yes. Hi, Claire. You're very welcome.'

'Bad day?' Claire asked.

Ken tipped his head. 'Well ... obviously, yes.'

Claire realized she'd overstepped. 'Sorry, just making conversation. So you wanted an update. I made a little progress over the past few days, but it's hard to talk to Nate himself, because of the whole kayfabe thing.'

'Right. I don't agree with Nate's old-school approach, but it is what it is. He's earned his respect in this business,' said Ken. But it sounded rehearsed, not like he meant it.

'People keep saying Eddie was old-school too, but he didn't do this kayfabe stuff?' Claire guessed.

Lila snorted. 'He didn't need to. He was exactly the same inside and outside the ring. Eddie was a Jerry Jarrett kind of booker,' she said.

Claire opened her mouth, but Ken got there first. 'Jerry Jarrett was a big name – a legend. He was a huge influence on wrestling from the seventies right through to the early 2000s. But his style of booking matches was to gauge what was going on behind the scenes and put that out on the mat. So if you didn't like someone in real life, you were more likely to end up in a six-month feud with them.'

'And end up hating them,' added Lila. 'Jerry even had a sign in his office: "PERSONAL ISSUES DRAW MONEY".'

'But you're not like that?' prompted Claire.

'It maybe sounds like an obvious statement, but I think you build a stronger promotion long-term if people actually like working there,' said Ken. 'I thought it made more sense to book good storylines that we wrote ourselves, and to behave professionally behind the scenes. It's not rocket science. The SWF was a stressful company to wrestle for, and Dad was a stressful person to work with.'

'Yeah, I suppose that's why it's proved harder than you'd think to pick out whoever killed him from the fucking stampede of everyone he knew,' said Sophie.

'Um, yes. So, on that note,' continued Claire. She took out her notebook and flipped through it, to make it look like she was organized and on top of things. 'Investigating Nate has so far yielded no *hard* evidence. The water is also a bit muddied by other suspicious parties, including the tag team known as Pink Champagne. And ...' she took a deep breath, 'I have to tell you, I've been unable to conclusively rule out your mother.' *Plus whatever is going on with your wife,* she silently appended, while trying hard not to look at Lila, in case Ken would notice and be able to read everything from that.

Ken steepled his hands. 'Anything else?'

'Yes, re Nate, I've sort of only got Eddie's word for that currently,' went on Claire. She chose to stare at her notebook, so she wouldn't see Lila's expression. Technically she wasn't lying, if she used 'sort of' to cover as many sins as a Travelodge duvet. 'Obviously there was the rumour that Nate was having an affair with Trudy, but I haven't found any evidence for that, either.'

'Don't forget Nate inherited the gym,' said Ken suddenly. 'That's a motive, surely?'

'I meant to ask, actually,' she said. 'Who actually *owned* the gym? Why didn't all three founders get an equal share?'

'All three of them put up the initial cash to buy this place,' Ken replied. 'But it was all cash, you understand; there was no official paperwork. Dad registered the business officially a little while after, and he did it in his name alone. He just didn't tell the other two. They found out a few years after the fact.'

'Wow, what a complete bastard,' said Sophie. 'I'm sort of impressed.'

'Didn't the others mind?' asked Claire.

'It was a while ago. Me and Ken were too young to remember, but probably. I think my dad did, for a while, but when I asked him about it, he said it turned out the SWF wasn't making much money, so he was happy taking what he got and not buying in on a potential risk,' said Lila. 'He was cautious like that.'

'Well, we know how Chaz got his own back, don't we?' said Sophie.

'Can I ask why you didn't mention Chaz? It seems like a big omission,' said Claire.

Lila swallowed. She exchanged glances with Ken, but Claire couldn't tell what emotion they were carrying.

'I told Ken we should have said—'

'Chaz had been gone for months by the time Dad died,' said Ken. 'I didn't think it made a difference.'

'That's exactly what people say in your stupid TV show when they know something that'll make an iceberg-hitting-the-*Titanic* difference,' commented Sophie.

'You have to see that it comes over as a bit odd, from my point of view,' said Claire.

Ken shrugged. 'Habit? Respect for my dad's memory? I dunno.' He looked sheepish. Like many idiosyncratic things that people do, 'I don't mention the existence of my wife's dad because my own, now-deceased father didn't like him' probably didn't sound stupid until you said it out loud to someone else.

Lila abruptly got up from the table and disappeared into another room, this time returning with a grainy framed photograph of a group of wrestlers. Eddie, in the front row, had one arm slung over the shoulder of a compact man who had the same sort of stance as a bulldog: wide, taut, overcompensating. He had jug ears and was grinning. Lila pressed her thumb on his chest. 'That's Dad,' she said. 'They argued, like Eddie argued with anyone, but they'd been through a lot together. I have no idea what happened to make them fall out like that.'

'You're sure there hadn't been tension or anything?'

Ken seemed to consider this honestly. 'Well, maybe a bit more than usual, but tension came and went like that with Dad. As we just explained, Dad thought personal problems were good for business. So whatever it was must have been pretty serious. He would never talk about it with me.'

'I mean, this put Lila in a pretty fucking awks position, I'd imagine,' said Sophie.

Claire looked at Lila, but she didn't have to say anything.

'I know what you're thinking,' Lila continued, 'and yes, obviously I still talked to my own dad. But Dad wouldn't talk about it, either. It felt like he was freezing me out.'

'How did they know each other, if you don't mind me asking?'

'They all went to school together, in Essex,' said Lila. 'Thick as thieves for years, and they trained and travelled around, doing shows as a group.'

'The way Dad told it, they did fine while travelling, but when he met Mum, she said she wanted a kid – me – and she didn't want Dad always to be on the road,' said Ken. 'The plan was to settle here and made a kind of local area hub for wrestling, a bit like how there used to be different pro-wrestling territories in America years ago. This was all happening in the nineties, just before I was born. Dad said refitting the place ate up most of what he'd saved up to that point. They ended up having to redo the flooring and some of the plaster because the roof had started leaking. I don't know what Nate thought about it all.'

'Well, I suppose he owns it all now, doesn't he? Did you all know that Eddie had changed his will?' Claire asked.

'Yes, of course,' replied Ken. 'Everyone knew. We had a fight about creative direction, again.' He smiled a little. 'That happened a lot.'

'Okay,' said Claire. She cleared her throat. 'We're also looking into Guy and Ruby, as I said, in connection with a Scottish promoter.' Neither of them appeared to notice she said 'we'.

'The Weegies?' said Ken. 'How could they be involved?'

'It's something we want to rule out,' continued Claire. *That sounded really professional*, she thought. *That sounded really good.*

'Wow, you're a real private-dick,' said Sophie, with weighty emphasis.

Ken leaned back in his chair again. 'Look, I'll be honest. This whole conversation has gone around the houses. It sounds like you're doing detective work that I never really expected of you. And the police told us that … well, I hate saying this in front of Lila, but we know who killed my dad now.'

Claire managed to stop herself wincing. 'Yes, I know what the police have said. But Eddie is still haunting the gym.

'Well, could we pivot away from whatever you're doing now, and towards other ways of helping my dad move on? That was what I originally asked you to do. I presume you can do things with herbs and ceremonies, and so on.'

'Um.' Claire was thrown. 'Yes, I am experienced in doing seances. We could look at, er, cleansing the space in some way.'

'Great. If you could send me some options, then we can arrange a time and hopefully draw a line under this whole thing. We've got a show coming up and I want it to be a memorial, so it would be great if you can, you know, help move Dad on before that.' Ken pushed his chair back, in a way that suggested the conversation was over and Claire was expected to leave now.

She looked at Lila, but Lila turned her head and looked absently at the wall.

Sophie flapped her hands as Claire stood. 'We can't go yet, Dickhead, we've only seen this one room. They could be hiding a whole secret room, with their plan to kill Eddie for obscure reasons meticulously written out on a whiteboard.'

'Claire hesitated, stymied once again by the difficulty she had in thinking on her feet, which flaw did nothing to recommend her as a detective.

'Just ask for a tour, Weirdo. Say you're thinking of moving. Losers like this love showing you an Ikea bookshelf and going, "Yeah, so we made this place into a kind of multi-purpose nook" and shit like that.'

'This is a weird question, but I'm thinking of moving soon,' she said. 'Er, so, would it be okay if I looked around? No worries, if not.'

'That's a lie you write in emails – that's not something you say in real life,' scoffed Sophie. But, as she had correctly predicted, Lila was positively delighted to give Claire a tour of the flat. She kept apologizing for it being 'such a mess', despite the fact that the whole place seemed to have gone though some sort of antimicrobial cleaning process that would render it safe to perform open-heart surgery on the bathroom floor.

The cleanliness meant that it was also quite boring to look around. Nothing was out of place, and although Sophie nosed around as much as she was able, there was nothing that indicated any foul play or suspicious circumstances. These flats weren't the sort of flats where anything untoward could happen. They were the sort of flats where the occupants all had, or were talking about buying, a multipurpose Ninja cooker. Claire wouldn't be surprised if Lila and Ken had sat down and solemnly signed a contract to never have sex in the immaculate beige flat. The master bedroom had a double bed and no sign of clothes thrown all over the floor in lieu of storing them or putting them in a hamper, which Claire found utterly unrelatable.

'I don't think this is an actual home someone lives in,' said Sophie. 'This is a safe house. This is a Mr & Mrs Smith situation. They're undercover agents of some description. None of this is real.'

The second bedroom was a neat office space. Claire made a show of looking around, saying, 'Yeah, great use of light' and comments of that nature, which she had picked up in a vague sort of way through TV shows about dentists buying multiple homes. Lila then showed her the kitchen, and Claire opened a random cupboard, expecting to be able to say, 'Oh, this is a nice amount of storage' on seeing a lot of pans, but instead she was lost under an avalanche of silicone.

'Argh,' she said.

'Oh, sorry!' said Lila. 'I make chocolates – these are all the moulds.'

Claire looked at her in open astonishment. She had trouble believing that, firstly, making chocolates was a thing one could do. Surely it was only possible to make chocolate in huge factories producing enough bars of Dairy Milk to euthanize every dog in the country. And, secondly, if she were to accept that making chocolates was possible, it was something she could only imagine being done by the sociopathic brand of TikTok influencer who wore smocks with big puffy sleeves and pretended they made cough syrup from scratch for their awful toddlers. It was not something she would have expected Lila, a muscular fan of alternative music and a trained professional wrestler, to do in her spare time to such a degree that she had a kitchen cupboard so precariously stuffed with chocolate moulds that they burst forth like something out of a *Looney Tunes* short.

'It helps me relax,' said Lila apologetically. 'I'm trying

to start a small business from home, because otherwise I'm only doing the wrestling. But I need to get my food-safety certs. Dad was helping with rent, but obviously...' She trailed off.

'Sorry! Sorry, I just didn't think. Let me get these.' Claire bent over to help tidy up.

'Don't worry, I'll sort it,' said Ken, stepping forward and taking a lilac-coloured hard-shell mould from her hands. 'Claire doesn't need to know the ins and outs of how we pay the rent.' He gave a small laugh to indicate that all was well, but it felt like a passive-aggressive eyebrow raise aimed at Lila – like when you tell people what your salary is, and someone clears their throat because apparently it's some sort of grave social faux pas to do that.

It was only after they'd left the building that Claire remembered she hadn't given Ken her invoice.

13

Depressing Shopping

Claire was staring morosely at the television in her flat. The only thing lunchtime had yielded was an extremely long voice-note from Alex. It described that Ken had called them and also they were just walking into town – wow, there was a cool new graffiti by the crossing near Sainsbury's – but anyway the boxes of costumes seemed fun, but Ken had said they weren't allowed to look in there until he knew them better, because it was proprietary stuff, a lot of it, which seemed a bit mean, but on the other hand Alex supposed Ken didn't know them really, but it was all gravy because they were allowed to hang out and watch training until their head was better, and Uncle B (here they did a very accurate impression) said: 'I have to say that so far my fears for you have been largely assuaged. You are spending time out of the house, and have been discouraged from going on massive benders, due to them having an adverse effect on your physical fitness. The benefits to me have been largely positive.'

'You should get out from under this duvet. Goblin-mode is out,' said Soph. 'Big salads are in.'

Claire ignored her, because while Sophie had been extremely on-trend – even ahead of trend – when she was a living popular girl, she now received her ideas on what was popular second-hand from Alex, or when it had breached youth-culture containment and was widely known enough to be a topic of discussion on the *Jeremy Vine* show, and then it was no longer cool or popular.

But Claire *was* hungry, so she went upstairs to the shop above the flat.

'Hi, Mr Przybylski,' she said. He looked up briefly from his station behind the counter and nodded at her.

'Hello, Claire. There are many Oasis bottles on the steps again,' he said.

'Put a bin outside your door, Mr Przybylski,' said Claire, walking with leaden steps to the dairy cabinet at the back. It didn't have doors; it had those thick plastic strips across, which made Claire uncomfortable.

'The council, they say it is not possible,' said Mr Przybylski. He waved his hands, as if to encompass the enormity of time he had spent discussing the need for a bin with the council. 'But I have installed the new camera system. You see, I can watch on my phone and make sure you are not leaving all of your pizza boxes on the steps, to ruin the cleanliness reputation of my shop!'

'Oh yeah?' said Claire. She returned to the counter with her shopping list of items (frozen pizza baguette, milk, single-portion toffee pudding that comes in packaging that makes it look like a yoghurt, so you don't feel as much of a loser, roll of tin foil, banana-flavoured KitKat of unknown international provenance).

'Yes!' said Mr Przybylski, beaming. 'My son did it for me. He is very good with technology. But he does not wish to work in this shop. But that is okay. I did not wish to do the same job as my father, so I told him, "Joseph, you work hard and I will leave this shop to you, and you can sell it to help your tech-review channel on YouTube!"'

'You should probably tell him that Joe isn't onto a winner, he needs to pivot to TikTok,' said Sophie.

'What did your dad do, Mr Przybylski?' asked Claire, with genuine interest.

'He was a sculptor! He tried to force me to go to art college, but I refused. I ran away to London when I was eighteen. I longed to be a small businessman, as you see me now, selling cans of cider and individually wrapped ice lollies to the people.'

Claire narrowed her eyes at him. She often suspected Mr Przybylski of being too clever by half. He smiled at her, but then tutted and looked sad.

'You need a nice young man or lady, Claire,' he said, shaking his head. 'Your shopping is very depressing – very depressing.'

'You're my landlord, not a therapist,' replied Claire.

She swept the items, which she had to admit he had assessed correctly, into her rucksack.

'Even to get a pet, that would help,' he went on, deep sadness in his voice. 'It is not allowed in the lease, but I will grant special dispensation.'

'Goodbye, Mr Przybylski,' she said, hurrying towards the door. A slightly mournful cry of 'A small cat!' chased her out.

Claire scampered back into her basement home and rubbed the radiator. The scalding heat soothed her smarting pride from Mr Przybylski's comments, knowing that he would have to pay for it. *Mmm, nice and toasty. Petty revenge served piping hot.*

'I didn't really think much about the footage from the security camera,' said Claire to Sophie. 'But it doesn't make sense. Most people who actually know the SWF don't go through that room, unless they need to, for some reason. So Nate going and standing there, it's almost like he wanted to be seen. But why would he? And if he did, why would he have deleted the video afterwards? It's weird.'

She turned on the oven and put the pizza baguette in immediately, rather than waiting for it to heat up to the recommended temperature, and ate the pudding while it warmed. Claire lived in fear of doing the wrong thing in any given social situation, but eating her pudding first when she wanted to was a small act of rebellion against normal behaviour that she could safely engage in when nobody else was looking.

'What's weird is that you eat that first, you know,' said Sophie.

Almost nobody was looking. Claire was developing a theory (which wasn't peer-reviewed, because so far she didn't have any peers, apart from a very angry terrier) that ghosts were actually a scientific phenomenon. After all, humans ran on electricity, right? Sort of. So maybe ghosts were like a residual energy from a person's life, and some people – that is, her – had some extra rods or cones, or something, that made her able to see them. And maybe Alex had a whisper of it as well.

Claire felt guilty about Sophie. She had disappeared during an open day-trip to Oxford University. They normally did everything together, but this time Claire hadn't been there. Sophie always told Claire she couldn't be held responsible for Sophie being extraordinary. Even if Claire didn't have any particular reason to fear posthumous punishment of any kind, that didn't mean she didn't deal with pre-humous guilt. She had expressed this to Alex once, and Alex said, 'At what point does that not explain all of religion?', which Claire did not find supportive.

Claire and Sophie arrived at Basher and Alex's flat at around half-past five that evening, whereupon Basher informed them they were having carbonara – Alex's second foray into vegetarianism having recently ended when it ran head-first into Alex's desire to have a kebab at 2 a.m.

'How did your conversation with Ken go?' Basher asked as he ushered Claire into the front room and moved a stack of books off the coffee table.

'It was fine, thanks,' replied Claire, immediately defensive. 'He wants me to do a seance to try to clear the SWF. Or not a seance. I guess an exorcism? Some kind of banishing ... ritual. Of some description. I'll have to make it up.'

'Excellent. No further investigations necessary,' said Basher.

Alex appeared from their bedroom, which was more a sort of nest papered with art supplies and second-hand designer clothes. They were wearing dungarees, which was exactly the sort of thing Alex could do and look good in.

'Well, I did find out from Lila that she was the one who cleaned up Eddie's death-scene. And she said her dad's suicide note, it said he was the one who killed Eddie,' continued Claire. 'Chaz says he poisoned Eddie with something called wolfsbane, and then took some himself. See, didn't I say Eddie was poisoned?'

'That is as may be, but it still doesn't warrant you getting involved,' said Basher.

'I just think that—'

'Ah-buh-buh-buh!' Basher cut her off and Claire sulked.

'Don't be annoying, Uncle B,' said Alex. 'Maybe you got a bit worked up, C,' they suggested and rubbed her shoulders.

This sort of undermining wasn't usual from Alex, and Claire found it upsetting. 'I'm not here for comfort,' she replied eventually.

'Oh, pardon us,' said Basher. He smiled.

'But something still isn't right. What if whoever killed Chaz staged it as a suicide because they also killed Eddie?'

'That is such a stupid a thing for the actual murderer to have done that I am inclined to put it down as a point in favour of Chaz having genuinely taken his own life,' replied Basher.

'How come?' asked Alex.

'Because obviously now the cops will have to investigate Eddie's death as well, even though they'd already cleared it as a natural death,' said Sophie. 'Bash is right: what kind of fucking spanner would come up with that?'

'Chaz left the SWF because Eddie found out that Chaz was stealing a bunch of money from them,' insisted Claire. 'But Chaz found out who Eddie was having an affair with. What if whoever it was didn't want me finding that out from Chaz? And they went round and spiked his beer with this wolfsbane, or something.'

'It would have to be someone d knew,' said Sophie.

'You are coming at this from the point of view of already being suspicious,' said Basher. 'Let us assume Eddie was having an affair with someone at the SWF. Who could that have been?'

'Well, one of the wrestlers, like Ruby,' suggested Claire. 'Or Lila. She did tell us she was having secret wrestling lessons with Eddie, but she seemed very grossed out by the idea.'

'But she didn't actually say no, did she?' pointed out Sophie. 'Plus, it makes more sense that she'd clean up the scene, get rid of the Viagra tablets, because she was actually covering up that she was shagging her disgusting father-in-law.'

'Quite so,' said Basher. 'And if you had found out that your oldest friend had somehow seduced your daughter, that would prompt an argument that might lead to a break from the business, even if you *had* been siphoning money from it for years.'

'And you might even be angry enough to kill over it,' finished Alex.

'So the sequence of events, as described by Chaz's note, may be entirely truthful,' said Basher.

Claire had to admit the logic in this, although she refused to do so out loud. 'But, I mean, how would he poison Eddie's tablets? That sounds quite hard.'

'On the contrary,' replied Basher, the fount of all general knowledge,' I think it would be surprisingly easy to poison someone with wolfsbane. The getting away with it would be the harder part, which evidently Chaz had not fully thought through. Perhaps you calling him was the last straw.'

'Well, what is wolfsbane then?' asked Claire.

'It is a plant, properly called aconite. You can buy aconitum as a substance, although that is of course controlled. But the plant itself you can get in a garden centre – it's quite common. And would be flowering about now, I think. The popular misconception is that it is an undetectable poison, but very little is undetectable in the twenty-first century. For our purposes, the interesting fact is that its effects mimic heart and blood-pressure problems.'

'Oh, well, that answers my first question,' said Claire. 'The second is how do you make a poison out of that and then turn it into pills?'

'That's two more questions,' said Basher.

'Why don't we call Mac and ask?' said Alex.

Mac was a vet they had met on holiday, and a vet was the closest thing to a scientist that Claire knew. Alex was still somewhat in touch with Mac and her little family. Mac confirmed she was free, and Alex called her immediately.

'Wotcher, M,' they said. 'You're on speaker. How's tricks?'

'Not bad, not bad,' replied Mac in her soft, slightly posh Edinburgh accent. 'Did you get that cake recipe herself sent?'

'I did, but I'm all business today, I'm afraid. We need your help.'

'*My* help? Have you lot got messed up in another murder?' It was clear from Mac's tone of voice that she was joking.

'No comment,' replied Basher. 'I am going to absent myself from this discussion, so as to provide plausible deniability.' He went into the kitchen and turned on the kettle, which was equal parts old and deafening. Claire thought it was less about plausible deniability and more that he wouldn't be able to stop himself getting further involved.

'Ignore him, he's a big party-pooper,' said Alex. They stuck their tongue out in the direction of the kitchen.

'I cannot hear you, but I know at least one of you is being rude!' shouted Basher, over a sound like an immersion heater about to explode.

'Um, hi, Mac. Nice to speak to you again. I was wondering how you would, you know, get a kind of concentration from a plant. You're a scientist, so I thought you'd know,' said Claire.

'I mean, I'm not exactly that sort of scientist. Sorry, I'm eating leftover pasta at the same time,' she replied, with her mouth full. 'You can powder basically anything – it's just a question of drying it out and smashing it up. If you have the roots, that's the easiest. You can slice up turmeric and air-dry it, for example. Loads of air cookers have a dehydration setting now too; that's how you make apple crisps or banana chips. Or you put it in the oven on a really low heat overnight – that's basically the same thing. And then you can powder it down in a pestle and mortar or a grinder.'

'Oh, right. That's way easier than I thought,' replied Claire. 'Okay, so what about ... how do you make that powder into a pill.'

'Gosh, now it sounds like *you're* trying to murder someone,' said Mac, laughing.

Basher walked in, put a couple of fresh mugs of tea on the coffee table and then walked out again to start his pasta properly. He paused at the doorway to mime zipping his mouth up and shaking his head in disapproval. Claire mouthed, 'Thank you.' Alex threw the Vs up at him.

'But believe it or not, this I am a bit more of an expert on,' continued Mac. 'It depends what sort of pills, though. If it's a hardcap – a gelatine capsule made of two halves stuck together with powder inside, you know, like the paracetamol ones you get that are like blue-and-white Tic Tacs – then you could very, very carefully pull them apart and replace the powder inside with whatever you wanted, if you had access. That's what they thought the Tylenol Killer did over in America, but now there are safety caps on pill bottles. Maybe the easier method now is with pressed-powder tablets, which are like the own-brand paracetamol tabs you get in Tesco. In the old days, vets used to make up a lot of the treatments for animals themselves, and the practice here still has quite a few old hand-presses for making pills. They come in all sorts of shapes and sizes.'

'So as long as you had the right sort of press, you could make nearly whatever pill you wanted?' asked Sophie.

Claire passed this on.

'Yeah, you can get some presses that are almost hand-screws that only make one tab at a time. Would fit in your pocket. Of course the easiest to make are just flat circles, like Berocca tablets. Making pills isn't illegal in itself; it depends on what's in them and what you do with them.

Some people make their own sweets to have at home, and things like that.'

'What's Berocca?' asked Alex.

'Tch. Kids today,' said Mac.

Claire ended the conversation, pleased that her theory was possible, but upset that it was *so* possible that anyone with sufficient stick-to-itness was capable of it.

'Hey,' said Sophie. 'What does this plant look like anyway?'

Alex tapped away on their phone. 'Huh, it's cool!' they replied. 'Nice flowers.'

'What colour is it?' asked Claire.

'Really nice, deep purple.'

14

No Flowers for Charlie

A good medium, Claire told herself, would perform the best seance possible by gathering all the facts she could. This was not, per Basher's edict, investigating a murder. This was investigating a dead man. It might behove her to know, for example, what flowers he would like best. The fact that one of these flowers might have been used to create a poison, and there was security footage of Trudy secretly stealing a bunch of posters from the gym that she allegedly never went to, was clearly by the by.

'Your attitude to this is flip-flopping all over the place,' said Sophie. She was dragging behind Claire as they walked towards Trudy's house, trying to stretch their tether out more. It felt a bit like dragging a child along when they got tired halfway through a walk, except that instead of carrying a discarded doll they had said they would definitely carry the whole way, you had to carry an inexplicably supernatural ache that gnawed at you from the inside out.

'Can you come closer, please, it's getting a bit much,' requested Claire. 'Anyway, I don't know *your* attitude. Do you think either Eddie or Chaz was murdered? And if so, who did it?'

'Eddie might not have been. Chaz might have been,' said Sophie. 'And if he was, my money is on Pink Champagne. Miller said they were a great source for him, and Ruby let slip that Chaz is a gossip. Maybe he knew something about them.'

'But *what* – and why would they bother to kill him? That's why I can't leave it alone,' grumbled Claire. 'None of it fits properly together. Basher had just about convinced me that Chaz might have killed Eddie, but now Trudy is back in the frame because of the flowers.'

'Maybe it's an *Orient Express* thing and they all did it,' said Sophie.

'Unlikely. I just wish any of them ever told the whole truth. Including Eddie.'

'He's the one who started this whole mess anyway; you were only ever supposed to be doing a seance. He's the one who kicked off about being murdered.'

'Hm, well. Let's ask Trudy about her plants.'

They had made it up the stairs to the King homestead and Claire knocked on the door.

'Ask in a subtle way, though,' Sophie added. 'In case she poisons your tea.'

She said this as Trudy opened the door, and Claire

tried to look pleased, as if there was nothing in the world she would rather do than say hello to Trudy.

'Hello, love,' said Trudy. 'What brings you back here then?'

'Well, er ... What's happening is that Ken would like me to progress with a seance to help Eddie pass over,' she said. 'And I was hoping to ask a few more quick questions that would help with that.' Trudy looked hesitant. 'It won't take long, only ten minutes, tops.'

'Go on then. I've got to head out in a minute – the police want me to give a statement about Chaz. Terrible that, isn't it? I would never have thought.' She stepped aside to let Claire in and shut the door almost in Sophie's face.

'Charming. No manners, people these days,' said Soph as she walked through it.

'I know. Horrible. I, er, I don't know if you know, but I was actually the one who found Chaz,' said Claire. 'I had made an appointment to see him, to ask him about Eddie. Do you believe what ... what the police said?'

'Oh, I don't know. I'm almost past caring. It wouldn't surprise me if any of them had killed each other. Go through to the back again, love,' responded Trudy.

'Why doesn't she want you anywhere else in the place?' Sophie asked.

'That's fine, I wanted to see the flowers again,' Claire replied. She went out to the purple jungle and hoped that Trudy would again take some time making tea, because she wanted to photograph as many of the flowers as she could.

'Maybe it's that one,' suggested Sophie, pointing to big spears of plants covered in purple bells.

'Those are foxgloves,' muttered Claire. 'They're also poisonous.'

'What was that?' asked Trudy, coming back through with a run-of-the-mill mug of tea, obviously less interested in rolling out the purple carpet this time.

'I was just talking about the flowers. My spirit guide, she was admiring the foxgloves. And I said that they're poisonous.'

Trudy nodded. 'They are, though not usually fatal. But I don't make salad with them, don't worry.'

'Are any others poisonous, do you know?'

'Yes, one I know definitely is. That one next to you there, that's monkshood.' She pointed to a large pot. The plant in it had a dense puff of thin green leaves at the base, and then long stalks clustered with deep-purple flowers. 'They look like little cowls, you see? Like the hood on a cloak. That's very poisonous, but they're so pretty. I think it's called wolfsbane sometimes.'

'If she did poison anyone, she's very confident about it, revealing it like that,' said Sophie.

They say poison is a woman's weapon, Claire remembered. She looked at her tea again.

'Did you give them to anyone?'

'The monkshood? Yes, as it happens. It grew like topsy, I ended up giving a pot to almost everyone. Except Nate. I take him bunches of flowers if I visit. And not Chaz, actually. He said he had a brown thumb.'

'Very convenient, eh?' said Sophie.

Trudy watched Claire take a picture of the monkshood. 'What's that got to do with Eddie?' she asked.

'Oh, nothing really. I was just wondering if any of these flowers were his favourites, and if they might be safe to, er, burn, or anything like that.'

'He wasn't arsed about them at all,' said Trudy. 'Except once, a few years back, he'd pulled some girl who loved gardening. I got home earlier than expected, but she and I actually had a nice chat. Eddie didn't like that,' she added and laughed.

'Didn't you ever want to leave?' asked Claire. She couldn't stop herself.

'When I was younger, yes, but Ken was young then, too. When he grew up, I kept thinking, "Next year, next year" and then there was always a reason not to. Divorce is expensive. I'd have to find somewhere new to live.' Trudy shook it off. 'Got sorted out for me, didn't it?'

'Yes, I suppose so,' replied Claire.

'She's awfully chipper still,' said Sophie.

'Was there anything else?' asked Trudy.

Claire looked down at the mug in her hands, which was still mostly full, and had the distinct impression she was being got rid of.

'I suppose not,' she said. 'I'll ... put this in the sink for you.'

'No need, love, I can do it.' Trudy held out her hand. Claire looked at her and then over her shoulder at the firmly-closed kitchen door.

'No, no, I'll save you a job,' she said, and made a break for it.

She didn't have to break far. It was a small home. Still, she had to get by Trudy to reach the kitchen, and the older woman had faster reactions than Claire had expected. She managed to hook her fingers around Claire's elbow as she dived for the door handle, and Claire sloshed most of the tea against the wall. She pushed her way into the kitchen in triumph.

'A-*ha!*' she shouted. And then wished she hadn't.

'Bit premature,' said Sophie. The kitchen was spotlessly clean.

'What the hell are you playing at?' asked Trudy, who could clearly only abide someone spilling tea in her house once.

'Ask about the CCTV,' said Sophie.

'Uh, yeah. Sorry, Trudy, it's just that I've been given access to the CCTV records from the front office, because of the potential for, er, spirits to be picked up on camera. And there's a video of you taking a lot of posters out of the SWF.'

'Oh, for— Is that all?'

'You were being evasive! Say she was being evasive,' said Sophie.

'You were being evasive,' Claire suggested, looking embarrassed.

'I like my kitchen to be clean. Sakes! Come up here.'

She gestured for Claire to follow, and walked upstairs in the cross way people do when they want you to know they're annoyed. Trudy puffed and sighed like an angry tea kettle.

'Here!' she said. She flung open the door to what had probably been Ken's old bedroom and was now a guest room. All over the floor and bed were snowdrifts of card stock, all ripped up, showing isolated muscles, fingers, an eye, an ear, a leg. Other posters were in half-rolls on the floor, like beetles on their backs. 'Here are the bloody posters. What's the problem?'

'Why have you taken them all? Why are they ripped up?'

'I was going to bloody mulch them!' she replied. 'Then I got a proper look at them and most of them are waxed. Can't compost any of them. But I'd got it into my head about shredding them, and I started and I couldn't stop ...' She trailed off. 'Anyway now I don't know what to do with the bastard things. All with Eddie's big, stupid face on them.' She put a cigarette in her mouth and tried to light it, sparking the lighter several times before giving up.

'Why did you take them all down then?' asked Claire.

'I did no such thing. I was talking to Ruby about needing paper for mulch and she said these were all out the back. So don't try making me seem like a thief, as they were already going to be thrown out.'

'But ... but you took them all secretly!' Claire protested. 'You said you never go to the SWF.'

'Well, all right. Maybe it was a bit secret. I waited until

Ken wasn't going to be there, because he cares about all this stuff and the history, and I thought he'd get upset if he knew I was going to shred them. That's all. Take one for your bloody seance if you like – see if I care.'

'Uh. No, that's okay, thanks. Sorry.'

'Don't apologize. Never admit wrongdoing!' said Sophie.

Trudy snorted. 'I'll thank you to leave. I want to be shot of this whole mess, and I want my son to be shot of it too. Don't bloody come back here.'

'Wow, you lost her fast,' said Sophie. 'She was well into you and your mystical medium ways the first time.'

Trudy almost physically pushed Claire out of the front door, and slammed it behind her.

'Do you believe her?' asked Sophie.

'I don't know. Yeah, probably. So does that mean Pink Champagne took down the posters?'

'They knew about them at least,' replied Claire. She walked down to street level and looked up aconite on her phone again, then compared it to the picture she'd just taken.

'That's definitely the stuff,' she said, showing Sophie.

'Agreed,' replied Sophie. 'But what now?

'Let's go over to the gym while we're here; maybe some of the posters are still around.'

'God, you might as well get a flat opposite – we're up and down from this place like a fucking yo-yo.'

*

They strolled along to the gym and Claire went to open the main door, but it rattled and remained shut. She rattled harder, but the door remained steadfast.

'I think it's closed,' said Sophie mildly.

'Ugh. Now we have to wait for the bus.'

But then the door opened. Ken was standing there, looking flustered. 'Oh, it's you. What do you want?'

'Sorry, Ken, we thought the place would be open.'

'You keep saying "we", you know,' Sophie observed. 'I think you have unresolved guilt about my death. Don't worry, I don't think he's noticed.'

'Can I help you?' Ken repeated, having been spoken over by a dead adolescent the first time, to the extent that Claire hadn't heard or answered his question.

'I, er, was going to look for some old memorabilia or costumes of Eddie's,' she said. 'To help with the seance stuff, like you said.'

'I can't let you right now. I've just got back from talking to the police about Chaz. I really only came to get some paperwork and lock up the place before I head back to see Lila again.'

'How's she doing?'

'She's doing fine. The police aren't suspicious about Chaz's death, so I'm concentrating on making the next show the best it can be. I've got a poster mock-up somewhere.' Ken patted his pockets down and produced a folded piece of A4, which had a sketchy design on it. At the top was the SWF logo, and then underneath was written 'KING OF THE RING' in block capitals, with many stars and embellishments. In the middle were some stick figures, with labels indicating that one would be Eddie, standing behind Ken with paternal hands laid on his son's shoulders.

'I want the show to be, you know, respectful continuity,' Ken said. 'What do you think? I think it's good.'

'Aw, he's showing off. It's sort of sweet,' said Sophie. 'Desperate for validation, even from someone who doesn't know or care about wrestling. He wants you to put his poster idea on the fridge.'

Claire coughed to cover her laugh and replied, 'Oh, yeah, that's great. Really strong image.'

'I was thinking I should be depicted wearing dad's classic singlet, you know?' Ken went on. He was clearly only half-listening to her. 'Although, speaking of costumes, tell Alex again that they can't go through the old boxes. I keep catching them at it.'

'Sure. Sure, I'll let them know,' said Claire.

Ken locked the door as he left and pushed past her without looking back.

'Ken, I still need to know where to send the invoice,' she called after him.

'Sorry, Clara, lot on. Can't hear you!'

'Ohmigod, that was on purpose,' said Soph. 'Prick! Also he wasn't holding any paperwork.'

'Maybe we could find an open window and— *Christ!* Miller!'

'I usually have to buy ladies a drink before they shout that at me,' said the portly little ghost. He smiled and smoothed down his beard.

'You can shove that sentiment right up your hole,' replied Sophie. 'As if.'

'No need for that,' said Miller. 'I merely wanted to reiterate that my services are always open.'

'Miller, you've been fucking useless,' said Claire. 'Did you know that Lila was secretly meeting Eddie here sometimes? No, you did not. Did you know that Eddie was taking Viagra? Also a no. You barely know anything. You've actually been less than no help.'

'Look, I'm doing what I can. I'm dead. I just want you to help me out.'

'People aren't entitled to my help because they're dead,' said Claire. 'I have a life – I have my own stuff going on. I have *her* to deal with!' She gestured at Sophie.

'All right, fucking hell, no need for the drive-by there,' said Sophie.

'I'm only saying: what's in this for me, huh?' Claire went on. 'Nothing. Merely transcribing a boring load of nonsense for you, which will take fucking ages to do, won't it? Me standing here in the cold, by myself, tapping stuff out on my phone for you.'

'You're sort of my Obi-Wan Kenobi here, though,' said Miller. 'Otherwise I might be stuck here for ever.

'So? Why is that my fucking problem? It's not my fault you're dead. Why do I have to deal with all this? I didn't ask for it.'

'I'm only trying to—'

'You know what else you didn't know?' said Claire. Her blood was up. She could feel the adrenaline in the set of her jaw. 'You didn't know that they, in there, all think you're an idiot. They think you're a poser. They think you're pathetic and useless. That's what they think. They don't respect you at all. Writing a last blog post won't change that. There's no point. Maybe you should just get over it by yourself. I can't help you.'

Miller didn't say anything. He just blinked very fast and worked his mouth a lot. Claire could feel her shoulders raising and falling in time with her laboured breath. It didn't feel as good as she thought it would.

'It's not you, pal,' said Sophie.

Miller nodded.

'Don't fucking apologize for me,' snapped Claire.

'I didn't.'

Claire turned and started walking away.

'Do you think it's possible that you weren't angry at *Miller* there,' said Sophie, jogging to keep pace.

'Shut up.'

'Do you think it's possible that you were feeling anger towards yoursel—'

'Fuck off!'

'LOL,' said Sophie. 'Can't.'

15

Dream Wedding

Claire was lying in bed, staring at the ceiling. Another day had passed without incident, and everyone else seemed happy enough with the unofficial-official explanation that Chaz had killed Eddie. Claire was still struggling to let it go. Partly because Ken was ignoring her calls and her requests for invoice details.

'Look, maybe they're right,' said Sophie. She was standing in the corner, looking at Claire with an expression somewhere between compassion and dispassion. '"Occam's razor", isn't that what it's called? You can leave the details to the police. Which is sort of what you wanted anyway.'

'I don't think they're getting it right,' grumbled Claire, speaking from less than two years of experience.

'So you keep saying. It's getting old. Just concentrate on finding a way to exorcize Eddie,' said Sophie.

'I'm neither an old priest *nor* a young priest,' said

Claire. 'I could cobble together bits and pieces from different exorcism methods. Bit of holy water here, bit of *qui habitat* there. But it's all religious, and I don't know if it would work. Plus, if it did, I might exorcize you by mistake, mightn't I?'

'Ah yes, caught in the spiritual crossfire,' replied Sophie.

Claire's phone rang, and she rolled over onto her stomach to look at it. It was an unknown number, which, being a millennial, immediately alarmed her, but she answered it anyway and put it on speaker.

'Is this Claire, the medium?' said a familiar theatrical voice.

'Yes. Is this *Nate*?' she asked, incredulous.

'This is Nate King, yes,' said he, pre-exhausted by the conversation he was about to have. Sophie clambered over the bed to get closer to the phone.

'What the hell, man?' Claire exclaimed. 'I've been trying to talk to you for days!'

'I'm under no obligation,' said Nate. 'I've been cooperating with the police, and they don't seem to find me at all suspicious.'

'Yeah, but they don't know what we do,' said Sophie. 'Or at least they don't believe it, which is rude of them. Why is he talking to you?'

'Yeah, why are you talking to me at all, if you've nothing to say to me,' said Claire.

Nate sighed heavily. 'Owing to recent events, we've decided to put on another show this week, on a tight turnaround, while interest in our promotion is still high.'

'Next question: why is he talking to you like a normal person and acknowledging that wrestling is a performance?' said Soph, which was a good point.

'So what?' Claire said. 'Ken already told me that; he wants me to get rid of your brother beforehand.'

'I'm in charge of booking the show while Ken is supporting Lila, and I have been thinking about it a lot. The SWF has a reputation for putting on the greatest shows in the country,' continued Nate. Here he almost lapsed back into being a showman. 'But we also have a reputation with our fans for integrity and honesty. I want to let them be a part of saying a final goodbye to my brother, now that we know what happened.' He paused. 'I want you to perform your seance – or energy-clearing ceremony, or whatever it is – live in the ring, on Thursday night. And to be present and visible at the show for the evening.'

'*What?* Is this you doing kayfabe at me again?'

'You'd already agreed to doing a seance with my nephew. I'm merely suggesting we change the terms of that agreement slightly,' said Nate.

'God, he sounds so strange when he's being formal,' observed Sophie.

'That's so weird,' said Claire. 'That's such a weird thing to do – to make a performance out of it.'

'I understand you hold yourself out to be a *real* medium, so I don't see why it would be disrespectful,' replied Nate. He sniffed. 'You can't understand this business unless you've lived it.'

'You know what: people keep saying that, and I don't

think it's actually true,' said Claire, finally exasperated enough to shout at someone about it. She threw her hands in the air. 'This isn't some unknowable fucking Lament Configuration; it's gymnastics with extra steps! It's dance-moms, if they were lads full of testosterone. Actually it's *exactly* like mums; it's like the smug ones who say, "You'll know once you have your own" sagely, as if people are incapable of real empathy until they've been knocked up by some boring fucking teaching assistant they were thinking of leaving anyway!'

'Did I touch a nerve?' asked Nate, after a pause.

'Honestly, you have so many, it's impossible to tell which one,' said Sophie.

'Yeah, yeah, fuck you very much,' replied Claire. She caught her breath after her outburst.

'Do you want to do it or not?' Nate pressed.

'Will I get paid?'

'Yes.'

'Fine. But I want to talk to you beforehand about everything that's happened. This has been a very intense few days, you know. And by the way, I don't buy all that rubbish about the fans getting to say goodbye to Eddie. What's the real reason?'

'We need to fill fifteen minutes,' said Nate promptly. 'We're short a match and can't find anyone to fill in. Pair of backstabbers left without warning, and nobody can get hold of them.'

Claire frowned at her phone. 'Who did? What are you talking about?'

'Pink Champagne of course! I was going to give them the headline spot, like they bloody wanted,' said Nate. 'But they've gone.'

'Gone?' asked Claire. 'Gone where?'

'Nobody knows,' replied Nate. 'They just disappeared after the training session they ran on Saturday. Anyway I have your contact info and will send you some more details this week. Please provide your own costuming and other accoutrements.' He hung up, quite abruptly.

'Jesus, he's different from his brother, isn't he? Nate's actually decent to talk to when he's not putting on that act,' said Sophie. 'When he's putting on the act, it's like he's pretending to be Eddie, almost.'

'Never mind that! Some suspects have fled the area. What happened to "Don't leave town" – isn't that a thing?'

'I think mostly in your TV shows.'

'I'm going to call Sami. This surely is *something* significant, for God's sake.'

Sami didn't pick up, so Claire left a long, rambling voice-message and then had a glass of not-quite-but-basically-in-date apple juice for breakfast.

'Can we please get out of the depression dungeon for a bit today?' Sophie mewled. 'Look, you need to buy some stuff for doing your performance seance. Maybe you can get a sage bundle and a pashmina, or something.'

'*Ugh*, fine. I'm not happy about it, though.'

'Well, you have to leave at some point, because you've run out of dry sliced bread to eat,' Soph observed. 'It won't even be that hard. There's a bunch of magic shops in Brighton, and they spell "magic" with a k, and everything. Come on, come on, come on.'

Claire got dressed and hurried past the shop door, lest Mr Przybylski notice her. Because it was a Tuesday daytime, the town was fairly empty, and Claire felt less scared about buying the supplies that regular psychics trafficked in. She'd bought a Tarot deck once, but every future she'd seen in the cards was unfailingly negative.</NI>

On the way towards what she thought of as the Weirdo Shops area of Brighton, which was a small warren of tight, cobbled streets, she was pulled up short by the sight of a wedding-dress shop.

'No way. Look. "Hannah's Belles!" It's the one that does the wrestling gear,' she exclaimed.

'Really? You're going to walk yourself down another dead-end and into a brick wall,' Sophie moaned.

'It's open, and it says, "No appointment necessary". It'll only take a few minutes and then—'

'Wotcher, C!'

'Oh, arses,' muttered Claire under her breath, but with deep emotion.

Alex and Basher were advancing from the other end of the street. There was no escape.

'My, my,' said Basher. 'We have just been out shopping to get some lovely local produce, and Alex expressed an interest in visiting this establishment to ask the proprietor about certain types of tailoring. So I know why *we* are about to go inside the shop that provides the SWF with its costumes, but I cannot imagine why *you* are …'

'Caught red-handed, innit,' said Soph.

'Because of course,' continued Basher, 'we have already had a discussion about how you do not need to continue looking into anything to do with Eddie's death, and so on.'

Claire tugged at her sleeves in an effort to make herself more presentable. 'I had absolutely no idea this place made costumes for wrestlers,' she lied. 'Honest, er, the thing is that, well, you know …'

'I am sure I do not,' said Basher.

'Well, every woman secretly thinks about what wedding dress she would like to wear one day,' said Claire. 'I'm allowed to look in a shop window in a vulnerable moment.'

'Not your worst lie,' commented Sophie.

Basher narrowed his eyes, and then seemed to cheer up immensely in the space of a few seconds. He made a great show of opening the door with a flourish.

'Well then, please,' he said. 'After you.'

'This feels like a trap,' said Sophie.

'*What is happening?*' asked Alex in a stage whisper.

The shop inside wasn't small, but it seemed like it was, because the walls were lined with rails full of wedding dresses. This gave the initial impression that the owner had tried to soundproof the room with king-sized duvets. A small, neat middle-aged blonde woman appeared. She was wearing black trousers and a coral shirt, which struck Claire as a good choice. She looked professional, but a dowdy kind of professional that wouldn't overshadow anyone trying on a dress, despite the fact that she had a pretty little rosebud sort of a face.

'Hello,' she said. 'Who's looking for a dress today?'

Alex opened their mouth, but Basher spoke first. 'My friend Claire here,' he replied. He slipped an arm around Claire's shoulders and gave her a little squeeze. 'I am her maid-of-honour. She is simply dying to try on some dresses.'

Claire turned to look at him, her mouth open. Sophie burst out laughing, the kind of all-consuming laughter that turns into a coughing fit.

'Yes,' agreed Claire. She took a moment to straighten up, and rearranged her face as she stared Basher down. 'I would *love* to.'

Basher didn't blink. 'Great,' he said. '*Perfect.*'

Claire's bravado belied the fact that Claire hadn't shaved her armpits or legs for some time, although presumably some brides chose to go all natural as well. Alex seemed delighted at the chance to play pretend at Claire's expense and actually clapped their hands together.

The woman did not seem alarmed by the tone of this exchange, and instead rang a bell, at which point another, similar woman appeared. She was almost identical, but twenty years younger.

'This is my daughter, Sharon. She can help you find your perfect dress,' said, presumably, Hannah, with a smile.

'Right this way,' said Sharon. She led them towards the back of the shop, where there was a small sofa, large mirrors and a little raised step for brides-to-be to stand on. 'Prosecco?' she asked.

'Ooh, yes,' said Alex.

'No,' said Basher firmly.

Claire waggled her eyebrows at Alex, trying to prompt them to ask their questions about the wrestling gear, but Alex resolutely refused to do this, and instead Claire had to fumble through a conversation about what kind of cut, colour and fabric she would like.

'How about we start with something simple and classic and go from there? I'll pull a couple of options,' said Sharon. She had affixed a slightly glassy smile that suggested she would later describe the group as nightmare customers.

Alex flopped down on the sofa and pulled an embroidery hoop and a mass of assorted thread out of their tote bag.

'What's that?' asked Claire.

'I am doing very important art,' they said. They were wearing a T-shirt that said 'PROTECT CM PUNK' in block letters in the colours of the trans-rights flag, a reference that Claire did not understand and felt she did not have time to ask about, but that she assumed was somehow to do with wrestling. Alex had a lot of strings to their weird bow and had previously made forays into dildo art – that is, making strange art pieces with cast-off dildos that hadn't cured properly. In the main, they were an embroiderer and seemed to have combined the two interests by making an embroidery of two colourful dildos. But, in accordance with their current hobby of choice, the dildos were depicted in the midst of a pro-wrestling match. One seemed to have just leapt from the top rope.

'It's good,' observed Sophie. 'But it's pretty fucking niche.'

'It's a low-percenter,' said Alex happily. 'Got time on my hands after Ken kicked me out of the costume corner, innit. I'm going to wrangle my way back in, though. Nate said someone needs to sort through it, and it might as well be me.'

'While I have the opportunity to air a grievance, may I lodge the complaint that you have ruined all my streaming profiles,' said Basher. His Netflix had previously been a machine that served up Korean films and quiet programmes about paper, and allowing Claire to use it while she was visiting had turned it into a meat-grinder that churned out dead mothers from Colorado.

'Maybe they'll make a documentary about me one day,' said Sophie. She cautiously stretched the tether out a little further and went towards the far side of the room to peer at a rack of satiny dresses.

'They'd have to find you first,' said Claire. 'And unless you were done in by a pervert who killed half a dozen girls in tracksuits, so they could call him The Juicy Killer, I dunno if you'd get a whole documentary to yourself.'

Basher did the second-long pause he did when he processed that she was replying to something Sophie had said. 'You know, I am often quite glad that I cannot hear the other half of your conversations.'

'Oh, are you talking about that new documentary everyone is watching?' asked Sharon. 'With the septic tank? I've not seen it yet. Still,' she went on, appearing to realize that this wasn't good shop talk, 'you've got your whole life ahead of you. Shall we try this one?'

She held up a slim champagne-coloured dress, which she then handed to Claire through the curtain of a pillowy changing room that had the sort of lamps that were pretending to be candles. Claire struggled out of her jeans and into the dress, which was closer to being a slip and therefore made her stand guarding her own body protectively.

'Did you ever think about your wedding?' she asked Sophie.

'No,' replied Sophie. Her eyes were black, like those of a shark.

Sharon brought her Claire of the changing room and trilled a 'What do we think?'

'I think you look like a plank in sexy pyjamas,' said Alex. 'It's doing nothing for you.'

'Did you know Ruby and Guy have done a runner?' asked Claire, as a defensive reflex. She felt bad for asking, because Alex's face fell as hard and fast as an apocryphally lethal penny dropped from the top of the Empire State Building. 'Er, sorry to be the one to tell you then,' she continued. 'Nobody has been able to get hold of them since the last lesson they ran, apparently.'

'Nah, it's fine. I mean, they said I had talent and

asked me to design some new costumes. I dunno. I would have thought they'd say something to me,' said Alex. Sometimes Claire forgot that Alex wasn't a completely matured adult, and then they did something like exhibit obvious hurt in a way that made their mouth crumple, and she saw they were actually very young.

'I'm sure it's nothing to do with you,' said Claire.

'Fuck 'em,' added Sophie.

'I'll try calling them or something,' muttered Alex.

'You don't think it's suspicious? Ruby was the one spreading all the gossip about Trudy and Nate and now they've just gone, after Chaz dies.'

'A-buh-buh-buh,' said Basher. 'We are here to get your wedding dress, remember.' He looked at her critically. 'I think we should try a puff sleeve. And a princess skirt. You know, the complete eighties picture.'

'Retro is very in right now,' said Sharon, nodding.

And soon Claire found herself being strapped into a heap of tulle and satin in bright, startling white. When she staggered out of the fitting room and onto the tiny dais, Sophie started laughing all over again.

'It's giving toilet-roll cover,' she said, when she was finally able to catch her breath.

'I'm wondering if there are *enough* sequins,' said Alex.

'Perhaps not,' said Basher.

Claire stared him down again.

'Yes,' she agreed. 'More sequins.'

'I'm not sure we have anything with more embellishments than this,' said Sharon. 'Depending on when the day is, we could make something custom, although of course that costs more.'

Alex cleared their throat. 'Oh, that reminds me,' they said. 'I wanted to ask about the work you do for the SWF.'

The effect this question had on Sharon was profound. She looked around hastily and then hopped over to Alex and raised her hand, as if she was about to clamp it over their mouth. 'Shhhh! You're supposed to call me directly! Mum doesn't mind me doing it, because of the extra money, but she won't have it talked about on the shop floor.'

'Oh, really? Why?'

'Says it creates the wrong impression,' replied Sharon.

'I guess,' said Alex dubiously. 'I only wanted to ask you about some of the techniques you use to sew the fabrics together. They're so stretchy.'

'Oh, well, it's not so hard once you get the hang of it,' said Sharon. She relaxed a bit. 'You need a ballpoint needle, and have to remember to measure very carefully. And never let the fabric hang when you cut it, because that can stretch it at that early stage and then you're licked before you even start.'

'Do you do a lot of it then?' asked Claire, the picture of innocence.

'Oh, here and there,' said Sharon. 'Less recently. It mostly came from Eddie. The last thing I did was a rush on some elements for Nate.'

'He wanted boots, right,' said Claire.

'Yes, boots and a new mask.'

'He got a mask?' said Claire. 'Why?'

'He always does,' responded Sharon. 'He's a luchador, I think they call it. A mask is part of his uniform.'

Claire stepped off the dais and strode over to Alex, then waved a finger under their nose. All pretence that she might be there to buy a wedding dress went out the window.

'So, so, so, so you're telling me,' she said, 'that whenever anyone has said they definitely saw Nate in his wrestling gear, going on and on about his bloody boots, that gear included a mask *covering his face*! Do these people have fucking screensavers instead of grey matter?'

'They're wrestlers,' said Alex.

'That's not an explanation,' shouted Sophie, who for once was united with Claire in outrage.

'I don't think it occurred to them that it might *not* be Nate,' Alex expanded. 'It would be a pretty big violation for anyone *but* Nate to put his mask on.'

'Oh my God. Sharon, get me out of this abomination.'

16

Technically Not Breaking and Entering

Getting wrapped up in the SWF had, if nothing else, given Claire a chance to tour the various socioeconomic strata that made up the Brighton and Hove area. Obviously the layer cake that was the city had quite a huge, squishy filling of the middle classes and a dense coating of the upper classes, but poor people still managed to find room around the edges.

Claire had observed previously that Brighton still had some of the weird mix of people you get in seaside towns – that is, retirees and tattoo enthusiasts – but Brighton's status as a London satellite meant there were also a lot of commuter yuppies with shiny hair and bespoke tech companies, and a frankly unstable number of coffee shops. Claire was starting to keep an eye on them, as she grew increasingly suspicious that indie coffee-roasters were the Brighton version of the CandyKing shops on

Oxford Street: you suspected they were a money-laundering front for some flavour of mafia, but you couldn't really prove it.

But she was struggling to figure out where Nate fitted in, based on the front of his house. It was off a street near an historically significant cinema. Claire looked at the street. The houses were compact, terraced and rundown, but in a clean, respectable way that spoke of working-class people who took care to maintain standards that rich people could afford not to care about.

Two up, two down. Probably all the houses would have been quite cheap when Nate's house was bought in the eighties or nineties, but would now command eye-watering prices of the kind that could only be contemplated by career landlords or MPs. But nobody who lived on this street would have sold, if they could help it, Claire thought. Everyone who lived here had been here for years, like furniture.

They weren't really very far from the main trunk road, but the noise from the traffic had disappeared almost entirely.

'Spooky,' said Sophie.

It was, somehow. The street was empty and bathed in sunshine – not unseasonable weather at all, because they were approaching high summer – but it was eerie. Somewhere a badly tuned radio was playing Classic FM with a lot of static, and it made Claire feel unmoored from time. She turned and looked at Sophie. The sunlight was making her dead friend faint and difficult to see, like an old, faded photograph. Claire could see the house on the other side of the street through Sophie and she closed one eye and squinted, because it was like an optical illusion she couldn't turn off. She looked down at her own hand and was surprised to see it was solid, and this was even more unnerving. She turned it over a couple of times, regarding it with suspicion.

'Are you Marty fucking McFly or something?' said Soph, once again able to read Claire's mind.

'I don't think that was his middle name in the films,' she replied.

'Shut up. Let's go, c'mon.' Soph waved her arms at Nate's front door, which was dark green and opened onto the street. His house was an end-of-terrace, sort of, in that it was next to an alley that cut through the terrace halfway down and joined up to the passage that ran between the back gardens of two terraces.

Claire knocked. She knocked several times. She put her face up to the window and cupped her hands around it, then tried to wipe away the smear that her skin left on the glass.

'I don't think he's in,' she said eventually.

Normally at this point Sophie would have walked into the house and had a proper look around, but the new, painful short length of their tether precluded this.

'Well, you never told him you were coming,' said Soph. 'You just tore out of that shop like a blue-arsed fly. But to be fair, if I knew you were coming round, I'd make sure to be out as well.'

Claire's furious and immediate desire to speak to Nate had largely dissipated after the walk to get to his house. 'I guess if he's not in, he's not in,' she said.

'So we're just fucking off home again? We had to come miles to get here,' moaned Sophie.

'Like, two miles,' said Claire.

'Right, more than one mile, which is what I said. Can we not at least see if there's a back garden we can get into? *Please.*'

Claire was unsure about this. On the one hand, she had technically engaged in some breaking and entering before, at Basher and Alex's family home, but she hadn't really been told off for this because she had unearthed a dead body as part of the process. Breaking into the house of a random normal person who, presumably, did not have a body on the premises would definitely warrant a telling-off.

On the other hand, it seemed often to turn out, in real life and on television, that cases are broken by physical evidence found in the suspect's home and if that were to happen, then nobody could be that cross with her. And if it didn't, then she wasn't likely to get caught by the police, because apparently the police basically weren't investigating any of the Kings. Plus, Basher would sort it out and collect them from the station anyway. The greatest danger was Nate coming home and catching her, and he was *literally* quite a large danger.

'Come o-o-o-n-n,' moaned Sophie. 'This so-called investigation has been so boring so far – we never do anything fun. Let's just look.'

'Ugh, fine.'

Claire looked around, presenting as the definition of furtive. If anyone *had* been looking, they would definitely have pegged her as suspicious and made a note of the time, in case at some point in the future they were asked if they'd seen anything out of the ordinary that day.

She assessed the area. Most of the back gardens on the row had gates that opened onto the passage running behind the terraces, but because Nate's home was at the end of the terrace, his garden was bigger and the gate was set into the side. This did at least mean it was marginally less likely someone would see her.

'Act like you're allowed to be here, Weirdo,' said Sophie. She strained at the limits of the tether, almost dragging Claire up to the gate.

Unfortunately for everyone concerned, Nate did not lock his garden gate. The latch lifted without a sound, as if it wanted her to go through. Claire stood perched on the balls of her feet, fearing she might need to run at any second.

The garden was a slightly depressing paved-over square, with the sort of detritus often found in unused garden spaces: a single plastic chair, an old round barbecue, a candy-striped beach windbreaker. But in one corner there was a washing-up bowl with rocks piled carefully around it, and a small log balanced inside. It was full of water. Claire bent over to examine it and was surprised to see a frog staring back at her.

'I think this is one of those, you know, bug-hotel

things,' said Sophie, who was similarly examining a stack of wood and old flowerpots.

They seemed like such caring touches – it felt incongruous. Claire was trying to map it over her understanding of Nate up to this point.

'Well, you've come this far,' said Sophie.

Claire sighed. In her heart she had known that even agreeing to test the garden gate was a given inch to Sophie. She pulled the sleeves of her hoodie down over her hands and looked at the back door. There wasn't a doormat, so that was out. There was a planter half full of dirt and some rocks, and she prodded them until she found the plastic one.

'God, I didn't realize people still did that,' said Sophie. 'Like, surely everyone knows that everyone knows about fake rocks.'

Claire prised the fake rock open while trying to not touch it and leave fingerprints, which was a challenge, and a spare key clattered onto the ground. 'Maybe Nate's just an old-fashioned sort of man,' she suggested.

'Yeah, right. Reckon he keeps all his money in the form of gold bullion stashed underneath a creaky floorboard in his bedroom cos he doesn't trust banks?'

Claire opened the back door and waited for any beeping that would suggest the presence of an alarm, although in fairness to Sophie, the fake rock was an indication that Nate eschewed the more modern kinds of security systems. When, after about thirty seconds, she still couldn't hear anything except the rushing of her own pulse in her ears, Claire crept forward and discovered she was in the kitchen, as evidenced by the hum of the refrigerator and the restrained dining table and chair set that she nearly walked straight into, because the single small window made it strangely gloomy inside. She was in danger of doing permanent damage to her knees during the course of this investigation.

'Light switch is here,' Sophie told her.

Turning it on revealed a room of such scrupulous neatness, and yet such comfortable homeliness, that it could have been on a wholesome renovation show hosted by someone in the genre of Nick Knowles. Every surface was dust-free, and yet the room was crowded with little knick-knacks. The table had a fruit bowl that was clearly made at one of those pottery-painting cafés. The sideboard had a wine bottle in a raffia holder, now repurposed as a candlestick. There was a novelty teapot in the shape of a tiny pub.

'Did we accidentally break into the wrong fucking house?' asked Sophie, looking around her in confusion. She was usually good at reading people – Claire was good at pulling things together into imagined stories, but Sophie was, aha-ha, the coldest of cold readers, so between them they added up to one only mildly incompetent medium – but it was hard to picture the Nate they'd met standing in this house.

'I used a key, so it's only "entering", all right?' said Claire. 'I dunno – people contain multitudes, I guess?'

'Not this many,' replied Sophie. 'You should keep

your voice down, by the way; the walls are probably thin enough for the neighbours to hear, if they're in.'

'It's weird whispering when you're talking at a normal volume,' whispered Claire, although she couldn't really complain, because the perks of being dead were inarguably so few, and anyway 'being able to talk loudly when you're in someone's house' was a side-effect of 'nobody can hear or see you'.

She examined the fridge. It was covered in gaudy 3D magnets from different holidays, mostly destinations that were close by, like Barcelona, Amsterdam, Berlin, and one long haul to San Francisco. There was a shopping list stuck to the fridge that included both tofu and beef.

'What exactly are we looking for?' Claire asked.

'You're the one who loves clues,' replied Sophie. She was evidently growing bored, now that the threat of discovery had waned. 'What about a bottle marked with a label saying, "The poison. The poison for Eddie, the poison chosen especially to kill Eddie – Eddie's poison"?'

Claire gritted her teeth and moved into the other room, which was a similarly homely living room, with a throw blanket on the sofa and a coffee table on which one could imagine placing a huge bowl of popcorn for movie nights in front of an old, creaking flatscreen – the sort of non-HD TV that was thick enough it was almost a CRT. There was a bookshelf of travel books, and DVDs. Everything was old and well used, but equally well looked after. But the living room didn't look like a place where you could easily hide evidence of a terrible murder, either.

The cupboard under the stairs had, at some point, been turned into a tiny toilet with a little fake sprig of lavender in a small vase and a lavender-scented candle that had never been lit, but helped create the illusion that the fake sprig was real. The carpet on the stairs was balding, but as clean as everything else. Nate evidently wasn't rich, but he was house-proud. And why not. It was a nice home.

Upstairs was a bedroom and a proper bathroom, featuring more purple flowers in a vase. Claire compared them to her photograph of wolfsbane.

'Possible Eddie poison located,' she said.

'All right, Special Ops, calm down. That's something, though. Trudy said she didn't give Nate a pot of them, so why does he have them?'

They continued their sweep into a tiny second bedroom that was currently serving as a general gubbins room. There was an empty fishtank and a desk, and a couple of cardboard boxes. Claire pulled her hoodie sleeves down again and opened the desk drawers, but they were empty. She carefully sifted through the boxes, which were filled with the bits of paper that you stash because you have a vague idea you'll need them again in the future. Old MOT forms, a printed-out Covid passport, a playbill from a wrestling show in the nineties.

She picked up a framed picture from down one side of a box. It showed a large group of wrestlers and was the same photo that Lila had shown them. The men's faces were shiny with exertion, and they all leaned on one another or strained their necks to make sure their smiling faces were in the frame. It was a strange collection of costumed men, almost like an extremely aggressive Village People. There was, indeed, someone who appeared to be dressed as a policeman. One man in the front was even wearing a Mexican lucha mask, which must be Nate, Claire now realized.

'He was kind of hot when he was young,' said Sophie. She leaned over with interest and pointed at the much younger Eddie in the middle. 'Like that picture of hot young Stalin, you know?'

'Bleh, he's a pig. If you were alive, you'd set feminism back by, like, thirty years,' replied Claire.

'How dare you! I thought feminism was sex-positive now? That's what Alex always says.'

'Yeah, and I'm positive you shouldn't have sex with gross fuckheads who think girls shouldn't swear,' replied Claire. She replaced the photo. 'There's nothing in here, is there?'

They took a cursory look around the bedroom (comfortable, shades of blue) and Claire opened any drawers she could find, but nothing jumped out. Certainly not any huge packets of rat poison. They headed back down the stairs and Sophie paused as they went past an end-table with a landline, because of course someone who had a fake rock for their back door key also bothered to have a landline phone.

'There's a message pad here,' said Sophie.

Claire looked. It was a little ring-flip book and the pages were nearly all flipped over – which meant there would be a lot of messages recorded on it. 'Have a look through, go on.'

'What about my fingerprints?' Claire replied.

'You completely forgot about that when you were scrabbling through the boxes upstairs like a little trash-goblin,' said Sophie. 'In for a fucking penny, babes.'

Claire tried to ignore a new and burgeoning fear that she would in fact be caught sneaking around someone's house, and started to flip through the message pad. 'There aren't any dates,' she muttered. 'It's hard to track any of it.'

'Keep going. How often do people call each other on a landline? The messages probably go back weeks at least.'

'Hey, look. Here's one.' Sophie leaned in to read it, as Claire ran a finger under the message, written in a neat, rounded hand. It was only a few words long. '"Call Chaz – Eddie. DANGER,"' she read aloud. 'DANGER' had been underlined twice. Sophie opened her mouth, but as she did so, a shadow appeared on the frosted glass in the front door.

Claire started like a cat and looked frantically around. The sound of keys, jangling as someone hoicked them out of their bag, only panicked her further.

'Fucking idiot – this way!' hissed Sophie.

She tapped Claire smartly on the shoulder, and the little jolt brought Claire back into her body. She spun round and ran on her tippy-toes through the kitchen and out of the back door, expecting an outraged shout any second. She heard the front door open as she closed the back door behind her, not bothering to relock it. She crossed the tiny garden area in two and a half strides and struggled to open the back gate as quickly as possible, while making as little noise as she could.

'Come on, come on, if he gets into the kitchen he'll see you through the window,' shouted Sophie.

'Not helping!' hissed Claire. She managed to slip through the gate and close the lock behind her. 'What do I do now?' she whispered.

'Fuck if I know,' replied Sophie. 'Wait, no. Er, don't run. Wait, do. Maybe.'

Claire settled on running out to the main street.

Unfortunately she ran straight into Sami, almost literally. Claire stepped back and began to formulate an excuse. She smiled sheepishly.

Sami looked at Claire with a strange mixture of both anger and sadness. 'Claire Hendricks,' she said, 'you're under arrest.'

17

Almost Solitary Confinement

Claire and Sophie were born-and-bred Londoners. As such, and even without Claire's involvement in other murder cases, they'd had run-ins with the police before. Specifically the Met, whom Sophie said 'were bigger fans of kettles than the PG Tips company'. Even so, Claire had never ended up in a cell before. It was about eight feet by eight, with a vaguely bed-shaped block against the wall opposite the door, on top of which was a sort of wipe-clean blue mattress with an incorporated pillow lump. Because Sophie was also in the cell, it was growing uncomfortably cold, even for Claire. Her breath misted in the air. Thank God she'd been wearing a jumper when Sami picked her up.</NI>

The arrest had been a great betrayal, and Sami had put her in handcuffs, but worse was the fact that she wouldn't even talk to Claire afterwards. Instead she was bundled into the back of a car and eventually presented to a duty sergeant in Brighton nick. He looked incredibly bored. 'There is nothing,' his expression said, 'that you could say or do that would shock me, so don't even bother to try.'

'Suspicion of breaking and entering,' said Sami, and she further outlined that Nate's home was fitted with a silent alarm, which had been tripped when Claire went through the back door – key or no key.

And then Claire had been booked and shown to her new digs. She kept muttering, 'They can only hold me for twenty-four hours' to herself.

'Just wait it out then, Weirdo,' said Sophie. 'They know someone broke in and that you were nearby at the time, but, as things currently are, they can't prove you were the one who did the breaking in.'

'Right, until they check for prints or find a strand of my hair on something in there,' replied Claire.

'Sure, but by that point you'll already be over the Mexican border. You can disappear in Mexico City and then resurface in Rio, where you might even be seen as an exotic and interesting.'

'Shut up,' she said.

'You should keep your voice down,' Sophie replied, amused. 'There are definitely cameras in here recording everything.'

Claire blanched. She hadn't realized that. Had she been talking to Sophie at a normal volume this entire time? She had thought that, when push came to shove, Sami wouldn't actually arrest her. But she had. And now Claire didn't know what would happen. She had visions of being refused bail, being brought before a high-court judge, being sent to real prison and never eating proper Cheddar cheese ever again.

There was a clang on the metal door. 'Hendricks,' called an anonymous policeman, his voice muffled by the thickness of the door, his tone limitlessly bored. 'Phone call.'

Claire got up as he opened the door and shuffled down the hall. There had been a brutally embarrassing moment when the duty sergeant had asked her if there was anyone she wanted to contact, and she hadn't known anyone's number by heart and asked if she could have her phone back to look at it, whereupon she had been allowed and had used a proper corded landline phone, like a grandparent, and had left a message for Basher. She had been too ashamed to say where she was.

'Hello, Claire,' he said now. He sounded distorted and tinny through the handset. 'I am returning your call.'

'Hello. Um, well. So the thing is …'

'I know where you are,' he replied. His voice was flat. Claire couldn't read the tone, exactly. 'I used to work there. I know the number of the custody desk when I see it. And if that were not enough, I also got a phone call from Sami. Do you know how embarrassing this is?'

'Well, yeah, obviously this isn't my proudest moment.'

'An understatement. It is embarrassing for *me*, Claire.' At this point Claire realized that Basher was very angry with her. It wasn't pleasant. She swallowed and found her mouth was suddenly very dry. What happened to calling her 'Strange' and joking about Netflix profiles and inviting her to dinner?

'I told Sami she would not have to worry about you doing anything wildly foolish because I trusted you,' Basher went on. 'I asked you if you trusted me, do you remember? And you said yes. Yet here we are. You appear to have broken into someone's house, convinced of your rightness, convinced that nobody else could possibly have a better grasp of the situation than you.'

'But Sami wasn't investi—'

'Please be quiet. If nothing else, at least if you are not speaking, then you will not say anything that further incriminates you.'

'Are you going to come and get me?' Claire asked. She said it in a very small voice, and she hadn't meant to. It had just slipped out. She was a little girl sitting outside the headmaster's office asking for a parent to save her, but her parents had both kept her at arm's length for twenty years. Now she was in trouble and was asking this kind, quiet man, who did not even know her that well, to reach out and pull a cold child to him and make things be okay.

'I am not. You have been arrested, and they are now able to hold you for twenty-four hours. I am sure that must have come up in one of the ridiculous detective shows you watch.'

'But ... but what do I do?'

Basher sighed. 'Ask for a lawyer, if they interview you. Do not answer any questions without one. Wait to see if you will be formally charged. I will speak to you tomorrow.'

'But ... I thought you'd help. We're friends.'

'Yes, exactly. And it does not seem to have occurred to you that taking people for granted isn't a friendly thing to do.'

He hung up without saying goodbye. Claire wordlessly replaced the handset and turned round, then made a feeble gesture at the desk sergeant.

Sophie had been hovering nearby, unable to hear Basher's half of the conversation. She peppered Claire with questions. 'Was that Basher? What did he say? When are we getting out of here?'

In response, Claire could only shake her head as she was escorted back to her cell. The fact that she thought of it as 'her' cell made her start crying. This seemed like a very trivial thing to start crying over, given everything that had happened up to that point.

'Try and get some sleep, love,' said the policeman.

The door clanged shut. There was a clatter as she was locked in again, which had a horrible finality. Somehow, until Basher had mentioned it, she hadn't considered that she might actually be charged with a crime. Without even having to think about it, Claire was able to conjure half of a conversation where Alex explained that not thinking you'd get into any trouble after breaking into someone's house was a manifestation of privilege, and this was exactly why Claire ought to come to more protests, since she was able to take heat from the police and was more likely to come out the other side unscathed. Claire thought she would much rather be at home, being told off by Alex for not memorizing the number of a lawyer or wearing a mask when participating in direct action, and this made her feel bad and also lonely.

'My toes are cold,' she mumbled. They had taken her trainers, rather than wait for her to unlace them fully. She sat on the bed lump and pulled her knees up to her chest. She'd been given a blanket, so she wrapped that around her and tried to make a little tent out of her own body. When she brought her arms up, she was breathing into the little enclosure formed by the blanket, and she imaged tents filling up with warm breath until the condensation ran down the insides of the canvas.

She closed her eyes and tried to imagine lots of hot things. A shower. Opening the oven while it's still going. Fluffy socks. Big jumpers. A woolly scarf wrapped right around your face. Dogs. The Amazon rainforest: she was in a cave in the Amazon somewhere; it was warm and the air was humid, and just being there was clearing out her sinuses because of the warm, wet air. Yes, nice and toasty.

'I'm fucking *bored*,' said Sophie.

'Well then, this is going to be a long night,' muttered Claire.

'I hate having to sit with you overnight while you sniff and cry,' Soph went on, as if Claire hadn't even spoken.

'I wouldn't be here if you hadn't made me—' she started to say and then cut herself off, remembering what

Basher had said and resolving not to admit to any crimes out loud.

'I didn't make you do anything!' said Sophie. She was indignant. 'I *can't* make you do anything – I literally can't make anyone do anything at all. You did it, you just don't want to take responsibility for any of this.'

'What do you mean "any of this"?' Claire asked.

'You started all this by agreeing to speak to Eddie, and then you escalated it! Nobody thought anything about his death, and you've gone and stirred things up, even though you didn't need to,' said Sophie. 'So that's number one. Number two, you told people you were going to speak to Chaz, so you'd better hope he actually did top himself, because if he didn't, then guess who tipped off his murderer?'

Claire felt a sudden chill in the pit of her stomach. She hunched her shoulders and drew the stiff, coarse blanket closer around her face.

'Sami and Basher both said it wasn't my fault,' she replied quietly.

'Yeah, of course they would. I bet a bunch of people would agree with them. Depends what you mean by "fault", doesn't it? Because I bet other people would say that your actions contributed to Chaz's death.'

Sophie was pacing from one side of the room to the other. She touched one wall, turned, took three strides, touched the other wall, turned, took three strides ... It was like watching a metronome.

'Why are you being horrible?' Claire asked her.

'Because this whole thing has been stupid and annoying. You stuck your nose in where you shouldn't, but then didn't commit; and you pissed off the only people who like you, by assuming you can do whatever you want,' said Sophie. She didn't turn to look.

'You're just making up reasons to be angry at me because you're bored and annoyed that we're stuck in here,' replied Claire.

'So what if I am? Doesn't mean it isn't true. What difference does it make?'

Claire tried to push down the hot feeling behind her eyes. Was it really her fault that Chaz was dead? Did Basher think that? Did Alex?

'It makes a difference whether you believe it or not,' she said eventually.

'You sound like a wellness influencer,' snapped Sophie. 'If we go to prison for any length of time, I will make it my personal quest to destroy any remaining shreds of your sanity.'

'Poetic,' said Claire. She closed her eyes and saw Chaz's chalk-white face, so she opened them almost immediately. There was no window and the lights were permanently on – buzzing fluorescents that made her teeth itch. She slid sideways down the wall like an oil spillage until she was lying down, then rolled over to face the wall, so she couldn't see Sophie pacing. Out of a vague curiosity, and a subconscious desire to check that she still existed, she pressed her palm to the yellowy paint in front of her. Her hand left a slightly greasy, shiny outline. She rocked her head ever so slightly to see it catch the light. Then she wondered if her hand was inordinately greasy – like, greasier than the average hand.

'This is just like you, you know,' Sophie said. 'Screwed everything up and drove away our friends *again*. And basically killed someone.'

'Stop saying that,' Claire hissed. 'I didn't kill anyone.' She stared resolutely at the wall.

'But you admit that you are, once again,' continued Sophie, 'alone.'

'I keep telling you: I'm weird because of you. You're the reason nobody wants to stay friends. I don't know how often you want to have this argument, because it isn't going to change unless you fuck off,' Claire replied. She was half-whispering, still talking into the painted wall in front of her.

'You know what?' said Sophie. Her tone was conversational, but studied. 'I think you probably got me killed as well.'

She had never actually said this before. Claire had always suspected Sophie thought it – if not that specifically, then something the same shape, something that carried the lead weight of responsibility. Claire held her breath, as if doing so would somehow stop time and prevent them from moving into the next moment, which might contain something worse.

'I wasn't there,' she said eventually. Her voice sounded like a dry gasp.

'Exactly,' replied Sophie. 'I asked you to come on that

open day and you didn't, and then I ended up wandering around by myself. It's hard to snatch *two* teenage girls – much harder than snatching one. Who knows where I'd be, if you'd bothered your arse to come with me.'

Claire realized then that Sophie really was saying things to upset her – to properly hurt her feelings. But the absolute worst part was that Sophie knew Claire blamed herself. She had done from the start, from the first day when Claire started being able to see Sophie. Claire had asked if it was her fault, because she thought maybe that was Sophie's unfinished business. Sophie had said no. But now she was picking at it, as if it was a fresh cut and not an old wound – as if the idea had only recently come to her. Claire knew that if she asked Sophie whether she remembered their conversation, from when Claire was scared and seventeen and her attempt at black-winged eyeliner was smudged and pooling under her eyes, Sophie would say no. Sometimes Claire wondered if Sophie was actually not a very good person.

Her breath was starting to mist in the air, Claire noticed. It was condensing on the wall in front of her face. She pulled the blanket up over her nose and then her head, so that she was nearly in darkness, and waited for her nose to warm up. She wanted to ask Alex what they thought about police-custody guidelines, and she wanted Basher to give her a cup of tea. She wanted not to disappoint people for once. She wanted to scream into the blanket, but she couldn't even manage that. She cried into the black void of her own self-loathing.

When Claire woke up, her face was hot and covered with her own hair, which stuck to her mouth. She clawed the blanket away, to find the room much the same. She couldn't tell how much time had passed. She couldn't tell if *any* time had passed. She was uncertain whether she'd been asleep. She felt unmoored. If there was anyone in the cells on either side of her, they were silent. There wasn't even any noise she could hear elsewhere in the building. What if the zombie apocalypse had started, like in *28 Days Later*? She'd never know and she'd starve to death.

Sophie was pacing still. How long had she been doing that?

'What's happening? What time is it?' Claire asked.

'*I* don't know,' replied Sophie. She didn't stop pacing and didn't look at Claire. 'Someone banged on the door about food, but you didn't move. He looked through the little window bit and waited until you snored or something, then he just left.'

'Was it breakfast or di—'

'I have no idea: he didn't read out the Daily Specials, either. It's fucked up, being in here. Alex is right about that prison abolition stuff.'

Claire didn't disagree, but she also thought Sophie was being slightly dramatic, given that they'd been in a cell for less than a day. At least she *hoped* it was less than a day, but maybe the zombies already roamed the country. Claire's parents had taken her to a zoo when she was little, and her dad, who often spoke to children as if they were adults, had told her about a tiger that was kept in a cage at the zoo so small that the only thing it had room to do was pace back and forth. And the tiger eventually went mad and had to be shot. Her father had not understood why this story upset Claire.

'I didn't kill you. And I didn't kill Chaz,' she told Sophie now. She had intended the words to sound decisive, but they came out in a rush.

'Did Chaz appear to you in a dream?' Sophie replied. Still moving. Ceaselessly. It was anxiety-inducing.

'Look. Even the police think Eddie was murdered now, right? But by Chaz.'

'I guess so, yeah. A technical victory for you.'

'But I don't think it makes sense.'

'So you're sticking to the idea that Eddie and Chaz were both murdered by someone else. You think the killer is still at large and may yet kill again?'

'Don't you think that? Wasn't that the point of you being mean to me?'

'If you do what you love, you'll never work a day in your life,' replied Sophie, with a kind of automatic nastiness like scratching an itch; none of the calculated nastiness of the night before. She stopped pacing back and forth and started pacing in a circle around the walls.

Claire shivered. The room was icy cold. Frost had formed on the inside of the door. She retreated to the blanket again.

'It's the timing, more than anything,' she said. 'Chaz agreed to meet me. I was giving him money. And before I show up, he kills himself out of guilt suddenly? He said he had to do something else first, which is why I had to wait a few hours. What if Chaz was trying to blackmail the actual murderer? He'd lost his main income.'

Sophie looked at her. She tipped her head on one side. *Ah, right, so we're not going to talk about it then. Coward.* Claire had often failed this sort of test when they were younger, too. Sometimes Sophie had pushed back because she wanted to feel resistance.

'Right, the small-business profit-skimming,' Sophie said eventually.

'So maybe Chaz is the one who accidentally tipped off his killer, not me.'

'Does that make you feel better?' Sophie asked.

Claire ignored her. 'Plus, Chaz didn't know about Trudy's garden, remember? So he wouldn't have got any poison from there.'

'I mean, we don't *know* the poison came from Trudy's garden,' Soph pointed out. She sounded quite pleased with herself. It was the sort of annoying rules-lawyering that Claire liked doing to *her*.

'No, we don't, but it being a purple flower does suggest that,' Claire said. Something was podding at her brain from the inside out. She wished she had a pen and paper to write things down. She stood up and started pacing as well, hoping the movement would shake something out of her grey matter.

'It's just ... really hard to put it all together. Because all the evidence points to different people.'

'Maybe that's the point,' said Sophie.

'What do you mean?'

'What if the murderer knew they might be implicated somehow, so they flooded the zone with a bunch of other stuff as well. So when the police came calling they wouldn't know where to look.'

'But the police *didn't* come calling,' replied Claire. 'I mean, not until now.'

'Yeah, because Lila cleaned up the crime scene, didn't she?' said Sophie patiently. 'Didn't even know she was doing it.'

'Oh, shit, I see what you're saying. So then the only clue that was picked up on was Nate, and that was picked up on by a dead man, because nobody checked the CCTV.'

'Exactly.'

'But that would mean the killer *wanted* everyone to know Eddie had been murdered. And that, in the words of Gwen Stefani, is B.A.N.A.N.A.S.'

Sophie and Claire looked at each other and were contemplating this, when the door to the cell screamed open again. There was now a uniformed policewoman standing there, the staff overnight having been replaced, and she seemed shocked at the frigid air that blasted from the cell like a freezer.

'Jesus, why didn't you say something?' she stammered. 'If you want to make a complaint, I—'

Claire waved a hand. 'Used to it. Am I being charged now?'

'No, you're being released. No charges. And someone has come to collect you.'

18

Jerking the Curtain

The process of getting released from a night in a police cell was as prescriptive and annoying as being put in one, but more frustrating because you had to do it while putting your shoes back on. There was also a notion that Claire should speak to a duty nurse, on the basis that she kept crying and talking to herself, but the duty nurse couldn't be found quickly enough and then the desk sergeant (also a different one from the night before) got distracted by a phone call.</NI>

'No charges at all?' Claire confirmed, for the nth time.

'Not at this time, although this does not preclude charges being filed in the future. We've been told it was a mix-up, so at this moment I am releasing you from custody.'

'A mix-up? What?' Sophie said. She tried to get a look at the paperwork on the sergeant's desk. 'Who's come to get you? Probably Basher, isn't it?'

Claire signed bits of paper stating that she'd got all her possessions back and that she understood her rights, and so on and so forth, then walked out of the station sheepishly. It was probably like going to hospital for a colonoscopy or something, she thought. They probably see far worse than you on a daily basis and won't be giving you a second thought.

The light outside was very bright. Claire winced and put her hand up to shield her eyes from the sun. Sophie snorted and said, 'All right, Shawshank, fucking hell,' her own extreme agitation at being locked up instantly forgotten.

Claire's mobile phone had run out of battery, but as far as she could tell it was early morning, so she'd been locked up for less than twenty-four hours, but her teeth felt fuzzy and her armpits sour. She looked around for whoever had come to collect her and saw the back window of a pigeon-grey car over the road open. Alex leaned out, without bothering to actually come over.

'Oi!' they shouted, and waved. 'Guess what? I made a break in your case!' They were holding Wyatt, but with difficulty, as she was trying to escape out of the window.

'Shhh!' hissed Claire. She jogged self-consciously over the road. 'I only just got let out. I don't think Sami knows, because otherwise she would have come down to shout at me first. What are you doing here? Did you convince Sami to let me out or something?'

'I can answer both of those questions if you get in the car,' said Alex.

Claire leaned over to see who was in the driver's seat and was extremely surprised.

'Er ...' she said, unsure what else she could possibly say.

'Hello,' replied Nate King, without turning around.

'Should we be alarmed that Alex is hanging around with a – well, if not a murderer, at least someone who was on the scene during a murder? Murder adjacent. Strongly implicated in a murder, type of person?' Soph said, although she sounded broadly unconcerned herself.

'Me and Nate get on all right,' said Alex with a grin. That wasn't necessarily an endorsement, because Alex got on well with most people until they decided they shouldn't.

Claire met eyes with Nate. Once again she had the sense that the man was changing gears.

'What is it you had to show me?' she asked. 'I was thinking very seriously about getting some chips with curry sauce, so it had better be good.'

'Just get in! I promise, it'll be worth your time,' said Alex. They pulled out their phone guiltily. 'Plus, if I'm honest, we have limited time before Uncle B finds out about this, so it'd be good to move things along.'

Claire dithered for a couple of seconds, but eventually did as she was told, sitting in the back next to Alex and watching Nate in the rear-view mirror. Sophie crawled into the front passenger seat and turned around to watch Alex, who reached between their feet and produced a shoebox. They tossed it towards Claire and then said,

'Oh, arseholes!' because the lid wasn't on properly and it tumbled over, spilling what Claire at first thought were dozens of rose petals all over the back of the car.

'They took fucking ages to collect,' grumbled Alex.

'What are we looking at here?' asked Soph. 'A gimp's wedding night?'

It did look a bit like confetti. Claire picked one up cautiously. It was leather – scores of pieces of red leather, or some plasticated approximation of it. At first she thought all the bits were the same size, about two inches long, but when she looked inside the shoebox she saw larger strips, some with obvious lines where stitches from seams used to be before they were pulled apart. She picked up a piece and noticed it had a white triangle on it.

'Alex,' she said cautiously. 'What is this?'

'It's the secret project I've been working on,' they replied. There was more than a note of smugness in their voice. 'You know they had me going through these boxes of clothes? I found some of these bits in the first box and just sort of … naturally collected them together. But then I found some in a second box. And a third. Every box I looked in. And I thought that was weird, so I started hunting for them specifically, because I got a hunch about what they were, but I didn't want to say anything in case I was wrong.'

Wyatt started snuffling around, and Alex scrambled over to stop her eating anything she shouldn't. 'Look, you can put them together, like a jigsaw.' They clamped Wyatt in one hand and took the piece of pleather Claire was holding in the other. Then they hunted around until they found some other pieces that also had flashes of white. Alex laid them out on the empty middle seat and pushed them into configuration until Claire was looking at a white star.

'Oh, you've got to be fucking kidding,' said Sophie.

Claire became aware that something was supposed to have dawned on her at this point, but it had not. She looked at Alex and felt somewhat embarrassed by this.

'Er. Sorry, I still don't get it,' she said.

'Ohmigod, you're hopeless,' huffed Sophie.

Alex rolled their eyes in a manner that was startlingly similar to Sophie and spent some moments slotting more bits of material into place. These had metal eyes in them. For laces.

'Oh my God,' she said at last. 'It's his fucking boots, isn't it? The smoking shoe!'

She looked at Nate. He was sitting quietly, hands at ten and two on the wheel and was not watching, in a resolute way that suggested he was not watching very deliberately.

'Hello? Nate?' she said. He didn't move.

'Be more assertive, Weirdo,' said Sophie.

Claire wasn't sure how assertive one should be with a potential murderer. She reached forward and tapped him on the shoulder.

'Oi! World's greatest method-actor! Did you do this?'

'Steady on, C,' said Alex, as Wyatt squirmed. 'I don't think Nate had anything to do with it. And I said you'd hear him out.'

Claire looked towards Nate again and to her surprise he was crying, in a silent, stoic, manly sort of way, as a Viking would cry at his dog's funeral.

'Well, he's not fucking saying anything,' she replied, although she was aware that sounded mean.

'He's a bit upset. They did his mask and everything,' said Alex. 'No need for it.'

'Oh, for—' exclaimed Claire, all human empathy having deserted her, in her annoyance. 'Are you crying for your brother or for your stupid gear?' she asked.

'I'll never wrestle again!' cried Nate.

'Well, that fucking answers that, doesn't it?' said Sophie.

'All right,' said Claire. 'Let's start from the beginning.'

They had decamped to Nate's house, at his insistence, and Claire was in two minds about texting Basher to let him know what was going on. She felt he would have strong views about the whole situation. It was possible he was going to storm in at any moment with a whole SWAT team behind him. He didn't look like he had the arm strength to swing through a window on a rope dropped from a helicopter, though. Claire wondered absently if regular police detectives had to take fitness tests, like doing the bleep test in the gym. She hadn't had to do that, because Sophie didn't want to, so they'd hid in the drama classroom, behind the old sets for *Grease*.</NI>

Claire was also extremely weirded out by the fact that she had, less than a day earlier, broken into this very house. She didn't know how she was supposed to act, but had a vague impulse to compliment the home, so kept saying things like 'What colour do you call these walls?', which was making Sophie say things like, 'I hate you, you're so embarrassing' in response.

They sat around the kitchen table and Nate offered them tea, and Claire watched him very carefully in case he put ricin or something in it, because she felt that, as a good detective, she shouldn't clear him as a suspect yet. Probably she should have refused the tea entirely, but she did really want a cup.

'When we were kids ...' Nate began.

Sophie immediately drowned him by shouting, 'Fuck off, Benjamin Button, don't start at the literal beginning!', which made Claire wince. This made Nate stop.

'Er, sorry,' said Claire. 'Is it necessary to go that far back? That's quite a long way. Actually, wait: my first thing first. Do you believe in ghosts?'

'Unusually direct for you,' said Alex, almost under their breath.

'Yes, I do,' replied Nate.

'Okay. So, um, the thing is, I'm followed around by one all the time. Her name is Sophie and she's here now, and she's quite impatient.'

'Only when people are being stupid,' said Sophie. She considered this to be most of the time.

'Oh. Right,' said Nate. He seemed slightly taken aback. There is, after all, a difference between saying you believe in ghosts and accepting that one is in front of you, making unheard judgements about your method of storytelling.

'Yeah. So I can repeat what she says, when she says something. And she doesn't want you to start that far back. That's all I'm saying,' replied Claire. She tried to look appropriately apologetic about Sophie.

'I'm not going to explain our entire childhoods,' said Nate. 'But some of the context is important. So, when we were kids, Eddie and I got on really well. Our mum was a housewife and Dad was in construction, but he got fucked during Right to Buy. You'd think that'd make him a socialist, but he was a true-blue Thatcherite all the way. It was a *traditional* family, is what I'm saying. And Eddie was a traditional man.'

'Right,' said Alex. 'I know what that's code for.'

The sound of the front door opening floated through to the kitchen, with a lack of urgency that indicated it hadn't been kicked in by Alex's concerned uncle. Claire leaned back in her chair and waited. The kitchen door swung open and a tall white man, with greying hair and the kind of musculature that indicated he was a normal person and not a wrestler, walked in. He was wearing a crumpled suit.

'Hello, love,' he said. He pecked Nate on the cheek and then turned to put some shopping in the fridge. Nate was watching Claire for a reaction.

'This is Oscar. I already told Alex about him,' he said. 'But you don't look surprised.'

'I'm not really,' replied Claire. 'It was pretty obvious you don't live alone.' She panicked, having said this. 'Sorry. I looked around. You've got a message pad by your phone, but people rarely leave messages for themselves when they answer a call. And your food list on the fridge has beef *and* tofu on it, which I suppose might be a protein-bulking thing, but ...' *And there are two toothbrushes in your upstairs bathroom, and two sets of clothes in your wardrobe, and so on*, she finished to herself, not wanting to reveal exactly how much rummaging around Nate's personal effects she'd done.

'Hey, nice work, Weirdo!' said Sophie, who had actually been surprised. 'Noticing stuff is usually my job. Don't start getting too good at it. Although if I had a nickel for every time a case has involved a man that I didn't realize was gay, I'd have two nickels, and all that.'

Three, thought Claire, remembering that it had taken several weeks for either of them to realize Basher was gay.

'But no pictures or anything,' said Alex. 'Nothing you can't explain away if someone drops in.'

'Yeah, dude's home is like a Marvel movie, ready to edit for foreign markets,' added Sophie. Claire did not repeat this.

Oscar sighed and closed the fridge. He turned and leaned against the kitchen sideboard, his mouth a line as he pressed his lips closed

'When I spoke to Trudy and mentioned the rumour that you two were having an affair, she laughed like it was the funniest thing she'd ever heard,' added Claire. 'So I'm guessing she knows as well.'

'She's the only one. She dropped round once without asking and walked in while we were making lunch, all couple-y,' said Nate. He was staring at the woodgrain on the table. 'I was terrified she'd tell Eddie, but she never did. I guess she understood why I hadn't. If I told any of the wrestling gang – even though I know loads of them wouldn't care – it would get about. Nobody there can keep secrets. I'd managed to get a house far away, so people wouldn't drop in on the off-chance, and I kept myself to myself, kept up the kayfabe. If Eddie heard about it ... I'm just ... scared of him.'

Still, Claire thought. Ingrained fear.

'I knew it was a part of me he wouldn't accept. And, worse, he would make it into a fucking storyline in the ring. We discovered wrestling at the same time, you know: Giant Haystacks and that generation of wrestlers. I was so – I dunno what you'd say. Mesmerized, I suppose. Right from the start. I love wrestling, partly because it lets me be a different Nate. I can be angry, I can fight'

'That's not who you are, Nan,' said Oscar suddenly. He came up behind Nate and leaned over him as he sat, put an arm around Nate's chest.

'Cute little pet-name,' said Soph. 'They've been together a while. Oscar must be very patient. Or love him a lot.'

Why not both? thought Claire.

Nate squeezed Oscar's arm. 'I know. But that's why I prefer to keep my wrestling separate from the real me. It protected me to compartmentalize. I learned about the lucha libre tradition, with the masks – that just made sense to me. I went down there for a couple of years in my twenties and trained properly to earn the right to be a luchador, and that helped me. But when I met Oz and we got serious, I wanted to say something,' he went on. Oscar moved to sit by him, frowning slightly. 'And after Eddie died, it was a weird mix of feelings. I was sad, but I started to feel safer. When Alex turned up, I watched them and they're so, you know, *out*. Just so confident in who they are – too bloody confident sometimes, if you ask their head injury – that it made me think it was worth doing.'

'Oh, don't,' replied Alex, fending off the tangential praise. 'Coming out is worth doing, but it's very personal. You do it whenever it's right for you. Are we not all on our own unique journeys of growth and self-acceptance?'

'Well, then it turned out that, according to you, I was a suspect in Eddie's murder, which I didn't even know was a bloody murder,' grumbled Nate. 'And it didn't feel like it was a good time. Oz kept saying I should talk to you, but that felt like it'd give you ammunition. And then Chaz died too …'

Nate leaned forward suddenly, towards Claire. 'I didn't have anything to do with it, I swear. My gear went missing ages ago: that's what I tried to tell you – everyone knows I don't wrestle without it, and I haven't wrestled in months. I even told Eddie! So when you were arrested after breaking in here, Alex called me and said to talk to you. I told the police you were a friend of mine that Oz didn't know, and that you'd set the alarm off by accident, so they let you go.'

'You make a compelling case,' replied Claire slowly. 'But we think Eddie was poisoned with wolfsbane flowers, and you have some of them upstairs.'

'They're from Trudy! She always brings some flowers from her little garden when she visits,' Oz interjected.

'But they're here, nonetheless,' said Claire.

'Well, it's only the flowers, not the roots,' Alex reminded her. 'The roots are the more poisonous part.'

'How about this: I can alibi Nate,' said Oz. 'He was with me that night. We watched The *NeverEnding Story* and went to bed early, and I was just leaving for work the next morning when Trudy called with the news.'

'Well, he would say that, wouldn't he? They're in love, and everything,' said Soph.

'I think it has something to do with Chaz,' pressed on Nate, sensing that Claire believed him. 'He called here the day he died, but I was out and Oz answered.'

'Chaz told me that he needed Nate to call him back as soon as possible because it was looking dangerous, and he wanted to talk about Eddie. I thought it was a figure of speech,' said Oz. 'Like when someone says things are getting tasty. After he died, we told the police of course.'

'The thing is, I think I worked out why Chaz left. Or why Eddie kicked him out, I should say.'

Claire rubbed a hand over her face absently. 'He was stealing, yeah. What has that got to do with Eddie dying?'

'Okay, how did you work *that* out?' exclaimed Alex.

'Eddie told us, but it was pretty obvious anyway. He and Nate were scraping by, but Chaz had a nice house;

Lila got lovely presents throughout her childhood; Chaz was helping her with rent, while she fannied about making chocolates,' said Sophie, ticking the items off on her hand. 'Plus, he stopped trying to get back the money he'd put up to buy the SWF.'

Claire repeated all this and Nate nodded. 'You – I mean, your ghost friend – is right. We left the accounts side of things to Chaz, because he said he had a head for numbers and that suited us, cos we didn't. It was all cash in hand anyway, specially in the early days. I was looking through things, and I'm no expert, but I think Chaz was skimming the whole time. What I don't know is why Eddie didn't tell anyone after he found out! I think Chaz knew something that he traded, tit-for-tat: you keep quiet about the money, I'll keep quiet about your thing.'

'Yeah, duh. That's obvious. And I bet we know what that was,' said Soph.

'Right. I'm supposed to be doing a sort of performative seance at the SWF tomorrow, and I think I sort of have a plan. But it's very stupid. Partly because I don't know what saging is, or how to do it.'

'Isn't it called smudging?' asked Sophie.

'I mean, I think that's a specific Native American ritual where you burn sage, whereas obviously I'm just going to burn sage and wave it around a bit,' replied Claire absently. 'Alex, I'm going to need your help especially.'

Alex frowned. 'Why me?'

'The thing about this is that the whole time I thought the killer was trying to hide the murder,' said Claire, talking to herself. 'But we just realized it was the opposite. Where their plan went wrong was in it *not* being found out. They wanted the drama. So it's someone with access to the flowers, access to your wrestling costu— gear, sorry. Someone who wants their potential recognized, and to feel clever.' Claire sighed, very heavily. 'I mean it really only leaves one person, doesn't it? And they're a very annoying person to have done it.'

19

The Show Must Go On

It was show night at the SWF. Claire was backstage, regretting every decision she had made that had led her to this point. But, as with many of her favourite Golden Age detective stories, she was in a situation where she knew who had committed the murder, but had no solid evidence for it. Everything was circumstantial, so the play they had left was to force the killer into a confession by putting them under psychological pressure. As has often been observed, despite being used in virtually every episode of a detective show ever produced in the history of broadcast television, in the real world this is not a good or reliable plan. But it was all she had to work with.</NI>

The larger problem Claire had now was that the plan hinged on Eddie cooperating – a trait that came as naturally to him as it did to a grizzly bear in feeding season. She was wandering around backstage trying to find him while holding a rather limp bundle of herbs that, similarly, was refusing to do its job of filling the halls with vaguely mystical smoke. Claire waved it around half-heartedly whenever anyone looked in her direction, but given that the only dried sage Basher had to hand was in small Sainsbury's jar form, she was left with some sticks of rosemary and thyme and some sprigs of fresh basil. Thus she had less of the air of a spirit-sensitive medium and more that of a home cook who had lost most of her roast.

'That fucker is avoiding us still,' she muttered to Sophie.

'I don't think he's even doing it because he's embarrassed,' said Sophie. 'I think he's doing it on purpose to be a prick, because you didn't bring him Nate's head, like he ordered.' They were passing the locker room again and Claire stuck her head in. There was no sign of Eddie, but Alex was there in some baggy black joggers doing some cursory stretches – pulling one elbow over their ear with the opposite hand and that sort of thing. They grinned and gave Claire the thumbs-up, but they looked nervous. Half a room and about a dozen semi-nude bodies away, Nate was sitting on a bench, leaning forward and staring intently at the floor. He was too zoned in on the tiles to notice Claire. But they were both in place, which meant the whole thing rested on Claire finding and convincing Eddie, and she was running out of time to do that.

She backed out and thudded into something.

'It's the Ken doll,' said Sophie, eyeing King Jr.

Claire turned and had a brief moment of panic that Ken might be about to throw her out. He looked less affable than normal, but possibly that was just the stress of show night.

'All ready for your bit tonight?' he asked.

Claire controlled herself. She kept forgetting, or maybe blocking out for self-preservation, that she was technically a performer that evening. She had asked to see the call sheet in the locker room earlier, and people had laughed at her for calling it a 'call sheet'. But in approximately ninety minutes she would be onstage, pretending to do an exorcism on Eddie's spirit.

A cloudy shape loomed out of the hallway behind Ken. It was Lila's enormous clown wig.

'We want everything to go smoothly tonight, don't we?' she said, looking significantly at Claire.

'Yeah. Actually, could I talk to you for a second? It's, uh, a girl thing,' replied Claire, employing a tactic that had always previously worked on insecure heterosexual men and confused PE teachers.

Lila looked at Ken automatically. 'Go ahead, babe,' he said. 'Just come back sharpish for the final checks. All good with you, Claire?'

'It's, um, going to be fine. Yeah. Looking forward to it,' said Claire. She glanced over her shoulder. 'I can't find Eddie, so it might be a very quiet exorcism.'

Ken breathed out. 'Honestly, I hope this place is ghost-free when you're done. It's a bit unnerving, isn't it? We all want to move on.'

Sophie stuck her tongue out at him. Ken walked into the locker room, and Claire grabbed Lila by the elbow and dragged her down the hallway, so they were out of earshot.

'This is your last chance to tell the truth, you know that?' she said. 'I'm so fed up with all of you. Were you not going to say that Eddie was your – you know – lover.'

Lila's face crumpled.

'God, "lover" is such a skeevy word,' said Sophie. 'Outside a romance novel, it makes you sound like an old-fashioned pervert.'

'What, would you prefer I said "fuckbuddy" instead?' snapped Claire, without thinking.

Sophie merely laughed, but Lila tensed up.

'You don't need to be rude,' she said. 'Obviously if nobody found out, then no, I wasn't going to fucking tell anyone.

'I know – I just like it,' said Sophie, grinning, as if Lila could hear her.

'Sorry,' Claire replied. 'That wasn't … I started this whole thing in good faith, and everyone's been fucking lying to me. Sorry. You could have said from the start and it would have been way easier.'

'Yeah, saying, "I was actually there because I'd been shagging my boyfriend's dad for the better part of eighteen months" would have made a brilliant impression,' said Lila. 'Fucking hell. I told you *most* of the truth.' For a moment she looked keyed up, fists clenched, mouth open, with white teeth showing. Then she deflated and put her face in her hands. 'God, I'm so fucking tired. I can't cry. This fucking make-up.'

'How did it start?' Claire asked. It had been quite easy to break Lila, as far as interrogations went. On TV, they implied it took hours of shouting and refusing to call lawyers.

'Like I told you,' replied Lila. She looked around quickly, but although wrestlers were passing in and out of the locker room further down the hall, nobody was paying her any attention. 'I was struggling with my gimmick; Ken and I were fighting about it a lot. And then Eddie started being really nice to me, he began giving me tips and we really did do some after-hours training. And one thing led to another.'

'No, no, no, I'm going to need a bit more than that,' said Sophie. 'You can't explain it away with "one thing led to another", when one of the things in question is a middle-aged overweight ham-man's penis – I'm sorry. Eddie's known her since she was a baby, for fuck's sake. These people are unhinged!' Sophie was working herself up. 'There are no hinges! Anywhere to be seen!'

'Uh, right. I mean, I sort of can see ... where you're coming from. I suppose I'm a bit stuck on ... It doesn't seem like a healthy dynamic, does it?' said Claire, in an attempt to translate Sophie's rage into a more Radio 4 mental-health panel-discussion language. 'And you're young and attractive, and Eddie's—' Claire stopped herself from saying anything about ham. 'He doesn't strike me as a particularly sensitive lover,' she finished.

Lila made a face. 'I won't go into details. I can't pretend to explain it, and yes, you're right, it was incredibly unhealthy, as you put it. I'd say I'm going to be talking about this in therapy for years, but I can't fucking afford therapy, can I? And the thing is, I don't even know how to feel about Eddie dying. Sometimes I'm sad, because I thought we were close and he cared about me. I thought he was going to leave Trudy!'

'Fuck me, that's one awkward Christmas dinner, isn't it?' observed Sophie.

'But it turned out he was only doing it for the wrestling. We had a big fight. I think I hated him when he died. It's a mess.'

'I don't understand: how could he have been doing it for the wrestling?'

'"Personal issues draw money",' said Lila. 'Remember? We've been telling you the whole time.

'So, wait, you're saying that Eddie, like ... I dunno, let's say he seduced you, because I don't have anywhere near the qualifications needed to diagnose this whole thing,' went on Claire, who had decidedly mixed feelings about whether or not she should just allow Eddie to stay trapped in his gym and gradually watch everyone forget him. 'Eddie seduced you to get a storyline out of it and make the in-ring drama more believable?'

'Weegie Pro had been winning the feud with SWF,' said Lila. 'Eddie and Ken got in a bust-up about it. Ken said Eddie was too old-school, and the sorts of storylines he was booking were dying a death. It was a proper knock-down, drag-out fight as well. They didn't speak to each other for a few days afterwards.'

'That must have been the fight that made Eddie change his will,' suggested Sophie. 'Remember, he said it was about the future of the company: that's what made him do it. I love it when stuff starts falling into place.'

'So an affair with you – that was Eddie being old-school?'

Lila nodded. 'Really vicious as well, although I didn't know it at the time. He was going to reveal it in-ring and book a bunch of feuds leading off from it – see who ended up hating who, who reconciled, all of that. I guess writing is less hard when you're just transcribing reality. "Personal issues draw money".'

'And that's a pretty fucking huge personal issue right there,' said Sophie.

'Really? He'd destroy everyone's lives for *that*?' asked Claire, still in disbelief.

'Others have done way worse,' said Lila. She twisted her lip. 'For what it's worth, I think Eddie massively miscalculated. It wouldn't have blown up the SWF, it would have taken it down. Torn the family apart and lost fans. It's a shit business.'

'Then why are you still in it?' asked Claire. She was genuinely curious.

Lila half-smiled. 'It's a great business too. There's nothing like it. For ill, but also for good.'

'And so, wait. Eddie *told* you all of this?'

'Yeah. That night. We'd been … together, and afterwards I asked him where things were headed one too many times and he blew up on me, told me it was all a work. From his point of view, anyway. It was like listening to a fucking Bond-villain monologue. I don't think it was part of his plan to tell me that early, and I was fucking furious and upset. But it's not like I could do anything.'

Lila lapsed into a deep silence. She gave a very different third impression than second or first, Claire thought. When they'd first met, Claire had assumed Lila was weak-willed and naive and, honestly, a bit daft. But it was becoming clear that Lila was one of the smarter people out of everyone Claire had met while investigating this case. In an industry still as dominated by loud, bull-necked, thick-bellied men as pro-wrestling, it wouldn't do to be obviously smarter than them.

'I knew nobody cleans up a dead body out of embarrassment,' said Claire. 'Unless there's really something to be embarrassed about.'

Lila sighed. 'When Eddie collapsed, I tried chest compressions. I honestly did. But I don't know how to do them. And he had said he was going to tell everyone!'

'So she didn't call an ambulance because she realized: "Well, shit, the massive fucking problem I had sixty seconds ago has just solved itself",' said Sophie. 'She got rid of the Viagra and hightailed it out of there. I like her way more now, you know.'

'What are you going to do?' asked Lila, anxiously. 'Are you going to tell Ken?'

'Hey! Lila!' Ken shouted from the locker-room entrance. 'Come on!'

'Are you going to do something? Claire?' hissed Lila.

Claire backed away from her and shook her head.

Sophie watched Lila scuttle back to the dressing room. 'Does she think that to exorcise a spirit you have to list everyone he has slept with, starting with the most recent?' she scoffed.

I mean, you might, thought Claire, who had the same general experience of Catholicism that most irreligious-but-technically-C-of-E English people had – i.e. the theme for horror films.

Claire waited for Lila and Ken to disappear through the open doorway and then stalked back towards the end of the hallway closest to the main entrance. She had borrowed a diaphanous black skirt from Alex, to look more like a stagey medium, and while she wasn't sure it really went with the slouchy sage cardigan, she did enjoy the sort of Grim Reaper aspect.</NI>

'If we can't find Eddie, this whole plan is fucked,' said Sophie.

'Yeah, I know – you don't need to keep saying,' said Claire.

She pressed her ear to the door separating her from the people pouring through the entrance into the main gym floor. She could hear all the rustling – a nest of chittering little insects scraping on metal as they took their seats. She opened the door a crack to peek through. It was the expected mix of alt kids and beefy boys, passing by her in a steady stream.

'Well, at least the cops have turned up,' said Sophie. 'But, honestly, that isn't going to count for much if Eddie isn't on board.'

Claire strained her eyes and eventually spotted Sami leaning up against the back wall, almost directly opposite. It had taken a few seconds to find her, because she was blending into the crowd in a more complete way than Claire had thought possible for a mum-of-two police detective who, prior to recent murder events, had known absolutely nothing about professional wrestling. She looked relaxed and was wearing a T-shirt that said 'AUSTIN 3:16', which was, crucially, an old, worn T-shirt, and as Claire watched, Sami peeled away from the wall with nonchalance, as if she'd just spotted the seat she wanted to take. Claire had no idea if Sami had seen her or not. She was quite impressed.

'Okay,' she muttered. 'One last job to do, and then we really have to find Eddie.'

She slipped out and joined the river of people, then left the current again as she got to the tech booth, where the young man who did the lighting and sound (for free, she had been told; for the love of the game) was busy looking at a clipboard.

'Um, hi,' she said, but so quietly that he didn't hear her. 'HELLO!' she tried again, this time far too loud, startling some nearby punters. Sophie was looking at her with an eyebrow raised, confident that she didn't even need to *say* the word 'Weirdo' out loud.

'What is it? We're super-busy,' said the lighting man.

'Um, hi, sorry. Yeah, I know. Nate asked me to pass this on to you. It's a VT from the, er, people at Weegie. You're supposed to play it before the final, um, match-thing tonight.'

The man looked at her. 'That looks like ... some sort of very sad bouquet.'

'Wrong hand, sorry,' said Claire, retracting her bundle. She was at least grateful that the low light of the room covered up her embarrassed blush. 'I meant this.' She brandished a USB stick.

'It's from Weegie? Ken didn't say anything about this,' replied the man, looking sceptical.

'Yeah, I know; it's, ah, setting up the next storyline with them. It was only recently agreed,' said Claire, trying to sound confident. 'It's not long, so it won't push everything out of schedule,' she added.

'Just a straight VT?' he enquired, holding his hand out.

'Yes! Yeah,' replied Claire, relieved. She handed the USB over. 'House-lights down, no music.' She gave him a thumbs-up, which she immediately regretted because she felt it probably made her look like a secondary-school teacher trying to be cool, then hurried off.

'I don't want to alarm you,' said Sophie. 'But I still haven't caught a glimpse of that dead shithead, LOL.'

Claire tried to bring a boot down on her rising panic. And then she heard a familiar, annoying noise: '*WOAH! RO-ROW-OW-OWWWW!*' Followed by, almost like it was a pantomime, someone saying, 'Who brought a fucking *dog*?'

'The cavalry!' shouted Sophie. 'Towards the entrance, look!'

Claire looked towards the front, but struggled because she was now heading in the opposite direction from everyone else and progressed with the continual mantra of 'Sorry, 'scuse me, sorry, can I just, sorry.' She looked around, frantic, but could not see Basher until she almost ran into him. He was in a faded grey hoodie, which turned him into a shadow. The combination of that and his grey eyes, blond hair and pale skin made him look like a black-and-white photo of a normal man. She glanced at him for a second, then grabbed Wyatt's lead out of his hands, with no explanation.

'Yes, hello, thank you!' he said, as she began to head back the other way. 'Can you at least assure me that Alex is not going to *die* in front of me tonight?' he called after her.

'Not really!' she yelled back.

Back in the relative quiet of the hallway, Claire was left with a confused and extremely angry small dog. Soph narrowed her eyes and crouched down so that she was facing Wyatt, who promptly tried to bite her face. Claire had to wrap the lead around her arm to stop Wyatt choking herself as she lunged forward.

'No, listen here, you useless disgrace of a genetically neutered wolf,' hissed Sophie. 'I know you can hear me, so you sit. Sit!' She flicked at Wyatt's nose and the dog, alarmed, promptly sat. 'Good. Now I don't like you and you don't like me, but we both have the same goal right now, which is to find your old owner and shout at him. So come on. Find him! Find Eddie! Where's Eddie? Where's Eddie?'

Wyatt got up and started dancing fretfully from paw to paw. She spun and got tangled in her lead, whined, spun some more, tried to dig into the wall and paced back and forth, while Sophie continued to berate her.

'I dunno if this is the best—' Claire started to say, when suddenly Wyatt stopped, dog-eyes dilated, and sniffed the air. Then she whipped forward and dragged the lead out of Claire's grip, leaving her with rope-burn in her hand.

'Thar she blows!' shouted Sophie triumphantly, as Wyatt pelted down the corridor.

'Oh my God,' said Claire. She was largely panicked that she was about to have to run. Chasing after a dog seemed like the ultimate slapstick indignity. She hitched up her skirt and gave chase, with Sophie pulling ahead at the very limit of the tether.

Wyatt stopped abruptly at the end of the corridor, and Claire nearly ran into Sophie's back. The little dog put her nose down and sniffed in a spaghetti-squiggle all around, tried to run into the wall again and then headed off back the way she had come. This process repeated itself several times, with Wyatt leading them back and forth, until they had managed to work their way right around the horseshoe corridor and into the main office. Wyatt began scratching at the door and Claire opened it, hoping the room would be empty, seeing as it was mostly surplus to requirements on show nights. But it was not.

'Hello, love,' said Trudy. She was sitting in the desk chair, gripping the arms. Wyatt ran over to her and Trudy picked her up. 'Aw, dolly bird. It's been a while. Give me a kiss.' Wyatt obligingly licked Trudy's face with great enthusiasm, which made Claire wonder what it tasted like, because it looked like it would taste of table varnish.

'Um, hello,' said Claire. 'What are you doing here?'

'Nate invited me,' said Trudy. 'Do you know, I haven't been to a show in decades. I suppose it makes sense that I'd come back after Eddie died.'

'I know Nate invited you,' replied Claire, thinking as she spoke. She looked around a little gingerly. She looked at Sophie and made wide eyes, but Sophie shrugged. 'I was wondering why you were in here, specifically?'

'I can't feel him,' said Trudy. She was still stroking and cuddling Wyatt, and it was almost like she was talking to the dog instead of Claire. 'I wanted to know if I could sense him. But I can't. Is Eddie here?'

'I can't *see* him,' replied Claire, deploying one of her patented technically-not-a-lie half-answers.

Trudy looked at Wyatt and planted a little kiss on the end of her snoot. 'You know what they say about ghosts – about people watching over you after they're gone?' she said.

'Um, yeah.'

'Is that true? Will he be able to watch me? When I've moved, when I get on with my life, will he be watching?'

'No,' answered Claire. 'He'll never be able to see you again. Unless you come into this building.'

Trudy gazed into Wyatt's eyes. Her fingers stopped stroking the little bullet head and her own expression glazed over a little. Finally she smiled.

'Good,' she said. She stood, gave Wyatt another little cuddle and put the dog down, before she strode to the office door.

'I dunno if she's going to get out of this night as drama-free as she's expecting,' commented Sophie.

As Trudy grasped the doorknob and opened the door to leave, Eddie suddenly materialized near Claire and took two long strides towards his widow, his face such a deep shade of furious puce that Claire worried it might be possible for a ghost to have a heart attack.

'Don't you turn your back on me, you—'

He stretched his hand out, but Sophie had managed to grab the back of his towel as he passed, and she tugged him back. His fingers nearly brushed Trudy's hair and Claire thought she saw Trudy suppress a shiver, but she did not look back – not even a glance – and the door slammed shut in Eddie's furious face. He spun round to Sophie, and Claire thought she saw his forearm twitch upwards a fraction, an instinctive move that he managed to stamp down on at the last second.

Soph didn't budge an inch. 'Make your move, *Mister* King,' she said. She managed to say 'Mister', the full two syllables, in a way that was suffused with such utter contempt that it was clear what she'd actually done was call Eddie King a pathetic little loser. Eddie seemed to be considering how to respond. He was breathing like a sow in labour, but the red of his face was gradually transitioning from strawberry to strawberry-milkshake, which Claire took as an encouraging sign.

'You've been avoiding us,' she said. 'Presumably because we found out how many people hate you and didn't do what you said, viz. getting Nate arrested, am I right?'

'Fat lot of good you were,' snorted Eddie. His jovial, boisterous manner as the head of a wrestling troupe had, Claire realized, sloughed off him, the longer she'd known him, with each conversation they'd had discarding another layer and revealing a little more of his unpleasant centre. Right now Eddie King was almost all dickhead, which made Claire slightly worried for the night's events. What was the morality, she wondered, of helping to solve the murder of a horrible bastard? What difference would it make, cosmically? Most everyone was happy that Eddie was gone. Maybe leaving his ghost to slowly and impotently suffer a gradual dimming of consciousness was bad form, but on the other hand, Claire wasn't exactly sure how much a ghost was a 'person'. It would have been useful if there was an episode of *Star Trek* about it, where Picard wrestled with the moral quandary of ghosts and did a good philosophical speech at the end.

But the thing was: Chaz had also been killed. And that was pretty morally unambiguous. So Claire was selling the evening's plan to herself as like teaming up with a baddie to catch another baddie – a feature of pop culture of some standing.

'Well, we found out who fucking killed you, idiot, if you still care about that,' said Sophie. 'But we don't have evidence that we can take to the police, because you got turned into a bag of cat litter, and nobody saw anything. So we have a plan to provoke the killer into confessing.'

Eddie narrowed his eyes and looked between them both, his bobbing head like that of a bloodhound wondering which animal to chase down. 'What sort of plan?'

'Well, I don't think you're going to like it,' admitted Claire. 'In fact you're probably going to hate it. But it involves you wrestling again.'

20

Worked into a Shoot

Claire waited nervously at what everyone at SWF called the 'stage door', a term that would – applied as it was to a pop-up curtain – draw the scorn of any Broadway revival cast you cared to name. There wasn't a stage manager with a clipboard making sure everyone hit their specific cue at the right time; rather, she had been told to wait until the wrestlers from the second-to-last match came off and then hang around listening until she was mentioned – at which point she was to glide through the curtain, looking very mysterious. So she was peering through a tiny gap in the curtain and trying to hear what Ken was saying.

I bet Matthew Broderick doesn't have to put up with this shit, she thought.

Not that Claire was the only person on edge. People who do live performances often like to say something along the lines of, 'Oh, it's good if you're nervous, because that means you care about your performance. It's the day I'm not nervous that I'll be really scared' (which struck Claire as the sort of thing you can say when your acting career has been funded by your upper-middle-class dentist parents paying for you to go to RADA and you don't ever have to be scared about – for instance – paying your fucking rent). But the SWF wasn't nervous in a good 'It'll be all right on the night' way. They were nervous in a 'Bro, what the fuck is happening?' kind of way. It was becoming a legendarily bad performance.

In the dressing room the clipboard holding the not-a-call-sheet had fallen off its hook on the wall three times in a row after being replaced, until a wrestler got annoyed and slammed it down on a bench. It had jumped off the bench onto the floor. At that point Ken had pulled the piece of paper off it and stuck the sheet to the wall with electrical tape, but none of the wrestlers wanted to look at it and they all gave it a wide berth.

In the locker room and all through the audience, people jumped and shivered in their seats as a sudden waterfall of cold rippled through them. It was happening enough that people were talking about it.

Wyatt barked non-stop through the entire show and escaped from wherever she was tied up, or the various arms that were holding her, so often that people gave up trying to contain her. The SWF building was filled with a Doppler-effect bark, as she ran the length of the horse-shoe and back. At one point a member of a male tag team (who were supposed to be being groomed to replace Pink

Champagne) stood up and roared, 'IF THAT FUCKING DOG DOESN'T SHUT UP, I'LL STRING IT UP BY ITS FUCKING LEAD!' He was bundled back to a seat by several other performers, who stifled his shouts because they were audible in the main room.

Because of the general air that a fight was about to break out between indeterminate parties, the wrestlers themselves were extremely keyed up and making mistakes; and the more mistakes were made, the more people made mistakes, as the unspoken but pervasive believe that the show was *obviously fucking cursed* took hold. Someone went completely blank and stopped talking when they were on mic and supposed to be cutting a promo. Someone else botched a table spot, reset and botched it again – said furniture remaining unentertainingly whole and resolute. The dog-hating tag wrestler, already up to here with the whole night, got into a scuffle with his own partner for being insufficiently responsive to his spot calls. Ken tried to play it off as if it were planned – as if it were the opening of a new storyline. But nobody seemed to buy it. The match was supposed to have been the big finale.

As Ken left the ring, someone in the back of the audience started a version of a ubiquitous football chant, 'There's only one Eddie King!', which was taken up by the whole crowd.

Ken found Claire backstage and pulled her aside. He looked quite scattered. He was blinking a lot. 'What's going on? Is this ... Is it *him*?' he stage-whispered at her.

'I dunno, I genuinely don't know where Eddie is right now,' Claire replied truthfully, slightly regretting that she hadn't been able to let more than a couple of living people and a couple of dead ones in on the full details of her ridiculous plan.

'Okay. Okay. It's fine, because we're about to do the big cleansing exorcism finale-thing, right?' said Ken. He looked like he was trying to convince himself. 'I'll play it up for the crowd, make it seem like one big meta-work. "Personal issues draw money." Nate! Lila! Get up here, we're on! "Personal issues draw money",' he muttered. '"Personal issues draw money ..."'

'*One Eddie Kiiiii-ing!*' came the muffled song of the crowd.

'They do say all men become their father,' Soph snorted.

'Yeah, well, they also say women become their mother, and I dunno how you'd fucking feel about that,' Claire snapped.

'Don't be mean because you're tense, LOL,' said Sophie. 'I'm the mean one.'

Claire watched a sliver of the action taking place in the ring. Although 'action' was a strong word. It was basically an extended promo. Ken stood in the middle of the ring, flanked by Lila and Nate. Nate was wearing a funereal-black suit, very appropriately, and Ken was supposed to be as well, but he'd spent his few allotted seconds backstage talking to Claire instead of getting changed, so he was in his little wrestling pants and a black blazer. Lila was still dressed as an entire clown, but her make-up was a big frowny face.

'At least you won't be the most stupid-looking one up there,' commented Sophie.

'Friends,' announced Ken to the audience. 'Thank you so much for joining us here tonight. It means so much to us that you continue to support our work – the great work that my father laid the foundations for, over decades of his life.'

He paused for a smattering of solemn applause. From the expression on his face, it looked like Ken got less than he'd been expecting.

'We want to build a temple on that foundation. And I know that, with the love of you all here tonight, we can do that. And I'm proud to say that my mother, Trudy King, joins us at the SWF tonight, for the first time in a *long* time, because she believes that we can get there. Stand up, Mum!'

There was another light dusting of applause, as of icing sugar on a WI Victoria sponge. Claire couldn't see, but Trudy obviously had not stood up, because Ken got in a jokey 'She's shy, ha-ha, she's shy – that's okay' to communicate that he was totally fine with his mum not standing up.

'Now, as I'm sure you've all noticed tonight, the SWF is not at peace. And many – if not all – of you will have heard by now that unfortunately my father, the great Eddie King, did not die of natural causes as we first thought. No, I'm afraid to say he was ... *murdered.*'

'Threw a lot of sauce on that little barbecue rib, didn't he?' said Sophie, talking over a collective muttering in the audience that made Claire feel like she was trapped in a hive. Sophie imitated Ken's dramatic pause: '... *moidered!*'

'Yes, yes, I know.' Ken lifted a hand, statesman-like, to calm the crowd. 'It was a shock to all of us, as much as to you. And I think – in fact, I *know* – that my father's spirit isn't at rest. You all felt it tonight, you saw the show. My father is here, and we need to help him pass on and find eternal peace. So tonight, with your help and the support of my uncle – my father's brother, Nate – and my beautiful love, Lila,' here he paused to squeeze Lila's hand, 'we're going to help Eddie King leave this place.'

Ken raised a hand out towards the entrance curtain and Claire was blinded by a spotlight shining almost directly in her face.

'Ohmigod! That's your cue, Weirdo,' said Sophie.

Claire suddenly felt like her shoes had melted to the floor and she couldn't move. This was a stupid plan. It was never going to work. She couldn't go out there.

Sophie gave her a shove, a brief connection that shocked Claire bolt upright and sent her stumbling forward into the curtain. She flailed with it a bit, but eventually fought her way past it and stood, squinting, in the glare of the spotlight, which was aimed directly at her face with the apparent intent of causing lasting retinal trauma. She raised a hand instinctively to block it out.

'Come forth, Raven!' shouted Ken. 'Mistress of the spirit realm!' He had not told Claire he was going to give her a fake and more pop-spiritualist-appropriate name, and the reveal of it caused Claire to make a frowny face without thinking.

'Don't just stand there – move,' prompted Sophie.

Claire took a few tentative steps forward and waved her dubious herb bundle about a few times. She pressed her other hand to her temple and tried to look as if she was channelling spirits beyond man's ken. Or, indeed, Ken's ken. She heard a titter from someone in the crowd, however, so obviously her act wasn't that ominous or pregnant with dread.

Luckily, because this was a regional independent show, the walk to the stage was incredibly short and was not broadcast live onto a huge LED megatron screen, so she reached the ring fairly quickly and climbed the metal steps at the corner without incident. But the ropes presented a sudden and unanticipated problem. Obviously she couldn't pull back and spring over the top rope, like she'd seen some wrestlers do. Her first instinct was to crawl underneath the middle rope, but that seemed like something she'd only pull off if she fully committed to the bit and crab-walked around the ring while shrieking about Satan, and Claire didn't have that many bits in her personal toolbox. The choice was made for her by Nate, who ambled over and held up the top rope and put one leg on the middle one, so that Claire could duck through. She still tripped over her skirt and landed on her hands and knees on the canvas, though.

'Oh, Raven!' said Ken. 'Dark, demented mistress of the Underworld!'

'One out of three ain't bad,' said Sophie, deadpan. She had managed to enter the ring without incident by dint of walking straight through the ropes.

'Tell me, what unearthly energies move among us tonight? Can we cleanse this place of my father's lingering spirit?'

Claire clambered to her feet and Ken pressed a mic into her hand. She looked down at it stupidly and then around her, outside the ring. The lights on the ring meant she couldn't see anything out in the crowd; she didn't know if everyone was where they were supposed to be. All she could see were occasional glints where a light caught a pair of glasses or a phone, but she could sense the crowd was restless. She turned and blinked, owlishly, trying to spot Alex. She heard a couple of chairs scraping back and realized that people were leaving.

'No, wait!' she shouted, without thinking. And then, quiet, embarrassed, 'Wait. Don't go.'

'Chin up, Buttercup,' said Sophie quietly. 'It's only a bigger seance, right? Look at me. We're just doing a seance.'

Claire turned back and focused on Soph. Her chestnut curls shone impossibly bright.

'Attagirl! Remember the new lines we were practising for regular seances? To add drama? You can do that.'

Claire took in a deep breath, tensed her shoulders as hard as she could for three seconds and let them drop. It was a technique Alex had taught her to relieve tension, but it also looked quite possession-y. She closed her eyes and breathed out slowly, and felt Sophie standing about half an inch in front of her, almost touching. She heard Lila whisper, 'What the fuck?' under her breath and some murmurs from the crowd, and she knew they had just seen her breath abruptly become an icy cloud in the air.

'There are spirits among us!' she shouted, growing in confidence. 'And we can cleanse this place … We can clean this place of evil, because there is evil here! The spirits tell me. They know the wrongs done at the SWF.'

She paused dramatically, and nothing happened for almost four seconds, until she looked over to where the sound desk was, in the corner, and flapped her free hand. The unpaid tech-intern must have got the message, because they were all plunged into sudden darkness, and the bank of screens hanging from the ceiling flicked into life. They showed TV static, like a ransom video, and then Pink Champagne appeared. They looked much as they ever had, although those in the audience who were faster on the uptake gasped, as they noticed their outfits were accented with pink-and-gold tartan. Those who were slow on the uptake gasped and booed as Michael Doolan, general manager of Weegie Pro-Wrestling, stepped in front of the camera.

'Well, hello to the King family. I understand it's a very important night for you down there,' he said. 'So I hope

I don't ruin it by taking the opportunity to reveal that Pink Champagne have accepted my offer and formally signed an *exclusive* contract with us here at Weegie Pro-Wrestling!'

There were more boos and a few whoops in the live audience at SWF – the crowd now getting into the panto spirit, as other wrestlers from Weegie moved into the frame of the video and applauded and slapped Ruby and Guy on the back.

'I want to say something. I want to say something!' said Guy, and Doolan handed him the mic. 'The King family *never* appreciated us. Pink Champagne are ready to take over the world of sports entertainment with the backing of a *real* manager who knows a once-in-a-generation talent when he sees it. But even then we weren't ready to leave the fans down in Brighton who supported us. There was one last straw that pushed us over the edge.'

Ruby grabbed the mic and, in a textbook Ruby display of impetuousness, seized the camera to focus it on herself. 'Yeah, it's because we know one of you is a murderer!' she spat, shouting into the lens. 'Eddie King's killer is free—'

The video stuttered with static as if the feed were cutting out, but then moved briefly to black-and-white security camera footage from the front ticket office, showing Nate – or at least a figure wearing his lucha mask and wrestling singlet – standing and staring at the camera. There was another buzz of static, and it cut to the figure putting down something small and white on the desk. Another wash of static and the figure was gone.

'What the fuck is happening?' asked Lila, at a normal volume.

Without warning the video cut back, with a sense of violence somehow, to Ruby shouting close into the camera. '... killer is there right now!' she screamed.

The video dropped entirely, leaving the room in sudden darkness.

'What the *hell* was that?' shouted Ken.

The audience applauded. It had been a good bit.

'That was really well edited – no wonder Weegie is doing better,' commented Sophie.

Claire turned and saw her friend, unnervingly solid, as if lit by a light coming from another world. Claire held her arm up, almost expecting Sophie to cast some light on it, but Claire still couldn't see her own hand in front of her face.

'Not a torch, Weirdo,' said Sophie. 'Don't forget your flowers – the lights will be on any second.'

'Shit. Wank. Argh,' replied Claire, fumbling in a very indelicate and unmystical way with her jumper.

The house-lights snapped on and Claire triumphantly brandished a bunch of slender flowers, their long green stalks ending with beautiful deep-purple hoods. They were only slightly the worse for wear from having been stuffed up her sleeve.

'Poison!' she cried dramatically.

'Don't wave them around, you look like that cunt Morrissey,' said Sophie.

'FuckoffPOISON!'

There were uneasy murmurings from the crowd again, not because they were bored, but because they had started to wonder whether the edges of this performance had begun to bleed into reality.

'Look!' someone shouted.

Alex, never knowingly not on cue, was stumbling down the aisle from the curtain, head lolling on their shoulders. And, invisible to everyone but Claire, Sophie and one particularly furious terrier backstage, Eddie King followed them.

'Eddie King will have vengeance!' said Claire, as Alex and Eddie reached the side of the ring.

'Are you sure about this?' asked Eddie.

'Eddie King will have vengeance right bloody now, thank you very much,' hissed Claire.

Alex, hearing this, tore off their baggy black sweats, revealing that they were dressed in exact copies of Eddie's wrestling singlet and boots. They threw their head back and spread their arms wide. And Eddie possessed them.

It looked really good, Claire thought afterwards. Alex slammed forward, nearly head-butting the edge of the ring, but brought their hands up at the last second. They pushed back, pirouetted on one leg like a drunken marionette and then charged into the ring.

'Oh my God!' screamed Lila. She started to make a run for it, but Ken grabbed her and pushed her into one corner, out of the way. Claire ducked into it as well, and Nate stepped in front of Ken, as Alex charged. They slammed into one another and grappled at the shoulder, like two cliffs crashing into one another, which was very strange to watch. Physically speaking, it was like watching a steak fight a noodle. And yet Alex flipped Nate over and picked him up, so that Nate was sitting on their shoulders, and slammed him heavily into the mat. Nate vamped and groaned and crawled into the corner opposite Claire and Lila. He gave Claire the tiniest, most infinitesimal nod.

Alex roared into the ceiling and beat their chest. It was, somehow, utterly convincing and the crowd had started to go wild again, as the idea that someone was being possessed by a dead wrestler did at least provide some solid ground to stand on, viz. this all being a very tasteless bit. But Lila was not on solid ground.

'Jesus Christ, it's him,' she squealed. 'It's him, it's Eddie – it's just like he used to do it.'

'It's an act,' snarled Ken. 'It's a cheap trick and it won't work. Dad is dead. He's fucking dead!'

'Gee it along, Weirdo, keep the momentum up!' yelled Sophie. She hopped from foot to foot in excitement.

'Uh, right, yeah – I mean, yes. He is dead!' shouted Claire, relieved that the mic was still live. 'Eddie is dead, but he is here with us. He has used this psychic as a vessel to wrestle one last time and enact his revenge!'

There was a cautious, but optimistic cheer from the crowd. Alex pounded their chest like a silverback. They prowled along the ropes, shaking them with fury in an effort to further whip up the crowd. Lila slid down to the mat and held onto the ring post, where she huddled up and mewled like a cat. Claire hoped she wasn't going to have a total breakdown. She hadn't expected Eddie's vicarious appearance to be so effective so quickly.

'You're no wrestler,' said Ken, pointing a shaking finger at Alex. 'And you're certainly no bloody King!'

He rushed Alex without warning, but Alex stepped swiftly to one side and raised their arm, which Ken ran into like it was a steel girder. He was knocked onto his arse, but he didn't sell it. This was for real. He jumped up and ran at Alex again and again, but every time they stepped aside or used momentum to flip Ken into the ropes. Veins began to braid over Ken's chest and arms. His jugular stood out against his straining neck. He was sweating profusely.

'There's only one Eddie King!' started up again from somewhere at the back. The chanting felt almost religious, as a backdrop to the strange drama playing out.

'Eddie King whispers to me even now, from beyond the thin veil that separates us from the dead,' declared Claire, as Alex spun out of the way of Ken's attack once again. They started to laugh. Claire tried once more to inject drama into her voice, but she didn't really have it in her. 'Eddie's killer was betrayed by him! And it was a betrayal they could not take. By chance they learned from Trudy that these flowers were poisonous, that very same day ...'

Ken finally caught hold of Alex long enough that they grappled in the ring. He roared in frustration as Alex pushed out of the grapple and reversed it, so they ended up holding Ken in a near choke-hold.

'The murderer wasn't smart enough to create a proper poison. They cut up the leaves from this plant and slipped them into Eddie's food on an impulse, but through sheer luck they had accidentally included enough of the root that the poison took effect later that night. They dressed as Nate, because they came across his gear in the boxes of old fabrics and thought it would be a good disguise. All of it was unplanned good fortune that helped them slip through the police's net.'

Ken pushed heavily backwards into Alex and used the movement to bring his own legs up. This gave him the momentum to land heavily and pull Alex forward to flip over Ken's head. They landed on the mat with an almighty *slam*. Ken pulled them up and gripped Alex around the neck with one arm. For an absurd moment, Claire thought he was going to give Alex a noogie, which would annoy them because they took great pride in their hair. But instead Ken spun them, leaving them flat on their back.

'Not enough, not enough,' said Sophie.

'That's enough,' shouted a voice that cut through the droning chants, and which Claire recognized as Basher's. 'Get Alex out of there right now!'

'Ohmigod, he's actually coming this way; he'll drag them out by their ankles if we don't wrap this up,' said Sophie.

'It was all uninspired,' said Claire, ad-libbing desperately. 'Eddie King's death was a foolish whim, unplanned and empty!'

Ken rolled up Alex's legs in an attempt to pin them, but they kicked away and roared again. Lila strangled back a sob and started to try to drag herself to her feet once more. Claire looked desperately at Nate, who was frozen in shock.

'For fuck's sake, he's no help,' shouted Sophie. 'We're going to have to cut this short – that fucker is trying to piledrive Alex!'

Ken had lifted Alex and was trying to wrangle them, but they were landing double-fisted blows on his shoulders – the hammers of gods. Lila had finally got to her feet and made to run forward.

'Eddie King's killer was just a spiteful, lucky fool! No creativity; genius hadn't touched them like it had touched Eddie.'

Basher slammed into the side of the ring, leaned through and grabbed Ken's ankle. Ken instinctively kicked out, and it put him off-balance long enough for Alex – their features twisted in unfamiliar, porcine rage – to flip forward using Ken himself as leverage. Lila slammed into Ken at the same time, her wig discarded, her make-up melting down her face to create a hideous impressionistic piece of art. They nearly fell together, but Ken righted himself against the ropes and threw Lila violently to the mat.

'You stupid bitch – it was all your fucking fault in the first place,' he spat. 'If you'd kept it in your pants, I wouldn't have had to fucking kill him!'

There was a sharp, collective indrawn breath from the audience, but Ken didn't notice.

'And another fucking thing, you fraud,' he said, turning to Claire. 'It took me months, so don't stand there calling me an idiot when you barely know what day it is.'

'It's a Thursday,' said Claire. She trembled slightly, suddenly very aware that the man in front of her was standing extremely close to her, and was extremely physically strong. 'And I might not be as clever as some people, but at least I haven't confessed to murder in a crowded room.'

Ken straightened up, as if suddenly aware of what had just happened, and where he was. 'But I – I didn't mean it; that was a … It was a work, it was a storyline. Yeah. Because everyone hated my dad, didn't they, so we were going to do a plot about his death. That was the whole reason you're here.'

'Nice try,' said Claire. 'But it's a reach. And besides, everyone might have hated your dad, and this whole place was falling apart, but you panicked and killed Chaz as well. And that man,' she took a deep breath and looked at Lila, 'that man had a family.'

Alex and/or Eddie took the opportunity presented by Ken's turned back to grab him in a chokehold. They picked him up, in what was almost a grotesque parody of someone cradling a baby, and slammed Ken to the mat, making sure to drive their knee into his back on the way down.

'KING OF THE RING!' they shouted. 'KING OF THE RING!'

21

Final Curtain

Claire's experience of solving a murder, based on the two incidents where this had happened to her so far, was that everyone said you were very clever and made you cups of tea and bought you Haribo Tangfastics when you asked for them. Therefore she was very upset that the successful wrapping up of this murder case included her and Alex, sitting next to each other on the sofa in Basher and Alex's living room like school children who had been caught ditching, being surround-sound told off by Basher and Sami simultaneously.</NI>

'I mean for fuck's sake, I didn't arrest you for my fucking health!' said Sami, throwing her hands in the air. 'You were told very clearly to leave things alone and that we were handling it.'

'... cannot believe that you would endanger Alex in that way – this is beyond what I expected from either of you,' Basher said, equally activated, but in his cold, white-lipped, quiet manner of fury that was somehow more terrifying.

'You have jeopardized a whole investigation with this ridiculous display,' Sami finished. 'It's not like on TV, you know, believe it or not: a – and please read the heavy sarcasm in my voice when I say the next two words – *citizen detective* blundering around really dicks the proper chain of evidence.'

'But you weren't—'

'What's that? So now you're having trouble mouthing off, are you?' Sami said. Her voice was at least returning to more normal decibels, but she was still very angry.

'I cannot believe I am saying this, but you are *grounded*,' hissed Basher. He waved a finger under Alex's nose, and they snapped at it with their neat teeth. 'This is not a joke!' he went on.

'Oh, please, Uncle B, I'm legally an adult and it all went fine, didn't it?' said Alex.

'What was it like for you, being possessed by Eddie?' asked Claire, her curiosity overcoming her horror at being told off.

'Well, obviously a large middle-aged man who almost certainly thinks Tommy Robinson has some good ideas wouldn't be my first choice of ghost to possess me,' said Alex. 'But it didn't feel like, you know, a violation or anything. It just felt like I had decided to do all that stuff myself and then I knew how to do it. Like I decided the time was right to do a back-breaker on Ken and I knew exactly how to do one. Didn't even have to think.'

Claire hoped they didn't start thinking about any of it too hard in fact, because that description sounded somehow more frightening than being possessed and knowing someone else was in control. What if there were people walking around today who were possessed by ghosts and didn't even know it? And then what happened if you died? Did you become a double ghost? Was it like in *Being John Malkovich*? It was a sobering thought. Still, Claire was glad Alex had agreed to it, because it had really unnerved Ken. She'd had an idea it would work on Alex because of their latent medium abilities, and the success of that aspect of her stupid plan was only further evidence that said abilities existed.

'It did not go *fine*, excuse me,' said Basher. 'Even if I were to accept that Alex was possessed by the ghost of a dead wrestler, they were still performing very dangerous stunts they are not trained to do, and which take an incredible physical toll!'

'Well, at least you accept that wrestling is real,' said Alex grumpily.

'Look, I'm very sorry, Bash, and I promise I won't ask Alex to do anything like that again,' replied Claire. 'Scout's honour.' She held up a hand.

'I think that's the Vulcan salute,' said Sami.

'Yeah, well, I wasn't a Scout, was I?' admitted Claire. 'It still counts. I promise that Alex will live long and prosper and whatever. Anyway, it doesn't look like Alex will be able to endanger their life in that very specific way ever again, does it?'

The SWF was on an indefinite hiatus while Ken was charged with two murders, although even if he wasn't, he should have been put in protective custody, judging by the volume and intensity of the threats shouted at him by his mother. Nate was reassessing his relationship with wrestling in general, and Lila was looking at charges for perverting the course of justice. This was also, Sami made clear, something that Claire might want to worry about as well.

'You need to refocus on how much trouble you're in,' she told her.

'But *you* weren't doing anything!' Claire said to Sami, trying for a bit of defiance.

'Oh, I'm sorry; clearly I should have been walking around in a trench coat with a giant fucking magnifying glass,' Sami replied. 'I have received emails from temporarily embarrassed African princes more convincing than Chaz's apparent suicide. How stupid do you think I am exactly?'

'Well, why didn't you arrest Ken?'

Sami pinched the bridge of her nose. 'Those shows you watch have so much to answer for. We interviewed Ken in connection with Chaz's death, but believe it or not, it isn't always good form to tell someone you suspect that you do, in fact, suspect them of doing a crime. You didn't even give me a week! It can take three days for fingerprints from a crime scene to come back, did you know that? And that's without any delays.'

Claire looked at her feet. She did not know that.

'There was CCTV covering the entrance to Chaz's house, but it was privately owned, and said owner wanted a warrant before he'd hand over the footage,' Sami continued. 'Nate also had a Ring doorbell, which required a separate warrant. We finally got all the footage late in the afternoon, which showed Ken, an idiot, going into Chaz's house with a bag of cans a couple of hours before you showed up. But that's *all* it showed, you understand? Not every suspect does the crime literally in front of me – unlike others that I could care to mention. But it gave us grounds for a warrant to search Ken's home and to arrest him, only we didn't want to cause a massive scene in the middle of a show watched by hundreds of people, so I was observing him last night when you, you know, caused a massive giant fucking scene!'

'Sorry, but I would have thought Ken confessing in front of a bunch of people would help, especially when physical evidence is lacking,' said Sophie.

'Or perhaps it might have occurred to you that Ken being verbally pressured by the woman who discovered Chaz's body, who is also a medium who claims to have spoken to his dead father, while he was being physically assaulted by someone related to the investigating officer's former partner, might muddy the waters at trial somewhat,' said Basher. He looked at Claire with his very piercing grey eyes, then rubbed his face for a full ten seconds.

'Oh. Right,' said Alex. 'Yeah, now you've put it like that ...' They flopped back on the sofa.

'This really isn't brain surgery, Claire,' continued Sami. Her face softened a bit and she sat down. 'Quite a lot of it is common sense. But now I need to untangle what you've been doing. Why were you suspicious of Ken?'

'I imagined this part would be much more triumphant,' observed Sophie.

'Well, it took a while,' said Claire. 'Because everything about Eddie's death pointed to all different people. He wore Nate's costume in case he was seen, and started rumours that Trudy was cheating with Nate. Then the poison came from flowers that Trudy grew, the pills were to do with Lila, and all the gossip being spread around suggested Ruby and Guy. Plus, everyone had reasons to dislike Eddie.'

'And then when Chaz died, that made it clear Chaz knew something that pointed to the actual murderer and he'd tried to blackmail them,' Sophie explained.

'That still didn't rule anyone out really. It could have been Lila, but she was so scared that she was going to be next, and she's not that good an actor. It could have been Nate, but then we found out that his gear included a mask, so did anyone actually see him? Trudy was open about not caring what Eddie did, so she wasn't a completely convincing suspect. Pink Champagne had beef with Eddie, and Ruby's explanation that she heard Eddie say he was "leaving" felt tenuous, but now I think she probably overheard him talking to Lila about leaving Trudy. Ruby just assumed it was about retirement.'

'I guess Occam's razor would tell you that the reason Pink Champagne left town was to relocate somewhere they felt they'd get better bookings.'

Claire nodded. 'Especially with the storylines that had been set up with Weegie Pro-Wrestling. In the end, that seemed more likely than them doing any murders.'

'Did you call them to organize that video, by the way?' asked Sami.

'Yeah, they did it really fast; we just had to stage some creepy-looking footage of Nate in the office, which took five minutes. They were only too happy to help. Eddie King really wasn't popular,' Claire replied. 'But they didn't know who the killer was,' she added quickly.

Sami waved a hand. 'They weren't going to get arrested anyway. But I'll need the contacts you have for them, to corroborate things.'

'The point is, nothing added up to one person, and everything felt so ... so *plotted* and theatrical, but in a stupid way. When Sophie said, "Maybe that's the point", I suddenly realized there's one person it *wasn't* pointing to. And when you put Ken in the middle of things, it made more sense.'

'How so?' asked Basher.

'Ken's the same build and height as Nate, so he could dress in Nate's gear, in case anyone saw him at the gym; and he's actively anti the old school, so he wouldn't care as much about wearing it. He kept trying to stop Alex from going through the boxes where he'd hidden the pieces of boots and mask too. I think he kept the pieces to prove to himself how clever he was – you know, the evidence was under everyone's nose! But Alex poking around meant the pieces might be discovered, and it made it harder to chuck those boxes out, now that someone was paying attention to them. Ken did eventually give us access to the CCTV footage, but that was *after* he tried to frame Chaz. I think he deleted the recording of him dressed as Nate, because that wouldn't add up with Chaz's suicide, would it?'

'That's not a lot to go on,' said Sami.

'It's not all,' continued Claire. 'Trudy mentioned that she wanted him to be a doctor, which suggested that he might have studied an amount of science or medicine before he went full-time on the wrestling. And when we were at his and Lila's flat, I saw a hard shell mould hidden amongst all her silicone chocolate moulds that he snatched off me. I think it was for the fake pills.'

Sami made a note of this. 'We've not been able to find the actual poison yet.'

'Yeah, Lila threw the pills away, so you'll probably never find them. She eventually told us she'd cleaned up around Eddie's death, and I didn't think much of it at first, although it was pretty obvious she *was* having an affair with Eddie. But if you work backwards again, that meant that the crime scene was meant to be discovered as it was – poisoned fake-Viagra and all.'

'Ohhhh,' said Alex. 'I'm getting it. The killer knew Eddie was having an affair, and shagging around wouldn't be a reason for Chaz to get that angry with Eddie, but shagging his daughter? That's something all right.'

Claire nodded. 'I think it was probably Chaz who told Ken, because Ruby said Chaz couldn't keep the piss between his legs, but then he didn't really think about it again because life went on as usual for months before Eddie died. Until I started asking about it, and then Chaz called Ken to blackmail him, and tried to speak to Nate for insurance. Of course it's possible that Ruby going to Ken to ask about Eddie retiring made him look into matters and discover what was happening with Lila. But we might never know for sure.'

'But why *did* Ken want Eddie's death to be investigated?' asked Alex. 'Like, until he got you involved and bumped off Chaz, Ken had literally got away with murder.'

'I don't think he did,' said Alex. 'I think Ken genuinely believed that Eddie was haunting the gym and wanted Claire to get rid of him. I keep saying: they're superstitious people.'

'Yeah, he did tell me to stop doing all the investigation stuff after Chaz died, but by then it was sort of too late and everything was unravelling.'

'I think there's a psychological factor,' said Sophie. 'Ken is a fucking idiot, but he thinks he's smart. He had been butting heads with his dad for years about who knew what was best for the business. Then he found out Eddie was shagging Lila, which he took as a massive insult, and he wanted to show how much smarter than his dad he really was, so he murdered Eddie and made what he thought was an unsolvable crime by framing about half a dozen people at once. So he didn't think Claire doing a seance, or whatever, would do any harm. Thing is, I bet if Eddie's death had actually been investigated at the time, he would have been caught in five minutes. He didn't know Nate had a secret boyfriend who could instantly alibi him, for example.'

'Yeah. I don't think killing Chaz was part of Ken's plan, either; obviously it was more of a defensive thing. Because then his cleverness got attributed to Chaz. That's why Ken was so frustrated and stressed,' said Claire. 'Which is why I could needle him into confessing.'

'That still isn't really physical evidence,' said Basher.

'Yeah, hence I thought we had to do the big, you know, dramatic scene,' said Claire. She chewed at her nails.

'Which is also why it would have been much better if you had done *nothing*, because there was a lot of evidence at Chaz's flat and potentially even more at Ken's,' said Sami. She gave Claire a massive slap on the back of the hand, which stung. 'Honestly, this is going to be a fucking nightmare, I'm warning you now. Unless we can get a proper confession.'

Basher shrugged. 'If Ken is as arrogant and stupid as Claire suggests, that should very much be on the cards.'

'It would help if he had any other history of violence or controlling behaviour,' said Sami, almost musing to herself.

'Er, well. Not to talk out of turn, but I think maybe Lila can help with that,' said Claire. 'Some of what she said about how Ken was with her ... I don't think he was a great husband, put it that way.'

'Massive bellend,' said Sophie. 'That's the greatest evidence against him, if you ask me.'

'Speaking of massive bellends,' said Alex, 'is Eddie still haunting the gym?'

'Dunno,' said Sophie. 'We haven't checked.'

Claire got off the bus and scraped her way along the alley to the SWF gym for what she hoped was the last time in her entire tiny life. She glanced briefly at Trudy's house, but the 'TO LET' sign in the hairdresser's window had been replaced by a 'LET' sign. Claire wondered where Trudy would end up. Maybe she'd move abroad permanently and never worry about topping up her tan again. Claire had caught a glimpse of her outside the gym on that last, weird night and Trudy hadn't looked surprised. She had just appeared grim and sad, and a little folded in on herself, like a crumpled tissue.</NI>

'What are you planning to do? Shout through a window?' asked Sophie. She skipped along next to Claire in a strangely good mood. 'Does this alley smell of piss? It looks like it smells of piss.'

It was getting dark and Claire regretted the choice to come, which she'd made on a whim after fixating for a full two days on what Sophie had said: she really hadn't bothered to check on Eddie. Whether Eddie deserved, or needed, to be checked on was a separate issue; like the violent hamster she'd had when she was eight, checking for signs of life was an act more about Claire's morality than his. Although in Eddie's case, signs of life weren't going to be present anyway. Or in the hamster's case, it had eventually turned out.

'Claire?'

She jumped out of her skin. Miller had been standing at the corner of the parking area in front of the gym. Against the half-light of the evening he looked almost alive.

'Oh. Hi, Miller,' said Claire. She rubbed the back of her neck.

'I was waiting for you,' he replied.

'Are you going to try to kill her? Other, better ghosts than you have failed,' said Sophie.

'Yeah, look, I'm actually glad that ... I'm sorry, Miller. About what I said. I took out a lot of my anger on you and that, you know – it wasn't nice. Or fair.'

Miller put his hands up. 'It's okay. That's what I wanted to tell you. After what you said, I was really down for a bit. But then I spent some time watching everyone coming back and forth. And thinking. I saw Ken getting arrested, and you know what someone in the crowd said?'

'What?'

'They said, "I wish Miller was still here – he'd be having a field day."'

'So?' Sophie asked.

'So maybe a lot of people didn't like me, but some people did. I wanted everyone to like me when I was alive, but that's not possible, is it? I wish I had focused more on the good things. Been more positive when I had the chance – been better to my girlfriend. I wanted to say it's okay. You don't need to apologize. I had a decent life; stupid sometimes. Maybe I didn't appreciate it, but it's too late for that now.'

'That's good. That's very philosophical of you,' said Claire.

'Yeah. I don't suppose you know what's next, do you?'

'No idea,' replied Sophie. 'Sorry. You heading off then?'

'Yeah, don't worry about the blog post. It was going to be a big, bitter rant, but I don't want that any more. People saying, "I wish Miller was still here" every so often: that's all right. I wanted to say goodbye to someone. To anyone really. And you're the only person I can say anything to.'

Claire found herself getting a tiny bit choked up, for this small, serious, hairy man and his wallet chain, and his too-late epiphany. Or maybe it was just in time. She cleared her throat. 'Well, goodbye, Miller. It was nice knowing you. I'll remember you.'

Miller nodded, and Claire turned and walked away.

'Good luck!' shouted Sophie, over her shoulder.

Claire glanced back, but there was nobody there any more.

To her surprise and alarm, the SWF had a light on. But Claire remembered that it was unlikely to be Ken, given that he was currently in custody. She pushed the door open awkwardly. The front office felt haunted, but in a different way. All the same T-shirts were still there: 'PINK CHAMPAGNE', 'KING OF THE RING', 'OP'.

'Creepy,' said Sophie.

Claire agreed. She pushed open the door to the main room. It was still full of chairs, many of them a confused jumble, knocked out of their neatly stitched rows when people had suddenly been forced to leave in a rush. The lights were on full, so it looked less like a show venue and more like a community theatre about to put on a play about peer pressure, written by and starring the nerds from the sixth-form drama class. In one seat, near the front, sat Nate. He turned round when the door clacked loudly in the empty space, but he'd clearly been sitting staring at the ring, which was still in the middle of the room. Claire swallowed.

'Fuck, you gave me a fright then,' he said.

'Um, sorry. Yeah. Didn't think anyone would be here.'

'Well, the place is mine, isn't it?' It didn't sound entirely rhetorical. 'What are you doing here anyway?' he asked.

'This is much easier now that he doesn't answer in fucking in-character riddles like a fucking Gollum Tumblr-account doing asks,' said Sophie.

'I ... I came to check. On – you know,' said Claire. She swallowed again.

'Oh, right. Me too, I suppose. I keep coming here and trying to decide what to do. Like he'll give me some inspiration.'

'Fuck off, the lot of you,' said Eddie King.

He was sitting slumped in the centre of the ring, legs splayed straight in front of him and shoulders hunched, his hands in his lap, like a toddler who'd dropped his ice cream.

'No one's been here for fucking days!' he shouted, not even bothering to turn his head. 'Except this miserable bastard. And all he does is sit there. What's he got to be miserable about, eh? He's not left sitting in the dark for hours at a time. Nothing to do. Nothing to look at. I'm going mad inside my own head here!' Eddie slapped his forehead with the heel of his hand, punctuating the words.

'I think Eddie is being forced to discover introspection,' said Sophie. 'LOL,' she added, for good measure.

'What are you looking at?' asked Nate suddenly. 'Is he here?'

'Um.' Claire weighed up her options. 'Yeah. And he's … I'll say "bored".'

'I'm fucking furious!' Eddie shouted.

'Oh, pipe down – when are you not?' snapped Sophie. 'You've only been dead five fucking minutes. Try almost as long as you were actually alive in the first place.'

'I think Eddie thought he'd move on, once his killer was caught,' said Claire. 'Er. But. Yeah, it appears not.' She turned to Eddie. 'You must have some other unfinished business,' she called. 'I don't make the rules. You're the one who started this whole thing. I don't know what you feel unfinished about unless you tell me.'

'Probably wishes he'd died on the job, the dirty old man,' muttered Sophie. 'I'm not wanking him off, I tell you that for nothing.'

'I heard that,' shouted Eddie. Still too despondent to get up or move, though, Claire noted.

Nate stood up and approached the ring. He hesitated. 'So ... so, whatever happens to this place, he'll still be here?'

'Um, yep. As far as I know. They hang around. Indefinitely. Some of them kind of forget who they are and they turn into like ... little clouds, sort of? But unhappy clouds, generally speaking.'

Different feelings passed behind Nate's eyes. His mouth worked for a few seconds. Then he straightened up.

'Good,' he said.

This wasn't exactly what Claire had been expecting him to say. Sophie laughed. It at least provoked Eddie into getting up. He lumbered to his feet and checked his towel was still secure.

'"Good." That's what I get for a lifetime of sacrifice! For giving him a job! Nate thinks it's good that I'm going to be stuck here, going off my nut for all time?'

'Do you not feel even slightly guilty for immediately suspecting your brother of murder?' asked Sophie.

'No, bugger that – you tell him what I said!' shouted Eddie, pointing at Claire. 'This is a fight now. I'm fighting with him.' Claire flinched, and Nate noticed.

'What's he saying?' asked Nate.

Claire sighed and repeated what Eddie had said, who opined that she was not expressing his anger with enough accuracy. Claire refused to shout at Nate, but said that Nate should be clear that Eddie was shouting.

'Oh, well, when was he not bloody shouting, eh?' said Nate. 'A lifetime of sacrifice, my arse. I worked as hard as him, and more. He just can't see past the end of his own dick. *You*, Eddie,' he said. 'I'm talking to you.' He pointed at the ring, and Claire wordlessly reached up and adjusted his arm so that it was actually pointing at Eddie. 'You're selfish,' Nate went on. 'You always were. You made it too hard to love you, and then hated people for stopping. I was afraid of you. We all were. Your own son killed you, for Christ's sake! And sometimes I think we're better off now you're gone.'

'What sort of thing is that to say about your own flesh and blood, huh?' shouted Eddie.

'Flesh and blood aren't enough,' said Nate. 'It's not the same as heart.'

Claire was quite impressed by this, but Sophie rolled her eyes. 'Bloody hell. It's like fucking *EastEnders* or something. Must be exhausting living with this much drama.'

It had worked on Eddie in some manner, though. He leaned on the ring ropes and dropped his head. 'What happened, eh? We got on when we were kids. Had each other's backs. Remember when you ... you ate a corner of the Christmas pud, two days before Christmas Day, and I said it was me, to save you the hiding from Mum?'

Claire dutifully repeated this.

'I don't know what happened, Ed,' said Nate. 'You never respected me. You pushed and I didn't push back, and I was scared of you. All my adult life I was. So I never pulled you back from how you treated your wife and your son, and, fuck, everyone else around you. My older brother, who looked out for me – I'll miss him. But not the man you became. You lost that kid somewhere along the way.'

'*Ohmigod*,' muttered Sophie. Claire shushed her.

Nate took a step towards the ring. He was trying to focus on something that wasn't there. Eddie raised his head and contemplated his brother.

'You really wanted to believe Nate killed you, didn't you?' said Soph. 'Did you think you'd deserved it?'

'The truth is, Eddie, that my life is worse in a lot of ways, but better in a lot of others. And the good outweighs the bad, in your passing. That's the truth. It's sad, but that's how it is,' said Nate.

Eddie climbed down out of the ring, and Claire reoriented Nate so that they were facing each other again. Nate was looking up automatically, because his brother was a few inches taller, but he still had nothing to focus on.

'Sorry, Nate. I'm sorry,' said Eddie. Claire got the sense it was the first time he'd said the word in a very long time.

Nate rubbed his eyes. 'I'm not,' he said.

'Yeah, that's fair enough,' replied Eddie. He stuck his hand out. Claire explained to Nate what was happening.

'Oh, go on, let's help them out,' said Sophie.

'I can't give Eddie my energy, remember?' whispered Claire.

'So let's do it in a chain – that's worked before.'

Claire sighed heavily and slipped her hand into Sophie's. It was like holding hands with a statue. She felt the *zip* of connecting with a ghost, felt her energy draining, and saw Sophie reach out and place her own hand on Eddie's shoulder. The drain doubled, and Sophie left her hand there long enough that when Nate reached forward and touched the air, he felt ... *something*. Something almost there. Something he could hold onto.

Claire snatched back her frost-burned hand and sat heavily in a nearby chair. She looked up to say something to Eddie, but he was gone.

'Eddie?' she called.

'I think he might be ... *gone*, gone,' said Sophie.

'What happened?' asked Nate.

'I think. Um, I think that did it,' she replied. 'So, yeah. Well done. One passed-over brother.'

Nate looked at his own hand and blinked. 'I felt ...'

'Can we go home now?' said Sophie.

They left Nate looking at his fingers as a dawning grief filled his face. Claire walked out of the room with unnatural speed, because if you see someone crying you're morally obligated to do something about it, but as long as you don't actually see it, then you bear no responsibility.

She yawned as soon as they got outside. Her mental concept of the bus stop down the road was that it was twenty-six miles away and the bus journey home would take eight years.

'I'm knackered,' she said. 'That was all too much. Let's go and see Mr Przybylski. I need a giant fucking Crunchie.'

'You always eat it too fast and then complain you have nothing to dunk in your tea,' said Sophie. She shook out her curls, smoothed down the front of her bright-blue tracksuit. She'd never looked more alive than when she was dead.

'Are you saying don't get a Crunchie?'

'Fuck, no! I'm saying get two, Weirdo.'

Claire bought two Crunchies. She ate both before she finished her tea. And then she threw one of the wrappers into the stairwell.

Acknowledgements

Want to know about Sophie and Claire's next case?

Sign up to

ALICE BELL'S
Newsletter

and get **news**, **giveaways** and **updates on new books** featuring your two favourite amateur sleuths coming soon!

SCAN TO JOIN TODAY